A STUDY IN SCARLET

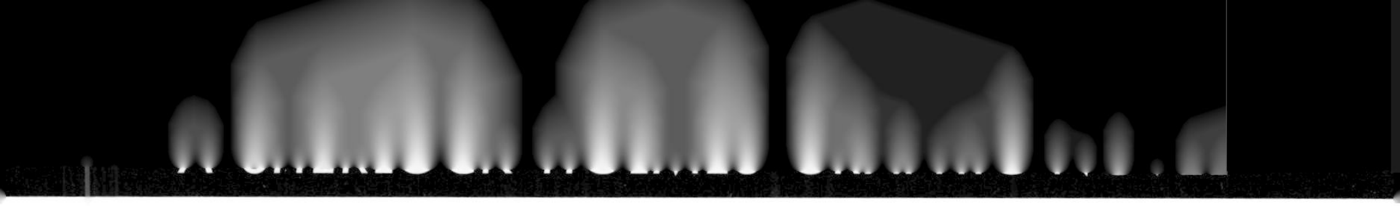

A STUDY IN SCARLET

ADAPTED FROM THE ORIGINAL NOVEL BY
SIR ARTHUR CONAN DOYLE
ILLUSTRATED BY
I. N. J. CULBARD
TEXT ADAPTED BY
IAN EDGINTON

STERLING

New York / London
www.sterlingpublishing.com

Published by Sterling Publishing Co., Inc.
387 Park Avenue South, New York, NY 10016

© 2010 SelfMadeHero

First published 2010
by SelfMadeHero
A division of Metro Media Ltd
5 Upper Wimpole Street
London W1G 6BP
www.selfmadehero.com

Illustrator: I. N. J. Culbard
Adaptor: Ian Edginton
Cover Designer: I. N. J. Culbard
Designer: Andy Huckle
Textual Consultant: Nick de Somogyi
Publishing Director: Emma Hayley
With thanks to: Catherine Cooke, John Corbett, Jane Laporte,
and Doug Wallace

Dedications
For Katy, Joseph, and Benjamin
– I. N. J. Culbard

*To the trio of lovely ladies in my life: my wife, Jane, and
daughters, Constance and Corinthia* – Ian Edginton

Distributed in Canada by Sterling Publishing
c/o Canadian Manda Group, 165 Dufferin Street,
Toronto, Ontario, Canada M6K 3H6

Printed and bound in China

ISBN: 978-1-4027-7082-1

10 9 8 7 6 5 4 3 2 1

For information about custom editions, special sales, premium
and corporate purchases, please contact Sterling Special Sales
Department at 800-805-5489 or specialsales@sterlingpub.com.

FOREWORD

"OBSERVATION WITH ME IS SECOND NATURE. . . ."

A Study in Scarlet is to the Sherlock Holmes canon what the book of Genesis is to the Bible—where it all begins.

Arthur Conan Doyle, a rising twenty-six-year-old doctor, wrote the story in six weeks in 1886, then sold the copyright for an unimpressive £25 and had to wait more than a year to see his work in print. *A Study in Scarlet* initially made little impression on the reading public, even though it was the debut of the world's most famous fictional detective, Sherlock Holmes.

What makes Holmes so perennially fascinating? It's true that his loyal friend Dr. John H. Watson, the narrator of this and most of the stories, talks up the detective's unique scientific reasoning and moral courage. But Holmes could hardly have been the easiest person to live with—he is arrogant, highly competitive, often melancholic, and wildly eccentric. He plays the violin at all hours, conducts noxious chemical experiments, and fires his revolver at the wall, never mind having a tendency to slip into unlikely disguises at the drop of a hat.

However, we see the detective's virtues clearly in *A Study in Scarlet*. He spots things that are missed by other people, including the professional policemen Lestrade and Gregson; he uses his imagination; he thinks outside the box, using, as Conan Doyle calls them in the original edition, "six dirty little scoundrels," later known as the Baker Street Irregulars, to do his, well, dirty work; and, most important, he gets his man.

For many readers, this makes Holmes a cold-blooded superhero, but the warm humor of the stories is often ignored. Watson's limited brain power is regularly mocked, but never maliciously; the same goes for police incompetence—though the officers always ask for it by getting above themselves.

Credit should be given to Conan Doyle, a much more profound writer than many literary critics believe. He took material that had been used by Edgar Allan Poe, Wilkie Collins, and numerous other writers, and made it completely his own. A Scot, he had the Celt's sense of the darkness that is never far from civilization. And he could set up a nerve-jangling mystery like nobody else. In *A Study in Scarlet*, the contorted corpse of a man is found, surrounded by bloodstains even though he has not been wounded. On a wall, the strange word "*Rache*" has been written in blood....

Eat your heart out, *CSI*.

— Paul Johnston
winner of the Sherlock Award for Best Detective Novel, 2004

PART 1.

(Being a reprint from the reminiscences of
JOHN H. WATSON, M.D.,
late of the Army Medical Department)

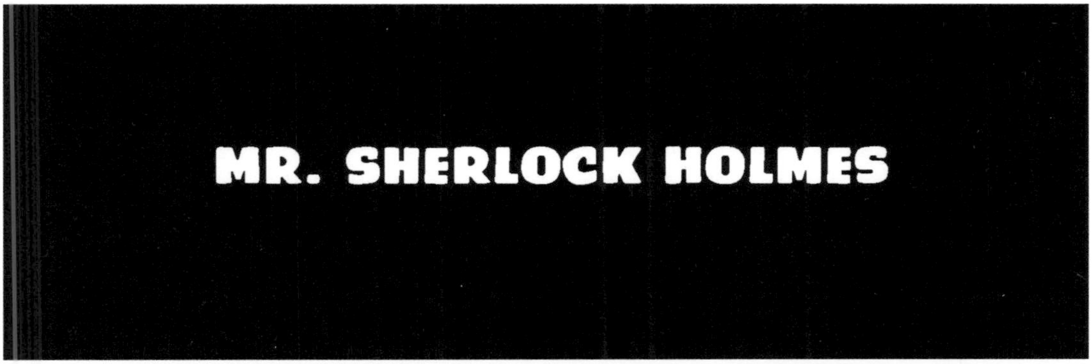
MR. SHERLOCK HOLMES

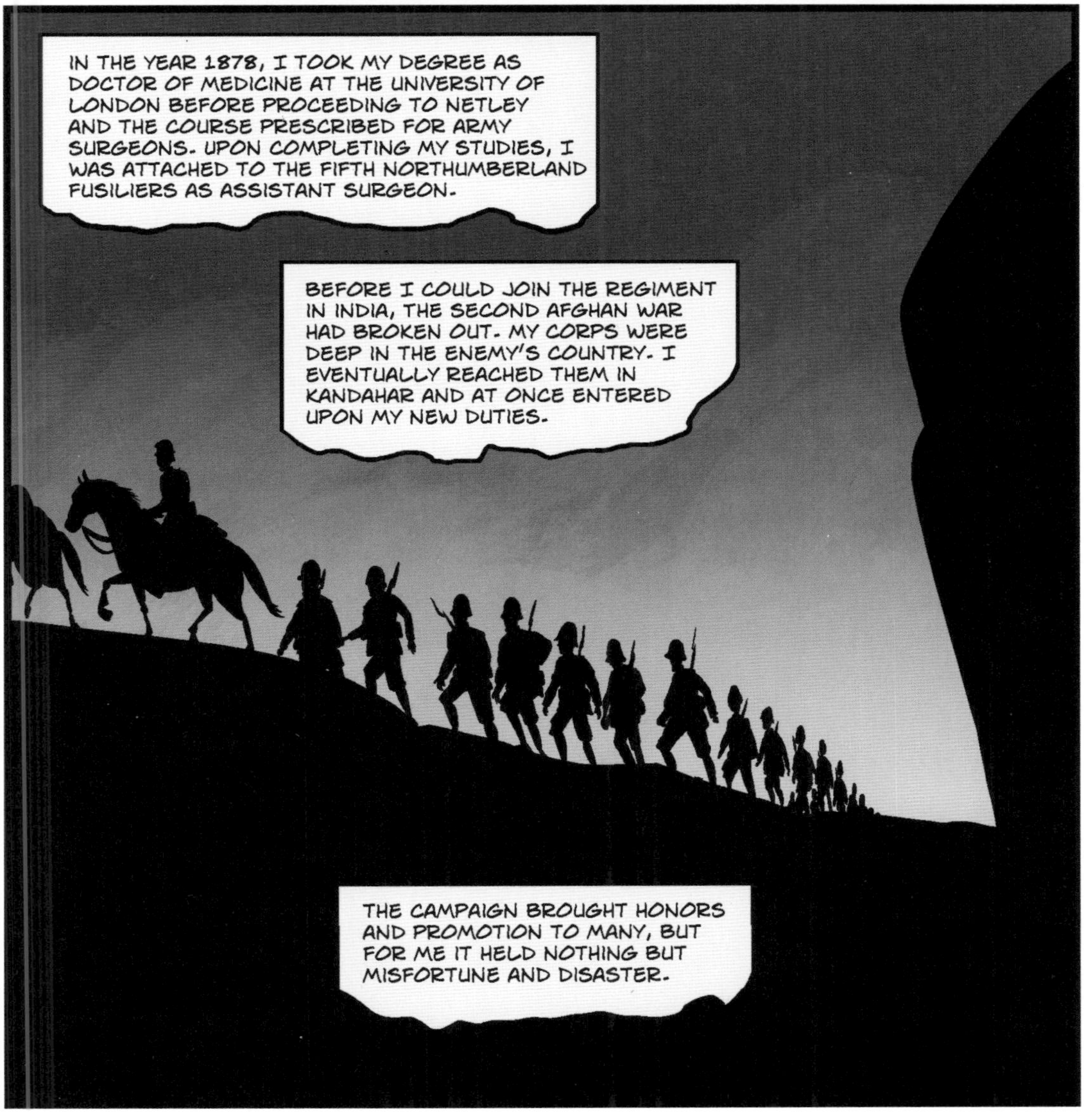
IN THE YEAR 1878, I TOOK MY DEGREE AS DOCTOR OF MEDICINE AT THE UNIVERSITY OF LONDON BEFORE PROCEEDING TO NETLEY AND THE COURSE PRESCRIBED FOR ARMY SURGEONS. UPON COMPLETING MY STUDIES, I WAS ATTACHED TO THE FIFTH NORTHUMBERLAND FUSILIERS AS ASSISTANT SURGEON.
BEFORE I COULD JOIN THE REGIMENT IN INDIA, THE SECOND AFGHAN WAR HAD BROKEN OUT. MY CORPS WERE DEEP IN THE ENEMY'S COUNTRY. I EVENTUALLY REACHED THEM IN KANDAHAR AND AT ONCE ENTERED UPON MY NEW DUTIES.
THE CAMPAIGN BROUGHT HONORS AND PROMOTION TO MANY, BUT FOR ME IT HELD NOTHING BUT MISFORTUNE AND DISASTER.

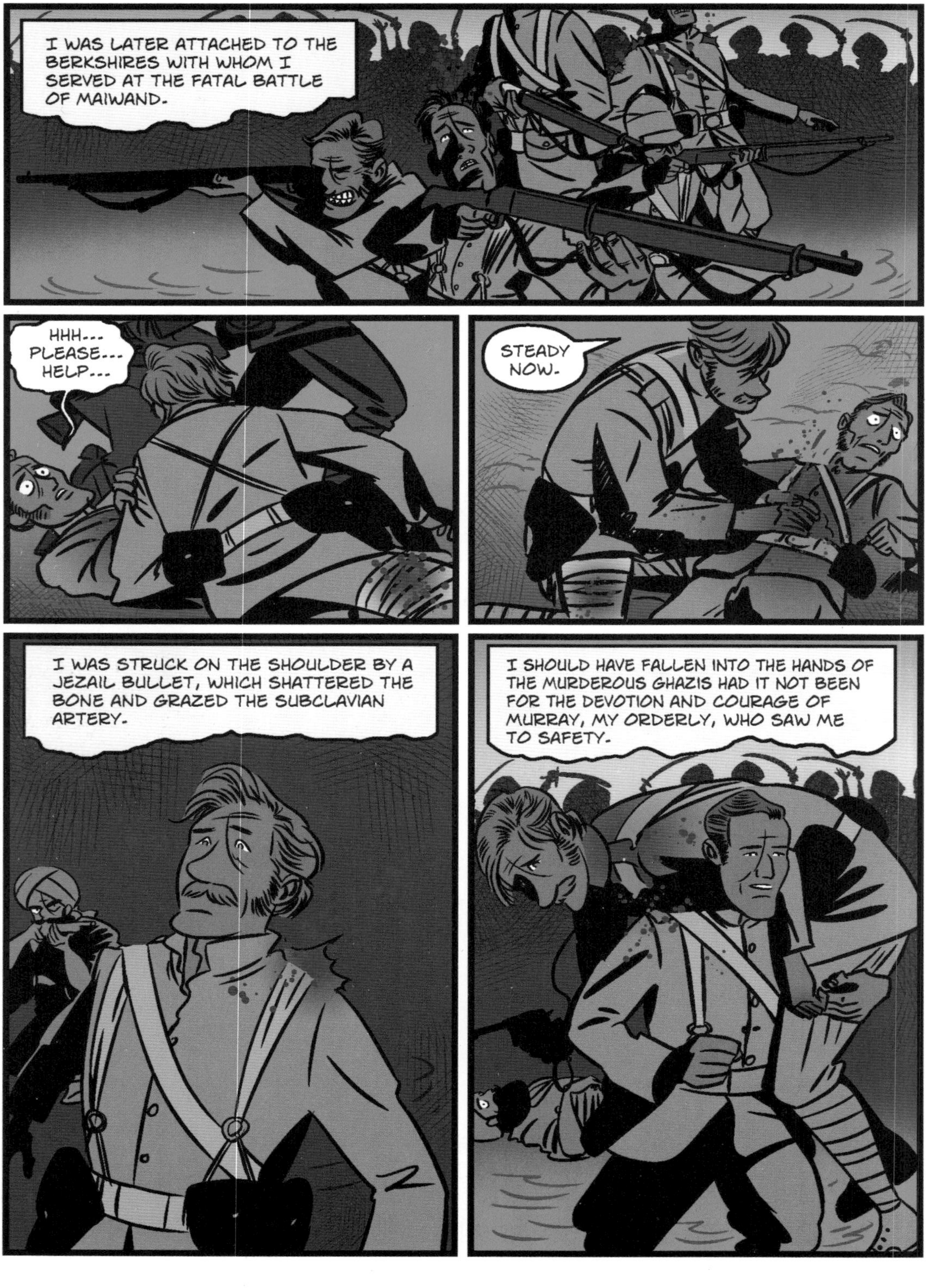
I WAS LATER ATTACHED TO THE BERKSHIRES WITH WHOM I SERVED AT THE FATAL BATTLE OF MAIWAND.
HHH... PLEASE... HELP...
STEADY NOW.
I WAS STRUCK ON THE SHOULDER BY A JEZAIL BULLET, WHICH SHATTERED THE BONE AND GRAZED THE SUBCLAVIAN ARTERY.
I SHOULD HAVE FALLEN INTO THE HANDS OF THE MURDEROUS GHAZIS HAD IT NOT BEEN FOR THE DEVOTION AND COURAGE OF MURRAY, MY ORDERLY, WHO SAW ME TO SAFETY.

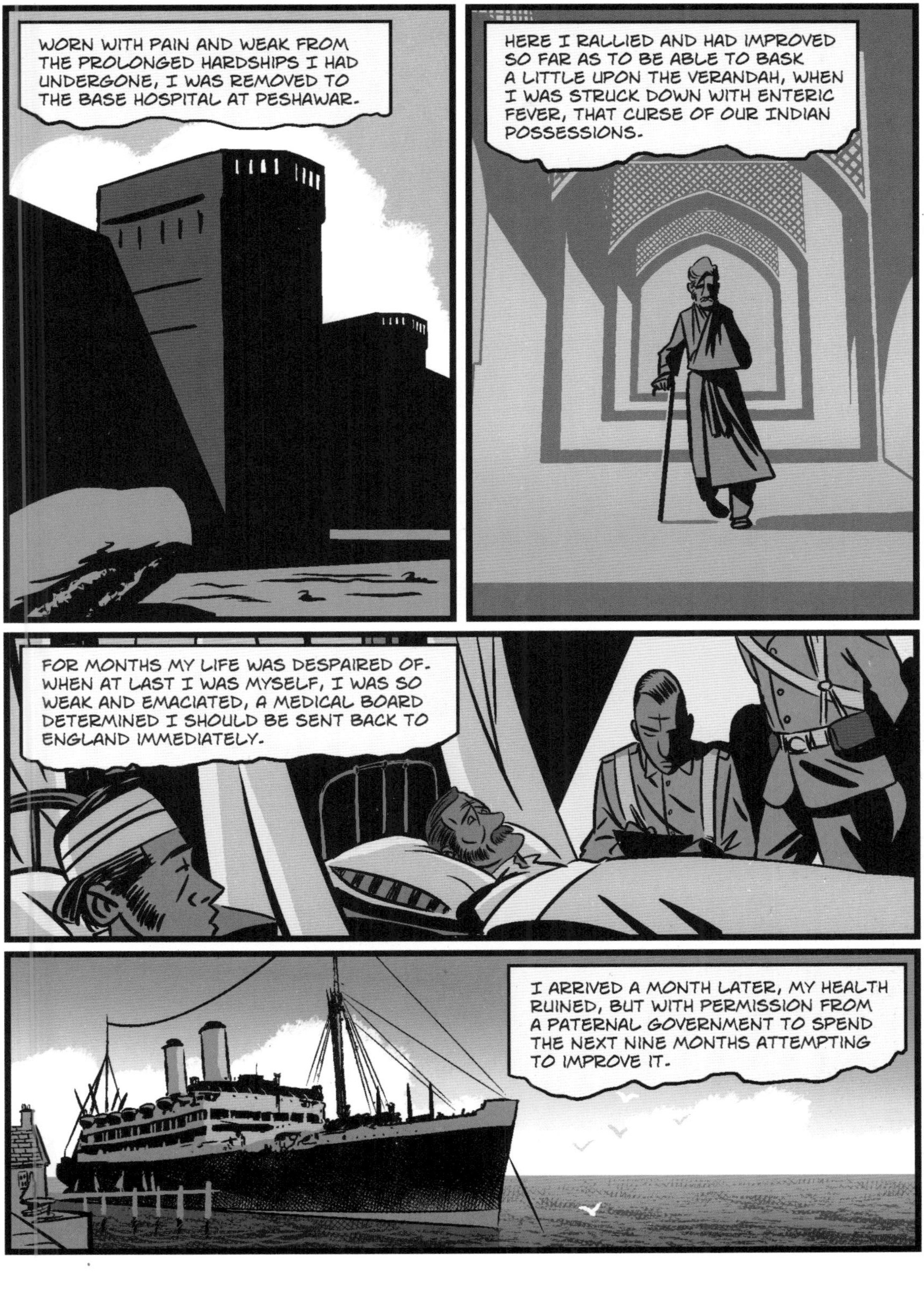
WORN WITH PAIN AND WEAK FROM THE PROLONGED HARDSHIPS I HAD UNDERGONE, I WAS REMOVED TO THE BASE HOSPITAL AT PESHAWAR.
HERE I RALLIED AND HAD IMPROVED SO FAR AS TO BE ABLE TO BASK A LITTLE UPON THE VERANDAH, WHEN I WAS STRUCK DOWN WITH ENTERIC FEVER, THAT CURSE OF OUR INDIAN POSSESSIONS.
FOR MONTHS MY LIFE WAS DESPAIRED OF. WHEN AT LAST I WAS MYSELF, I WAS SO WEAK AND EMACIATED, A MEDICAL BOARD DETERMINED I SHOULD BE SENT BACK TO ENGLAND IMMEDIATELY.
I ARRIVED A MONTH LATER, MY HEALTH RUINED, BUT WITH PERMISSION FROM A PATERNAL GOVERNMENT TO SPEND THE NEXT NINE MONTHS ATTEMPTING TO IMPROVE IT.

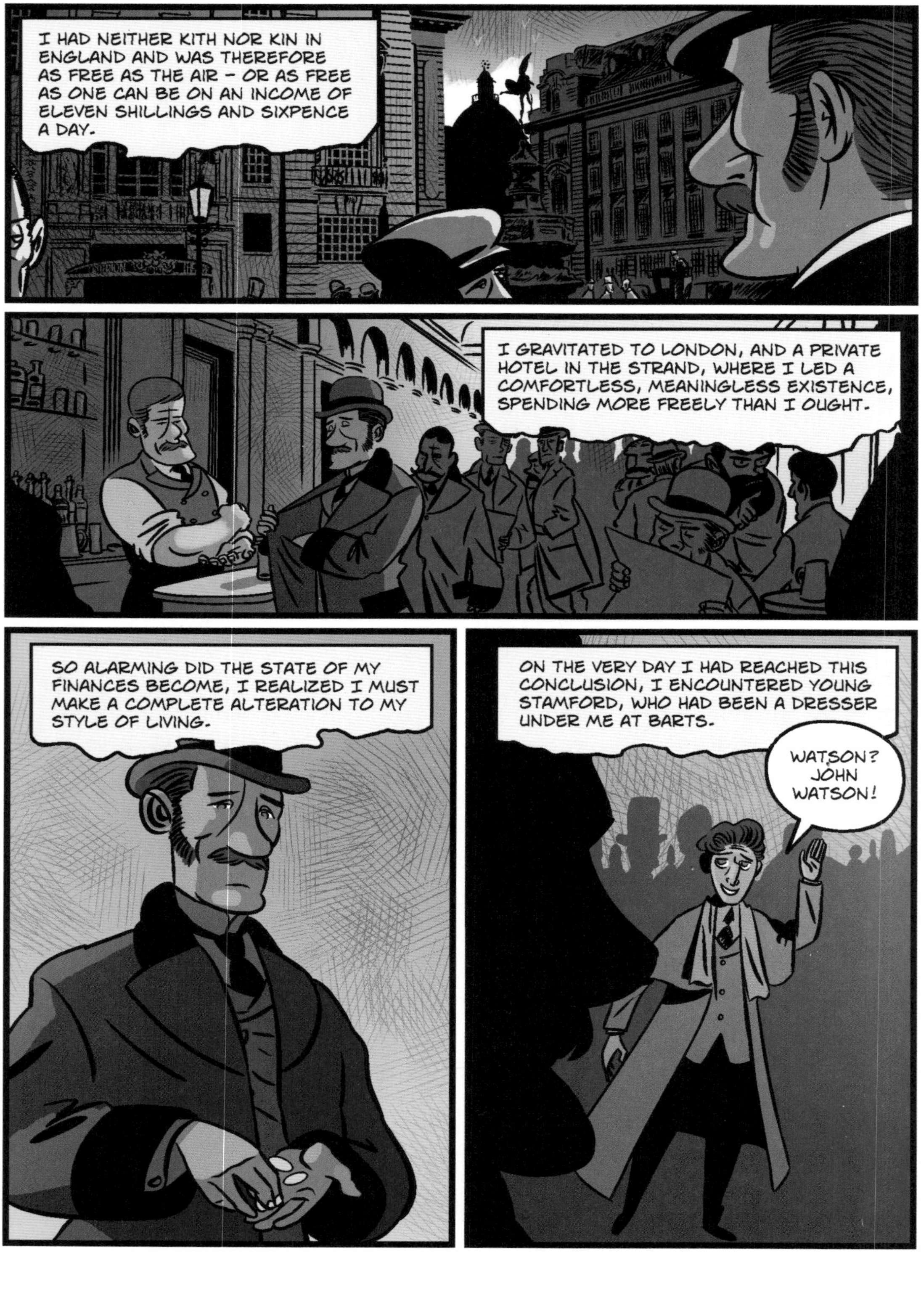
I HAD NEITHER KITH NOR KIN IN ENGLAND AND WAS THEREFORE AS FREE AS THE AIR – OR AS FREE AS ONE CAN BE ON AN INCOME OF ELEVEN SHILLINGS AND SIXPENCE A DAY.
I GRAVITATED TO LONDON, AND A PRIVATE HOTEL IN THE STRAND, WHERE I LED A COMFORTLESS, MEANINGLESS EXISTENCE, SPENDING MORE FREELY THAN I OUGHT.
SO ALARMING DID THE STATE OF MY FINANCES BECOME, I REALIZED I MUST MAKE A COMPLETE ALTERATION TO MY STYLE OF LIVING.
ON THE VERY DAY I HAD REACHED THIS CONCLUSION, I ENCOUNTERED YOUNG STAMFORD, WHO HAD BEEN A DRESSER UNDER ME AT BARTS.
WATSON? JOHN WATSON!

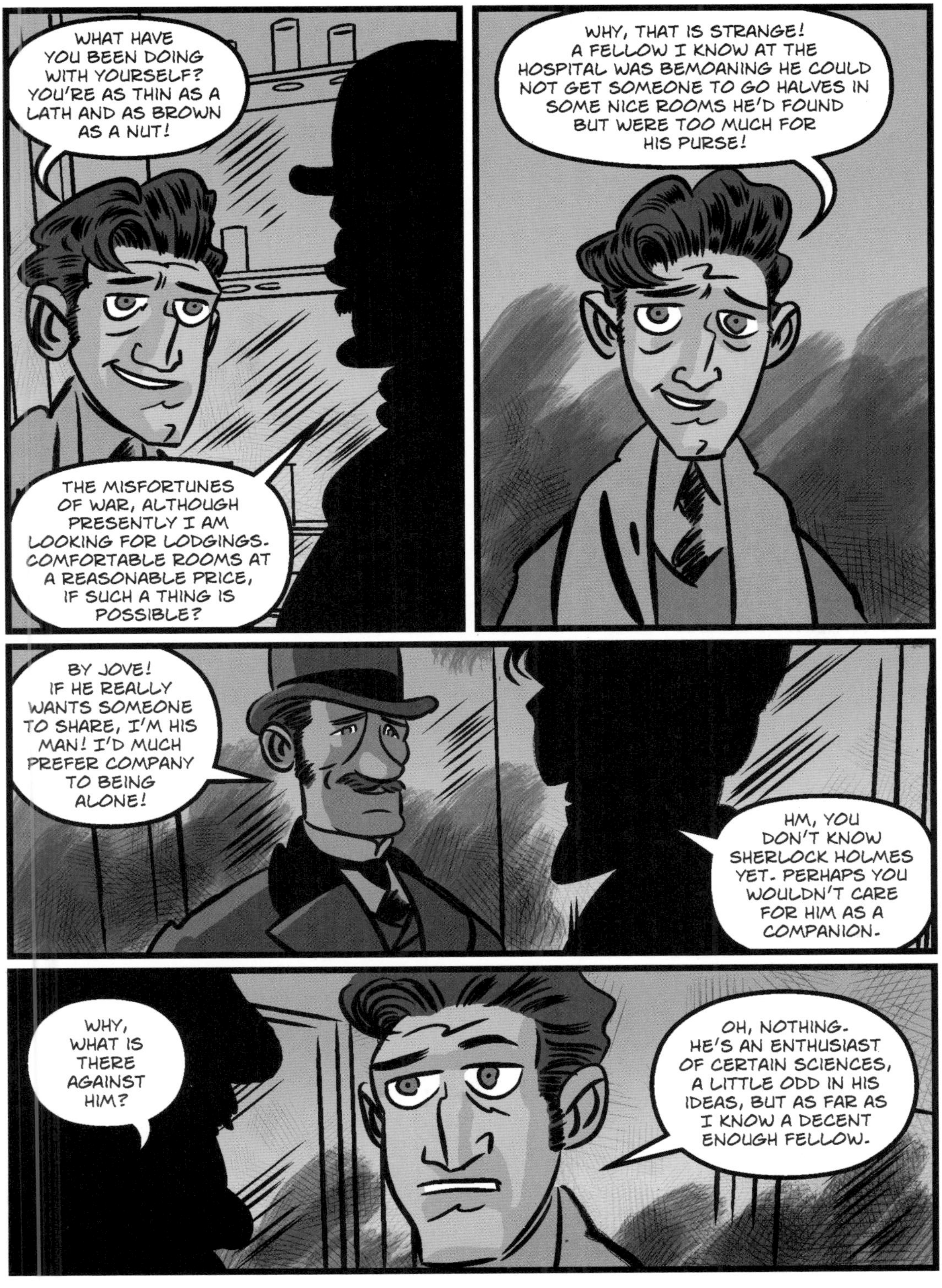
WHAT HAVE YOU BEEN DOING WITH YOURSELF? YOU'RE AS THIN AS A LATH AND AS BROWN AS A NUT!
THE MISFORTUNES OF WAR, ALTHOUGH PRESENTLY I AM LOOKING FOR LODGINGS. COMFORTABLE ROOMS AT A REASONABLE PRICE, IF SUCH A THING IS POSSIBLE?
WHY, THAT IS STRANGE! A FELLOW I KNOW AT THE HOSPITAL WAS BEMOANING HE COULD NOT GET SOMEONE TO GO HALVES IN SOME NICE ROOMS HE'D FOUND BUT WERE TOO MUCH FOR HIS PURSE!
BY JOVE! IF HE REALLY WANTS SOMEONE TO SHARE, I'M HIS MAN! I'D MUCH PREFER COMPANY TO BEING ALONE!
HM, YOU DON'T KNOW SHERLOCK HOLMES YET. PERHAPS YOU WOULDN'T CARE FOR HIM AS A COMPANION.
WHY, WHAT IS THERE AGAINST HIM?
OH, NOTHING. HE'S AN ENTHUSIAST OF CERTAIN SCIENCES, A LITTLE ODD IN HIS IDEAS, BUT AS FAR AS I KNOW A DECENT ENOUGH FELLOW.

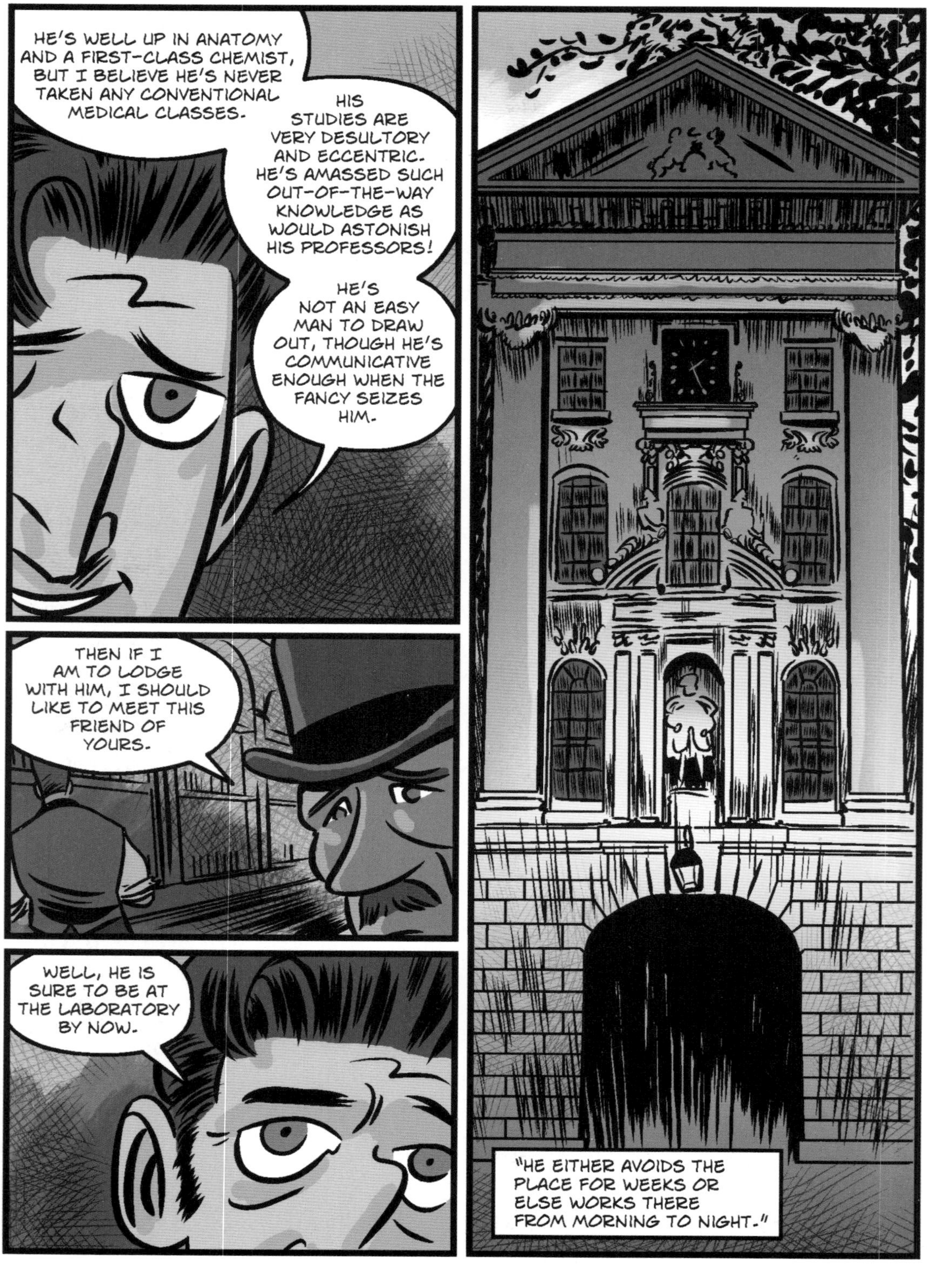
HE'S WELL UP IN ANATOMY AND A FIRST-CLASS CHEMIST, BUT I BELIEVE HE'S NEVER TAKEN ANY CONVENTIONAL MEDICAL CLASSES.
HIS STUDIES ARE VERY DESULTORY AND ECCENTRIC. HE'S AMASSED SUCH OUT-OF-THE-WAY KNOWLEDGE AS WOULD ASTONISH HIS PROFESSORS!
HE'S NOT AN EASY MAN TO DRAW OUT, THOUGH HE'S COMMUNICATIVE ENOUGH WHEN THE FANCY SEIZES HIM.
THEN IF I AM TO LODGE WITH HIM, I SHOULD LIKE TO MEET THIS FRIEND OF YOURS.
WELL, HE IS SURE TO BE AT THE LABORATORY BY NOW.
"HE EITHER AVOIDS THE PLACE FOR WEEKS OR ELSE WORKS THERE FROM MORNING TO NIGHT."

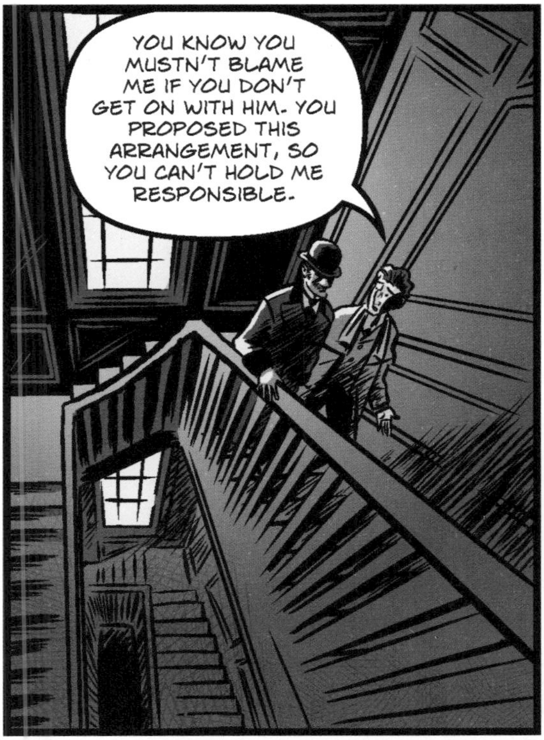
YOU KNOW YOU MUSTN'T BLAME ME IF YOU DON'T GET ON WITH HIM. YOU PROPOSED THIS ARRANGEMENT, SO YOU CAN'T HOLD ME RESPONSIBLE.

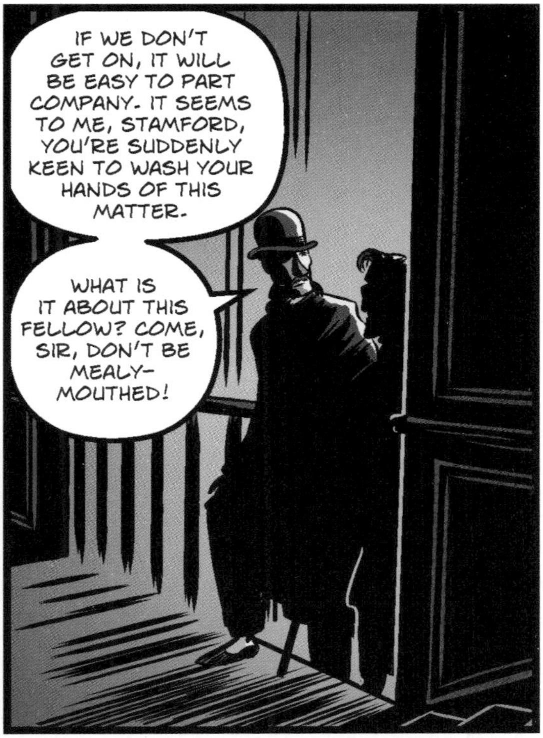
IF WE DON'T GET ON, IT WILL BE EASY TO PART COMPANY. IT SEEMS TO ME, STAMFORD, YOU'RE SUDDENLY KEEN TO WASH YOUR HANDS OF THIS MATTER.
WHAT IS IT ABOUT THIS FELLOW? COME, SIR, DON'T BE MEALY-MOUTHED!

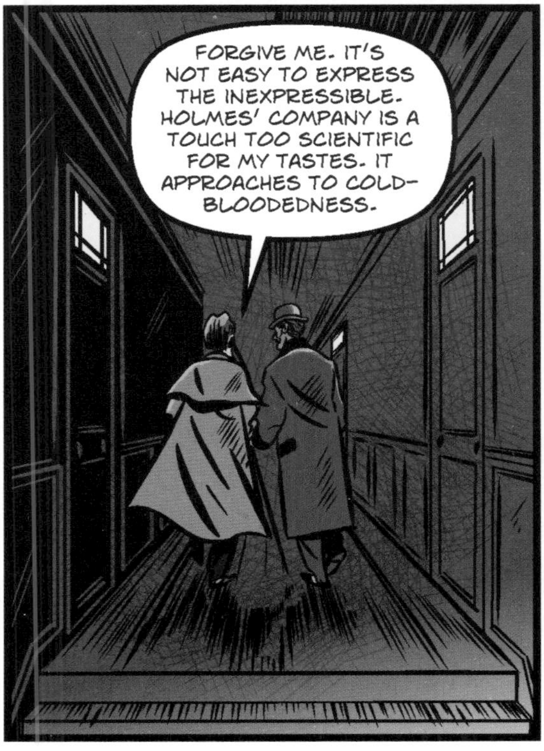
FORGIVE ME. IT'S NOT EASY TO EXPRESS THE INEXPRESSIBLE. HOLMES' COMPANY IS A TOUCH TOO SCIENTIFIC FOR MY TASTES. IT APPROACHES TO COLD-BLOODEDNESS.

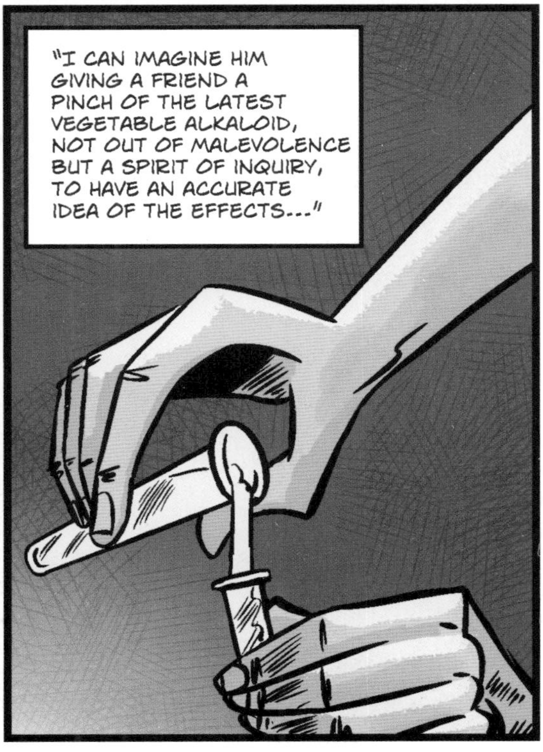
"I CAN IMAGINE HIM GIVING A FRIEND A PINCH OF THE LATEST VEGETABLE ALKALOID, NOT OUT OF MALEVOLENCE BUT A SPIRIT OF INQUIRY, TO HAVE AN ACCURATE IDEA OF THE EFFECTS..."

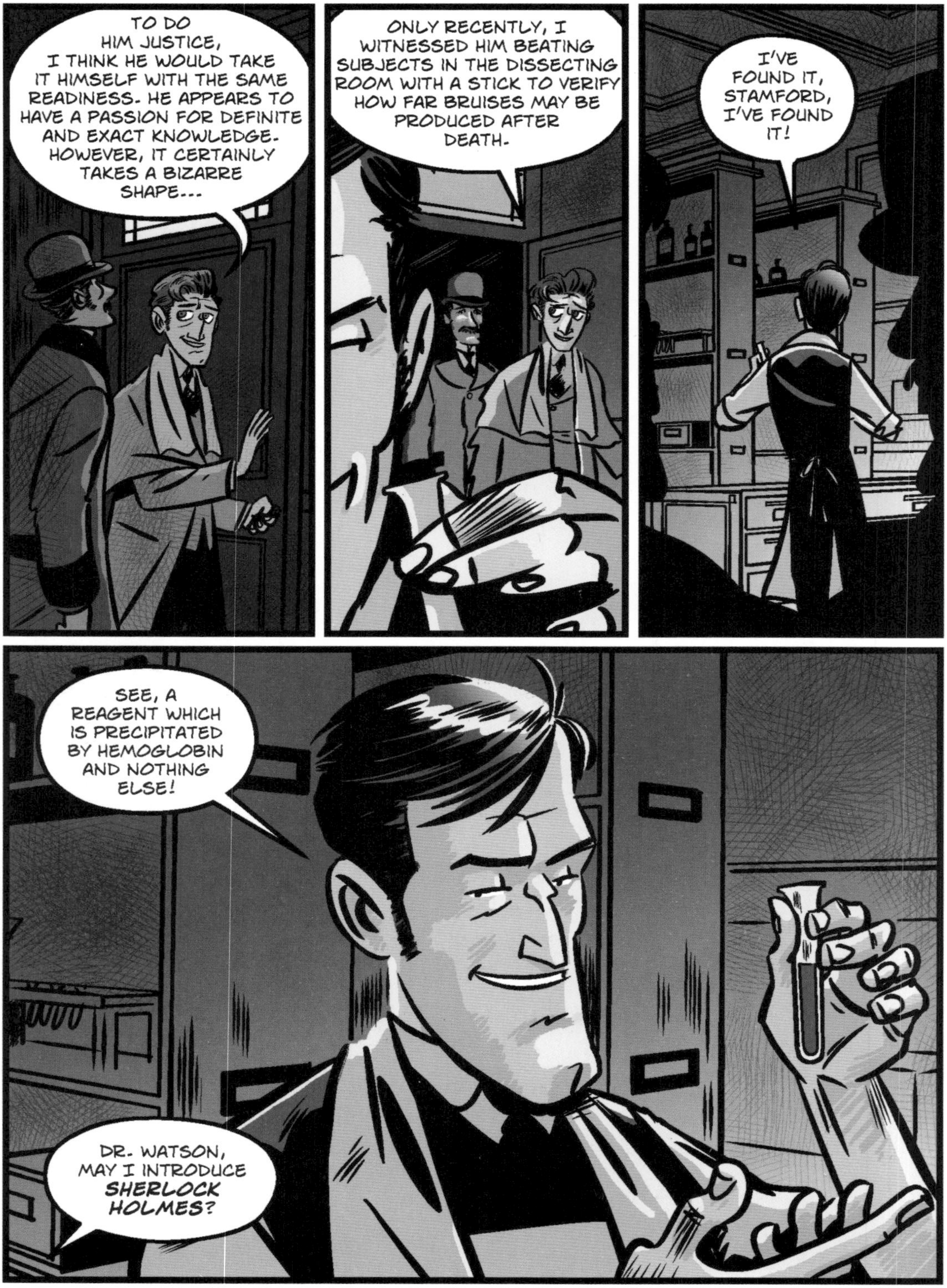
TO DO HIM JUSTICE, I THINK HE WOULD TAKE IT HIMSELF WITH THE SAME READINESS. HE APPEARS TO HAVE A PASSION FOR DEFINITE AND EXACT KNOWLEDGE. HOWEVER, IT CERTAINLY TAKES A BIZARRE SHAPE...
ONLY RECENTLY, I WITNESSED HIM BEATING SUBJECTS IN THE DISSECTING ROOM WITH A STICK TO VERIFY HOW FAR BRUISES MAY BE PRODUCED AFTER DEATH.
I'VE FOUND IT, STAMFORD, I'VE FOUND IT!
SEE, A REAGENT WHICH IS PRECIPITATED BY HEMOGLOBIN AND NOTHING ELSE!
DR. WATSON, MAY I INTRODUCE SHERLOCK HOLMES?

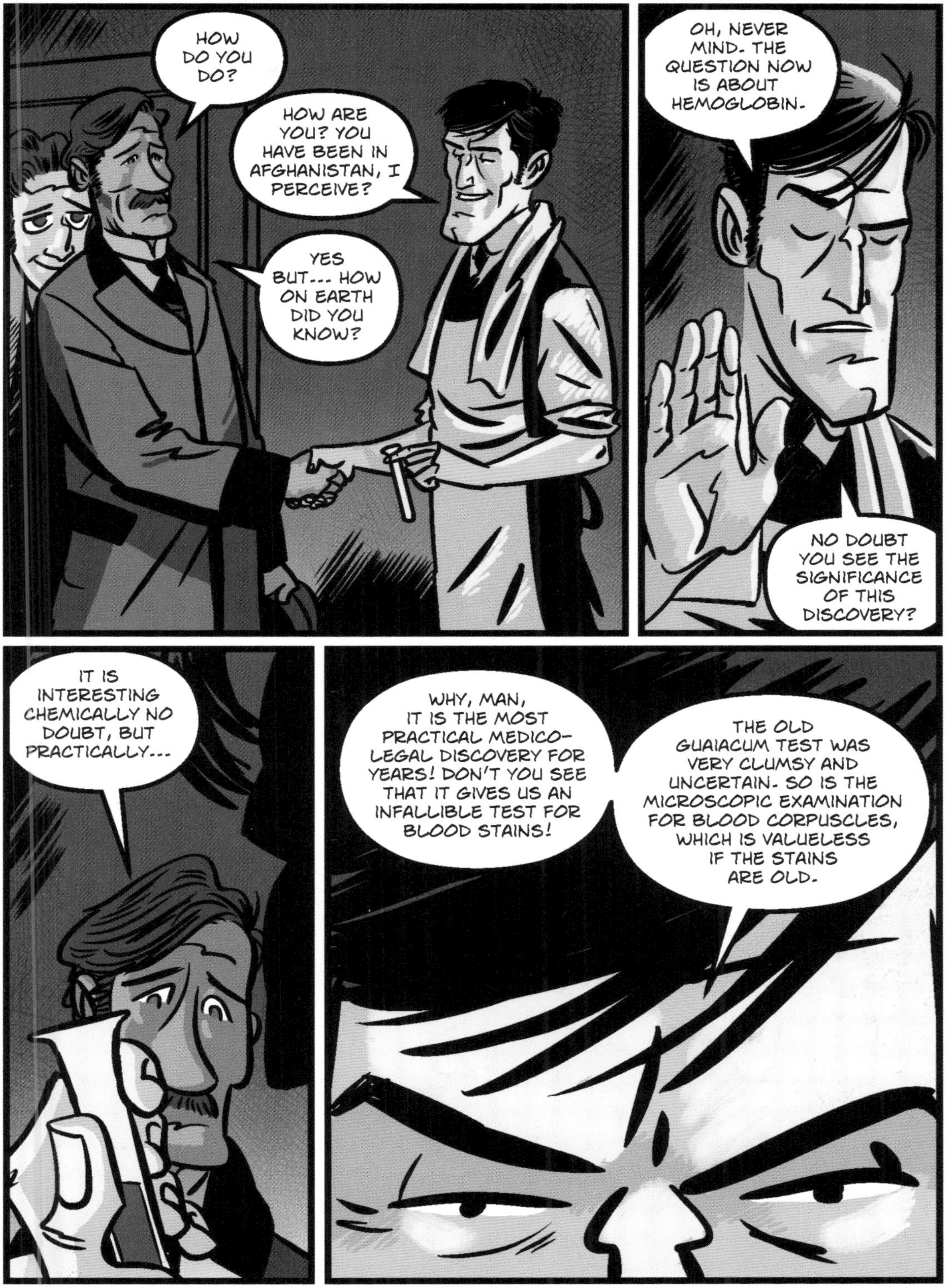
HOW DO YOU DO?
HOW ARE YOU? YOU HAVE BEEN IN AFGHANISTAN, I PERCEIVE?
YES BUT... HOW ON EARTH DID YOU KNOW?
OH, NEVER MIND. THE QUESTION NOW IS ABOUT HEMOGLOBIN.
NO DOUBT YOU SEE THE SIGNIFICANCE OF THIS DISCOVERY?
IT IS INTERESTING CHEMICALLY NO DOUBT, BUT PRACTICALLY...
WHY, MAN, IT IS THE MOST PRACTICAL MEDICO-LEGAL DISCOVERY FOR YEARS! DON'T YOU SEE THAT IT GIVES US AN INFALLIBLE TEST FOR BLOOD STAINS!
THE OLD GUAIACUM TEST WAS VERY CLUMSY AND UNCERTAIN. SO IS THE MICROSCOPIC EXAMINATION FOR BLOOD CORPUSCLES, WHICH IS VALUELESS IF THE STAINS ARE OLD.

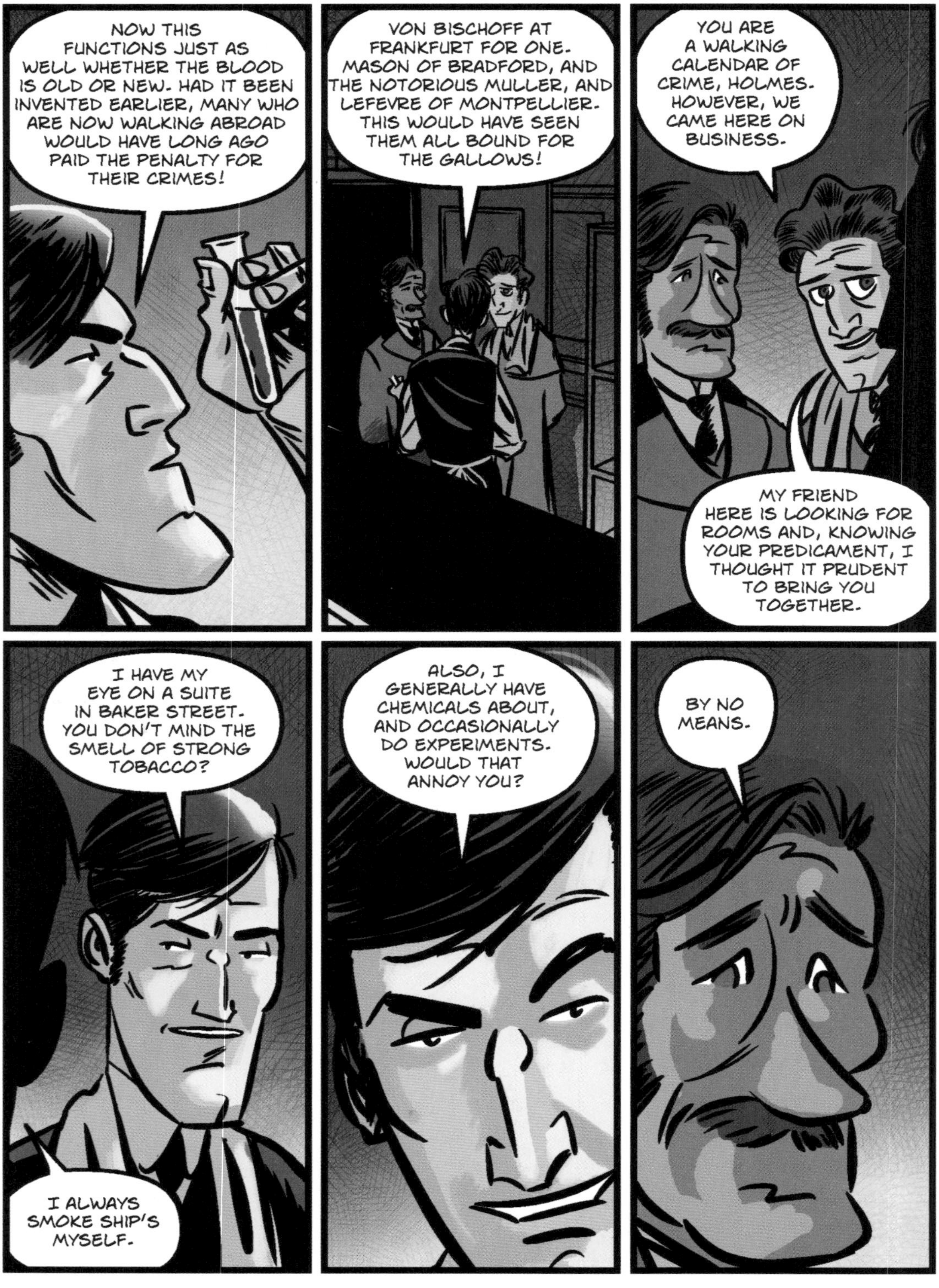
NOW THIS FUNCTIONS JUST AS WELL WHETHER THE BLOOD IS OLD OR NEW. HAD IT BEEN INVENTED EARLIER, MANY WHO ARE NOW WALKING ABROAD WOULD HAVE LONG AGO PAID THE PENALTY FOR THEIR CRIMES!
VON BISCHOFF AT FRANKFURT FOR ONE. MASON OF BRADFORD, AND THE NOTORIOUS MULLER, AND LEFEVRE OF MONTPELLIER. THIS WOULD HAVE SEEN THEM ALL BOUND FOR THE GALLOWS!
YOU ARE A WALKING CALENDAR OF CRIME, HOLMES. HOWEVER, WE CAME HERE ON BUSINESS.
MY FRIEND HERE IS LOOKING FOR ROOMS AND, KNOWING YOUR PREDICAMENT, I THOUGHT IT PRUDENT TO BRING YOU TOGETHER.
I HAVE MY EYE ON A SUITE IN BAKER STREET. YOU DON'T MIND THE SMELL OF STRONG TOBACCO?
I ALWAYS SMOKE SHIP'S MYSELF.
ALSO, I GENERALLY HAVE CHEMICALS ABOUT, AND OCCASIONALLY DO EXPERIMENTS. WOULD THAT ANNOY YOU?
BY NO MEANS.

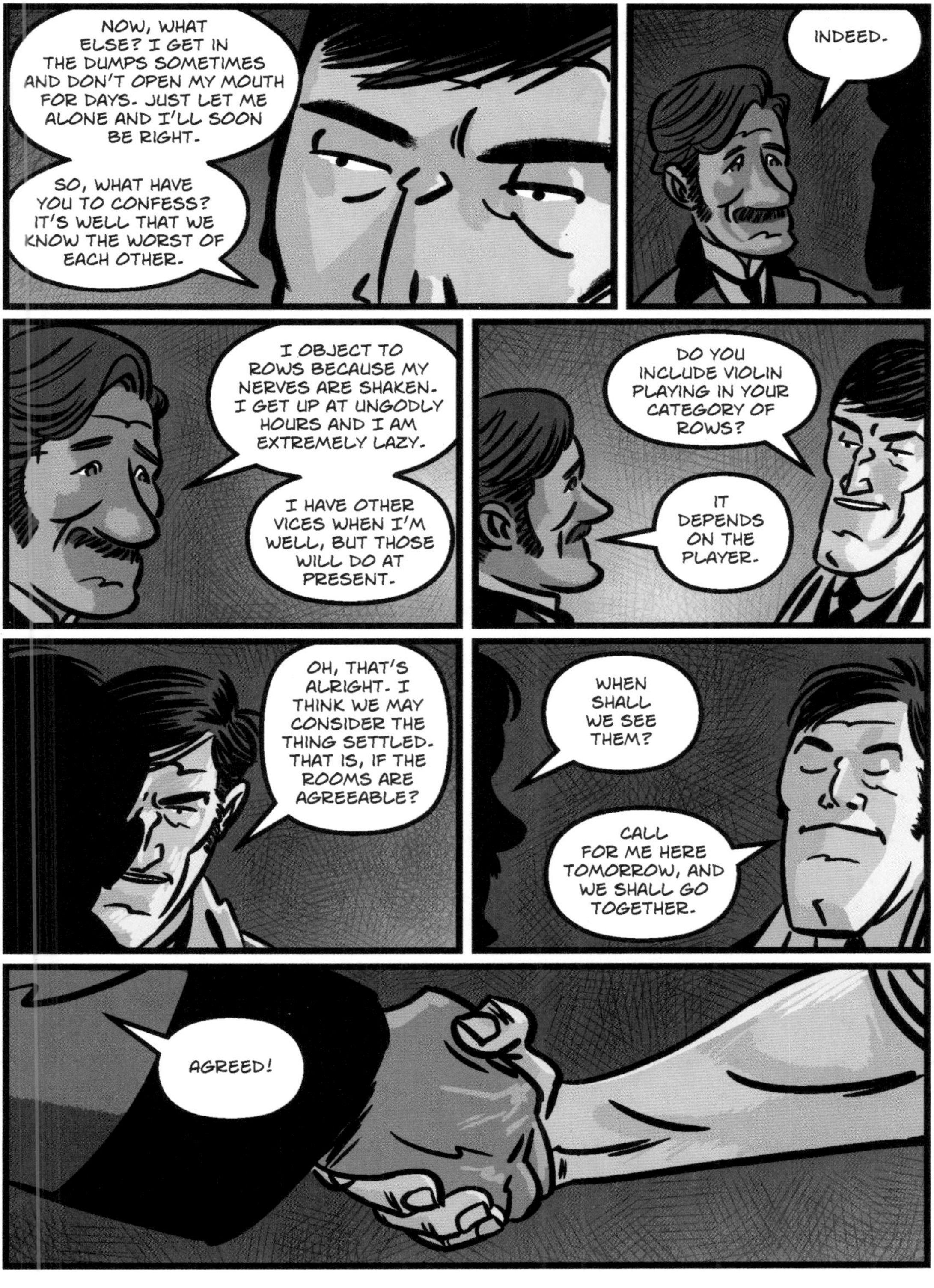
NOW, WHAT ELSE? I GET IN THE DUMPS SOMETIMES AND DON'T OPEN MY MOUTH FOR DAYS. JUST LET ME ALONE AND I'LL SOON BE RIGHT.
SO, WHAT HAVE YOU TO CONFESS? IT'S WELL THAT WE KNOW THE WORST OF EACH OTHER.
INDEED.
I OBJECT TO ROWS BECAUSE MY NERVES ARE SHAKEN. I GET UP AT UNGODLY HOURS AND I AM EXTREMELY LAZY.
I HAVE OTHER VICES WHEN I'M WELL, BUT THOSE WILL DO AT PRESENT.
DO YOU INCLUDE VIOLIN PLAYING IN YOUR CATEGORY OF ROWS?
IT DEPENDS ON THE PLAYER.
OH, THAT'S ALRIGHT. I THINK WE MAY CONSIDER THE THING SETTLED. THAT IS, IF THE ROOMS ARE AGREEABLE?
WHEN SHALL WE SEE THEM?
CALL FOR ME HERE TOMORROW, AND WE SHALL GO TOGETHER.
AGREED!

THE SCIENCE OF DEDUCTION

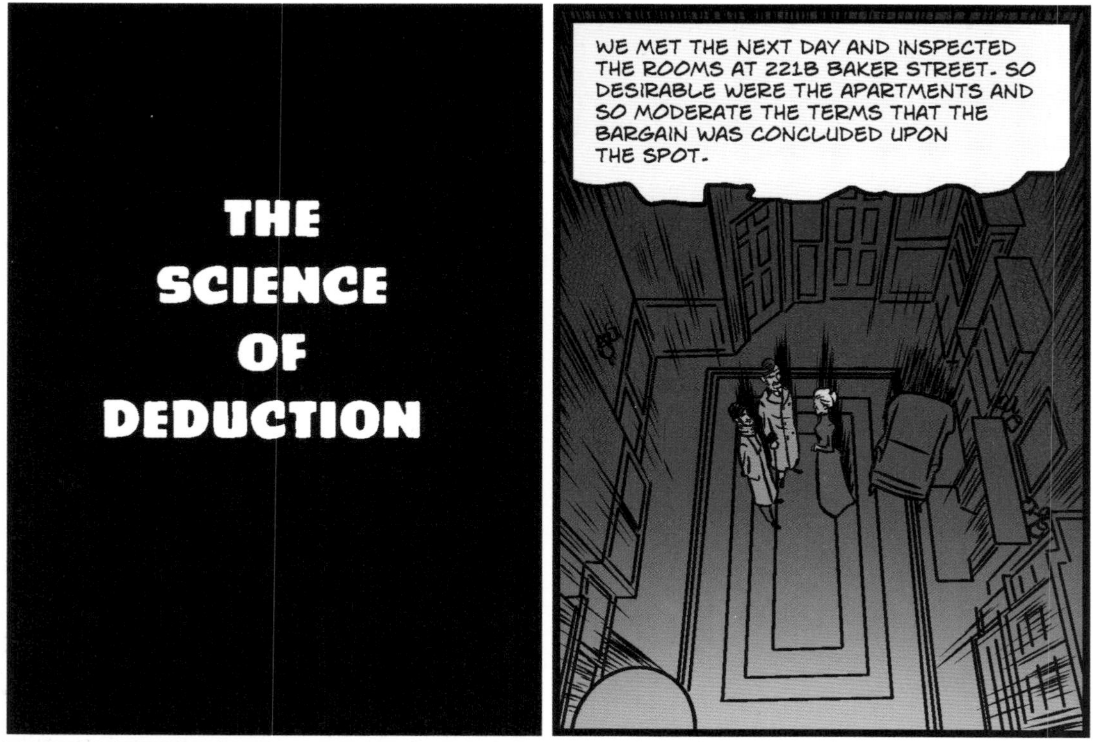
WE MET THE NEXT DAY AND INSPECTED THE ROOMS AT 221B BAKER STREET. SO DESIRABLE WERE THE APARTMENTS AND SO MODERATE THE TERMS THAT THE BARGAIN WAS CONCLUDED UPON THE SPOT.

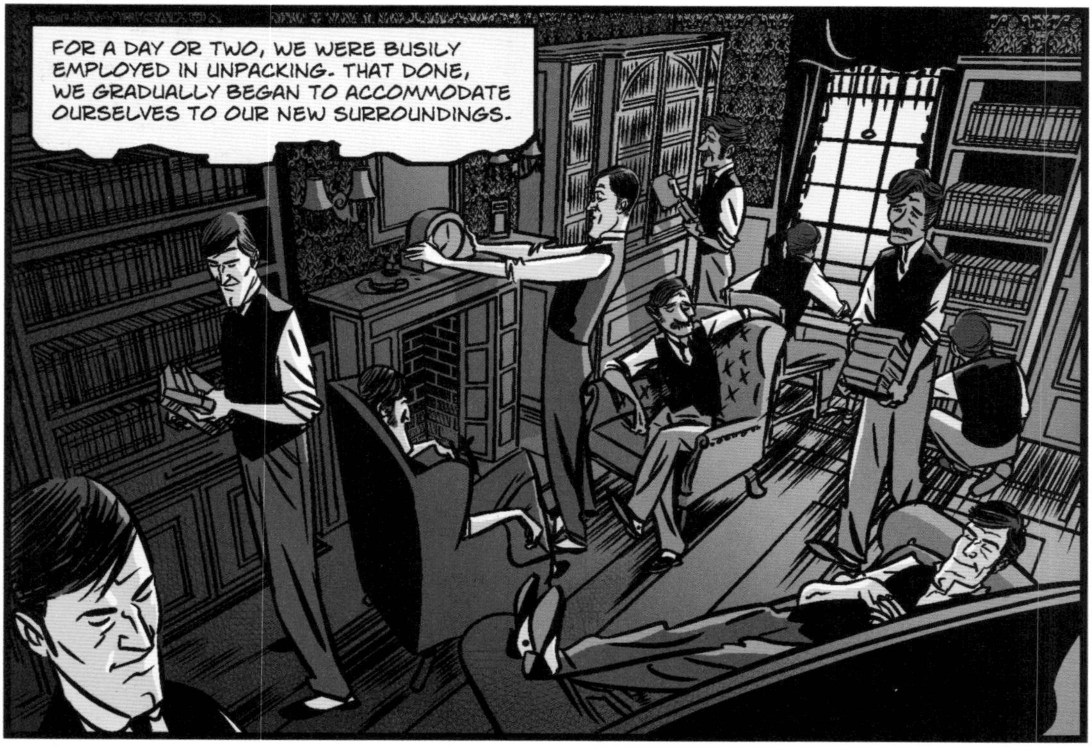
FOR A DAY OR TWO, WE WERE BUSILY EMPLOYED IN UNPACKING. THAT DONE, WE GRADUALLY BEGAN TO ACCOMMODATE OURSELVES TO OUR NEW SURROUNDINGS.

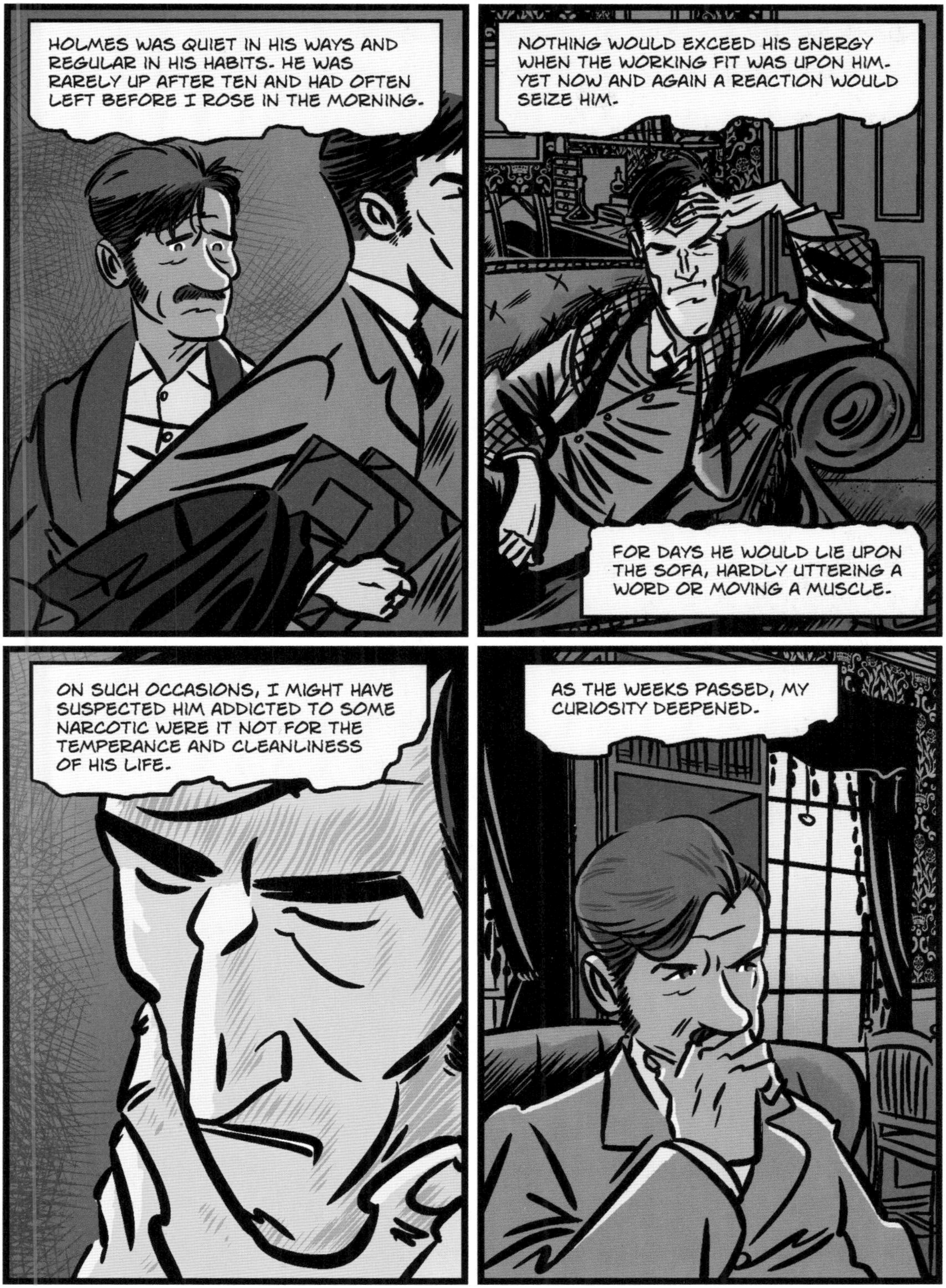
HOLMES WAS QUIET IN HIS WAYS AND REGULAR IN HIS HABITS. HE WAS RARELY UP AFTER TEN AND HAD OFTEN LEFT BEFORE I ROSE IN THE MORNING.
NOTHING WOULD EXCEED HIS ENERGY WHEN THE WORKING FIT WAS UPON HIM. YET NOW AND AGAIN A REACTION WOULD SEIZE HIM.
FOR DAYS HE WOULD LIE UPON THE SOFA, HARDLY UTTERING A WORD OR MOVING A MUSCLE.
ON SUCH OCCASIONS, I MIGHT HAVE SUSPECTED HIM ADDICTED TO SOME NARCOTIC WERE IT NOT FOR THE TEMPERANCE AND CLEANLINESS OF HIS LIFE.
AS THE WEEKS PASSED, MY CURIOSITY DEEPENED.

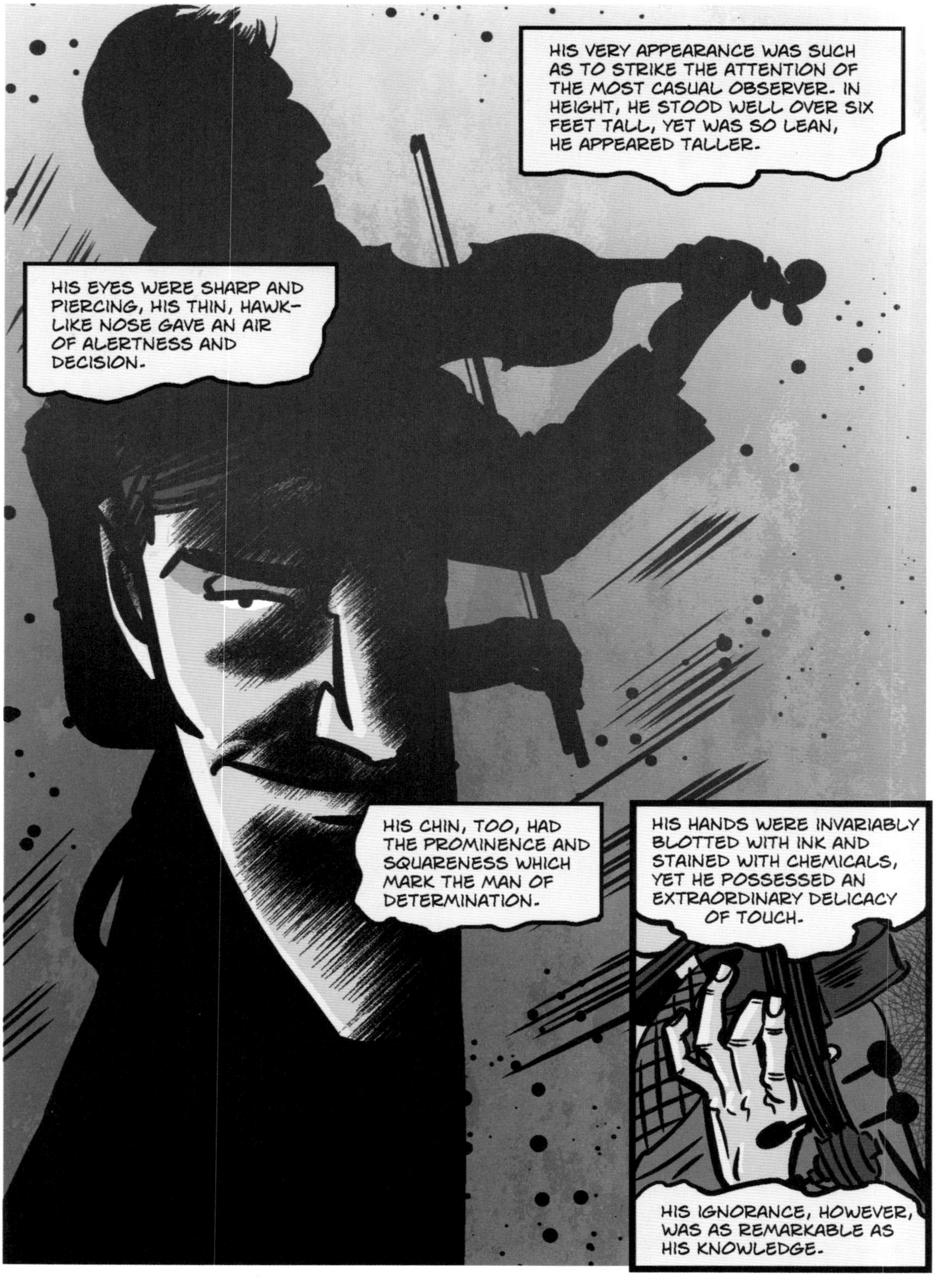
HIS VERY APPEARANCE WAS SUCH AS TO STRIKE THE ATTENTION OF THE MOST CASUAL OBSERVER. IN HEIGHT, HE STOOD WELL OVER SIX FEET TALL, YET WAS SO LEAN, HE APPEARED TALLER.
HIS EYES WERE SHARP AND PIERCING, HIS THIN, HAWK-LIKE NOSE GAVE AN AIR OF ALERTNESS AND DECISION.
HIS CHIN, TOO, HAD THE PROMINENCE AND SQUARENESS WHICH MARK THE MAN OF DETERMINATION.
HIS HANDS WERE INVARIABLY BLOTTED WITH INK AND STAINED WITH CHEMICALS, YET HE POSSESSED AN EXTRAORDINARY DELICACY OF TOUCH.
HIS IGNORANCE, HOWEVER, WAS AS REMARKABLE AS HIS KNOWLEDGE.

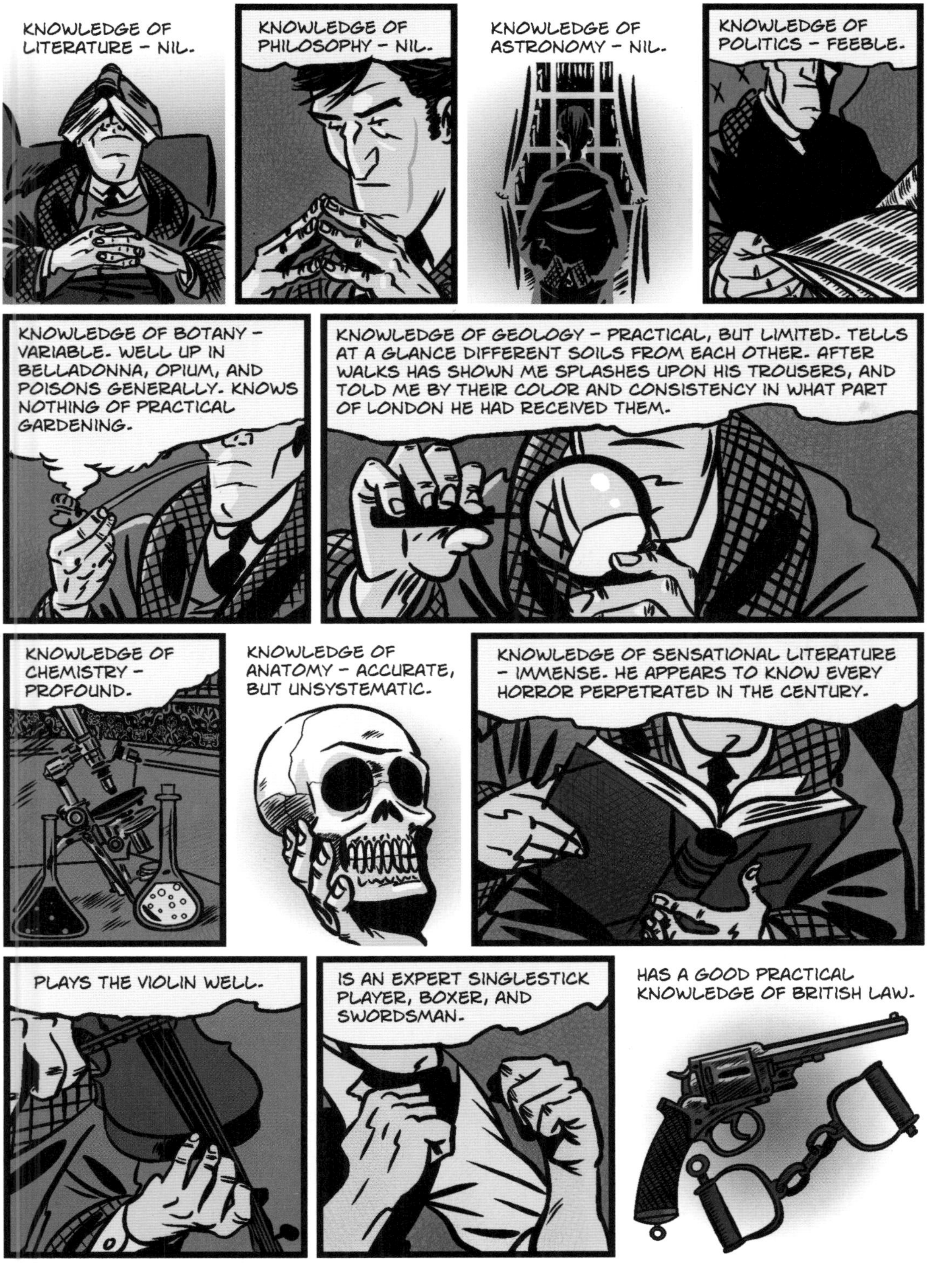
KNOWLEDGE OF LITERATURE – NIL.
KNOWLEDGE OF PHILOSOPHY – NIL.
KNOWLEDGE OF ASTRONOMY – NIL.
KNOWLEDGE OF POLITICS – FEEBLE.
KNOWLEDGE OF BOTANY – VARIABLE. WELL UP IN BELLADONNA, OPIUM, AND POISONS GENERALLY. KNOWS NOTHING OF PRACTICAL GARDENING.
KNOWLEDGE OF GEOLOGY – PRACTICAL, BUT LIMITED. TELLS AT A GLANCE DIFFERENT SOILS FROM EACH OTHER. AFTER WALKS HAS SHOWN ME SPLASHES UPON HIS TROUSERS, AND TOLD ME BY THEIR COLOR AND CONSISTENCY IN WHAT PART OF LONDON HE HAD RECEIVED THEM.
KNOWLEDGE OF CHEMISTRY – PROFOUND.
KNOWLEDGE OF ANATOMY – ACCURATE, BUT UNSYSTEMATIC.
KNOWLEDGE OF SENSATIONAL LITERATURE – IMMENSE. HE APPEARS TO KNOW EVERY HORROR PERPETRATED IN THE CENTURY.
PLAYS THE VIOLIN WELL.
IS AN EXPERT SINGLESTICK PLAYER, BOXER, AND SWORDSMAN.
HAS A GOOD PRACTICAL KNOWLEDGE OF BRITISH LAW.

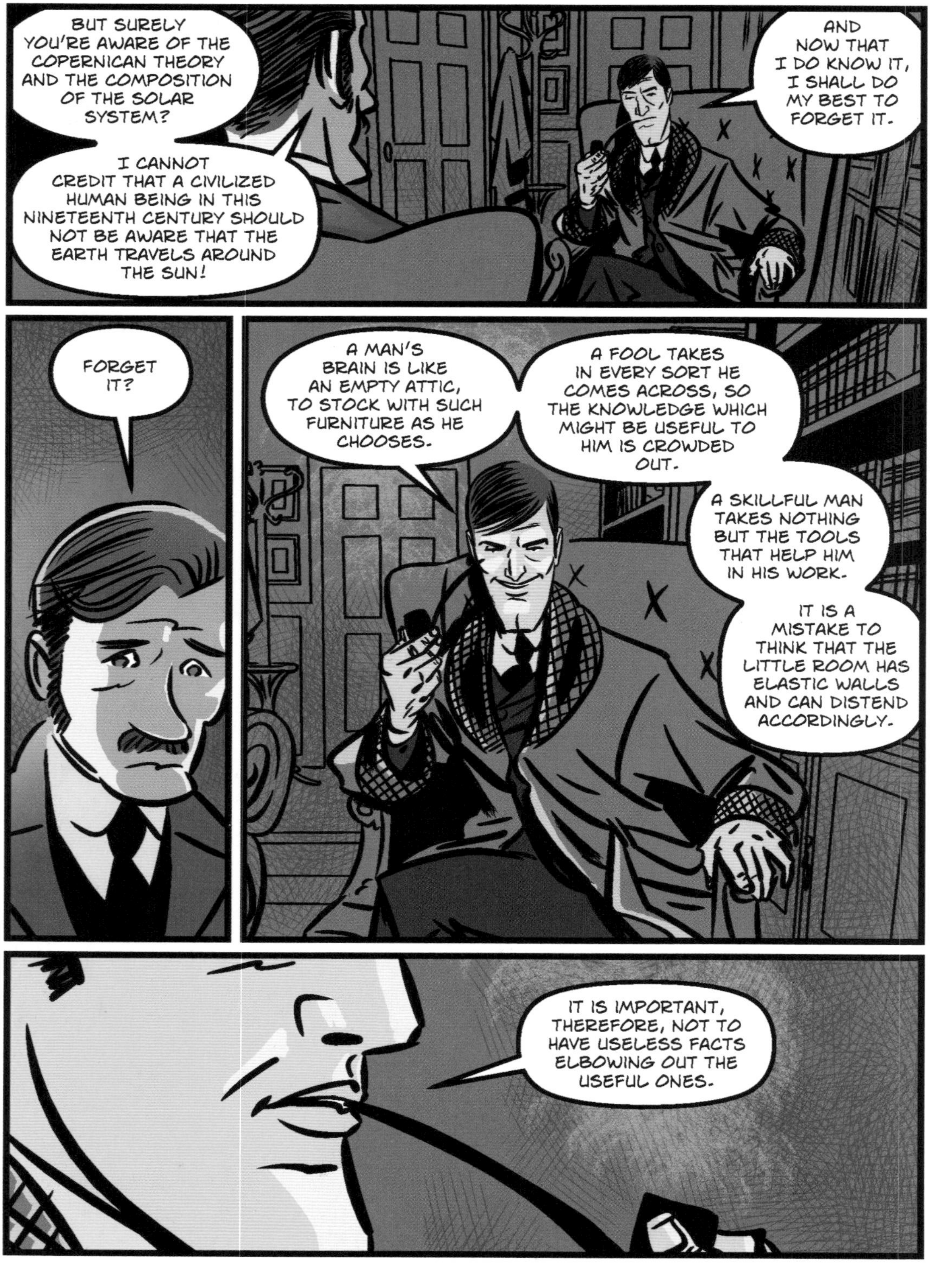
BUT SURELY YOU'RE AWARE OF THE COPERNICAN THEORY AND THE COMPOSITION OF THE SOLAR SYSTEM?
I CANNOT CREDIT THAT A CIVILIZED HUMAN BEING IN THIS NINETEENTH CENTURY SHOULD NOT BE AWARE THAT THE EARTH TRAVELS AROUND THE SUN!
AND NOW THAT I DO KNOW IT, I SHALL DO MY BEST TO FORGET IT.
FORGET IT?
A MAN'S BRAIN IS LIKE AN EMPTY ATTIC, TO STOCK WITH SUCH FURNITURE AS HE CHOOSES.
A FOOL TAKES IN EVERY SORT HE COMES ACROSS, SO THE KNOWLEDGE WHICH MIGHT BE USEFUL TO HIM IS CROWDED OUT.
A SKILLFUL MAN TAKES NOTHING BUT THE TOOLS THAT HELP HIM IN HIS WORK.
IT IS A MISTAKE TO THINK THAT THE LITTLE ROOM HAS ELASTIC WALLS AND CAN DISTEND ACCORDINGLY.
IT IS IMPORTANT, THEREFORE, NOT TO HAVE USELESS FACTS ELBOWING OUT THE USEFUL ONES.

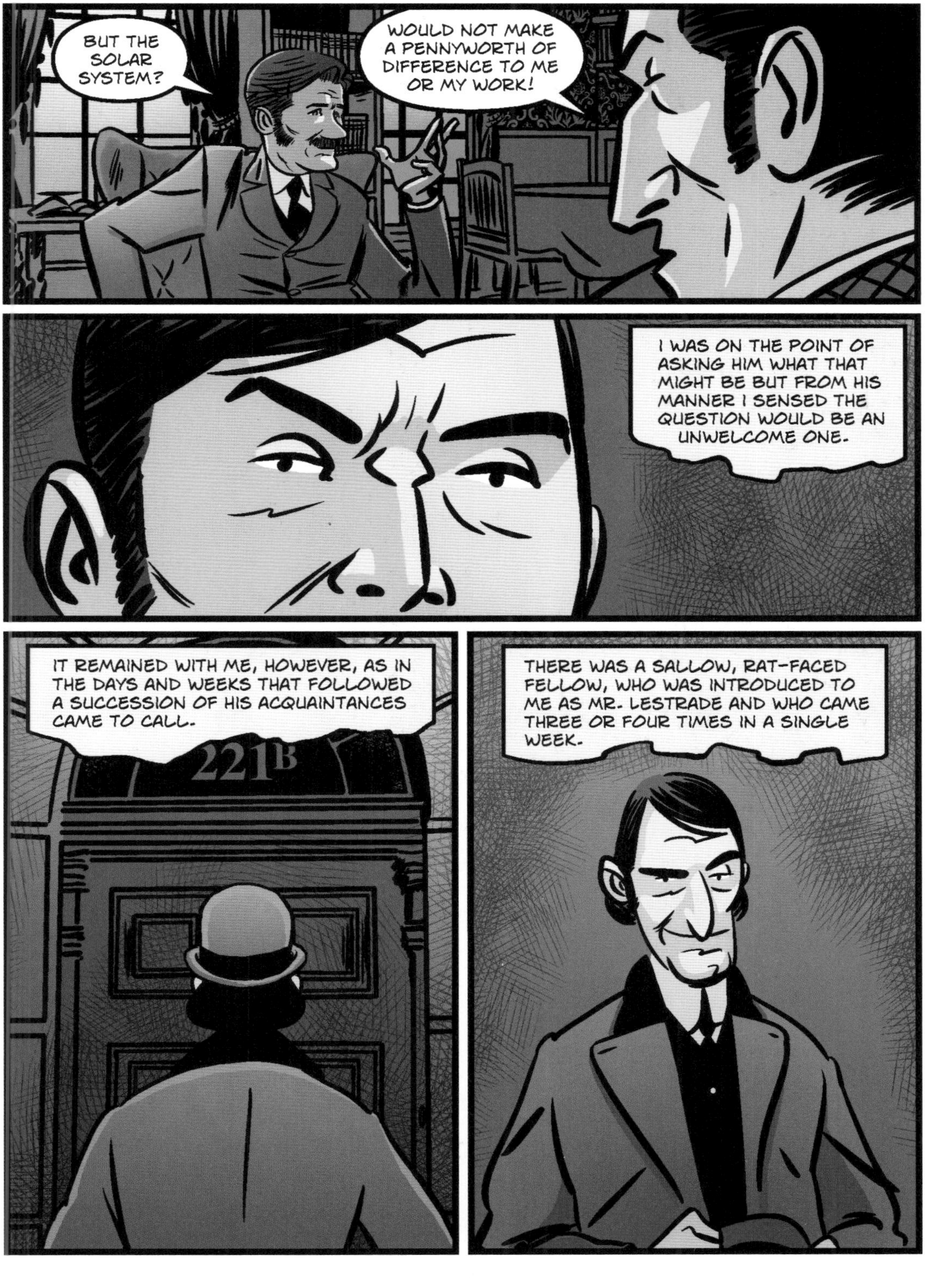
BUT THE SOLAR SYSTEM?
WOULD NOT MAKE A PENNYWORTH OF DIFFERENCE TO ME OR MY WORK!
I WAS ON THE POINT OF ASKING HIM WHAT THAT MIGHT BE BUT FROM HIS MANNER I SENSED THE QUESTION WOULD BE AN UNWELCOME ONE.
IT REMAINED WITH ME, HOWEVER, AS IN THE DAYS AND WEEKS THAT FOLLOWED A SUCCESSION OF HIS ACQUAINTANCES CAME TO CALL.
221B
THERE WAS A SALLOW, RAT-FACED FELLOW, WHO WAS INTRODUCED TO ME AS MR. LESTRADE AND WHO CAME THREE OR FOUR TIMES IN A SINGLE WEEK.

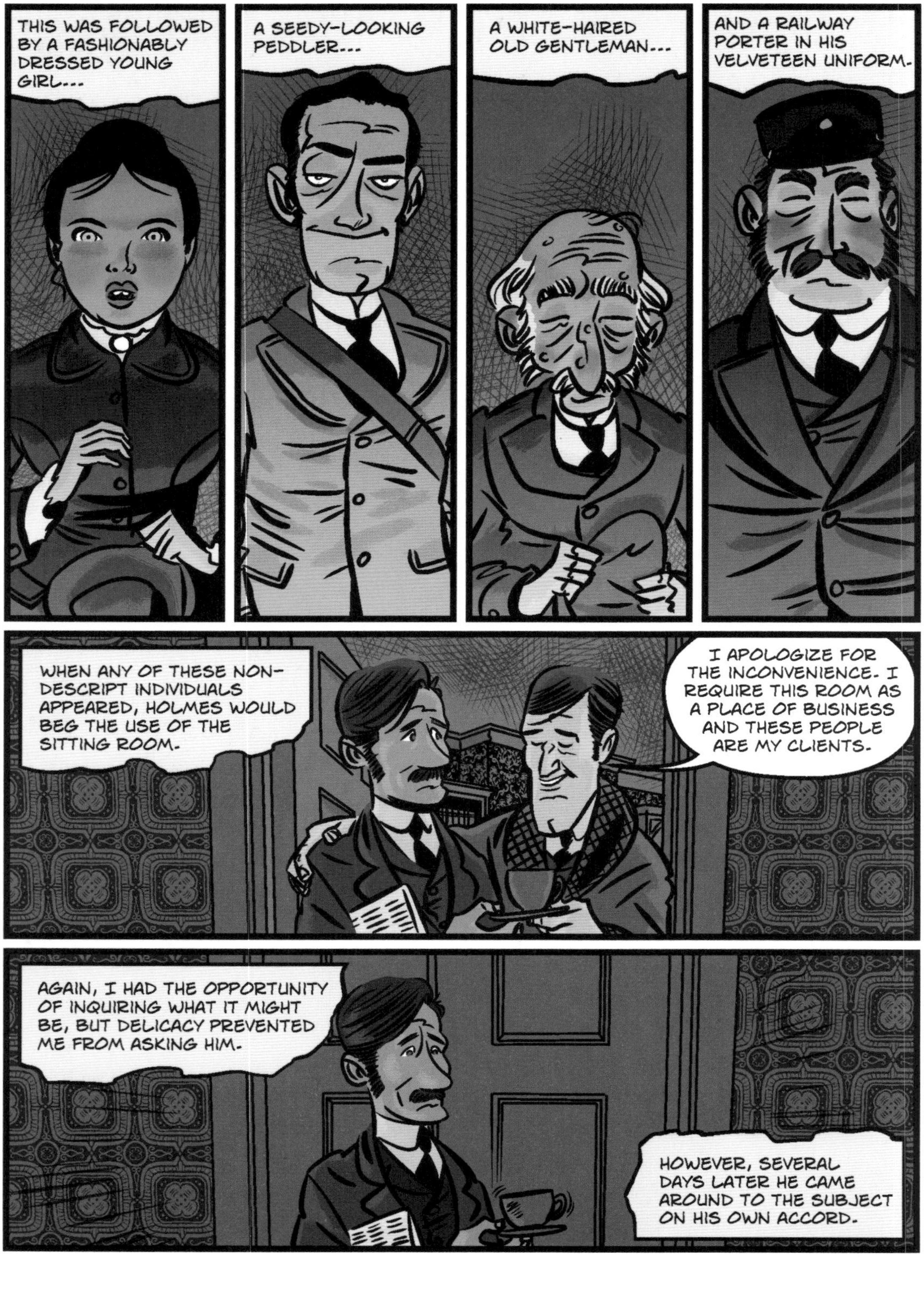
THIS WAS FOLLOWED BY A FASHIONABLY DRESSED YOUNG GIRL...
A SEEDY-LOOKING PEDDLER...
A WHITE-HAIRED OLD GENTLEMAN...
AND A RAILWAY PORTER IN HIS VELVETEEN UNIFORM.
WHEN ANY OF THESE NON-DESCRIPT INDIVIDUALS APPEARED, HOLMES WOULD BEG THE USE OF THE SITTING ROOM.
I APOLOGIZE FOR THE INCONVENIENCE. I REQUIRE THIS ROOM AS A PLACE OF BUSINESS AND THESE PEOPLE ARE MY CLIENTS.
AGAIN, I HAD THE OPPORTUNITY OF INQUIRING WHAT IT MIGHT BE, BUT DELICACY PREVENTED ME FROM ASKING HIM.
HOWEVER, SEVERAL DAYS LATER HE CAME AROUND TO THE SUBJECT ON HIS OWN ACCORD.

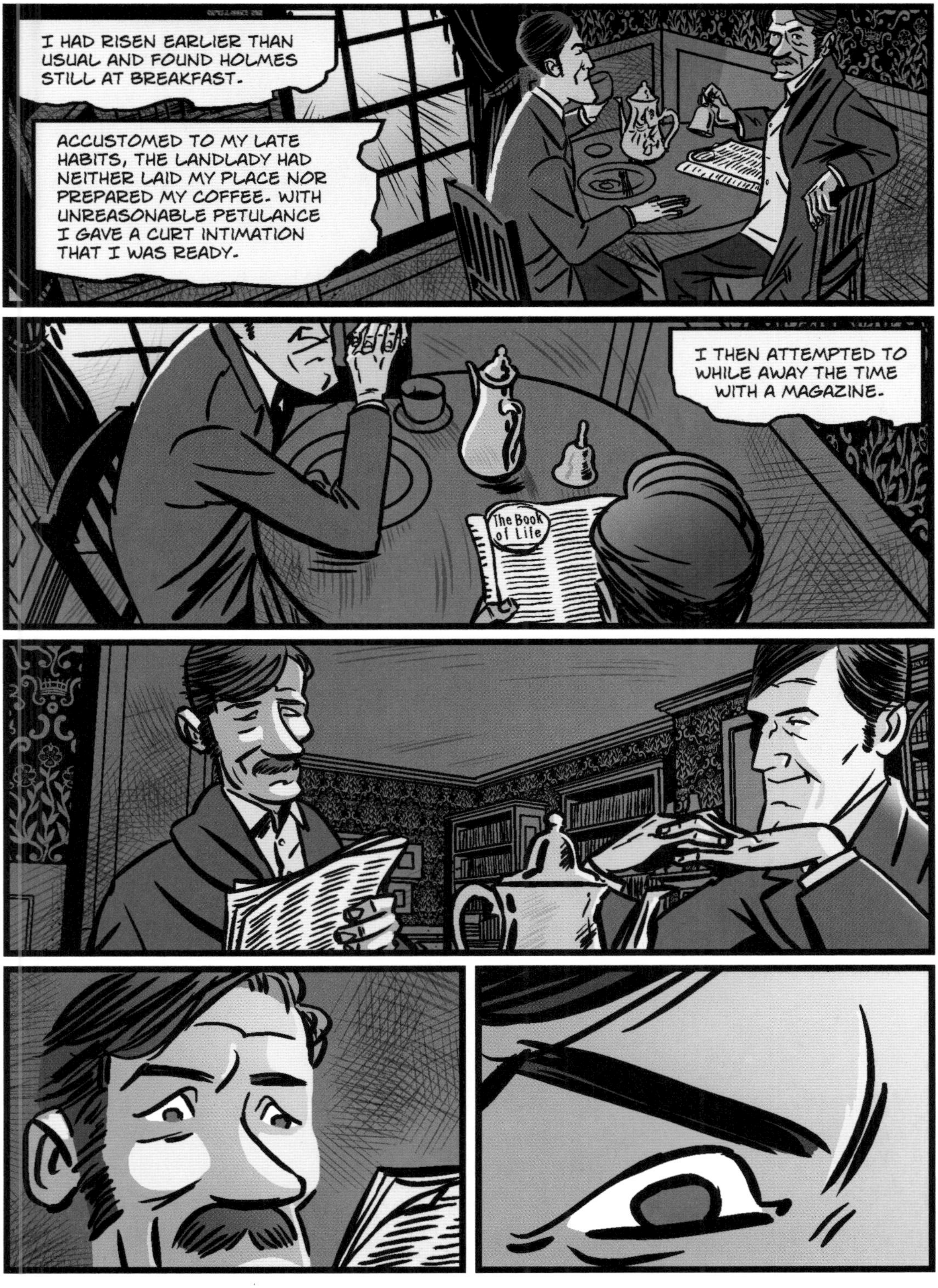
I HAD RISEN EARLIER THAN USUAL AND FOUND HOLMES STILL AT BREAKFAST.
ACCUSTOMED TO MY LATE HABITS, THE LANDLADY HAD NEITHER LAID MY PLACE NOR PREPARED MY COFFEE. WITH UNREASONABLE PETULANCE I GAVE A CURT INTIMATION THAT I WAS READY.
I THEN ATTEMPTED TO WHILE AWAY THE TIME WITH A MAGAZINE.
The Book of Life

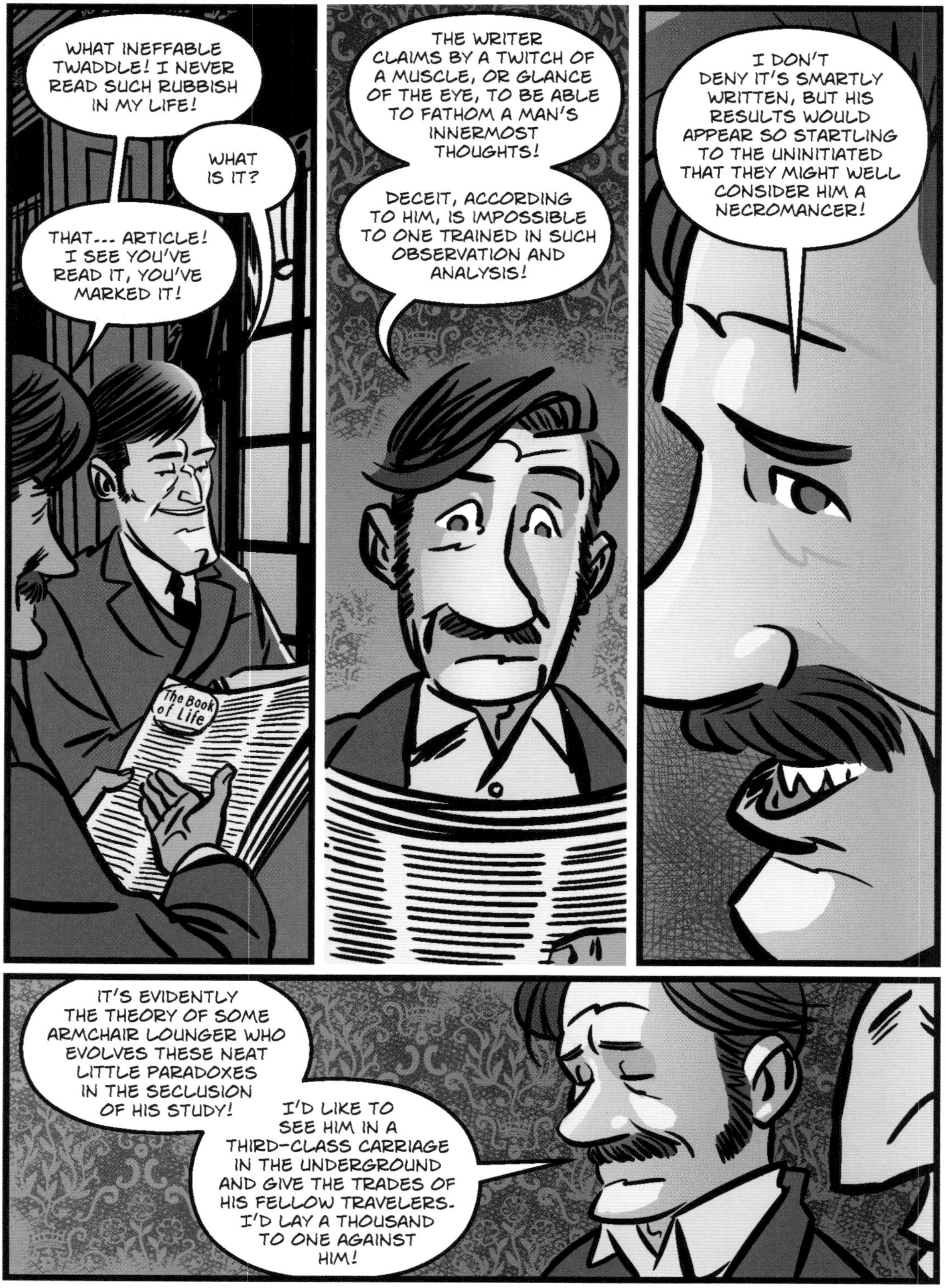
WHAT INEFFABLE TWADDLE! I NEVER READ SUCH RUBBISH IN MY LIFE!
WHAT IS IT?
THAT... ARTICLE! I SEE YOU'VE READ IT, YOU'VE MARKED IT!
The Book of Life
THE WRITER CLAIMS BY A TWITCH OF A MUSCLE, OR GLANCE OF THE EYE, TO BE ABLE TO FATHOM A MAN'S INNERMOST THOUGHTS!
DECEIT, ACCORDING TO HIM, IS IMPOSSIBLE TO ONE TRAINED IN SUCH OBSERVATION AND ANALYSIS!
I DON'T DENY IT'S SMARTLY WRITTEN, BUT HIS RESULTS WOULD APPEAR SO STARTLING TO THE UNINITIATED THAT THEY MIGHT WELL CONSIDER HIM A NECROMANCER!
IT'S EVIDENTLY THE THEORY OF SOME ARMCHAIR LOUNGER WHO EVOLVES THESE NEAT LITTLE PARADOXES IN THE SECLUSION OF HIS STUDY!
I'D LIKE TO SEE HIM IN A THIRD-CLASS CARRIAGE IN THE UNDERGROUND AND GIVE THE TRADES OF HIS FELLOW TRAVELERS. I'D LAY A THOUSAND TO ONE AGAINST HIM!

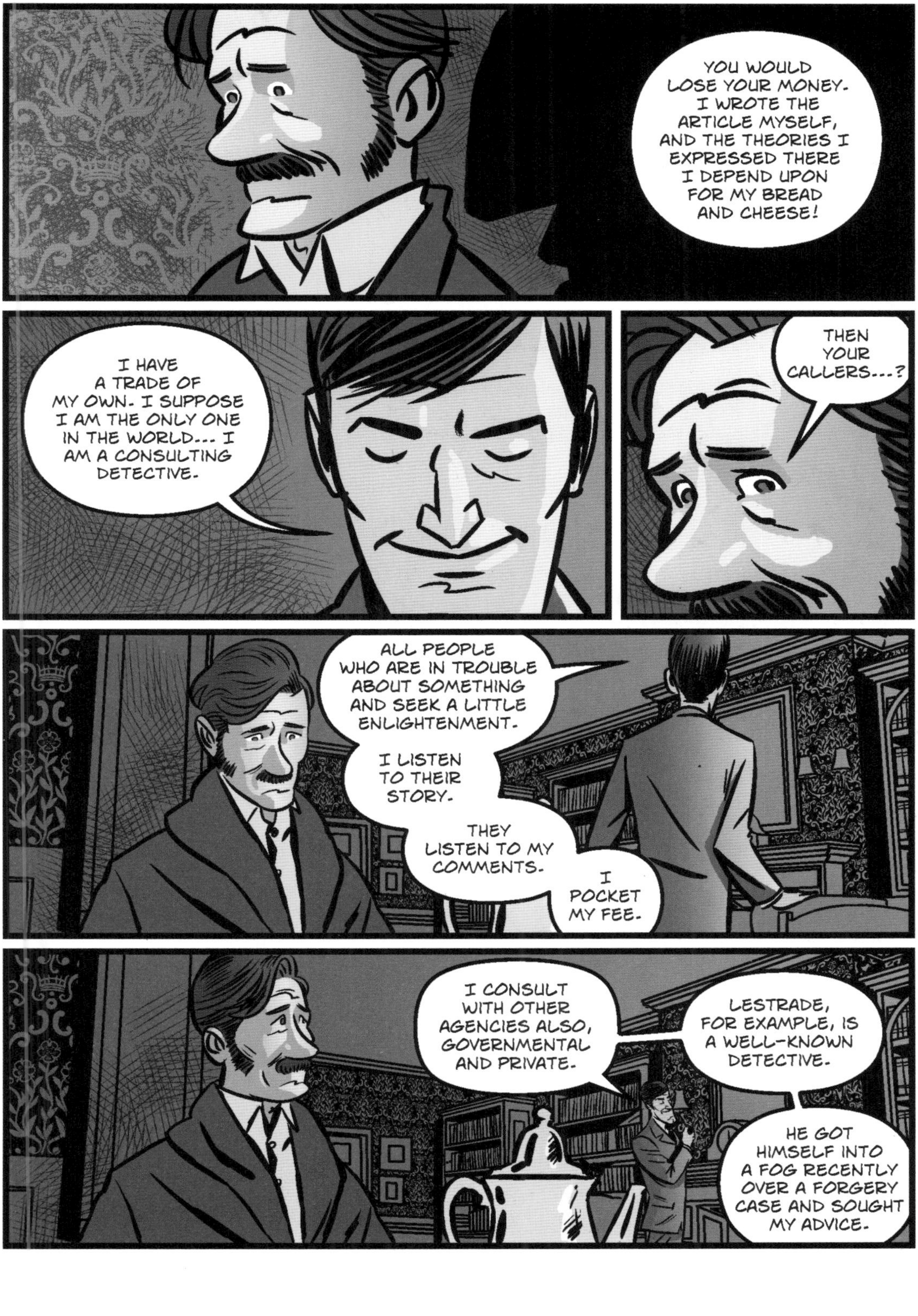
YOU WOULD LOSE YOUR MONEY. I WROTE THE ARTICLE MYSELF, AND THE THEORIES I EXPRESSED THERE I DEPEND UPON FOR MY BREAD AND CHEESE!
I HAVE A TRADE OF MY OWN. I SUPPOSE I AM THE ONLY ONE IN THE WORLD... I AM A CONSULTING DETECTIVE.
THEN YOUR CALLERS...?
ALL PEOPLE WHO ARE IN TROUBLE ABOUT SOMETHING AND SEEK A LITTLE ENLIGHTENMENT.
I LISTEN TO THEIR STORY.
THEY LISTEN TO MY COMMENTS.
I POCKET MY FEE.
I CONSULT WITH OTHER AGENCIES ALSO, GOVERNMENTAL AND PRIVATE.
LESTRADE, FOR EXAMPLE, IS A WELL-KNOWN DETECTIVE.
HE GOT HIMSELF INTO A FOG RECENTLY OVER A FORGERY CASE AND SOUGHT MY ADVICE.

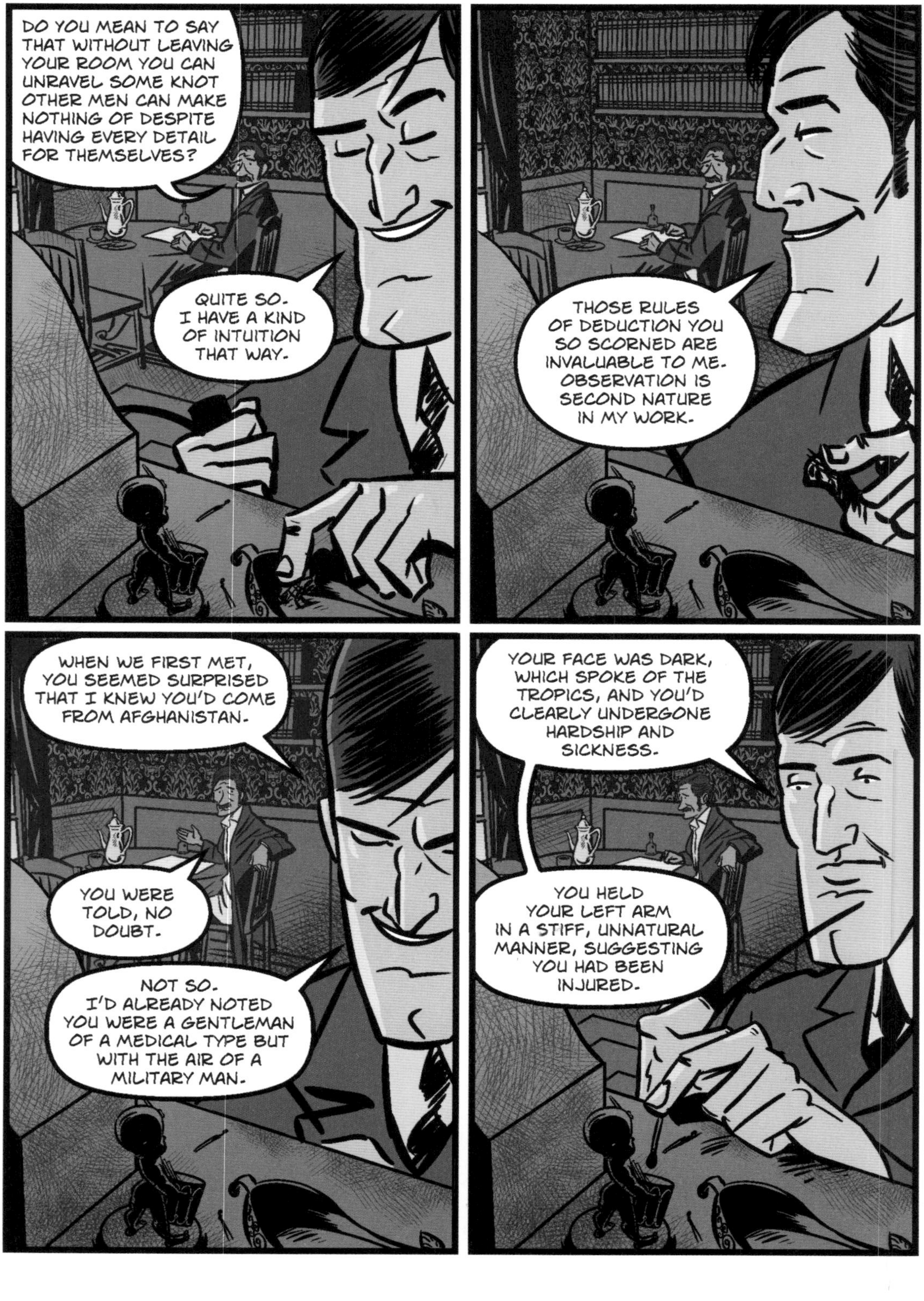
DO YOU MEAN TO SAY THAT WITHOUT LEAVING YOUR ROOM YOU CAN UNRAVEL SOME KNOT OTHER MEN CAN MAKE NOTHING OF DESPITE HAVING EVERY DETAIL FOR THEMSELVES?
QUITE SO. I HAVE A KIND OF INTUITION THAT WAY.
THOSE RULES OF DEDUCTION YOU SO SCORNED ARE INVALUABLE TO ME. OBSERVATION IS SECOND NATURE IN MY WORK.
WHEN WE FIRST MET, YOU SEEMED SURPRISED THAT I KNEW YOU'D COME FROM AFGHANISTAN.
YOU WERE TOLD, NO DOUBT.
NOT SO. I'D ALREADY NOTED YOU WERE A GENTLEMAN OF A MEDICAL TYPE BUT WITH THE AIR OF A MILITARY MAN.
YOUR FACE WAS DARK, WHICH SPOKE OF THE TROPICS, AND YOU'D CLEARLY UNDERGONE HARDSHIP AND SICKNESS.
YOU HELD YOUR LEFT ARM IN A STIFF, UNNATURAL MANNER, SUGGESTING YOU HAD BEEN INJURED.

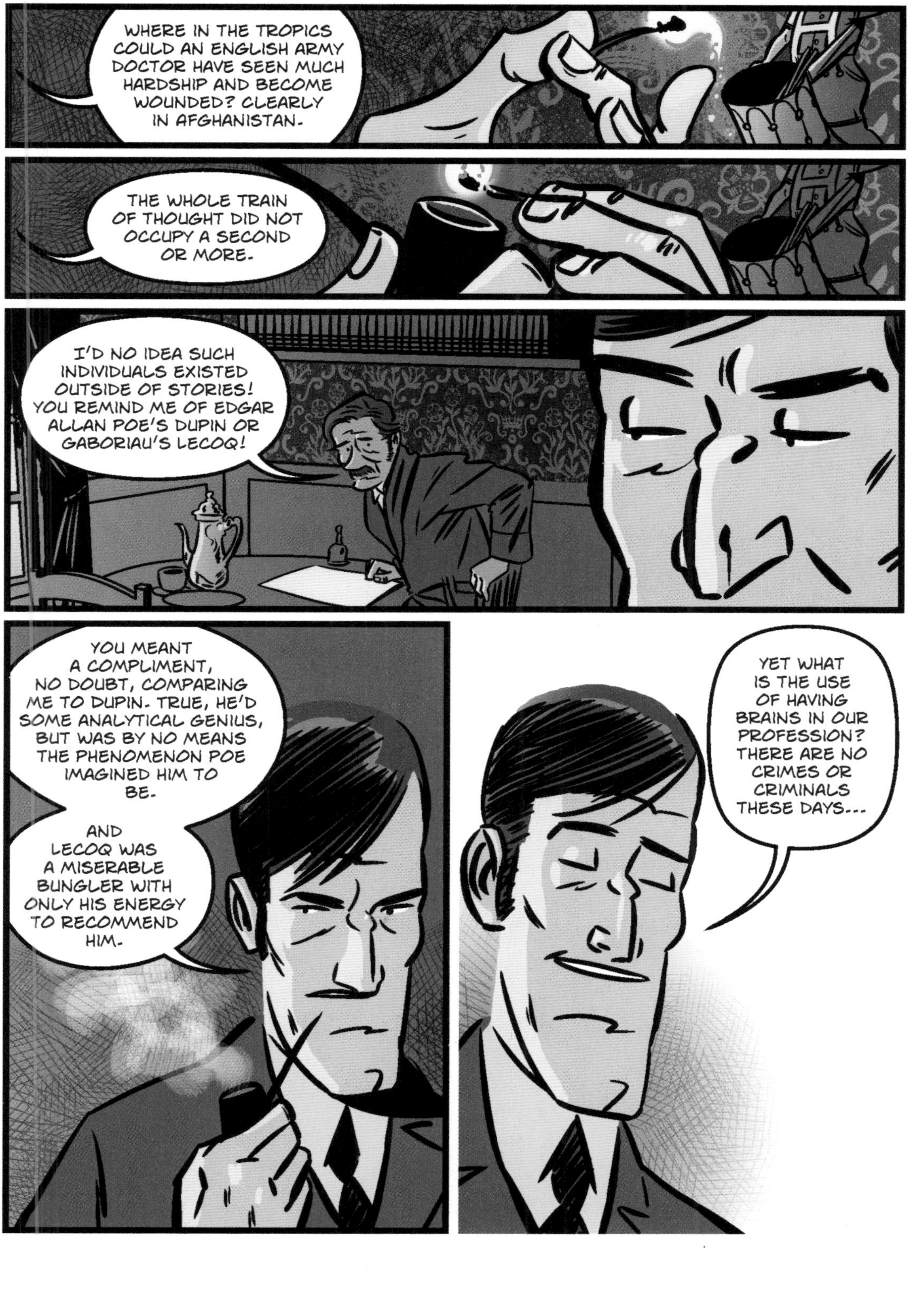
WHERE IN THE TROPICS COULD AN ENGLISH ARMY DOCTOR HAVE SEEN MUCH HARDSHIP AND BECOME WOUNDED? CLEARLY IN AFGHANISTAN.
THE WHOLE TRAIN OF THOUGHT DID NOT OCCUPY A SECOND OR MORE.
I'D NO IDEA SUCH INDIVIDUALS EXISTED OUTSIDE OF STORIES! YOU REMIND ME OF EDGAR ALLAN POE'S DUPIN OR GABORIAU'S LECOQ!
YOU MEANT A COMPLIMENT, NO DOUBT, COMPARING ME TO DUPIN. TRUE, HE'D SOME ANALYTICAL GENIUS, BUT WAS BY NO MEANS THE PHENOMENON POE IMAGINED HIM TO BE.
AND LECOQ WAS A MISERABLE BUNGLER WITH ONLY HIS ENERGY TO RECOMMEND HIM.
YET WHAT IS THE USE OF HAVING BRAINS IN OUR PROFESSION? THERE ARE NO CRIMES OR CRIMINALS THESE DAYS...

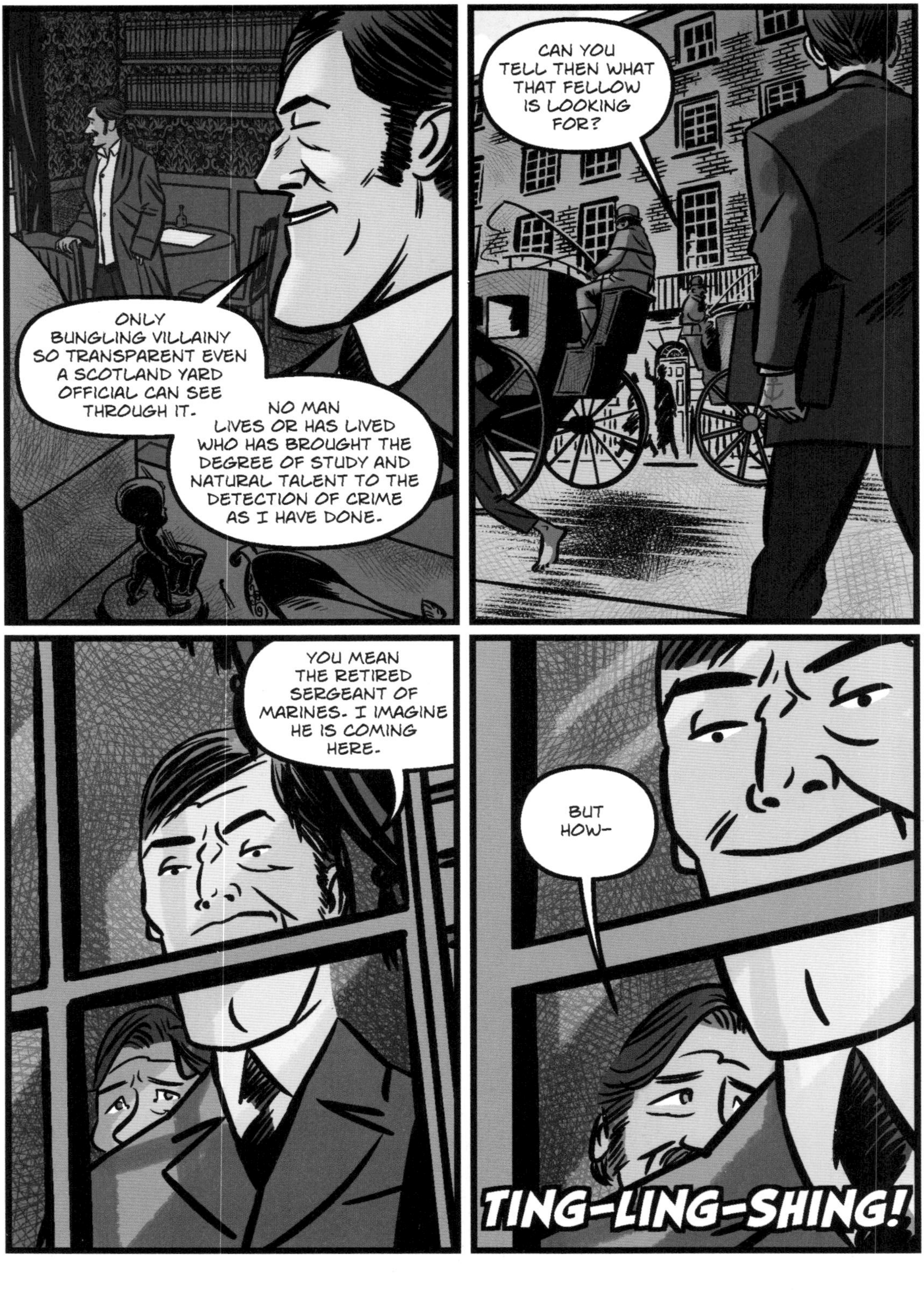
ONLY BUNGLING VILLAINY SO TRANSPARENT EVEN A SCOTLAND YARD OFFICIAL CAN SEE THROUGH IT.
NO MAN LIVES OR HAS LIVED WHO HAS BROUGHT THE DEGREE OF STUDY AND NATURAL TALENT TO THE DETECTION OF CRIME AS I HAVE DONE.
CAN YOU TELL THEN WHAT THAT FELLOW IS LOOKING FOR?
YOU MEAN THE RETIRED SERGEANT OF MARINES. I IMAGINE HE IS COMING HERE.
BUT HOW—
TING-LING-SHING!

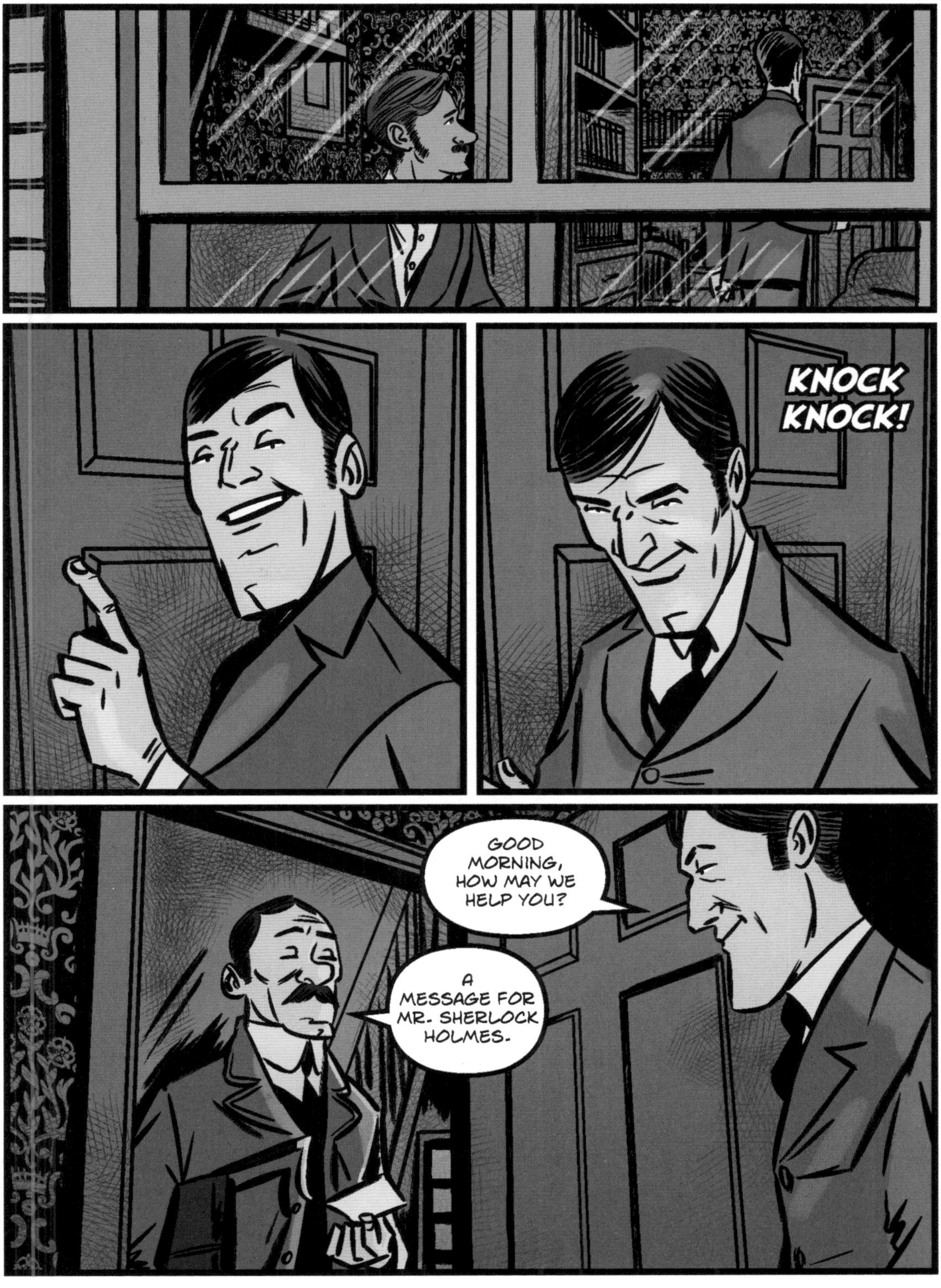
KNOCK KNOCK!
GOOD MORNING, HOW MAY WE HELP YOU?
A MESSAGE FOR MR. SHERLOCK HOLMES.

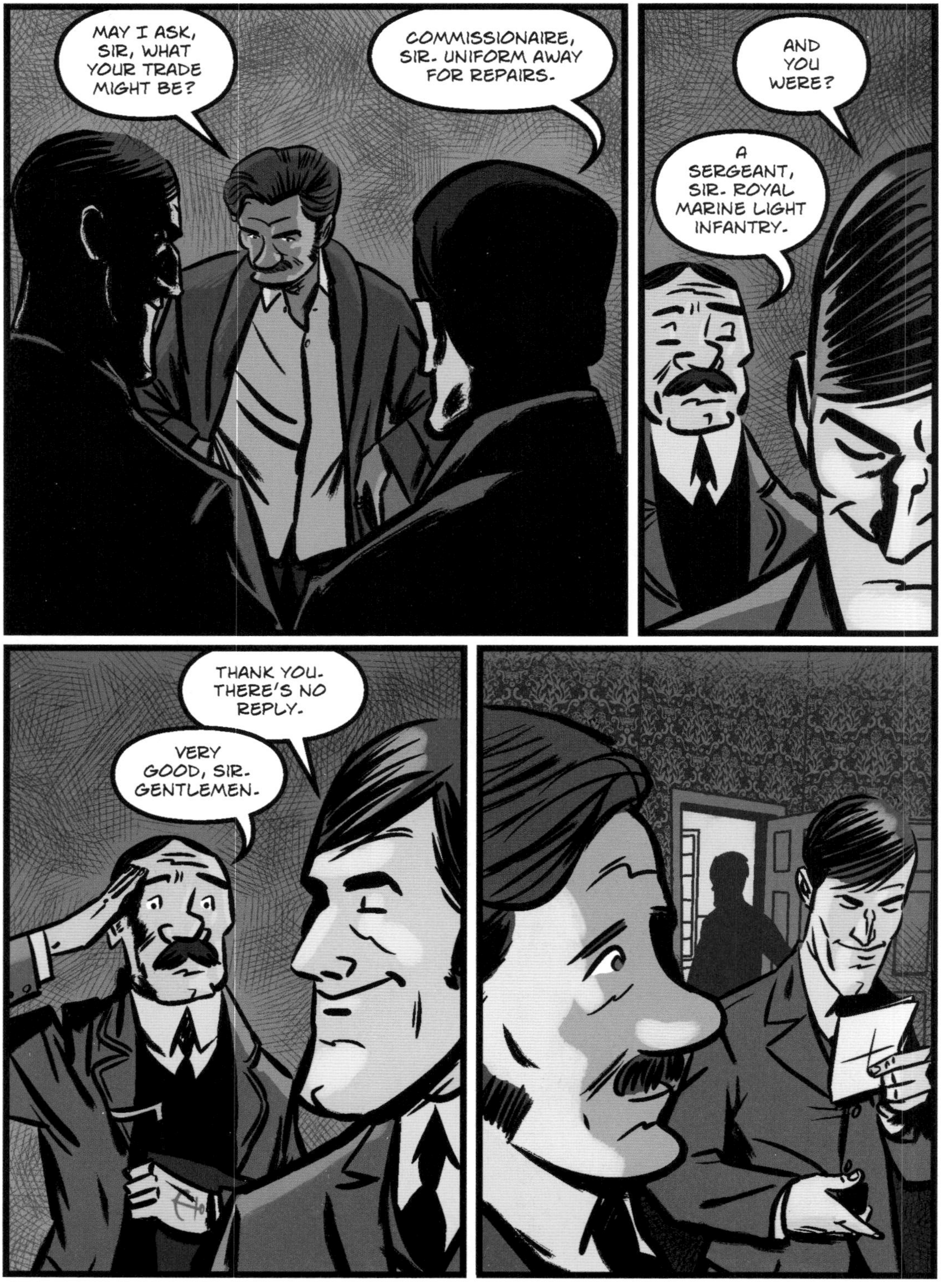
MAY I ASK, SIR, WHAT YOUR TRADE MIGHT BE?
COMMISSIONAIRE, SIR. UNIFORM AWAY FOR REPAIRS.
AND YOU WERE?
A SERGEANT, SIR. ROYAL MARINE LIGHT INFANTRY.
THANK YOU. THERE'S NO REPLY.
VERY GOOD, SIR. GENTLEMEN.

THE LAURISTON GARDENS MYSTERY

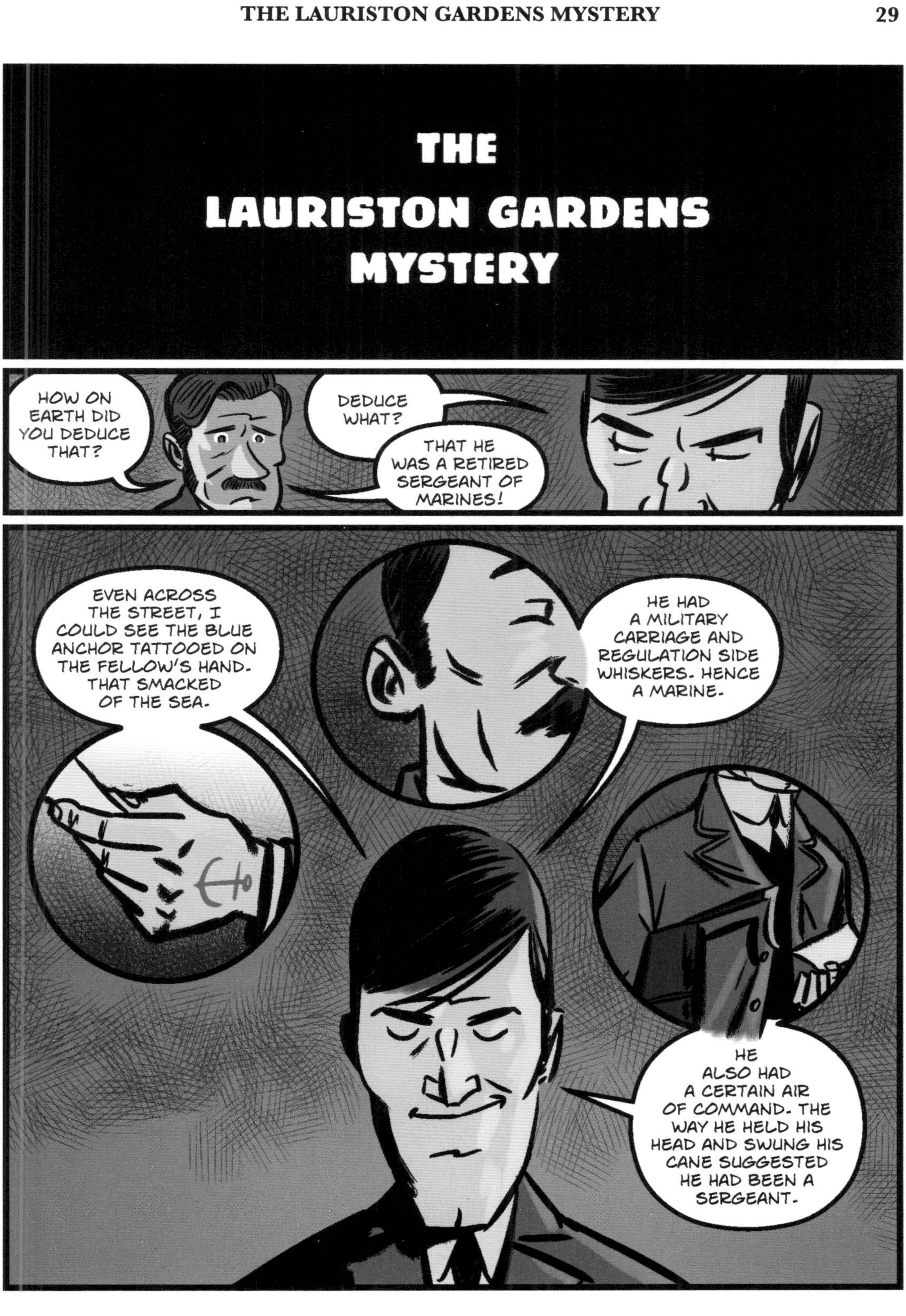
HOW ON EARTH DID YOU DEDUCE THAT?
DEDUCE WHAT?
THAT HE WAS A RETIRED SERGEANT OF MARINES!
EVEN ACROSS THE STREET, I COULD SEE THE BLUE ANCHOR TATTOOED ON THE FELLOW'S HAND. THAT SMACKED OF THE SEA.
HE HAD A MILITARY CARRIAGE AND REGULATION SIDE WHISKERS. HENCE A MARINE.
HE ALSO HAD A CERTAIN AIR OF COMMAND. THE WAY HE HELD HIS HEAD AND SWUNG HIS CANE SUGGESTED HE HAD BEEN A SERGEANT.

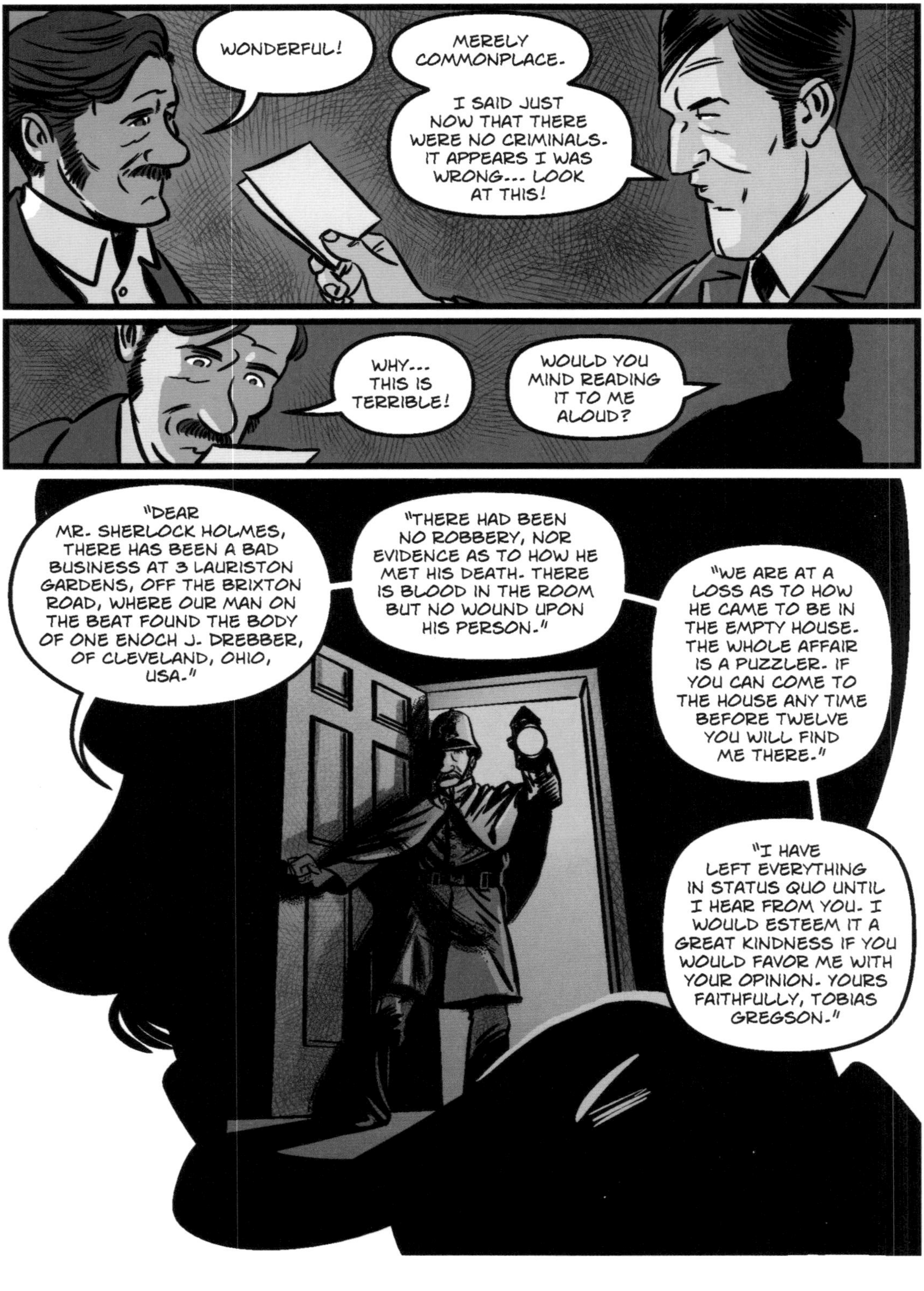
WONDERFUL!
MERELY COMMONPLACE.
I SAID JUST NOW THAT THERE WERE NO CRIMINALS. IT APPEARS I WAS WRONG... LOOK AT THIS!
WHY... THIS IS TERRIBLE!
WOULD YOU MIND READING IT TO ME ALOUD?
"DEAR MR. SHERLOCK HOLMES, THERE HAS BEEN A BAD BUSINESS AT 3 LAURISTON GARDENS, OFF THE BRIXTON ROAD, WHERE OUR MAN ON THE BEAT FOUND THE BODY OF ONE ENOCH J. DREBBER, OF CLEVELAND, OHIO, USA."
"THERE HAD BEEN NO ROBBERY, NOR EVIDENCE AS TO HOW HE MET HIS DEATH. THERE IS BLOOD IN THE ROOM BUT NO WOUND UPON HIS PERSON."
"WE ARE AT A LOSS AS TO HOW HE CAME TO BE IN THE EMPTY HOUSE. THE WHOLE AFFAIR IS A PUZZLER. IF YOU CAN COME TO THE HOUSE ANY TIME BEFORE TWELVE YOU WILL FIND ME THERE."
"I HAVE LEFT EVERYTHING IN STATUS QUO UNTIL I HEAR FROM YOU. I WOULD ESTEEM IT A GREAT KINDNESS IF YOU WOULD FAVOR ME WITH YOUR OPINION. YOURS FAITHFULLY, TOBIAS GREGSON."

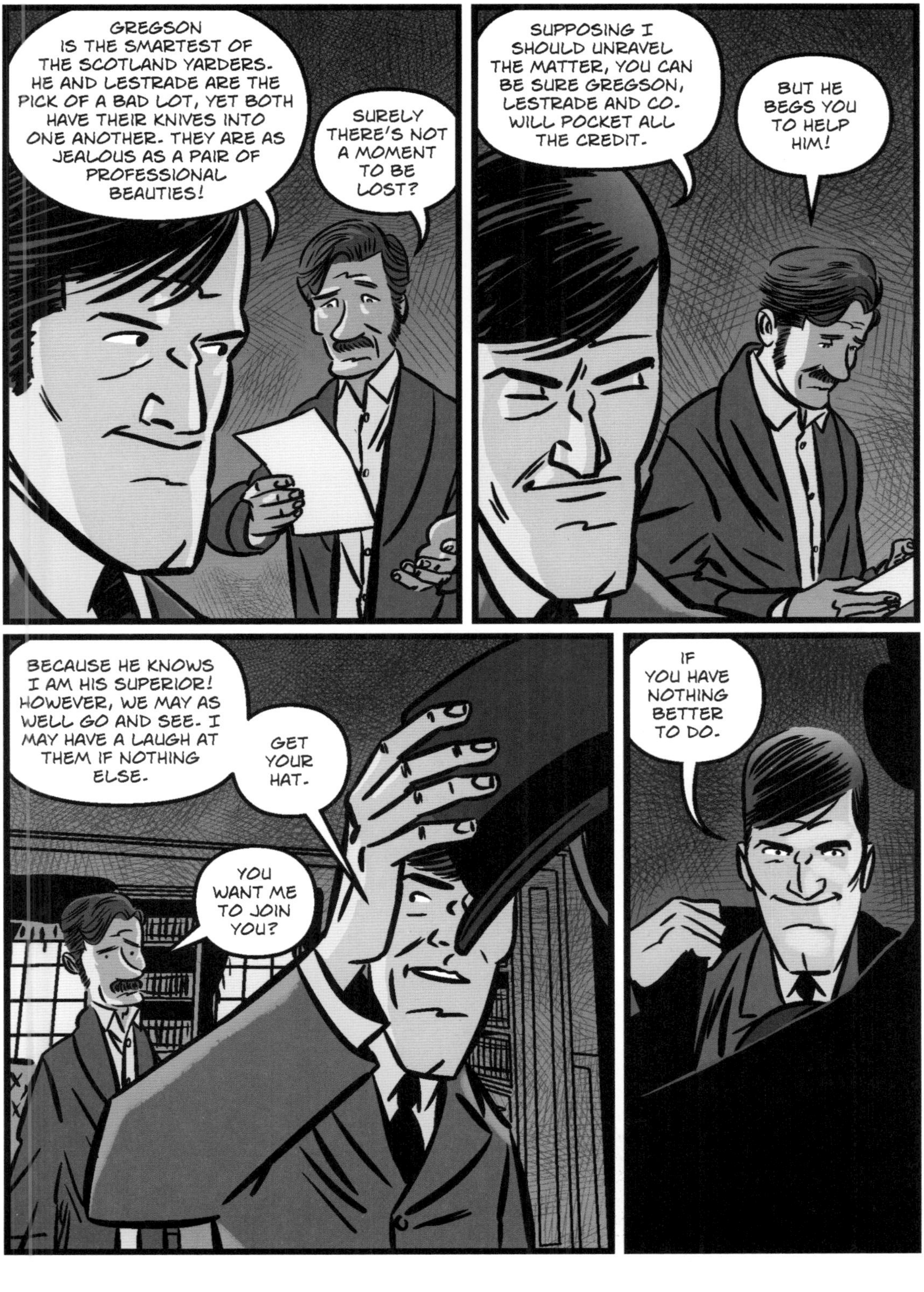
GREGSON IS THE SMARTEST OF THE SCOTLAND YARDERS. HE AND LESTRADE ARE THE PICK OF A BAD LOT, YET BOTH HAVE THEIR KNIVES INTO ONE ANOTHER. THEY ARE AS JEALOUS AS A PAIR OF PROFESSIONAL BEAUTIES!
SURELY THERE'S NOT A MOMENT TO BE LOST?
SUPPOSING I SHOULD UNRAVEL THE MATTER, YOU CAN BE SURE GREGSON, LESTRADE AND CO. WILL POCKET ALL THE CREDIT.
BUT HE BEGS YOU TO HELP HIM!
BECAUSE HE KNOWS I AM HIS SUPERIOR! HOWEVER, WE MAY AS WELL GO AND SEE. I MAY HAVE A LAUGH AT THEM IF NOTHING ELSE.
GET YOUR HAT.
YOU WANT ME TO JOIN YOU?
IF YOU HAVE NOTHING BETTER TO DO.

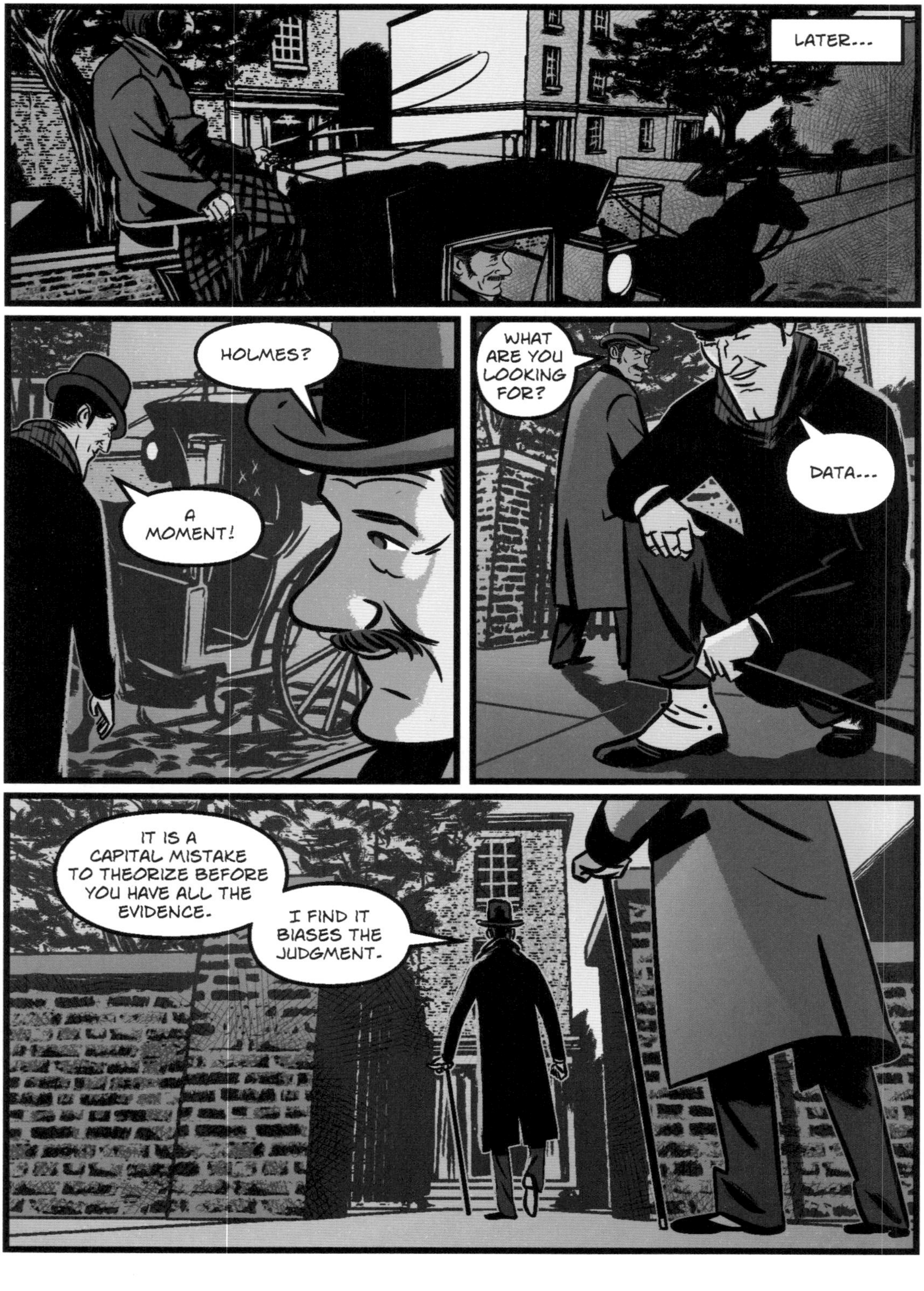
LATER...
HOLMES?
A MOMENT!
WHAT ARE YOU LOOKING FOR?
DATA...
IT IS A CAPITAL MISTAKE TO THEORIZE BEFORE YOU HAVE ALL THE EVIDENCE.
I FIND IT BIASES THE JUDGMENT.

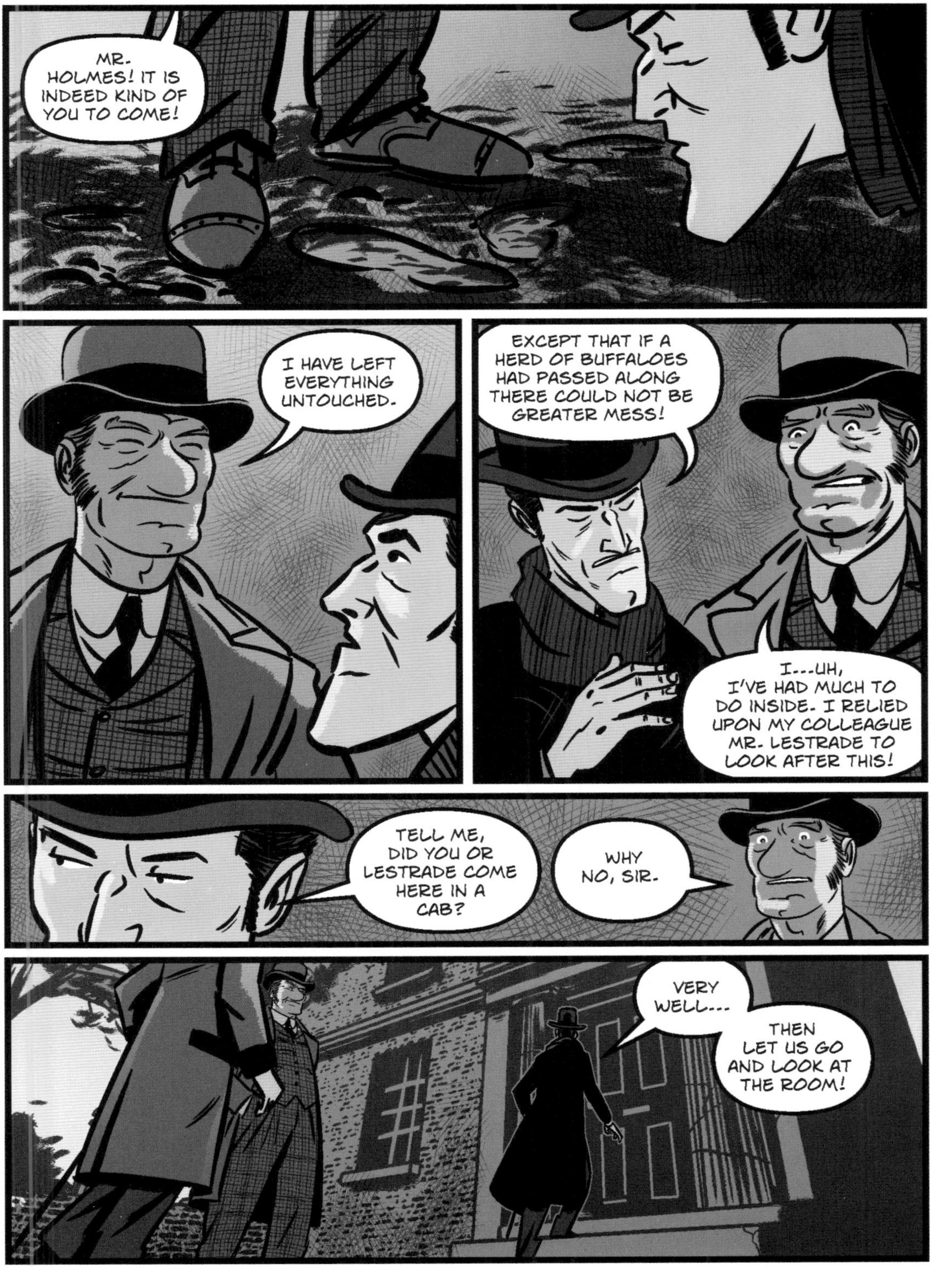
MR. HOLMES! IT IS INDEED KIND OF YOU TO COME!
I HAVE LEFT EVERYTHING UNTOUCHED.
EXCEPT THAT IF A HERD OF BUFFALOES HAD PASSED ALONG THERE COULD NOT BE GREATER MESS!
I...UH, I'VE HAD MUCH TO DO INSIDE. I RELIED UPON MY COLLEAGUE MR. LESTRADE TO LOOK AFTER THIS!
TELL ME, DID YOU OR LESTRADE COME HERE IN A CAB?
WHY NO, SIR.
VERY WELL...
THEN LET US GO AND LOOK AT THE ROOM!

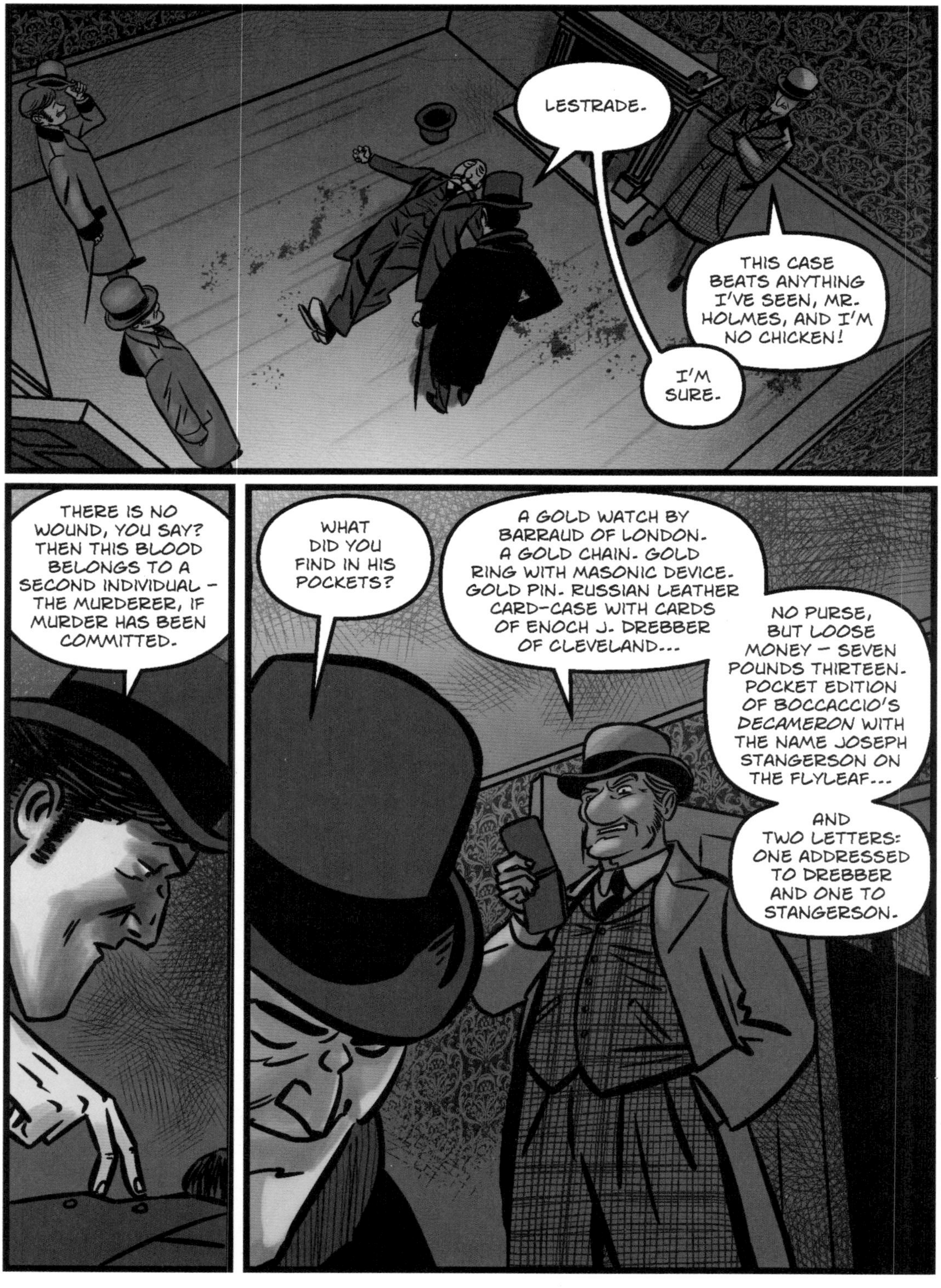
LESTRADE.
THIS CASE BEATS ANYTHING I'VE SEEN, MR. HOLMES, AND I'M NO CHICKEN!
I'M SURE.
THERE IS NO WOUND, YOU SAY? THEN THIS BLOOD BELONGS TO A SECOND INDIVIDUAL – THE MURDERER, IF MURDER HAS BEEN COMMITTED.
WHAT DID YOU FIND IN HIS POCKETS?
A GOLD WATCH BY BARRAUD OF LONDON. A GOLD CHAIN. GOLD RING WITH MASONIC DEVICE. GOLD PIN. RUSSIAN LEATHER CARD-CASE WITH CARDS OF ENOCH J. DREBBER OF CLEVELAND...
NO PURSE, BUT LOOSE MONEY – SEVEN POUNDS THIRTEEN. POCKET EDITION OF BOCCACCIO'S *DECAMERON* WITH THE NAME JOSEPH STANGERSON ON THE FLYLEAF...
AND TWO LETTERS: ONE ADDRESSED TO DREBBER AND ONE TO STANGERSON.

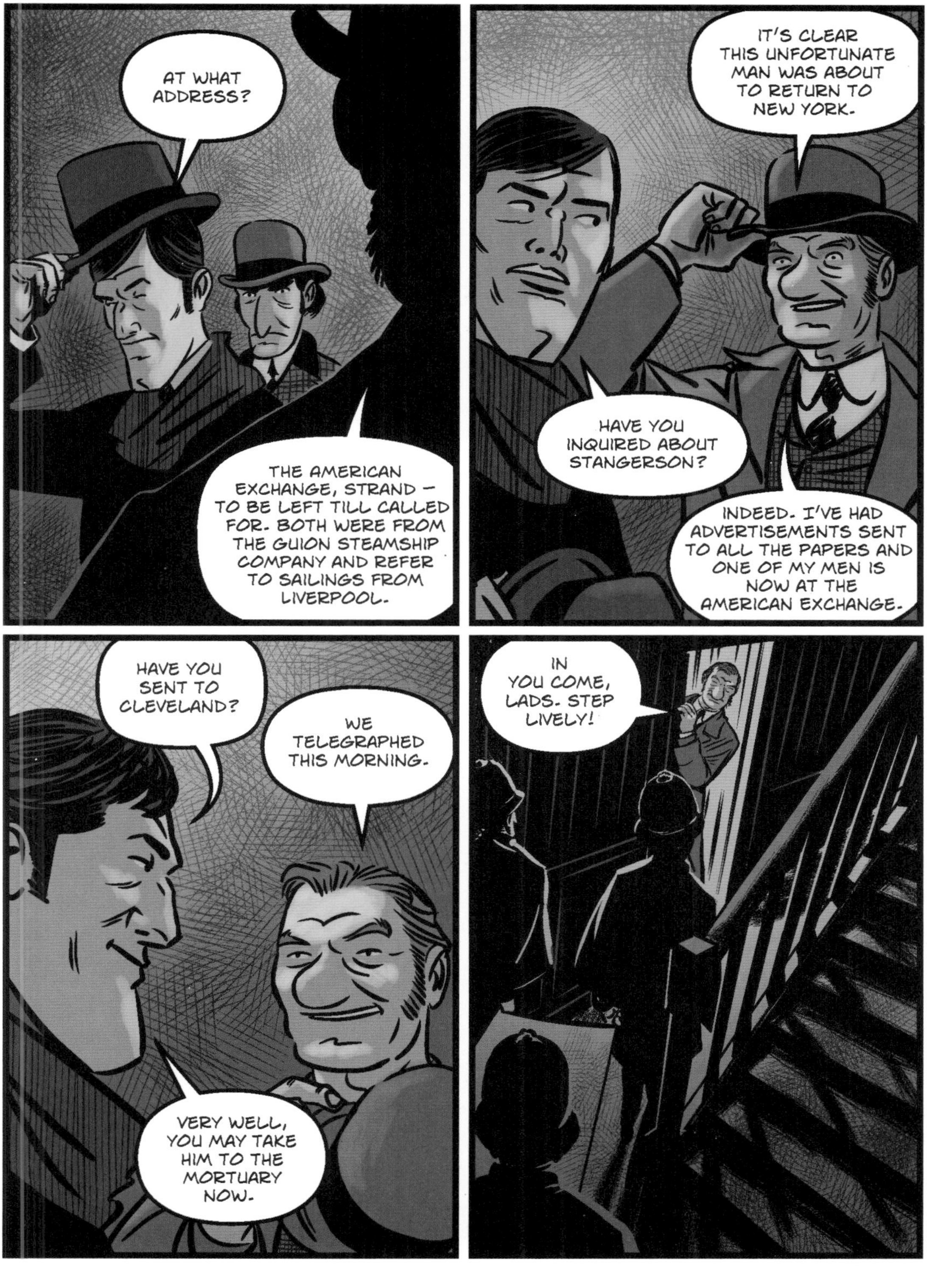
AT WHAT ADDRESS?
THE AMERICAN EXCHANGE, STRAND — TO BE LEFT TILL CALLED FOR. BOTH WERE FROM THE GUION STEAMSHIP COMPANY AND REFER TO SAILINGS FROM LIVERPOOL.
IT'S CLEAR THIS UNFORTUNATE MAN WAS ABOUT TO RETURN TO NEW YORK.
HAVE YOU INQUIRED ABOUT STANGERSON?
INDEED. I'VE HAD ADVERTISEMENTS SENT TO ALL THE PAPERS AND ONE OF MY MEN IS NOW AT THE AMERICAN EXCHANGE.
HAVE YOU SENT TO CLEVELAND?
WE TELEGRAPHED THIS MORNING.
VERY WELL, YOU MAY TAKE HIM TO THE MORTUARY NOW.
IN YOU COME, LADS. STEP LIVELY!

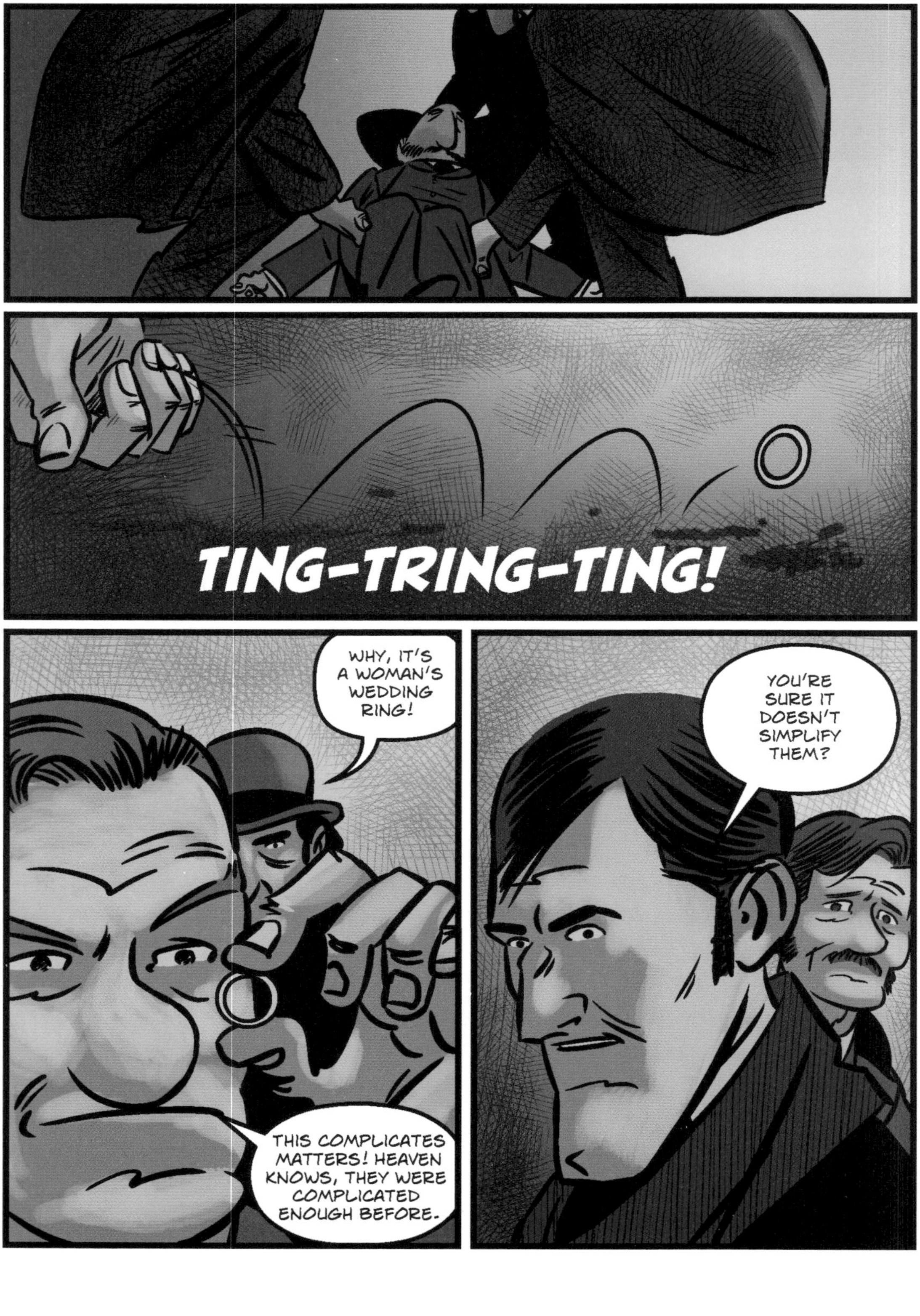
TING-TRING-TING!
WHY, IT'S A WOMAN'S WEDDING RING!
THIS COMPLICATES MATTERS! HEAVEN KNOWS, THEY WERE COMPLICATED ENOUGH BEFORE.
YOU'RE SURE IT DOESN'T SIMPLIFY THEM?

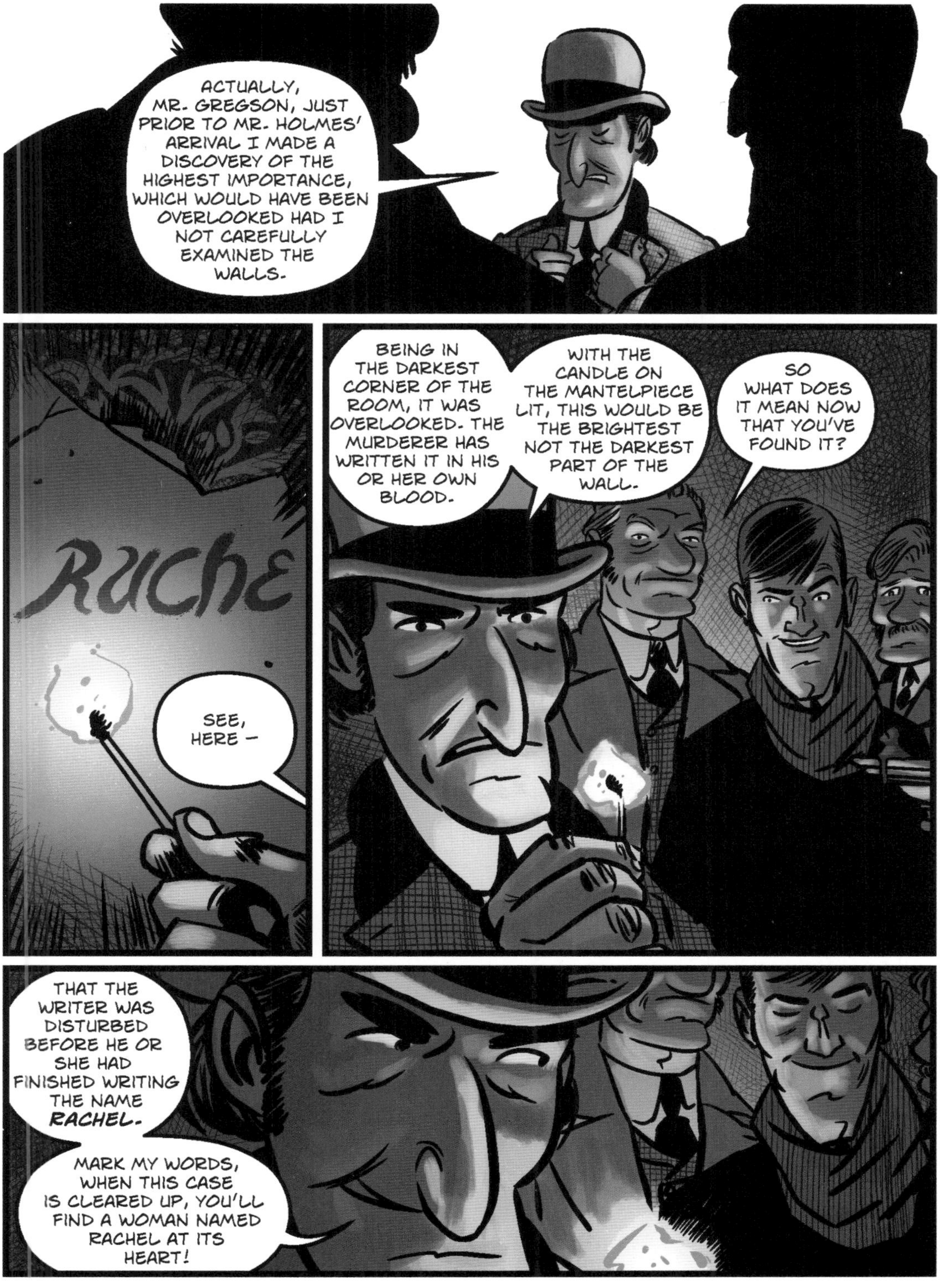
ACTUALLY, MR. GREGSON, JUST PRIOR TO MR. HOLMES' ARRIVAL I MADE A DISCOVERY OF THE HIGHEST IMPORTANCE, WHICH WOULD HAVE BEEN OVERLOOKED HAD I NOT CAREFULLY EXAMINED THE WALLS.
RACHE
SEE, HERE –
BEING IN THE DARKEST CORNER OF THE ROOM, IT WAS OVERLOOKED. THE MURDERER HAS WRITTEN IT IN HIS OR HER OWN BLOOD.
WITH THE CANDLE ON THE MANTELPIECE LIT, THIS WOULD BE THE BRIGHTEST NOT THE DARKEST PART OF THE WALL.
SO WHAT DOES IT MEAN NOW THAT YOU'VE FOUND IT?
THAT THE WRITER WAS DISTURBED BEFORE HE OR SHE HAD FINISHED WRITING THE NAME RACHEL.
MARK MY WORDS, WHEN THIS CASE IS CLEARED UP, YOU'LL FIND A WOMAN NAMED RACHEL AT ITS HEART!

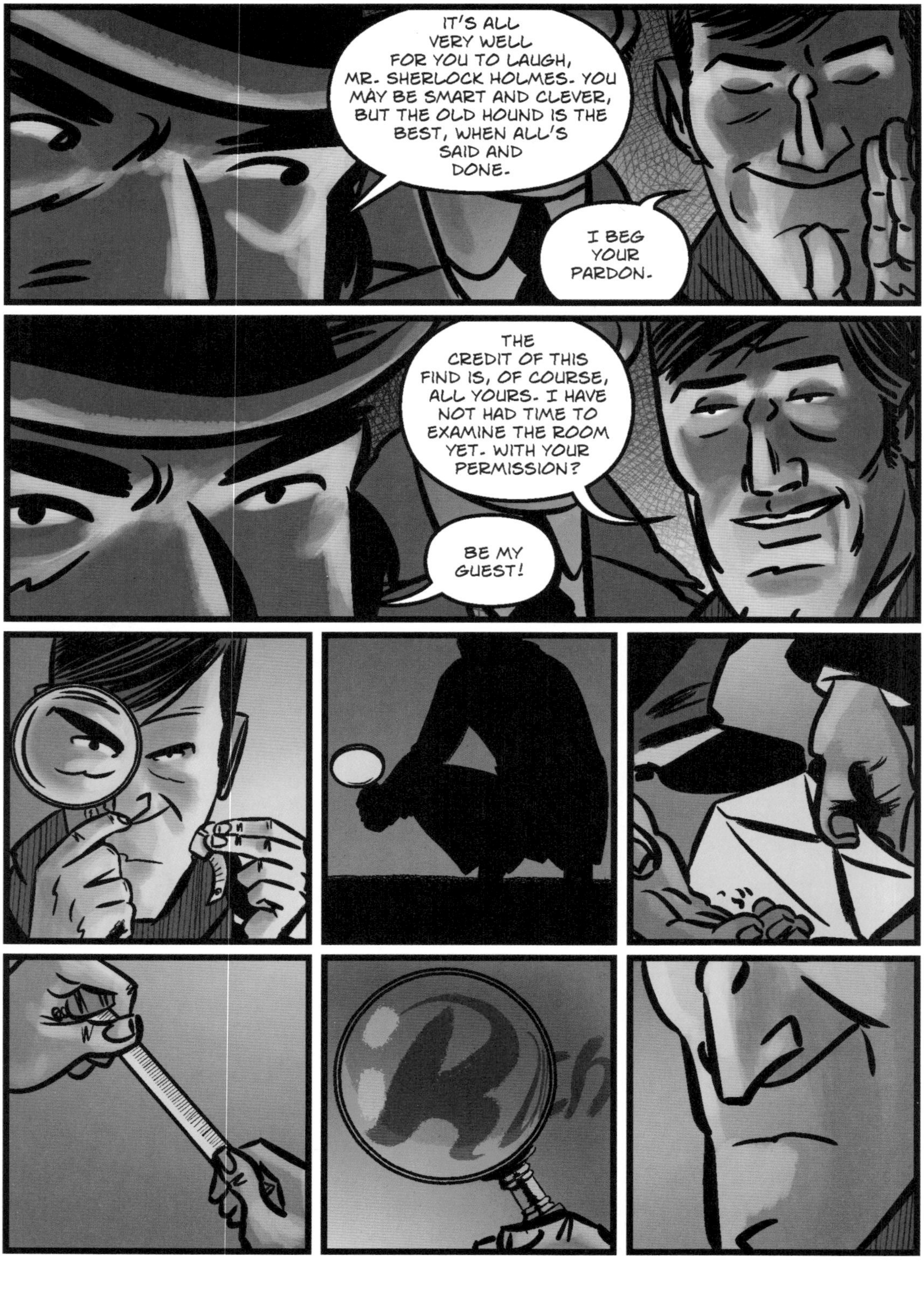
IT'S ALL VERY WELL FOR YOU TO LAUGH, MR. SHERLOCK HOLMES. YOU MAY BE SMART AND CLEVER, BUT THE OLD HOUND IS THE BEST, WHEN ALL'S SAID AND DONE.
I BEG YOUR PARDON.
THE CREDIT OF THIS FIND IS, OF COURSE, ALL YOURS. I HAVE NOT HAD TIME TO EXAMINE THE ROOM YET. WITH YOUR PERMISSION?
BE MY GUEST!

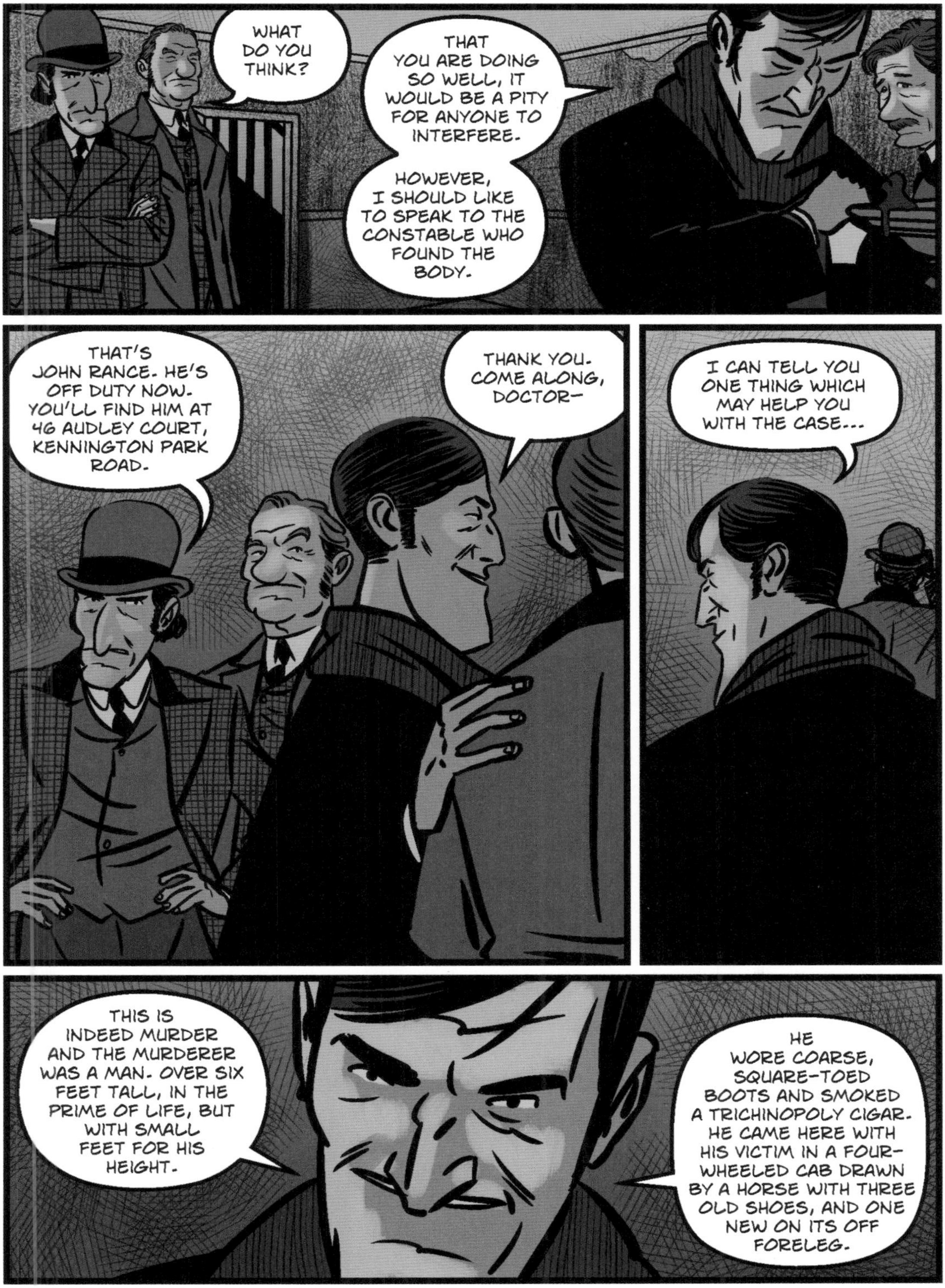
WHAT DO YOU THINK?
THAT YOU ARE DOING SO WELL, IT WOULD BE A PITY FOR ANYONE TO INTERFERE.
HOWEVER, I SHOULD LIKE TO SPEAK TO THE CONSTABLE WHO FOUND THE BODY.
THAT'S JOHN RANCE. HE'S OFF DUTY NOW. YOU'LL FIND HIM AT 46 AUDLEY COURT, KENNINGTON PARK ROAD.
THANK YOU. COME ALONG, DOCTOR—
I CAN TELL YOU ONE THING WHICH MAY HELP YOU WITH THE CASE...
THIS IS INDEED MURDER AND THE MURDERER WAS A MAN. OVER SIX FEET TALL, IN THE PRIME OF LIFE, BUT WITH SMALL FEET FOR HIS HEIGHT.
HE WORE COARSE, SQUARE-TOED BOOTS AND SMOKED A TRICHINOPOLY CIGAR. HE CAME HERE WITH HIS VICTIM IN A FOUR-WHEELED CAB DRAWN BY A HORSE WITH THREE OLD SHOES, AND ONE NEW ON ITS OFF FORELEG.

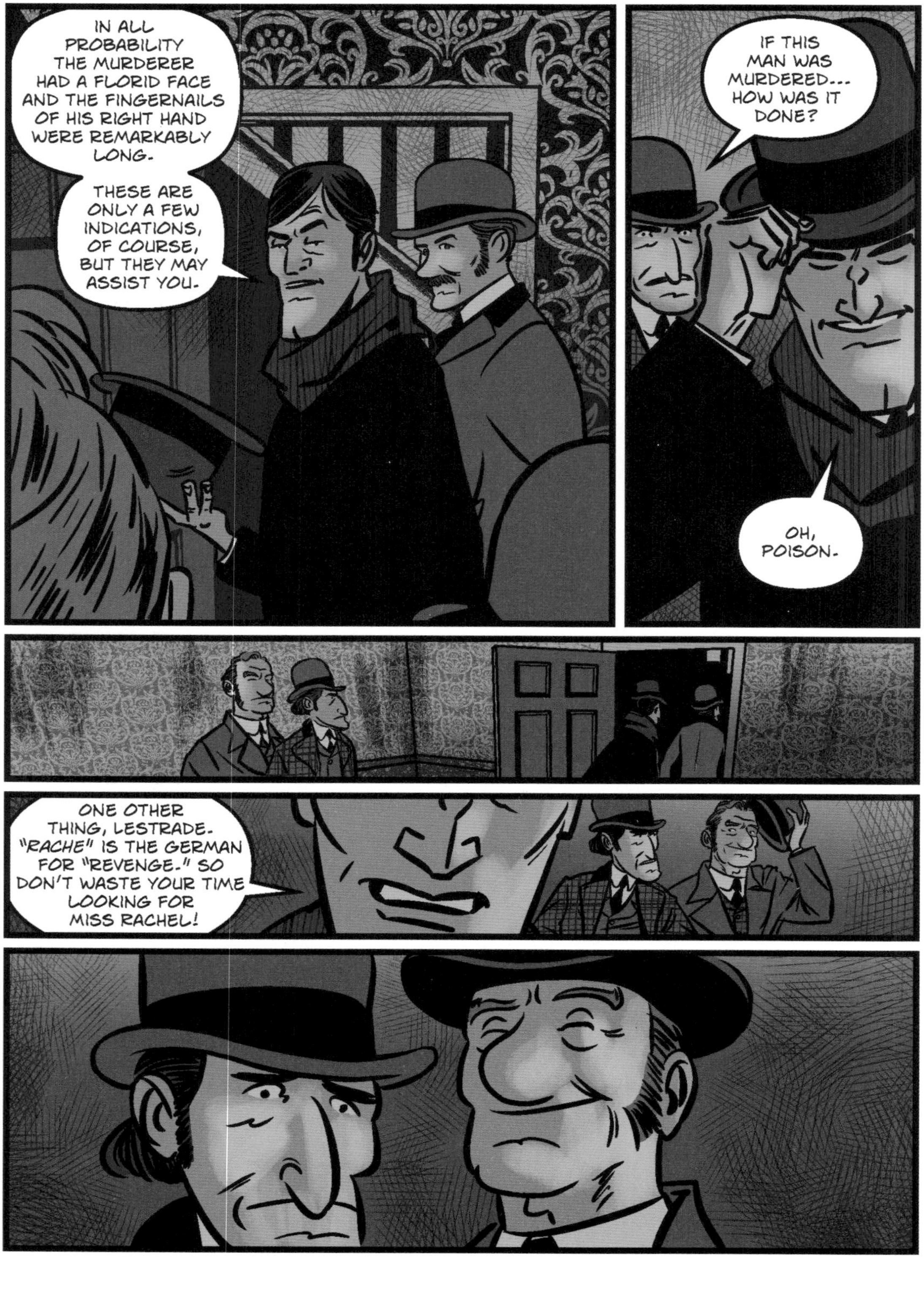
IN ALL PROBABILITY THE MURDERER HAD A FLORID FACE AND THE FINGERNAILS OF HIS RIGHT HAND WERE REMARKABLY LONG.
THESE ARE ONLY A FEW INDICATIONS, OF COURSE, BUT THEY MAY ASSIST YOU.
IF THIS MAN WAS MURDERED... HOW WAS IT DONE?
OH, POISON.
ONE OTHER THING, LESTRADE. "RACHE" IS THE GERMAN FOR "REVENGE." SO DON'T WASTE YOUR TIME LOOKING FOR MISS RACHEL!

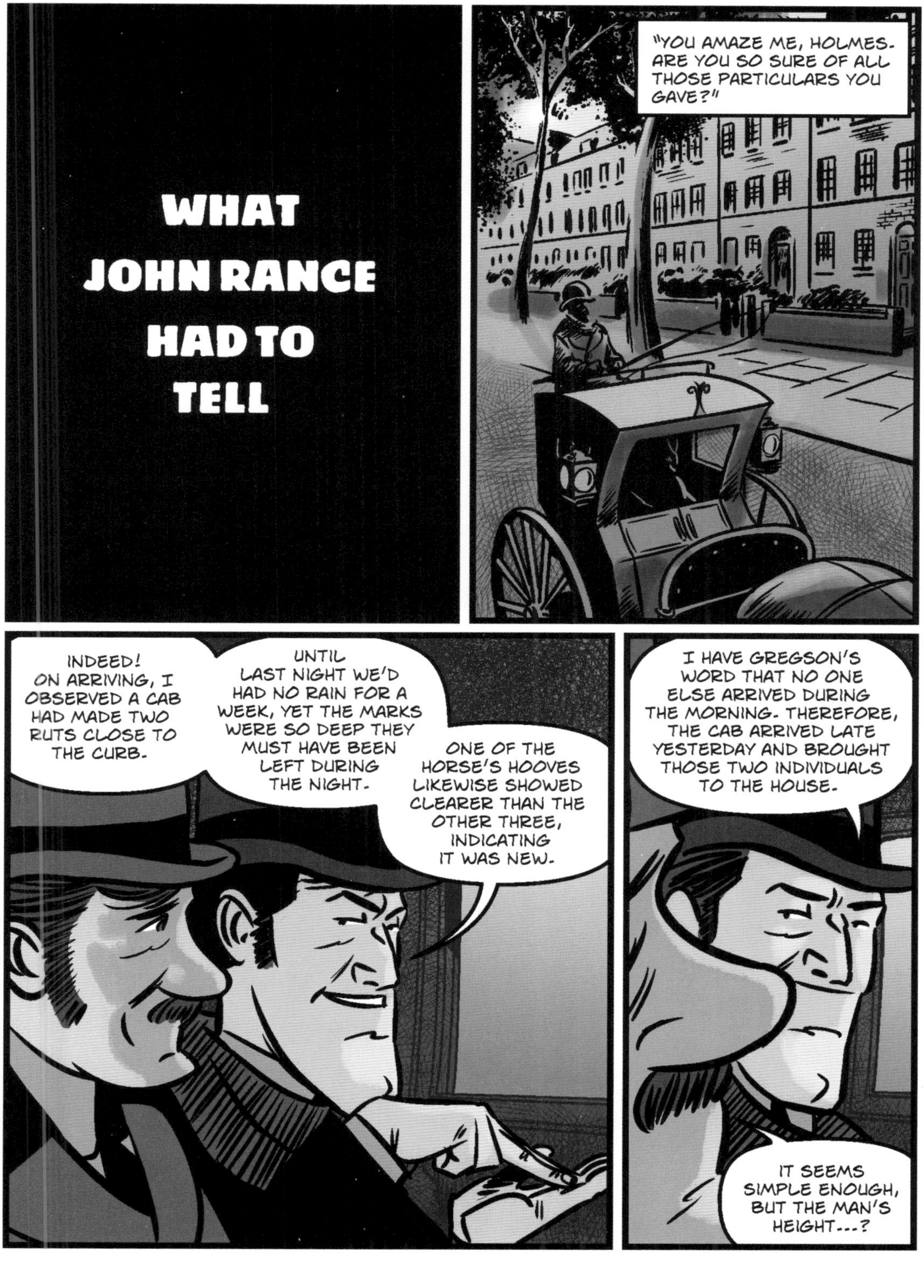
WHAT JOHN RANCE HAD TO TELL
"YOU AMAZE ME, HOLMES. ARE YOU SO SURE OF ALL THOSE PARTICULARS YOU GAVE?"
INDEED! ON ARRIVING, I OBSERVED A CAB HAD MADE TWO RUTS CLOSE TO THE CURB.
UNTIL LAST NIGHT WE'D HAD NO RAIN FOR A WEEK, YET THE MARKS WERE SO DEEP THEY MUST HAVE BEEN LEFT DURING THE NIGHT.
ONE OF THE HORSE'S HOOVES LIKEWISE SHOWED CLEARER THAN THE OTHER THREE, INDICATING IT WAS NEW.
I HAVE GREGSON'S WORD THAT NO ONE ELSE ARRIVED DURING THE MORNING. THEREFORE, THE CAB ARRIVED LATE YESTERDAY AND BROUGHT THOSE TWO INDIVIDUALS TO THE HOUSE.
IT SEEMS SIMPLE ENOUGH, BUT THE MAN'S HEIGHT...?

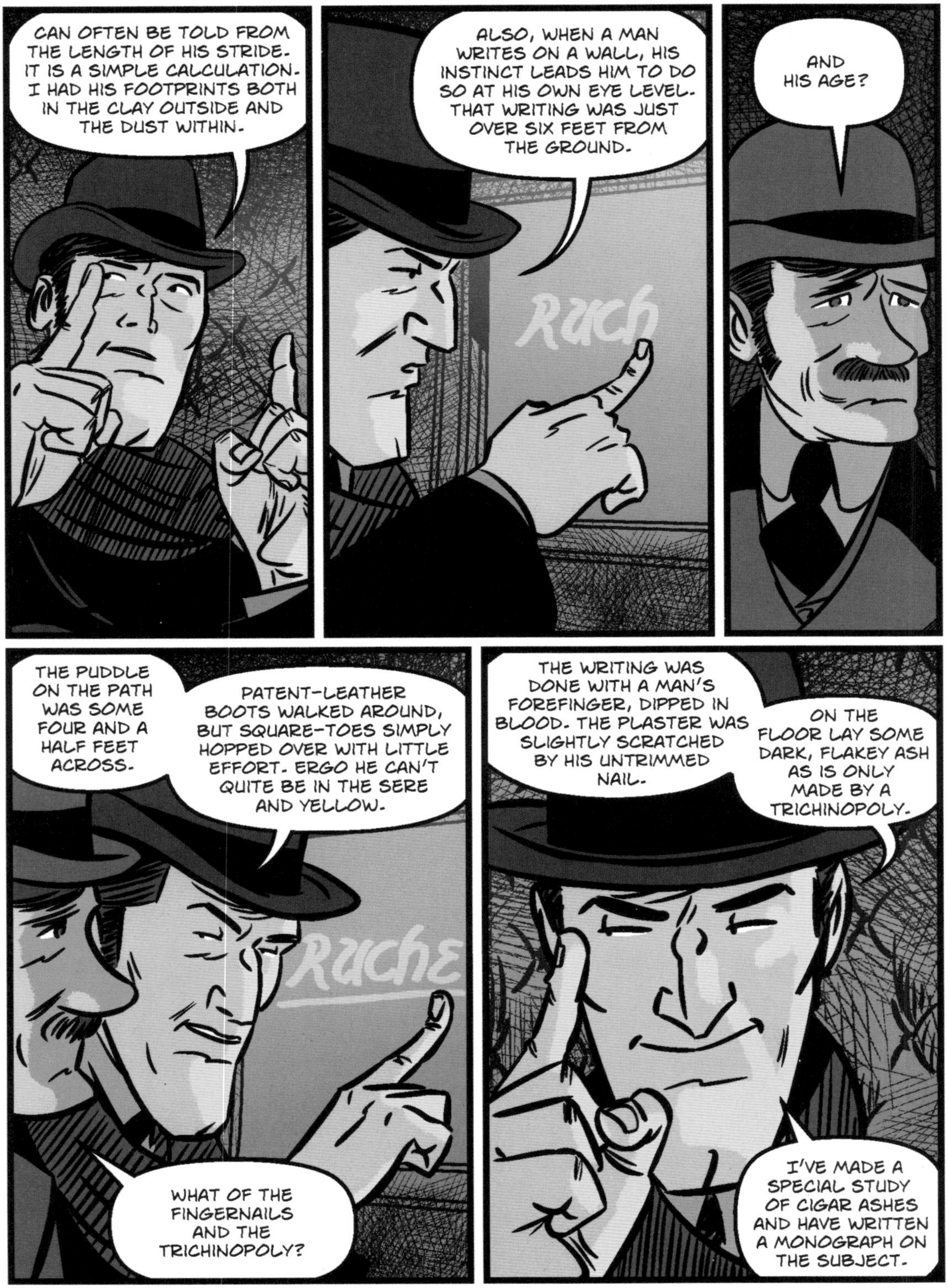
CAN OFTEN BE TOLD FROM THE LENGTH OF HIS STRIDE. IT IS A SIMPLE CALCULATION. I HAD HIS FOOTPRINTS BOTH IN THE CLAY OUTSIDE AND THE DUST WITHIN.
ALSO, WHEN A MAN WRITES ON A WALL, HIS INSTINCT LEADS HIM TO DO SO AT HIS OWN EYE LEVEL. THAT WRITING WAS JUST OVER SIX FEET FROM THE GROUND.
RACH
AND HIS AGE?
THE PUDDLE ON THE PATH WAS SOME FOUR AND A HALF FEET ACROSS.
PATENT-LEATHER BOOTS WALKED AROUND, BUT SQUARE-TOES SIMPLY HOPPED OVER WITH LITTLE EFFORT. ERGO HE CAN'T QUITE BE IN THE SERE AND YELLOW.
RACHE
WHAT OF THE FINGERNAILS AND THE TRICHINOPOLY?
THE WRITING WAS DONE WITH A MAN'S FOREFINGER, DIPPED IN BLOOD. THE PLASTER WAS SLIGHTLY SCRATCHED BY HIS UNTRIMMED NAIL.
ON THE FLOOR LAY SOME DARK, FLAKEY ASH AS IS ONLY MADE BY A TRICHINOPOLY.
I'VE MADE A SPECIAL STUDY OF CIGAR ASHES AND HAVE WRITTEN A MONOGRAPH ON THE SUBJECT.

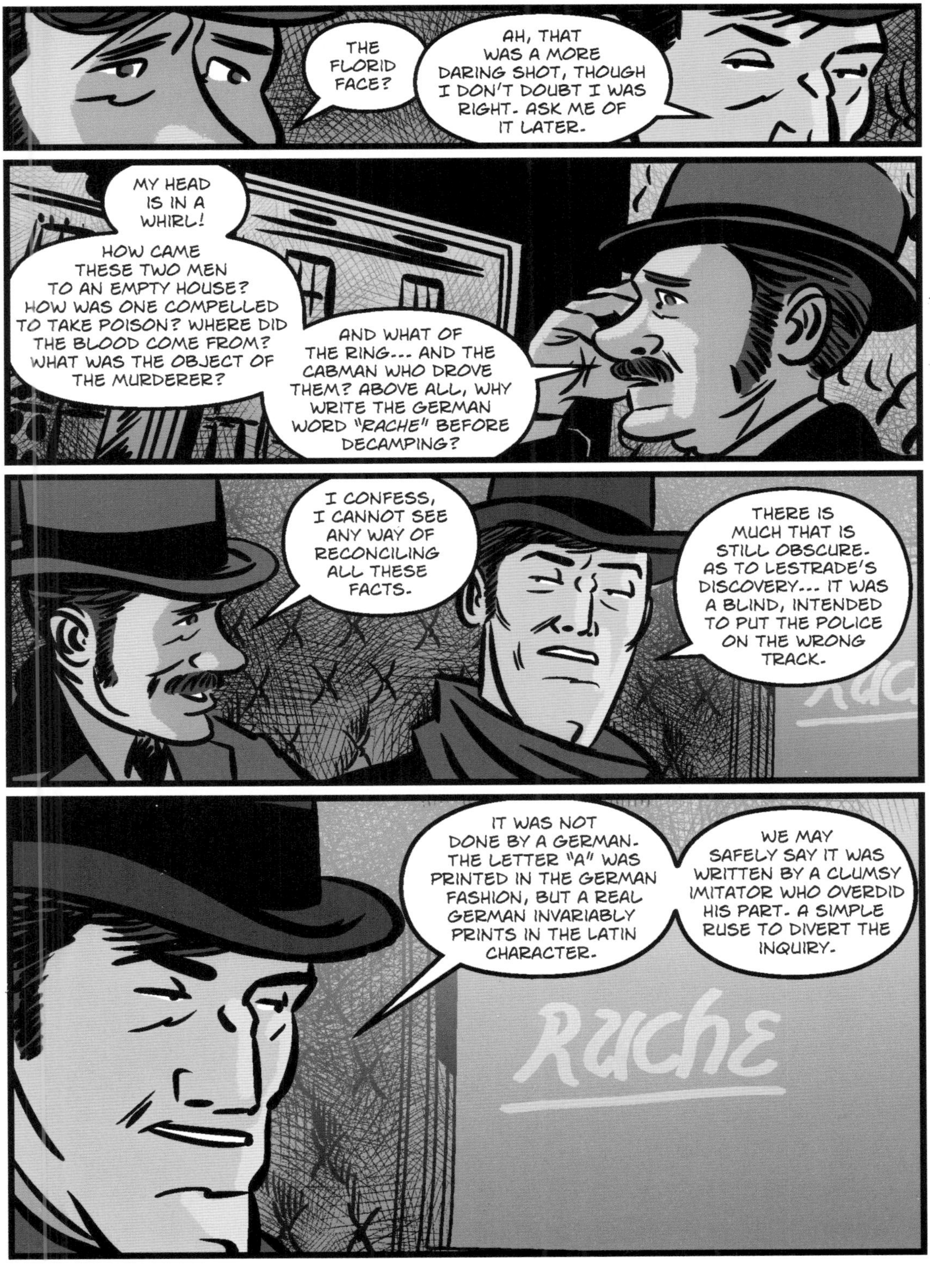
THE FLORID FACE?
AH, THAT WAS A MORE DARING SHOT, THOUGH I DON'T DOUBT I WAS RIGHT. ASK ME OF IT LATER.
MY HEAD IS IN A WHIRL!
HOW CAME THESE TWO MEN TO AN EMPTY HOUSE? HOW WAS ONE COMPELLED TO TAKE POISON? WHERE DID THE BLOOD COME FROM? WHAT WAS THE OBJECT OF THE MURDERER?
AND WHAT OF THE RING... AND THE CABMAN WHO DROVE THEM? ABOVE ALL, WHY WRITE THE GERMAN WORD "RACHE" BEFORE DECAMPING?
I CONFESS, I CANNOT SEE ANY WAY OF RECONCILING ALL THESE FACTS.
THERE IS MUCH THAT IS STILL OBSCURE. AS TO LESTRADE'S DISCOVERY... IT WAS A BLIND, INTENDED TO PUT THE POLICE ON THE WRONG TRACK.
IT WAS NOT DONE BY A GERMAN. THE LETTER "A" WAS PRINTED IN THE GERMAN FASHION, BUT A REAL GERMAN INVARIABLY PRINTS IN THE LATIN CHARACTER.
WE MAY SAFELY SAY IT WAS WRITTEN BY A CLUMSY IMITATOR WHO OVERDID HIS PART. A SIMPLE RUSE TO DIVERT THE INQUIRY.
RACHE

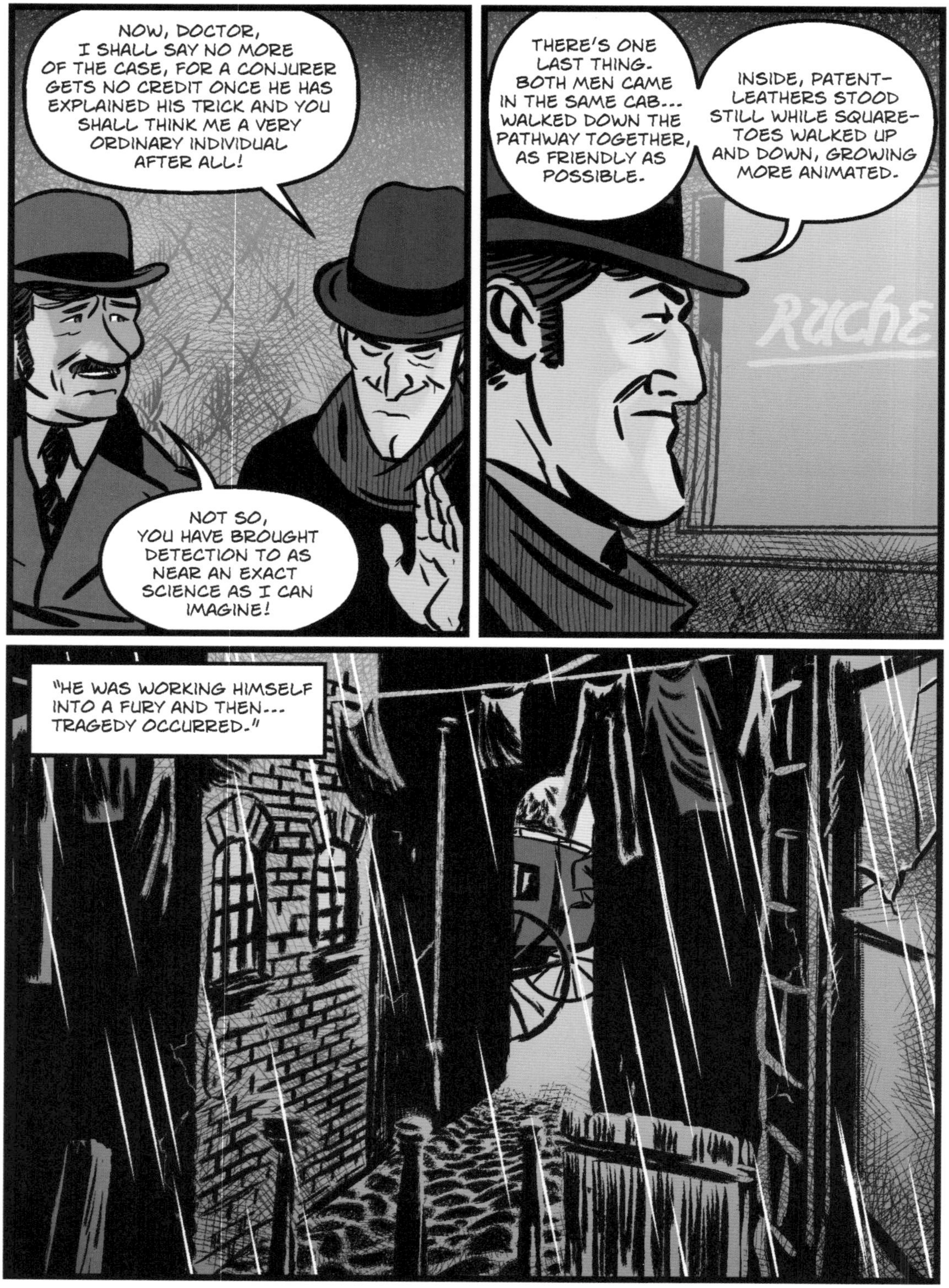
NOW, DOCTOR, I SHALL SAY NO MORE OF THE CASE, FOR A CONJURER GETS NO CREDIT ONCE HE HAS EXPLAINED HIS TRICK AND YOU SHALL THINK ME A VERY ORDINARY INDIVIDUAL AFTER ALL!
NOT SO, YOU HAVE BROUGHT DETECTION TO AS NEAR AN EXACT SCIENCE AS I CAN IMAGINE!
THERE'S ONE LAST THING. BOTH MEN CAME IN THE SAME CAB... WALKED DOWN THE PATHWAY TOGETHER, AS FRIENDLY AS POSSIBLE.
INSIDE, PATENT-LEATHERS STOOD STILL WHILE SQUARE-TOES WALKED UP AND DOWN, GROWING MORE ANIMATED.
RACHE
"HE WAS WORKING HIMSELF INTO A FURY AND THEN... TRAGEDY OCCURRED."

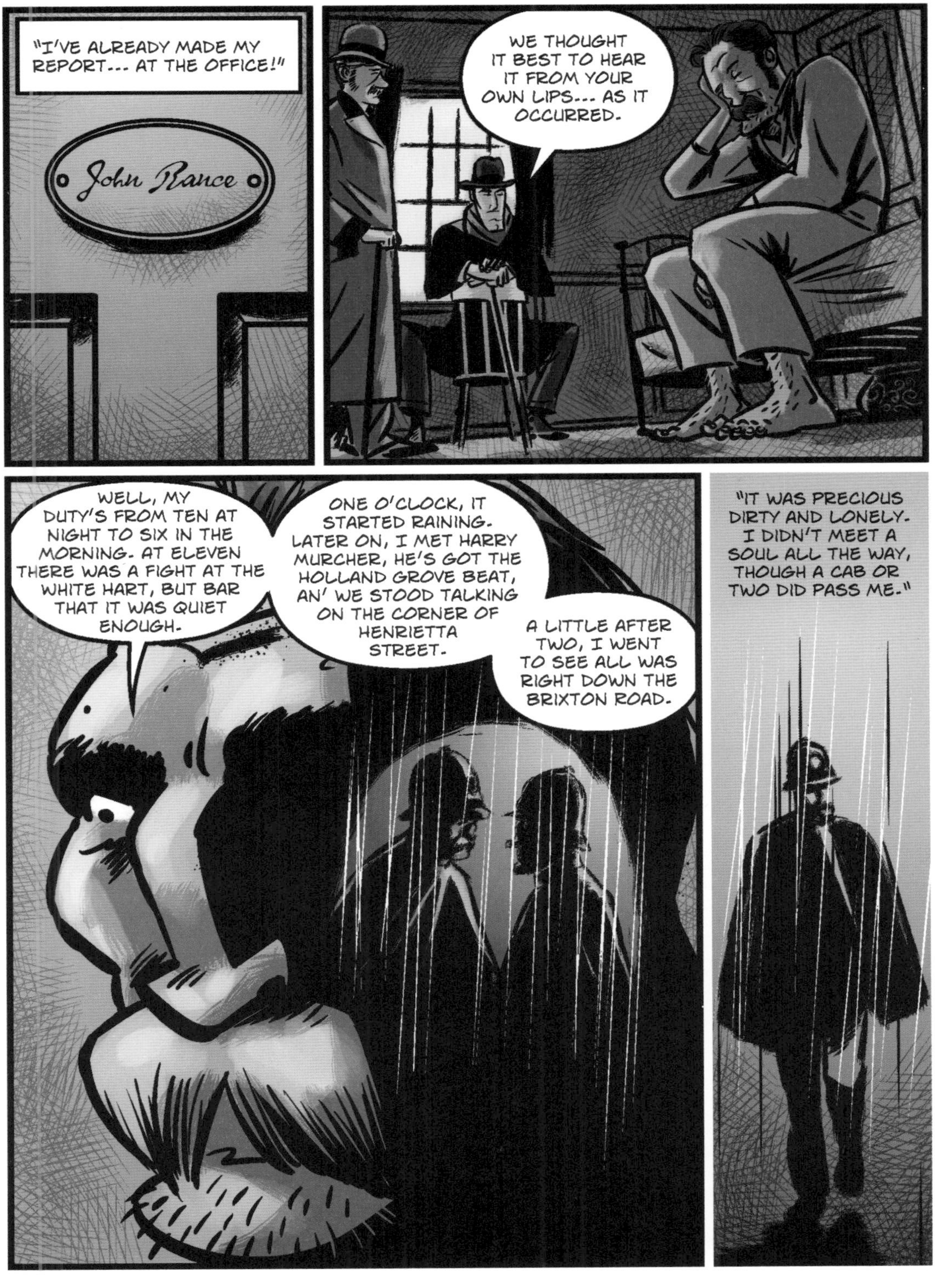
"I'VE ALREADY MADE MY REPORT... AT THE OFFICE!"
John Rance
WE THOUGHT IT BEST TO HEAR IT FROM YOUR OWN LIPS... AS IT OCCURRED.
WELL, MY DUTY'S FROM TEN AT NIGHT TO SIX IN THE MORNING. AT ELEVEN THERE WAS A FIGHT AT THE WHITE HART, BUT BAR THAT IT WAS QUIET ENOUGH.
ONE O'CLOCK, IT STARTED RAINING. LATER ON, I MET HARRY MURCHER, HE'S GOT THE HOLLAND GROVE BEAT, AN' WE STOOD TALKING ON THE CORNER OF HENRIETTA STREET.
A LITTLE AFTER TWO, I WENT TO SEE ALL WAS RIGHT DOWN THE BRIXTON ROAD.
"IT WAS PRECIOUS DIRTY AND LONELY. I DIDN'T MEET A SOUL ALL THE WAY, THOUGH A CAB OR TWO DID PASS ME."

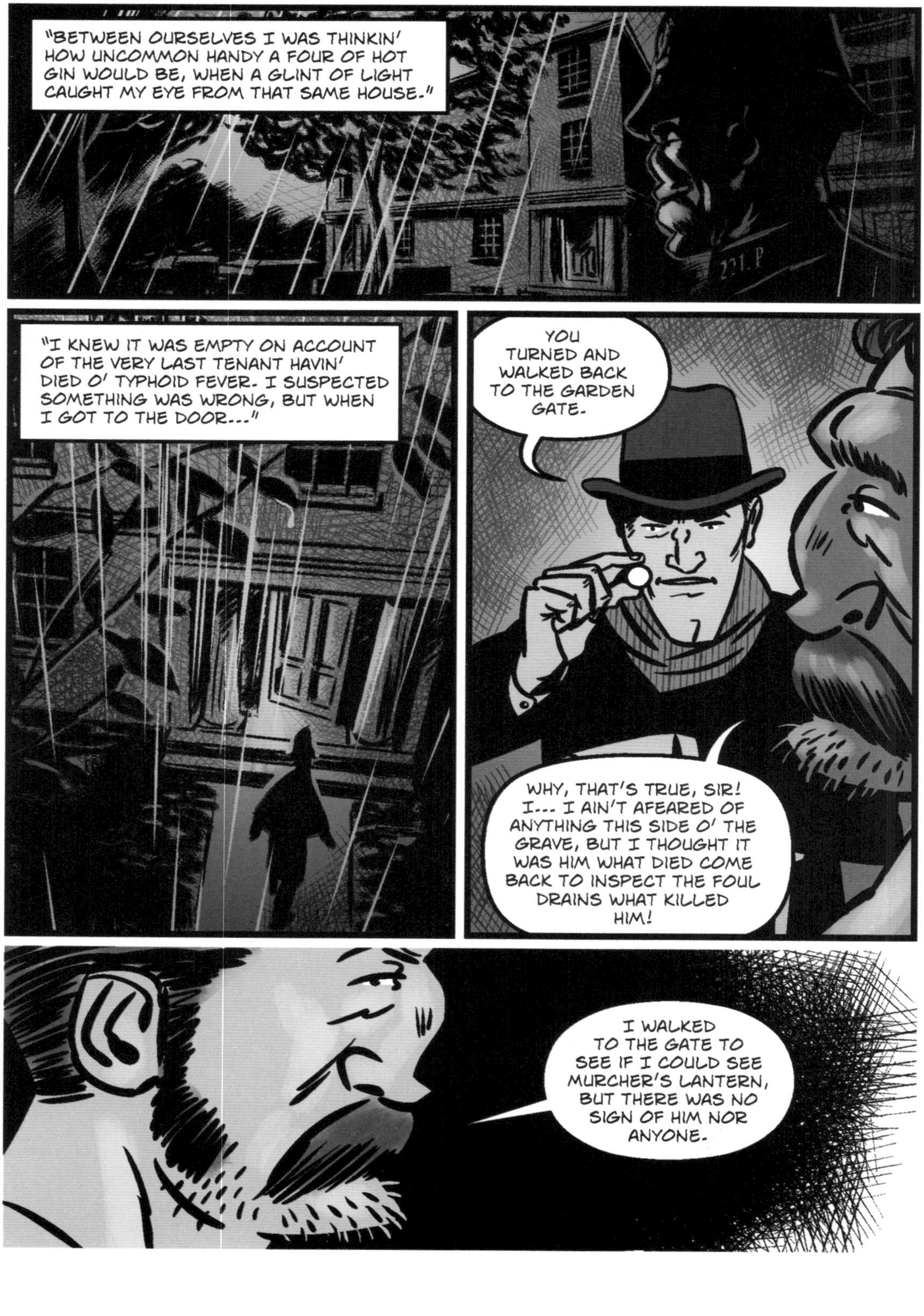
"BETWEEN OURSELVES I WAS THINKIN' HOW UNCOMMON HANDY A FOUR OF HOT GIN WOULD BE, WHEN A GLINT OF LIGHT CAUGHT MY EYE FROM THAT SAME HOUSE."
221 P
"I KNEW IT WAS EMPTY ON ACCOUNT OF THE VERY LAST TENANT HAVIN' DIED O' TYPHOID FEVER. I SUSPECTED SOMETHING WAS WRONG, BUT WHEN I GOT TO THE DOOR..."
YOU TURNED AND WALKED BACK TO THE GARDEN GATE.
WHY, THAT'S TRUE, SIR! I... I AIN'T AFEARED OF ANYTHING THIS SIDE O' THE GRAVE, BUT I THOUGHT IT WAS HIM WHAT DIED COME BACK TO INSPECT THE FOUL DRAINS WHAT KILLED HIM!
I WALKED TO THE GATE TO SEE IF I COULD SEE MURCHER'S LANTERN, BUT THERE WAS NO SIGN OF HIM NOR ANYONE.

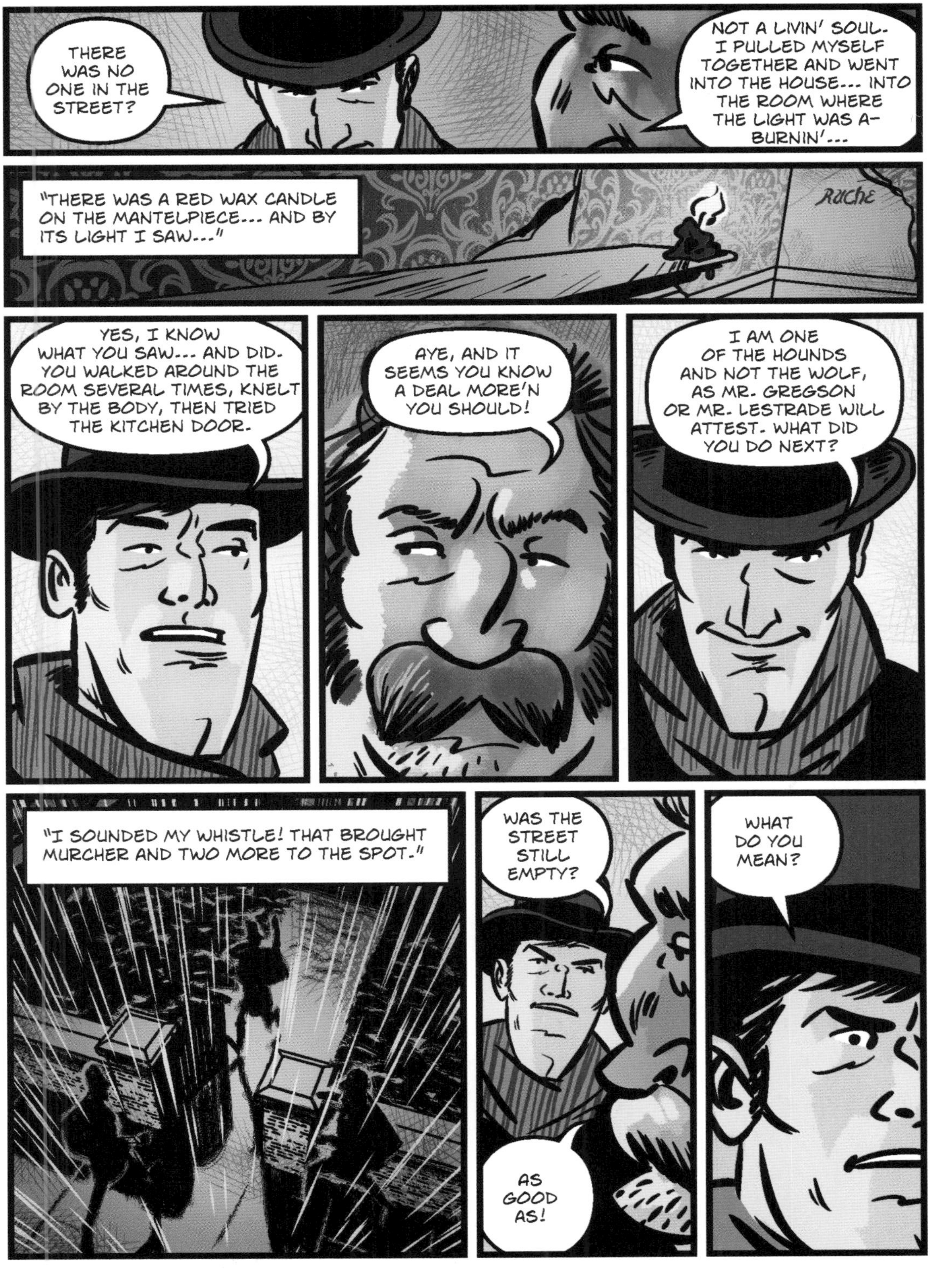
THERE WAS NO ONE IN THE STREET?
NOT A LIVIN' SOUL. I PULLED MYSELF TOGETHER AND WENT INTO THE HOUSE... INTO THE ROOM WHERE THE LIGHT WAS A-BURNIN'...
"THERE WAS A RED WAX CANDLE ON THE MANTELPIECE... AND BY ITS LIGHT I SAW..."
RUCHE
YES, I KNOW WHAT YOU SAW... AND DID. YOU WALKED AROUND THE ROOM SEVERAL TIMES, KNELT BY THE BODY, THEN TRIED THE KITCHEN DOOR.
AYE, AND IT SEEMS YOU KNOW A DEAL MORE'N YOU SHOULD!
I AM ONE OF THE HOUNDS AND NOT THE WOLF, AS MR. GREGSON OR MR. LESTRADE WILL ATTEST. WHAT DID YOU DO NEXT?
"I SOUNDED MY WHISTLE! THAT BROUGHT MURCHER AND TWO MORE TO THE SPOT."
WAS THE STREET STILL EMPTY?
AS GOOD AS!
WHAT DO YOU MEAN?

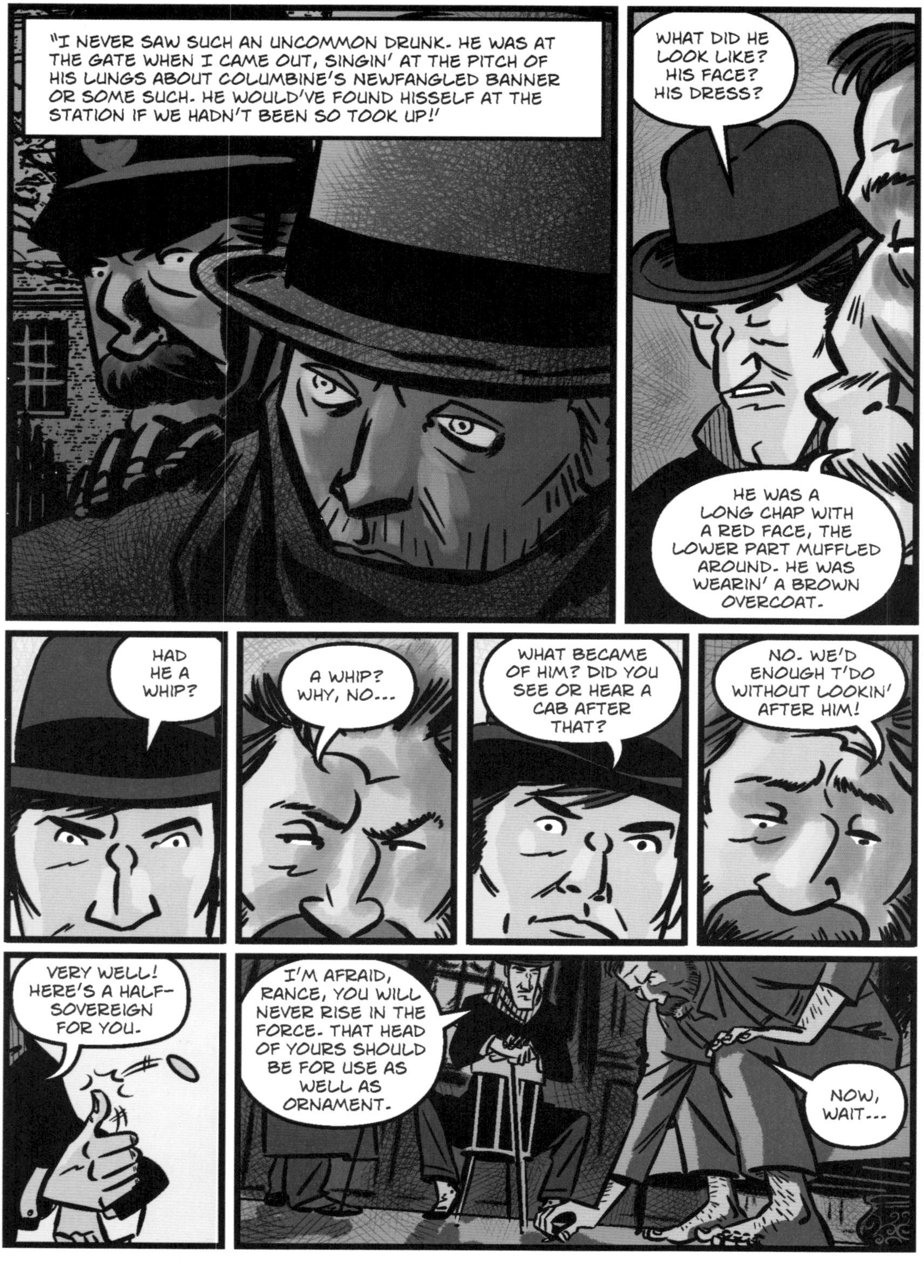
"I NEVER SAW SUCH AN UNCOMMON DRUNK. HE WAS AT THE GATE WHEN I CAME OUT, SINGIN' AT THE PITCH OF HIS LUNGS ABOUT COLUMBINE'S NEWFANGLED BANNER OR SOME SUCH. HE WOULD'VE FOUND HISSELF AT THE STATION IF WE HADN'T BEEN SO TOOK UP!'
WHAT DID HE LOOK LIKE? HIS FACE? HIS DRESS?
HE WAS A LONG CHAP WITH A RED FACE, THE LOWER PART MUFFLED AROUND. HE WAS WEARIN' A BROWN OVERCOAT.
HAD HE A WHIP?
A WHIP? WHY, NO...
WHAT BECAME OF HIM? DID YOU SEE OR HEAR A CAB AFTER THAT?
NO. WE'D ENOUGH T'DO WITHOUT LOOKIN' AFTER HIM!
VERY WELL! HERE'S A HALF-SOVEREIGN FOR YOU.
I'M AFRAID, RANCE, YOU WILL NEVER RISE IN THE FORCE. THAT HEAD OF YOURS SHOULD BE FOR USE AS WELL AS ORNAMENT.
NOW, WAIT...

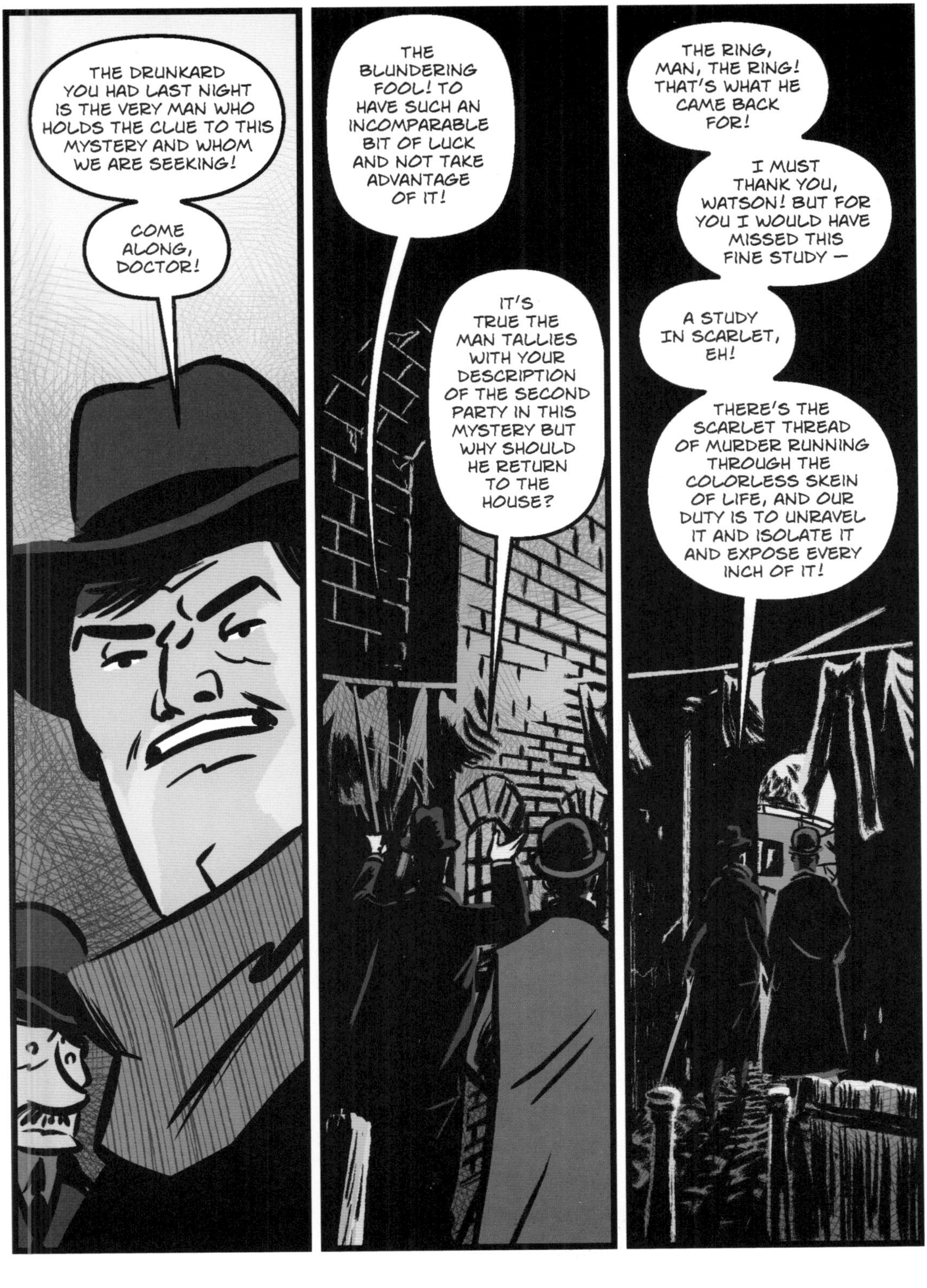
THE DRUNKARD YOU HAD LAST NIGHT IS THE VERY MAN WHO HOLDS THE CLUE TO THIS MYSTERY AND WHOM WE ARE SEEKING!
COME ALONG, DOCTOR!
THE BLUNDERING FOOL! TO HAVE SUCH AN INCOMPARABLE BIT OF LUCK AND NOT TAKE ADVANTAGE OF IT!
IT'S TRUE THE MAN TALLIES WITH YOUR DESCRIPTION OF THE SECOND PARTY IN THIS MYSTERY BUT WHY SHOULD HE RETURN TO THE HOUSE?
THE RING, MAN, THE RING! THAT'S WHAT HE CAME BACK FOR!
I MUST THANK YOU, WATSON! BUT FOR YOU I WOULD HAVE MISSED THIS FINE STUDY —
A STUDY IN SCARLET, EH!
THERE'S THE SCARLET THREAD OF MURDER RUNNING THROUGH THE COLORLESS SKEIN OF LIFE, AND OUR DUTY IS TO UNRAVEL IT AND ISOLATE IT AND EXPOSE EVERY INCH OF IT!

OUR ADVERTISEMENT BRINGS A VISITOR

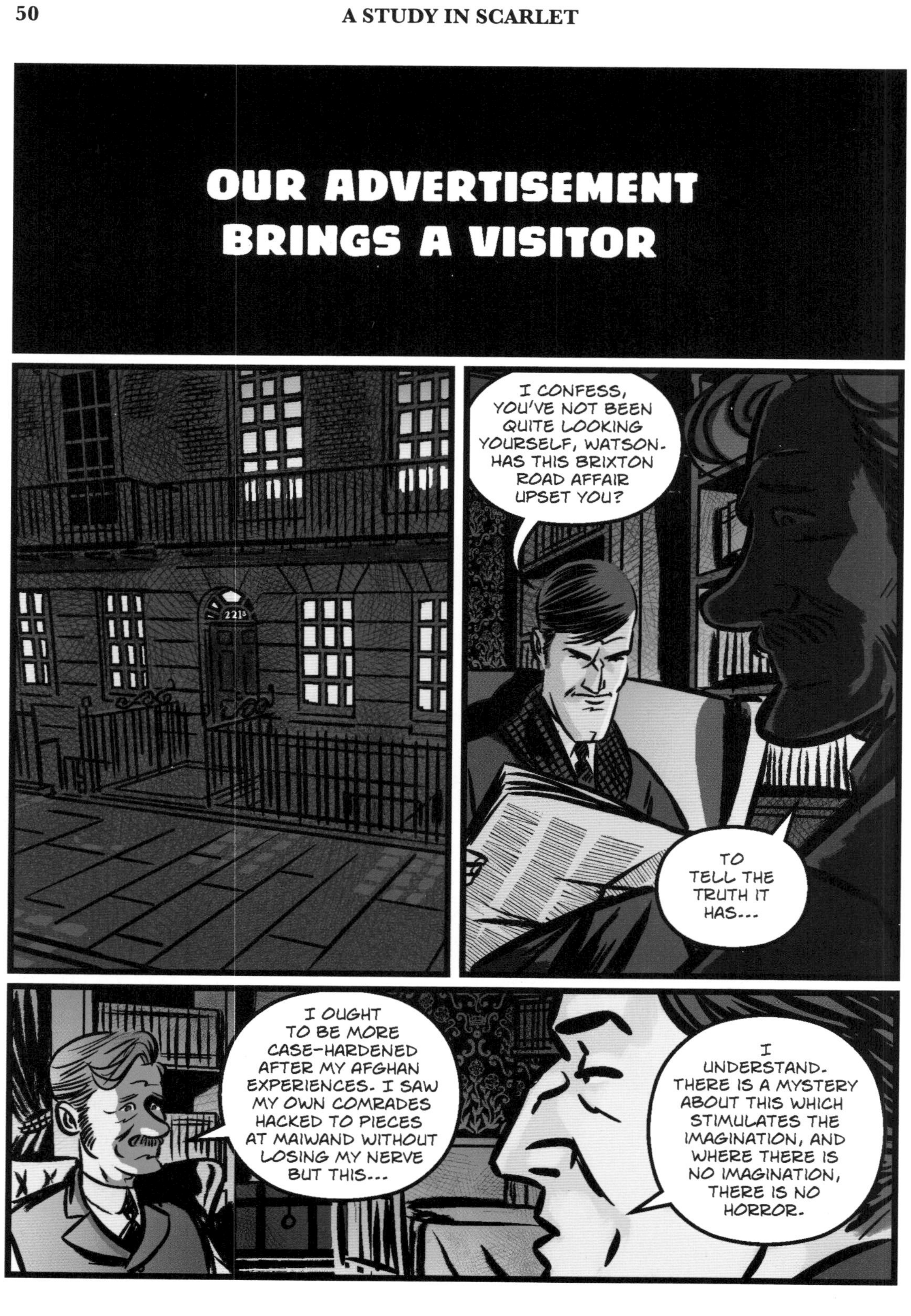
221B
I CONFESS, YOU'VE NOT BEEN QUITE LOOKING YOURSELF, WATSON. HAS THIS BRIXTON ROAD AFFAIR UPSET YOU?
TO TELL THE TRUTH IT HAS...
I OUGHT TO BE MORE CASE-HARDENED AFTER MY AFGHAN EXPERIENCES. I SAW MY OWN COMRADES HACKED TO PIECES AT MAIWAND WITHOUT LOSING MY NERVE BUT THIS...
I UNDERSTAND. THERE IS A MYSTERY ABOUT THIS WHICH STIMULATES THE IMAGINATION, AND WHERE THERE IS NO IMAGINATION, THERE IS NO HORROR.

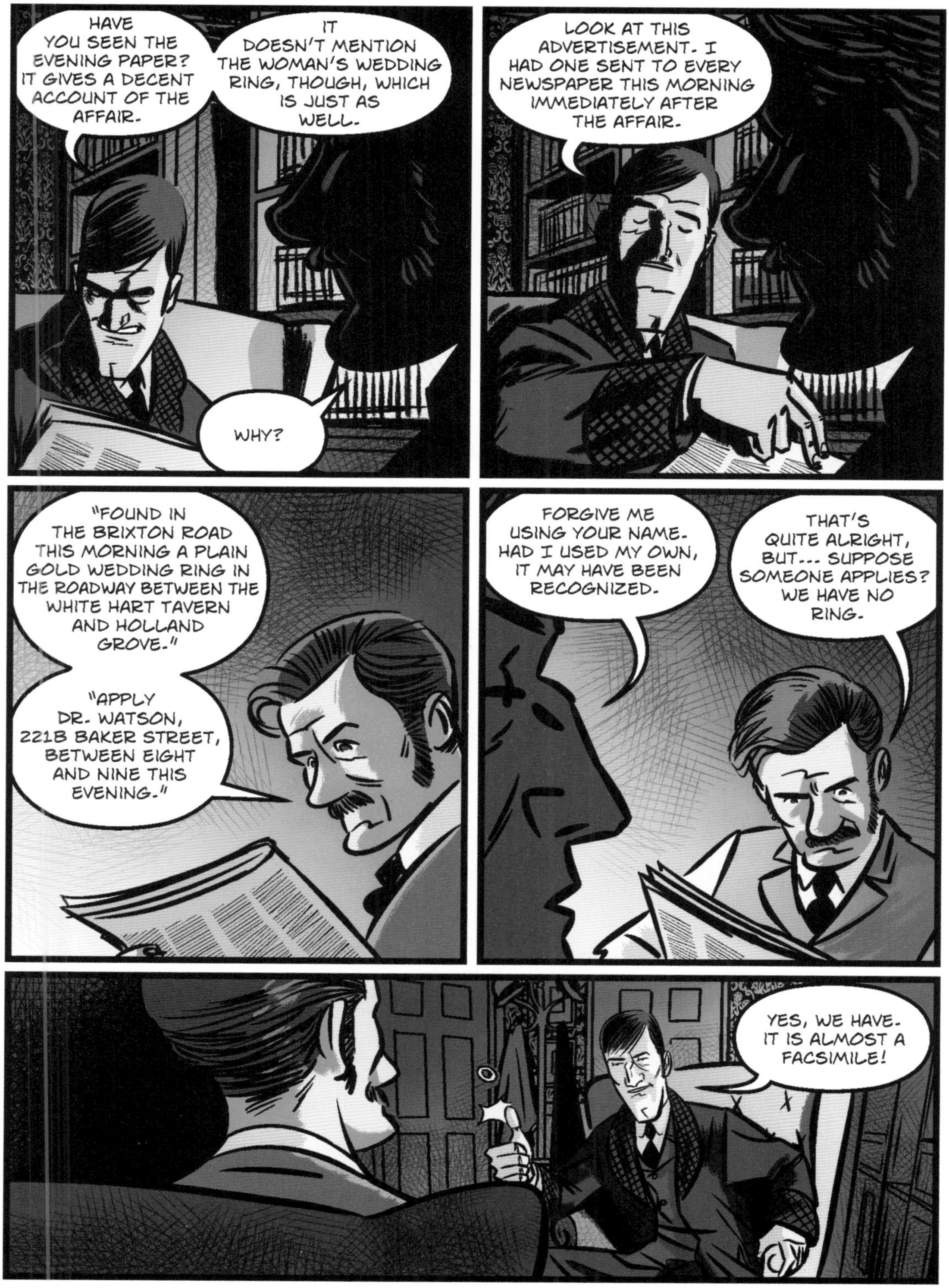
HAVE YOU SEEN THE EVENING PAPER? IT GIVES A DECENT ACCOUNT OF THE AFFAIR.
IT DOESN'T MENTION THE WOMAN'S WEDDING RING, THOUGH, WHICH IS JUST AS WELL.
WHY?
LOOK AT THIS ADVERTISEMENT. I HAD ONE SENT TO EVERY NEWSPAPER THIS MORNING IMMEDIATELY AFTER THE AFFAIR.
"FOUND IN THE BRIXTON ROAD THIS MORNING A PLAIN GOLD WEDDING RING IN THE ROADWAY BETWEEN THE WHITE HART TAVERN AND HOLLAND GROVE."
"APPLY DR. WATSON, 221B BAKER STREET, BETWEEN EIGHT AND NINE THIS EVENING."
FORGIVE ME USING YOUR NAME. HAD I USED MY OWN, IT MAY HAVE BEEN RECOGNIZED.
THAT'S QUITE ALRIGHT, BUT... SUPPOSE SOMEONE APPLIES? WE HAVE NO RING.
YES, WE HAVE. IT IS ALMOST A FACSIMILE!

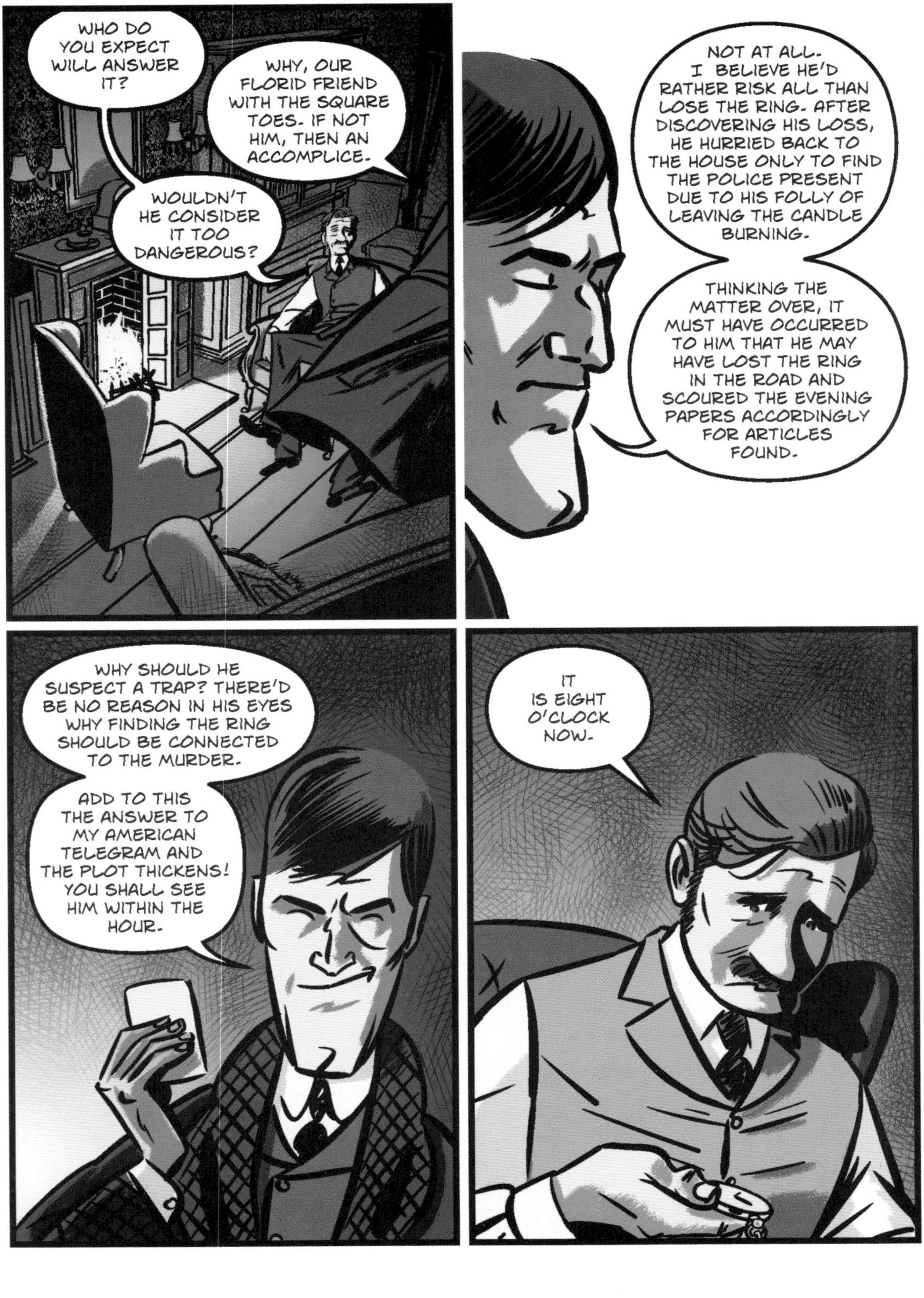
WHO DO YOU EXPECT WILL ANSWER IT?
WHY, OUR FLORID FRIEND WITH THE SQUARE TOES. IF NOT HIM, THEN AN ACCOMPLICE.
WOULDN'T HE CONSIDER IT TOO DANGEROUS?
NOT AT ALL. I BELIEVE HE'D RATHER RISK ALL THAN LOSE THE RING. AFTER DISCOVERING HIS LOSS, HE HURRIED BACK TO THE HOUSE ONLY TO FIND THE POLICE PRESENT DUE TO HIS FOLLY OF LEAVING THE CANDLE BURNING.
THINKING THE MATTER OVER, IT MUST HAVE OCCURRED TO HIM THAT HE MAY HAVE LOST THE RING IN THE ROAD AND SCOURED THE EVENING PAPERS ACCORDINGLY FOR ARTICLES FOUND.
WHY SHOULD HE SUSPECT A TRAP? THERE'D BE NO REASON IN HIS EYES WHY FINDING THE RING SHOULD BE CONNECTED TO THE MURDER.
ADD TO THIS THE ANSWER TO MY AMERICAN TELEGRAM AND THE PLOT THICKENS! YOU SHALL SEE HIM WITHIN THE HOUR.
IT IS EIGHT O'CLOCK NOW.

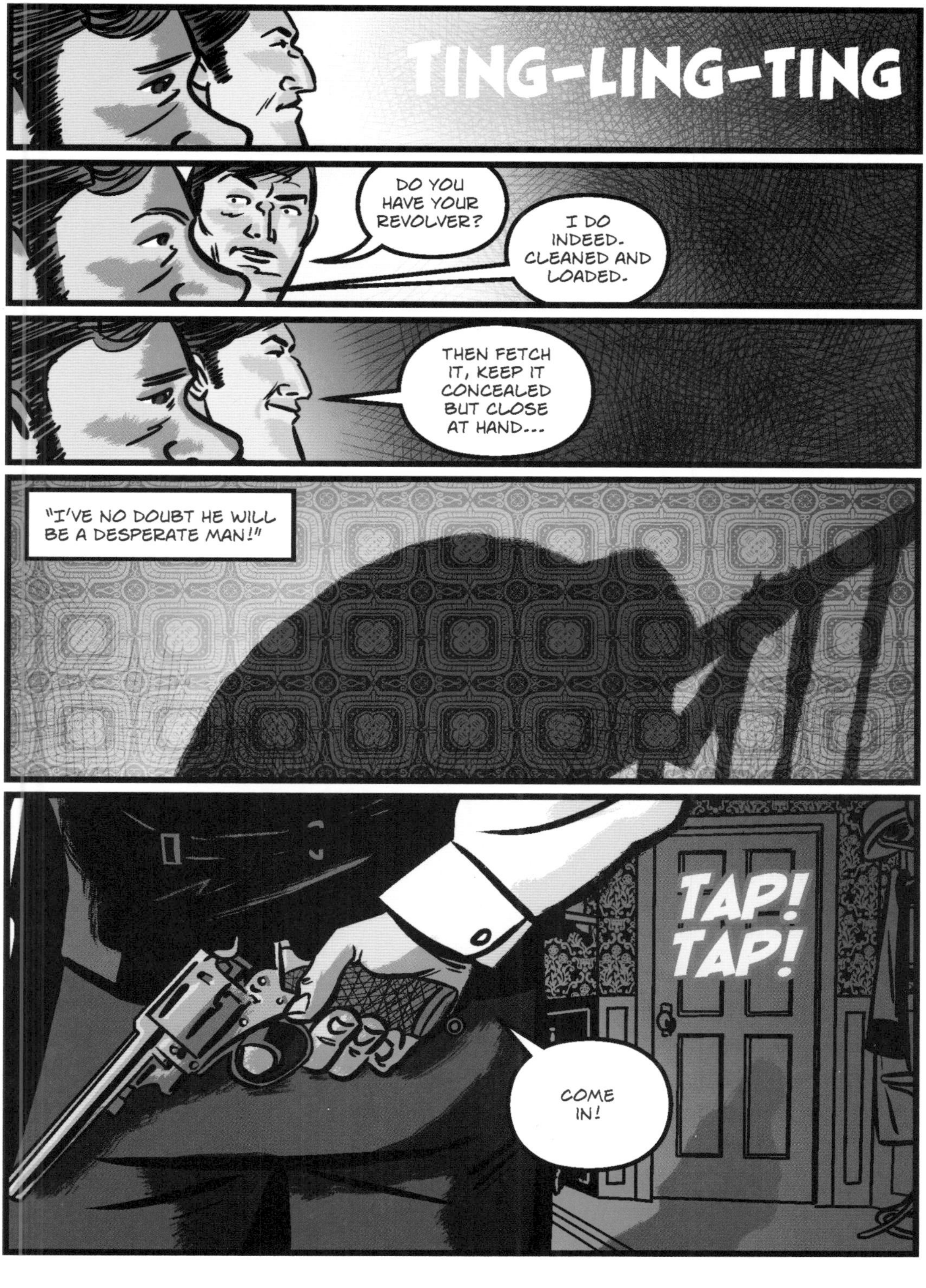
TING-LING-TING
DO YOU HAVE YOUR REVOLVER?
I DO INDEED. CLEANED AND LOADED.
THEN FETCH IT, KEEP IT CONCEALED BUT CLOSE AT HAND...
"I'VE NO DOUBT HE WILL BE A DESPERATE MAN!"
TAP! TAP!
COME IN!

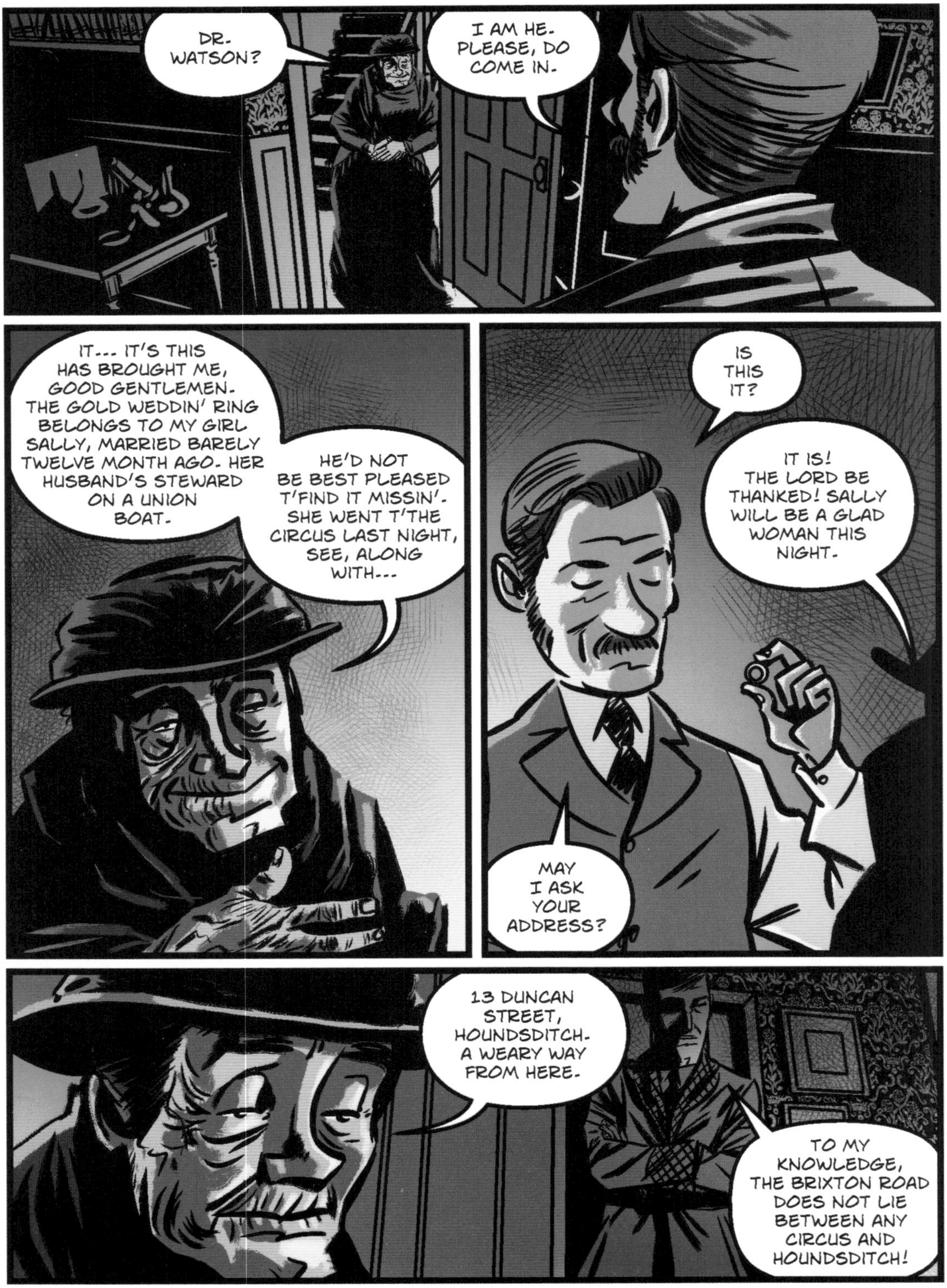
DR. WATSON?
I AM HE. PLEASE, DO COME IN.
IT... IT'S THIS HAS BROUGHT ME, GOOD GENTLEMEN. THE GOLD WEDDIN' RING BELONGS TO MY GIRL SALLY, MARRIED BARELY TWELVE MONTH AGO. HER HUSBAND'S STEWARD ON A UNION BOAT.
HE'D NOT BE BEST PLEASED T'FIND IT MISSIN'. SHE WENT T'THE CIRCUS LAST NIGHT, SEE, ALONG WITH...
IS THIS IT?
IT IS! THE LORD BE THANKED! SALLY WILL BE A GLAD WOMAN THIS NIGHT.
MAY I ASK YOUR ADDRESS?
13 DUNCAN STREET, HOUNDSDITCH. A WEARY WAY FROM HERE.
TO MY KNOWLEDGE, THE BRIXTON ROAD DOES NOT LIE BETWEEN ANY CIRCUS AND HOUNDSDITCH!

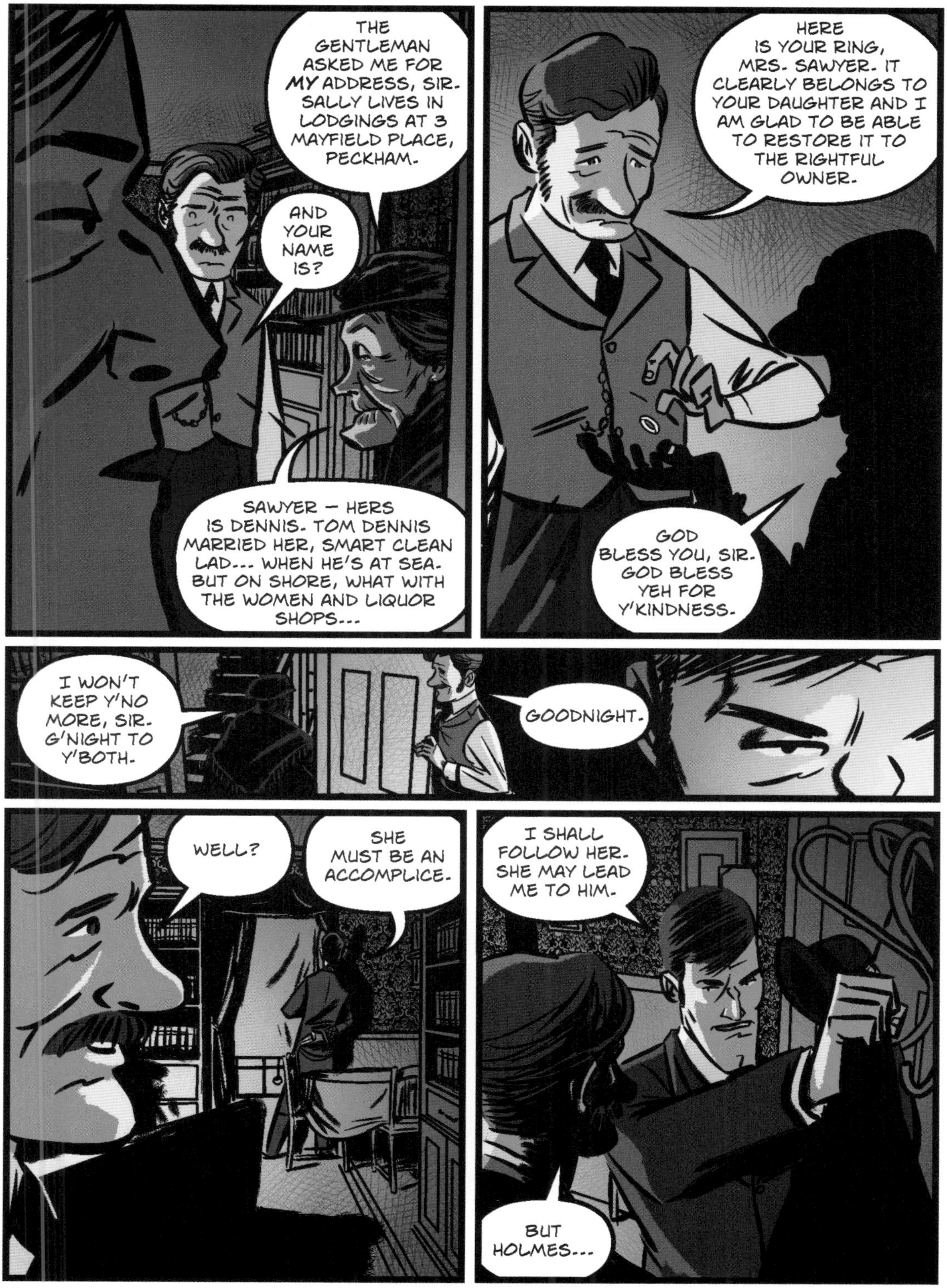
THE GENTLEMAN ASKED ME FOR MY ADDRESS, SIR. SALLY LIVES IN LODGINGS AT 3 MAYFIELD PLACE, PECKHAM.
AND YOUR NAME IS?
SAWYER — HERS IS DENNIS. TOM DENNIS MARRIED HER, SMART CLEAN LAD... WHEN HE'S AT SEA. BUT ON SHORE, WHAT WITH THE WOMEN AND LIQUOR SHOPS...
HERE IS YOUR RING, MRS. SAWYER. IT CLEARLY BELONGS TO YOUR DAUGHTER AND I AM GLAD TO BE ABLE TO RESTORE IT TO THE RIGHTFUL OWNER.
GOD BLESS YOU, SIR. GOD BLESS YEH FOR Y'KINDNESS.
I WON'T KEEP Y'NO MORE, SIR. G'NIGHT TO Y'BOTH.
GOODNIGHT.
WELL?
SHE MUST BE AN ACCOMPLICE.
I SHALL FOLLOW HER. SHE MAY LEAD ME TO HIM.
BUT HOLMES...

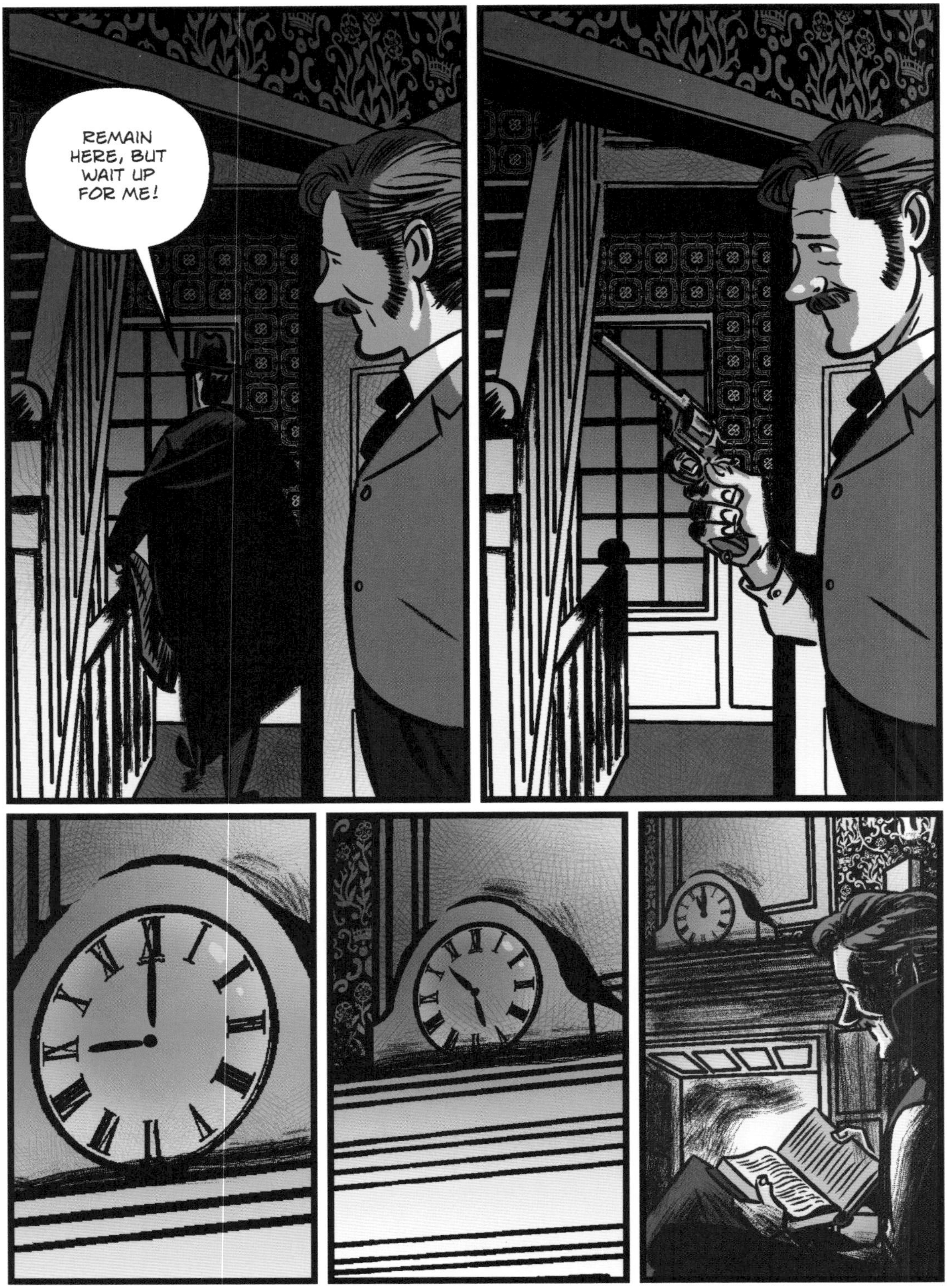
REMAIN HERE, BUT WAIT UP FOR ME!

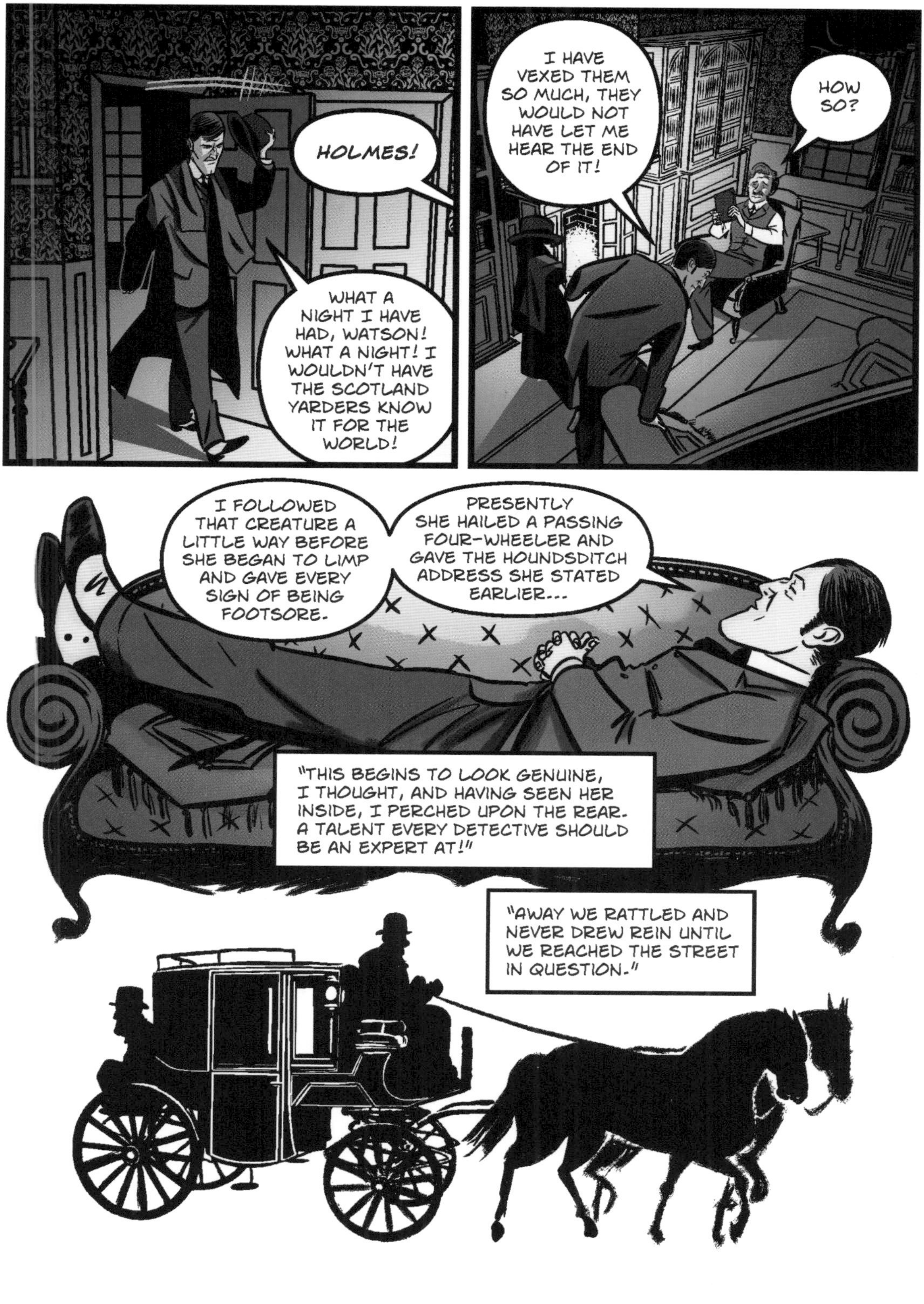
HOLMES!
WHAT A NIGHT I HAVE HAD, WATSON! WHAT A NIGHT! I WOULDN'T HAVE THE SCOTLAND YARDERS KNOW IT FOR THE WORLD!
I HAVE VEXED THEM SO MUCH, THEY WOULD NOT HAVE LET ME HEAR THE END OF IT!
HOW SO?
I FOLLOWED THAT CREATURE A LITTLE WAY BEFORE SHE BEGAN TO LIMP AND GAVE EVERY SIGN OF BEING FOOTSORE.
PRESENTLY SHE HAILED A PASSING FOUR-WHEELER AND GAVE THE HOUNDSDITCH ADDRESS SHE STATED EARLIER...
"THIS BEGINS TO LOOK GENUINE, I THOUGHT, AND HAVING SEEN HER INSIDE, I PERCHED UPON THE REAR. A TALENT EVERY DETECTIVE SHOULD BE AN EXPERT AT!"
"AWAY WE RATTLED AND NEVER DREW REIN UNTIL WE REACHED THE STREET IN QUESTION."

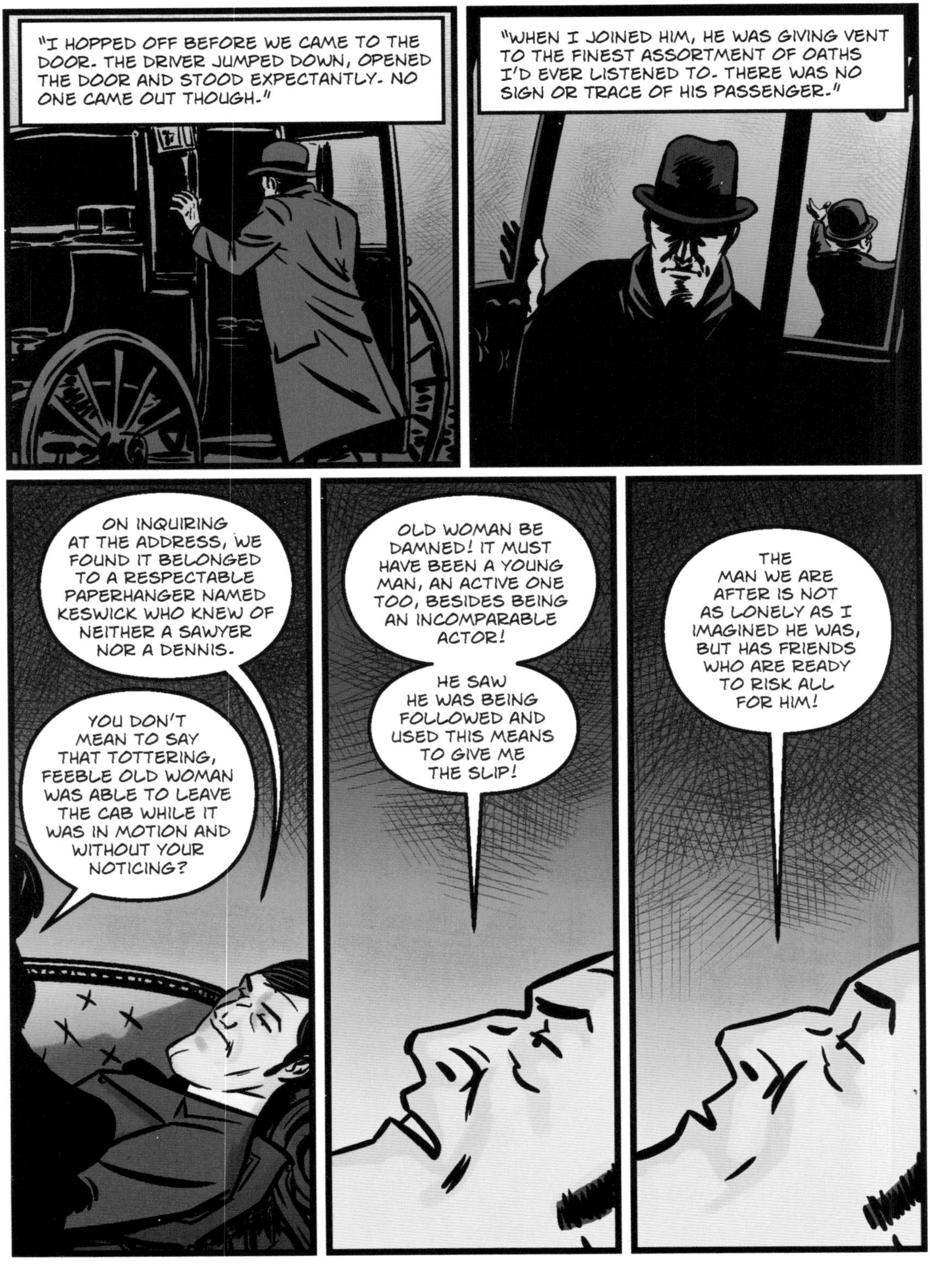
"I HOPPED OFF BEFORE WE CAME TO THE DOOR. THE DRIVER JUMPED DOWN, OPENED THE DOOR AND STOOD EXPECTANTLY. NO ONE CAME OUT THOUGH."
"WHEN I JOINED HIM, HE WAS GIVING VENT TO THE FINEST ASSORTMENT OF OATHS I'D EVER LISTENED TO. THERE WAS NO SIGN OR TRACE OF HIS PASSENGER."
ON INQUIRING AT THE ADDRESS, WE FOUND IT BELONGED TO A RESPECTABLE PAPERHANGER NAMED KESWICK WHO KNEW OF NEITHER A SAWYER NOR A DENNIS.
YOU DON'T MEAN TO SAY THAT TOTTERING, FEEBLE OLD WOMAN WAS ABLE TO LEAVE THE CAB WHILE IT WAS IN MOTION AND WITHOUT YOUR NOTICING?
OLD WOMAN BE DAMNED! IT MUST HAVE BEEN A YOUNG MAN, AN ACTIVE ONE TOO, BESIDES BEING AN INCOMPARABLE ACTOR!
HE SAW HE WAS BEING FOLLOWED AND USED THIS MEANS TO GIVE ME THE SLIP!
THE MAN WE ARE AFTER IS NOT AS LONELY AS I IMAGINED HE WAS, BUT HAS FRIENDS WHO ARE READY TO RISK ALL FOR HIM!

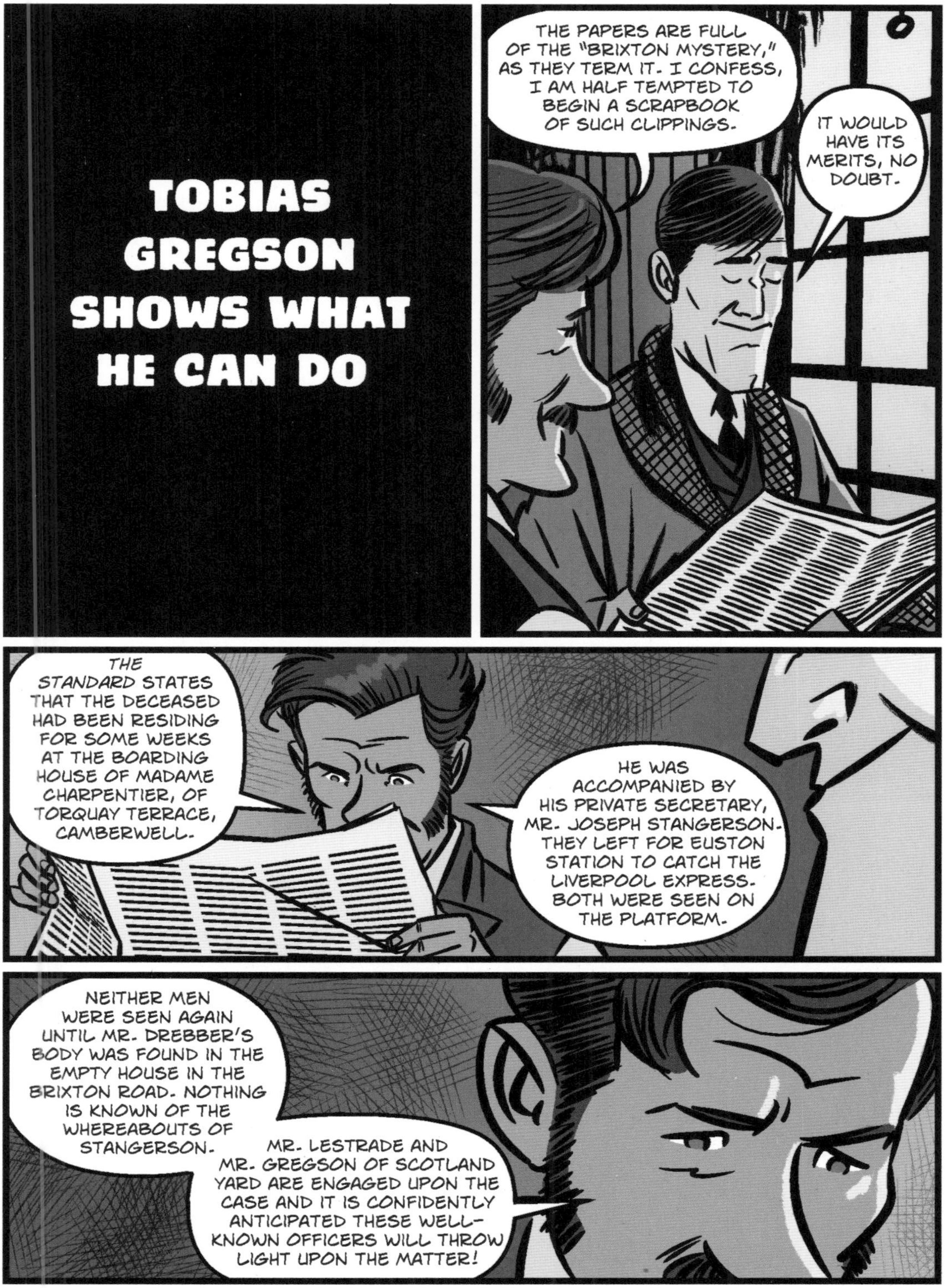
TOBIAS GREGSON SHOWS WHAT HE CAN DO
THE PAPERS ARE FULL OF THE "BRIXTON MYSTERY," AS THEY TERM IT. I CONFESS, I AM HALF TEMPTED TO BEGIN A SCRAPBOOK OF SUCH CLIPPINGS.
IT WOULD HAVE ITS MERITS, NO DOUBT.
THE STANDARD STATES THAT THE DECEASED HAD BEEN RESIDING FOR SOME WEEKS AT THE BOARDING HOUSE OF MADAME CHARPENTIER, OF TORQUAY TERRACE, CAMBERWELL.
HE WAS ACCOMPANIED BY HIS PRIVATE SECRETARY, MR. JOSEPH STANGERSON. THEY LEFT FOR EUSTON STATION TO CATCH THE LIVERPOOL EXPRESS. BOTH WERE SEEN ON THE PLATFORM.
NEITHER MEN WERE SEEN AGAIN UNTIL MR. DREBBER'S BODY WAS FOUND IN THE EMPTY HOUSE IN THE BRIXTON ROAD. NOTHING IS KNOWN OF THE WHEREABOUTS OF STANGERSON.
MR. LESTRADE AND MR. GREGSON OF SCOTLAND YARD ARE ENGAGED UPON THE CASE AND IT IS CONFIDENTLY ANTICIPATED THESE WELL-KNOWN OFFICERS WILL THROW LIGHT UPON THE MATTER!

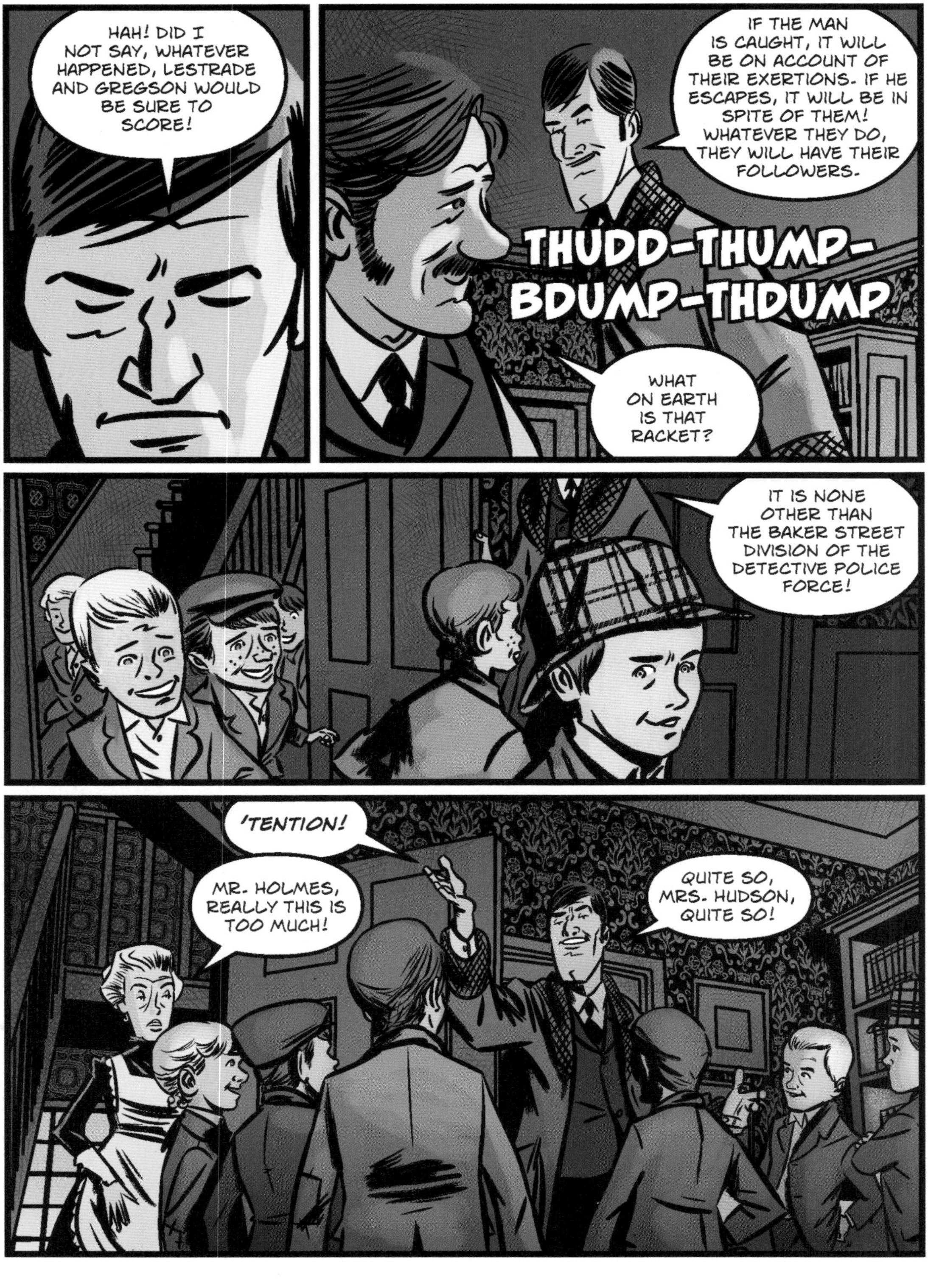
HAH! DID I NOT SAY, WHATEVER HAPPENED, LESTRADE AND GREGSON WOULD BE SURE TO SCORE!
IF THE MAN IS CAUGHT, IT WILL BE ON ACCOUNT OF THEIR EXERTIONS. IF HE ESCAPES, IT WILL BE IN SPITE OF THEM! WHATEVER THEY DO, THEY WILL HAVE THEIR FOLLOWERS.
THUDD-THUMP-BDUMP-THDUMP
WHAT ON EARTH IS THAT RACKET?
IT IS NONE OTHER THAN THE BAKER STREET DIVISION OF THE DETECTIVE POLICE FORCE!
'TENTION!
MR. HOLMES, REALLY THIS IS TOO MUCH!
QUITE SO, MRS. HUDSON, QUITE SO!

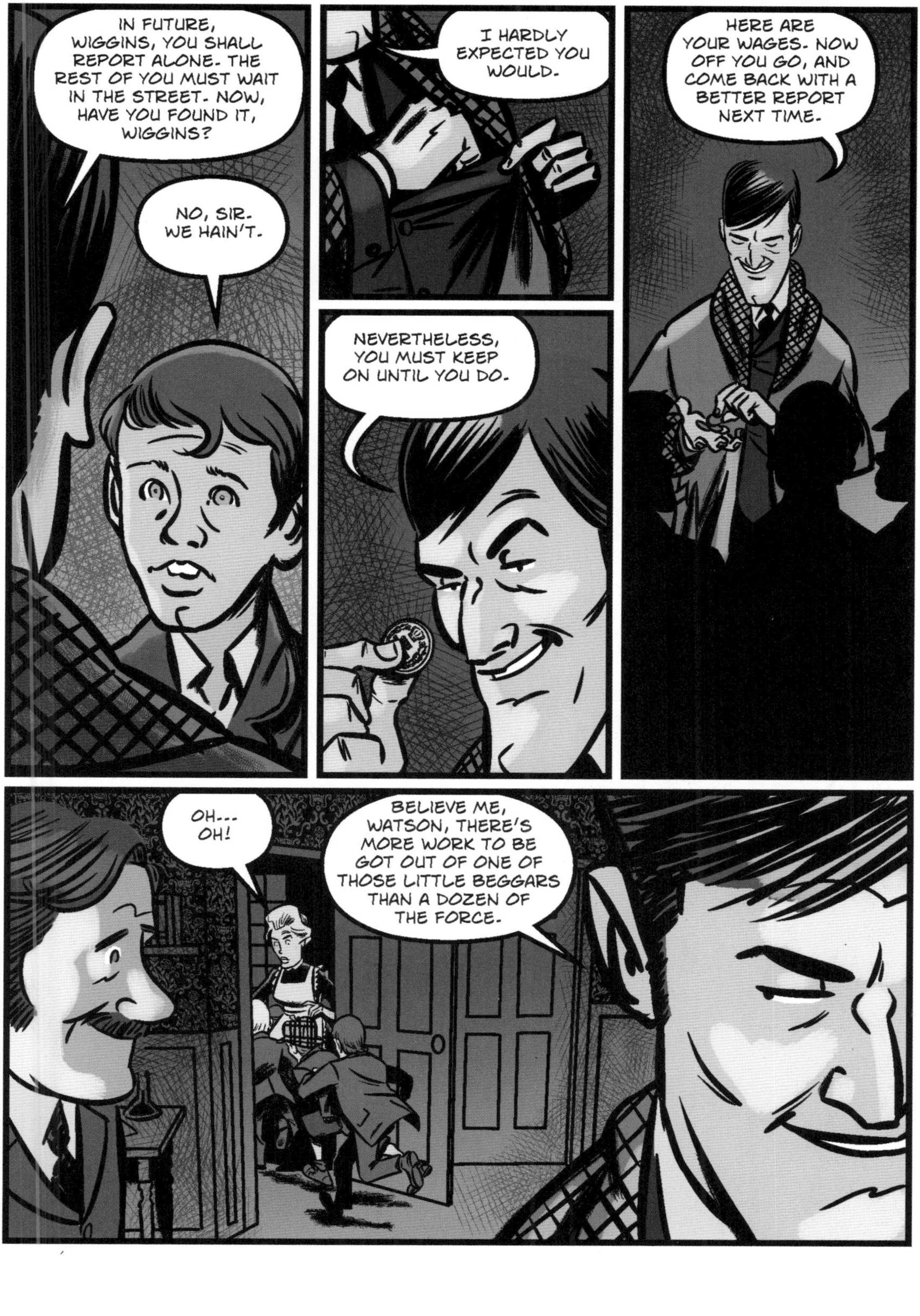
IN FUTURE, WIGGINS, YOU SHALL REPORT ALONE. THE REST OF YOU MUST WAIT IN THE STREET. NOW, HAVE YOU FOUND IT, WIGGINS?
NO, SIR. WE HAIN'T.
I HARDLY EXPECTED YOU WOULD.
NEVERTHELESS, YOU MUST KEEP ON UNTIL YOU DO.
HERE ARE YOUR WAGES. NOW OFF YOU GO, AND COME BACK WITH A BETTER REPORT NEXT TIME.
OH... OH!
BELIEVE ME, WATSON, THERE'S MORE WORK TO BE GOT OUT OF ONE OF THOSE LITTLE BEGGARS THAN A DOZEN OF THE FORCE.

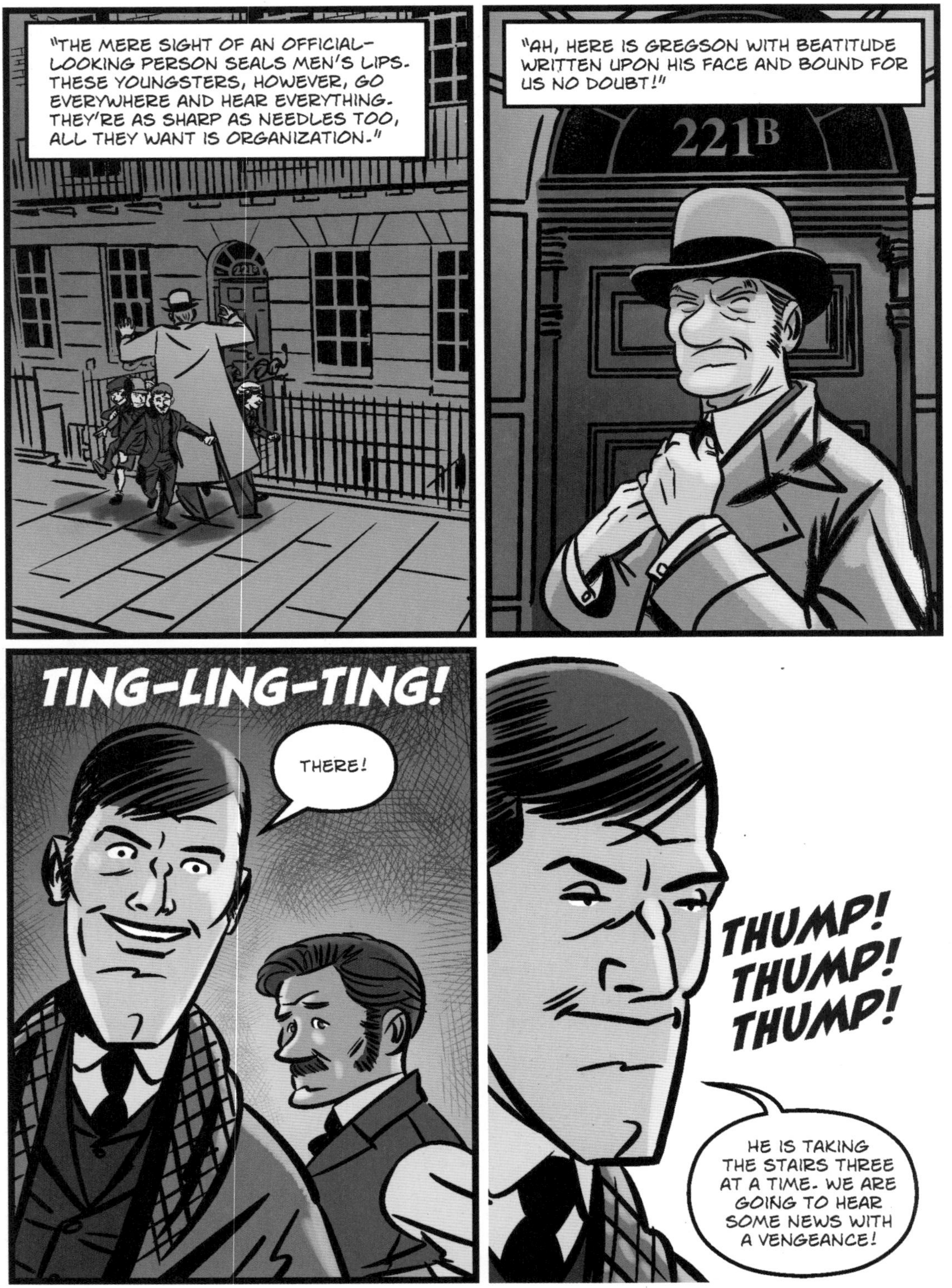
"THE MERE SIGHT OF AN OFFICIAL-LOOKING PERSON SEALS MEN'S LIPS. THESE YOUNGSTERS, HOWEVER, GO EVERYWHERE AND HEAR EVERYTHING. THEY'RE AS SHARP AS NEEDLES TOO, ALL THEY WANT IS ORGANIZATION."
"AH, HERE IS GREGSON WITH BEATITUDE WRITTEN UPON HIS FACE AND BOUND FOR US NO DOUBT!"
221B
TING-LING-TING!
THERE!
THUMP! THUMP! THUMP!
HE IS TAKING THE STAIRS THREE AT A TIME. WE ARE GOING TO HEAR SOME NEWS WITH A VENGEANCE!

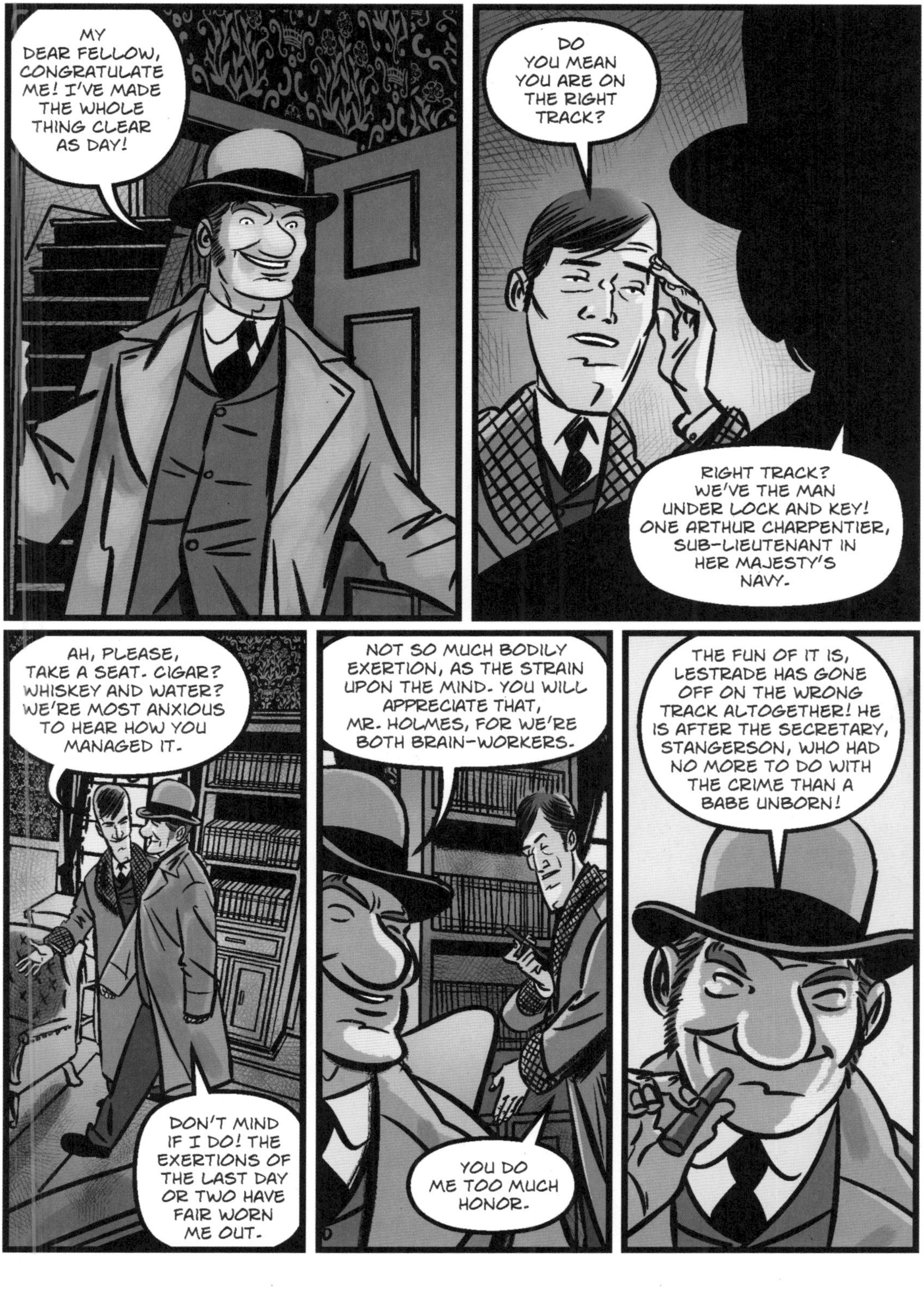
MY DEAR FELLOW, CONGRATULATE ME! I'VE MADE THE WHOLE THING CLEAR AS DAY!
DO YOU MEAN YOU ARE ON THE RIGHT TRACK?
RIGHT TRACK? WE'VE THE MAN UNDER LOCK AND KEY! ONE ARTHUR CHARPENTIER, SUB-LIEUTENANT IN HER MAJESTY'S NAVY.
AH, PLEASE, TAKE A SEAT. CIGAR? WHISKEY AND WATER? WE'RE MOST ANXIOUS TO HEAR HOW YOU MANAGED IT.
DON'T MIND IF I DO! THE EXERTIONS OF THE LAST DAY OR TWO HAVE FAIR WORN ME OUT.
NOT SO MUCH BODILY EXERTION, AS THE STRAIN UPON THE MIND. YOU WILL APPRECIATE THAT, MR. HOLMES, FOR WE'RE BOTH BRAIN-WORKERS.
YOU DO ME TOO MUCH HONOR.
THE FUN OF IT IS, LESTRADE HAS GONE OFF ON THE WRONG TRACK ALTOGETHER! HE IS AFTER THE SECRETARY, STANGERSON, WHO HAD NO MORE TO DO WITH THE CRIME THAN A BABE UNBORN!

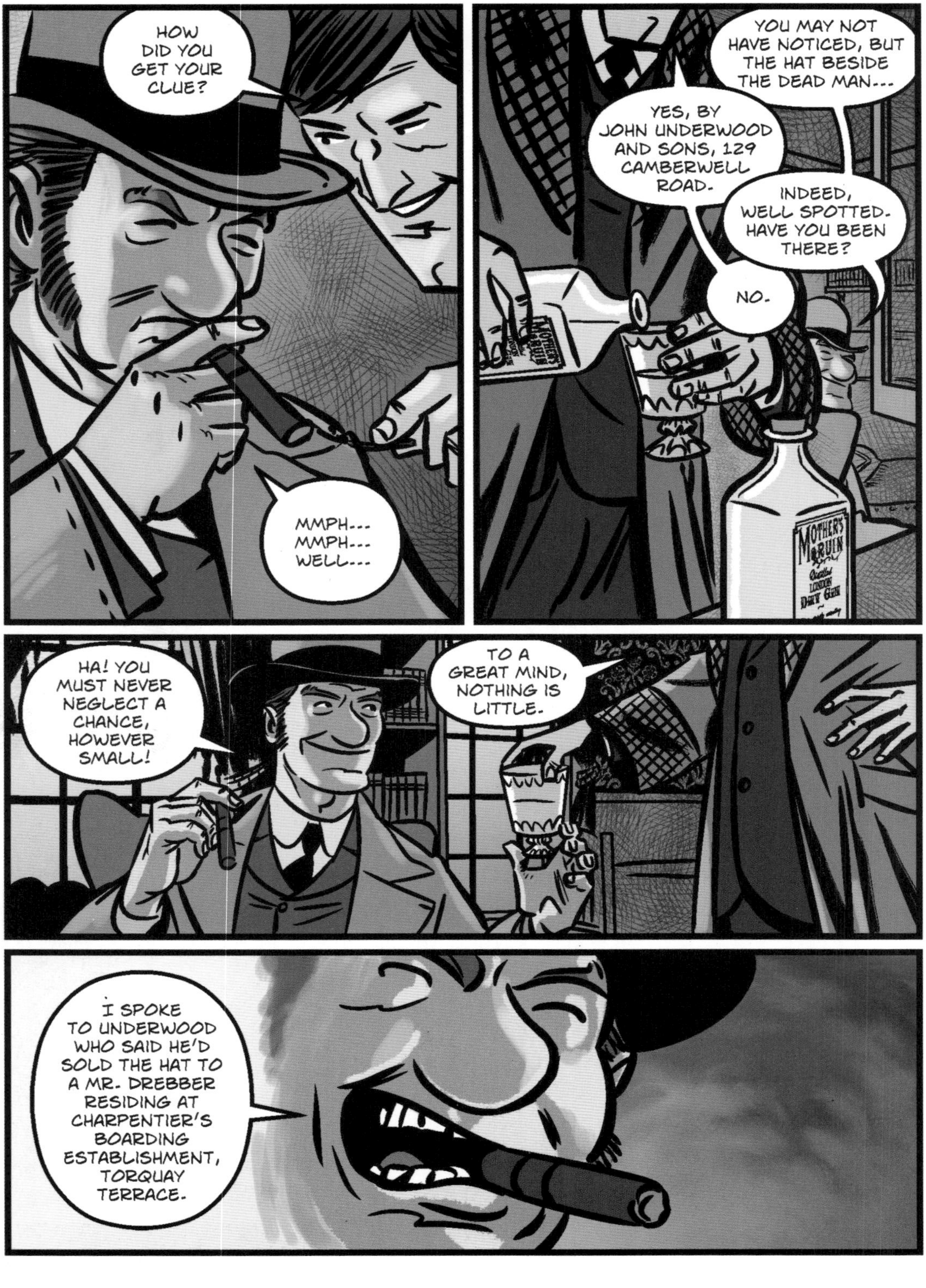
HOW DID YOU GET YOUR CLUE?
MMPH... MMPH... WELL...
YOU MAY NOT HAVE NOTICED, BUT THE HAT BESIDE THE DEAD MAN...
YES, BY JOHN UNDERWOOD AND SONS, 129 CAMBERWELL ROAD.
INDEED, WELL SPOTTED. HAVE YOU BEEN THERE?
NO.
MOTHER'S RUIN
LONDON
DRY GIN
HA! YOU MUST NEVER NEGLECT A CHANCE, HOWEVER SMALL!
TO A GREAT MIND, NOTHING IS LITTLE.
I SPOKE TO UNDERWOOD WHO SAID HE'D SOLD THE HAT TO A MR. DREBBER RESIDING AT CHARPENTIER'S BOARDING ESTABLISHMENT, TORQUAY TERRACE.

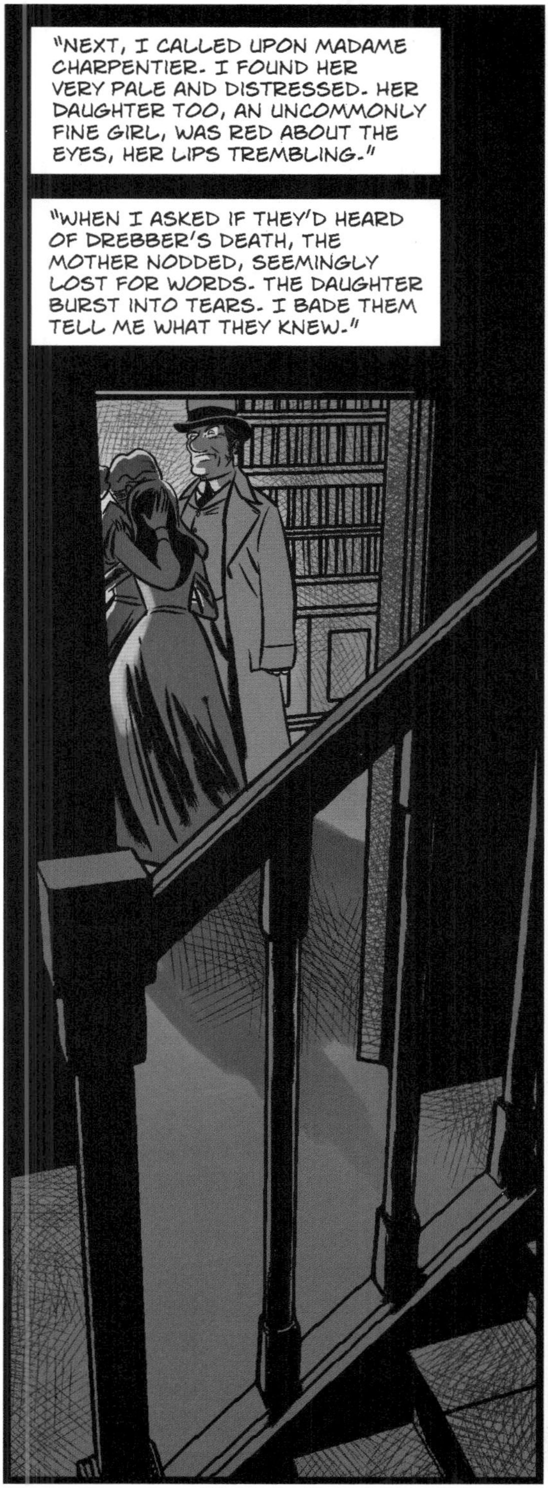
"NEXT, I CALLED UPON MADAME CHARPENTIER. I FOUND HER VERY PALE AND DISTRESSED. HER DAUGHTER TOO, AN UNCOMMONLY FINE GIRL, WAS RED ABOUT THE EYES, HER LIPS TREMBLING."
"WHEN I ASKED IF THEY'D HEARD OF DREBBER'S DEATH, THE MOTHER NODDED, SEEMINGLY LOST FOR WORDS. THE DAUGHTER BURST INTO TEARS. I BADE THEM TELL ME WHAT THEY KNEW."

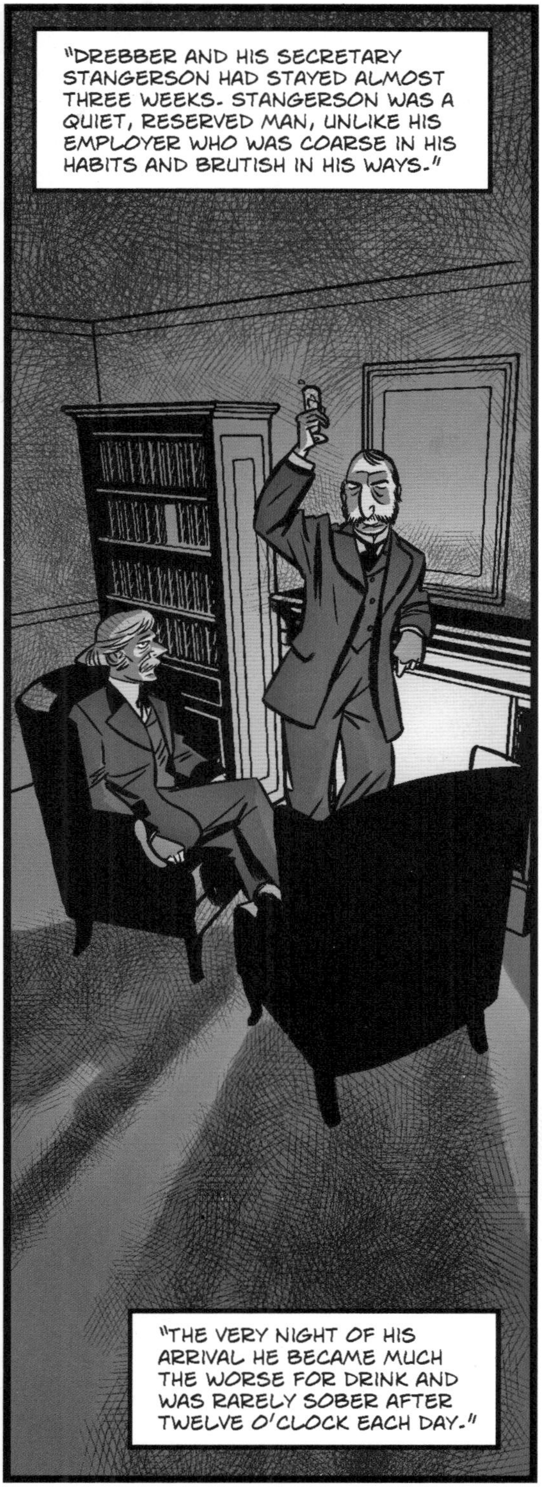
"DREBBER AND HIS SECRETARY STANGERSON HAD STAYED ALMOST THREE WEEKS. STANGERSON WAS A QUIET, RESERVED MAN, UNLIKE HIS EMPLOYER WHO WAS COARSE IN HIS HABITS AND BRUTISH IN HIS WAYS."
"THE VERY NIGHT OF HIS ARRIVAL HE BECAME MUCH THE WORSE FOR DRINK AND WAS RARELY SOBER AFTER TWELVE O'CLOCK EACH DAY."

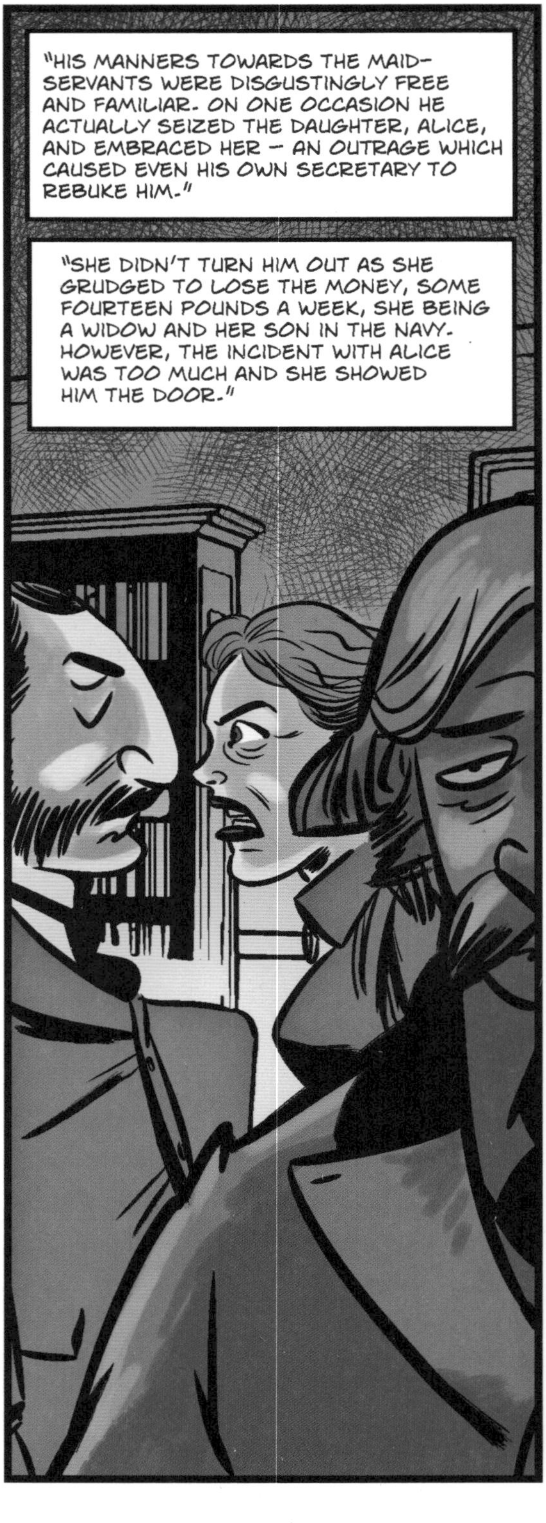
"HIS MANNERS TOWARDS THE MAID-SERVANTS WERE DISGUSTINGLY FREE AND FAMILIAR. ON ONE OCCASION HE ACTUALLY SEIZED THE DAUGHTER, ALICE, AND EMBRACED HER — AN OUTRAGE WHICH CAUSED EVEN HIS OWN SECRETARY TO REBUKE HIM."
"SHE DIDN'T TURN HIM OUT AS SHE GRUDGED TO LOSE THE MONEY, SOME FOURTEEN POUNDS A WEEK, SHE BEING A WIDOW AND HER SON IN THE NAVY. HOWEVER, THE INCIDENT WITH ALICE WAS TOO MUCH AND SHE SHOWED HIM THE DOOR."

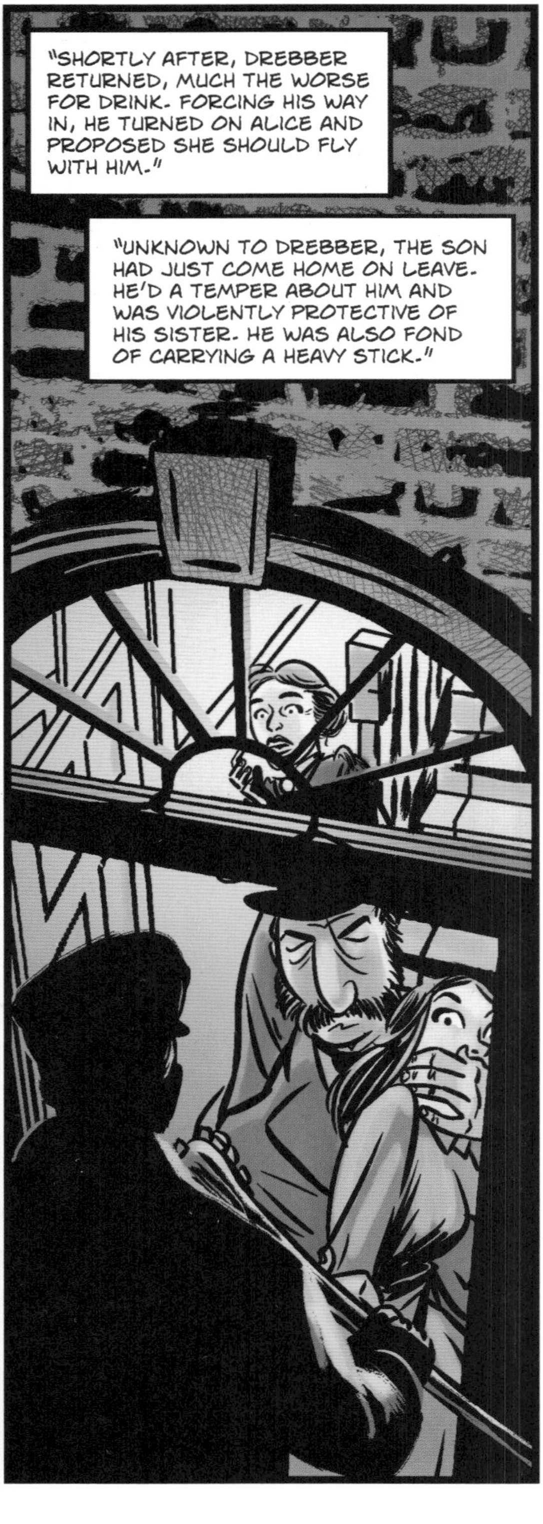
"SHORTLY AFTER, DREBBER RETURNED, MUCH THE WORSE FOR DRINK. FORCING HIS WAY IN, HE TURNED ON ALICE AND PROPOSED SHE SHOULD FLY WITH HIM."
"UNKNOWN TO DREBBER, THE SON HAD JUST COME HOME ON LEAVE. HE'D A TEMPER ABOUT HIM AND WAS VIOLENTLY PROTECTIVE OF HIS SISTER. HE WAS ALSO FOND OF CARRYING A HEAVY STICK."

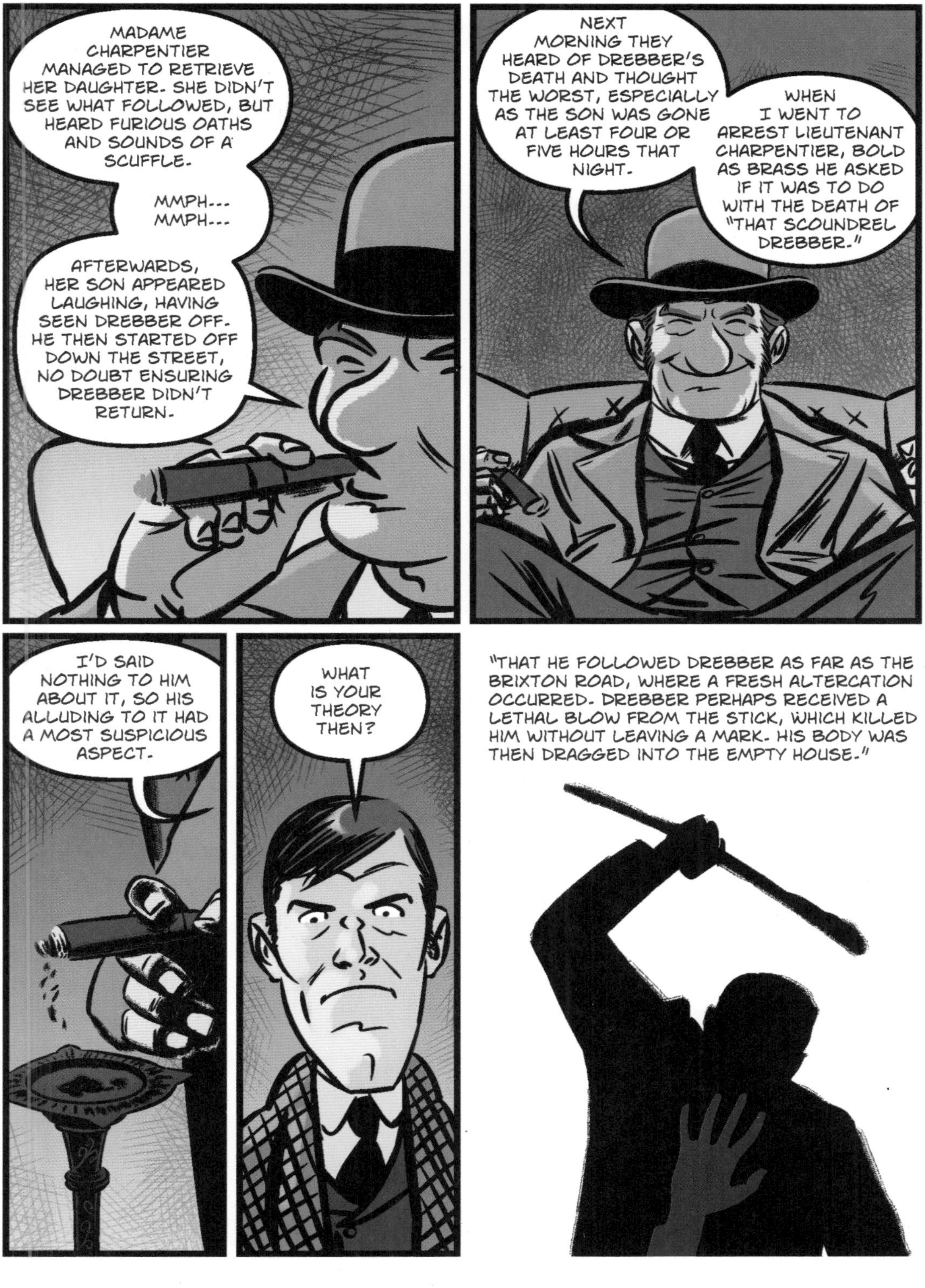
MADAME CHARPENTIER MANAGED TO RETRIEVE HER DAUGHTER. SHE DIDN'T SEE WHAT FOLLOWED, BUT HEARD FURIOUS OATHS AND SOUNDS OF A SCUFFLE.
MMPH... MMPH...
AFTERWARDS, HER SON APPEARED LAUGHING, HAVING SEEN DREBBER OFF. HE THEN STARTED OFF DOWN THE STREET, NO DOUBT ENSURING DREBBER DIDN'T RETURN.
NEXT MORNING THEY HEARD OF DREBBER'S DEATH AND THOUGHT THE WORST, ESPECIALLY AS THE SON WAS GONE AT LEAST FOUR OR FIVE HOURS THAT NIGHT.
WHEN I WENT TO ARREST LIEUTENANT CHARPENTIER, BOLD AS BRASS HE ASKED IF IT WAS TO DO WITH THE DEATH OF "THAT SCOUNDREL DREBBER."
I'D SAID NOTHING TO HIM ABOUT IT, SO HIS ALLUDING TO IT HAD A MOST SUSPICIOUS ASPECT.
WHAT IS YOUR THEORY THEN?
"THAT HE FOLLOWED DREBBER AS FAR AS THE BRIXTON ROAD, WHERE A FRESH ALTERCATION OCCURRED. DREBBER PERHAPS RECEIVED A LETHAL BLOW FROM THE STICK, WHICH KILLED HIM WITHOUT LEAVING A MARK. HIS BODY WAS THEN DRAGGED INTO THE EMPTY HOUSE."

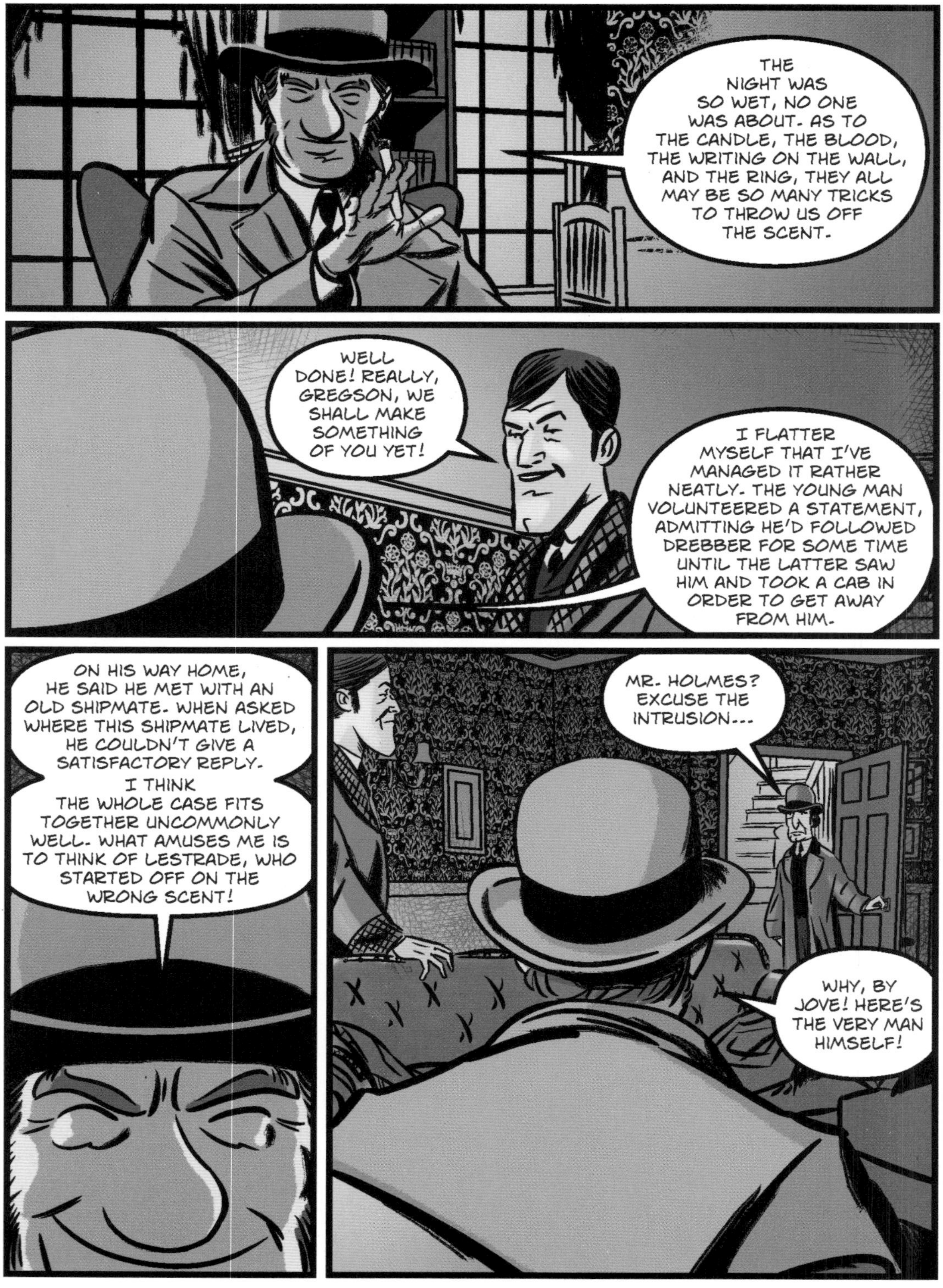
THE NIGHT WAS SO WET, NO ONE WAS ABOUT. AS TO THE CANDLE, THE BLOOD, THE WRITING ON THE WALL, AND THE RING, THEY ALL MAY BE SO MANY TRICKS TO THROW US OFF THE SCENT.
WELL DONE! REALLY, GREGSON, WE SHALL MAKE SOMETHING OF YOU YET!
I FLATTER MYSELF THAT I'VE MANAGED IT RATHER NEATLY. THE YOUNG MAN VOLUNTEERED A STATEMENT, ADMITTING HE'D FOLLOWED DREBBER FOR SOME TIME UNTIL THE LATTER SAW HIM AND TOOK A CAB IN ORDER TO GET AWAY FROM HIM.
ON HIS WAY HOME, HE SAID HE MET WITH AN OLD SHIPMATE. WHEN ASKED WHERE THIS SHIPMATE LIVED, HE COULDN'T GIVE A SATISFACTORY REPLY.
I THINK THE WHOLE CASE FITS TOGETHER UNCOMMONLY WELL. WHAT AMUSES ME IS TO THINK OF LESTRADE, WHO STARTED OFF ON THE WRONG SCENT!
MR. HOLMES? EXCUSE THE INTRUSION...
WHY, BY JOVE! HERE'S THE VERY MAN HIMSELF!

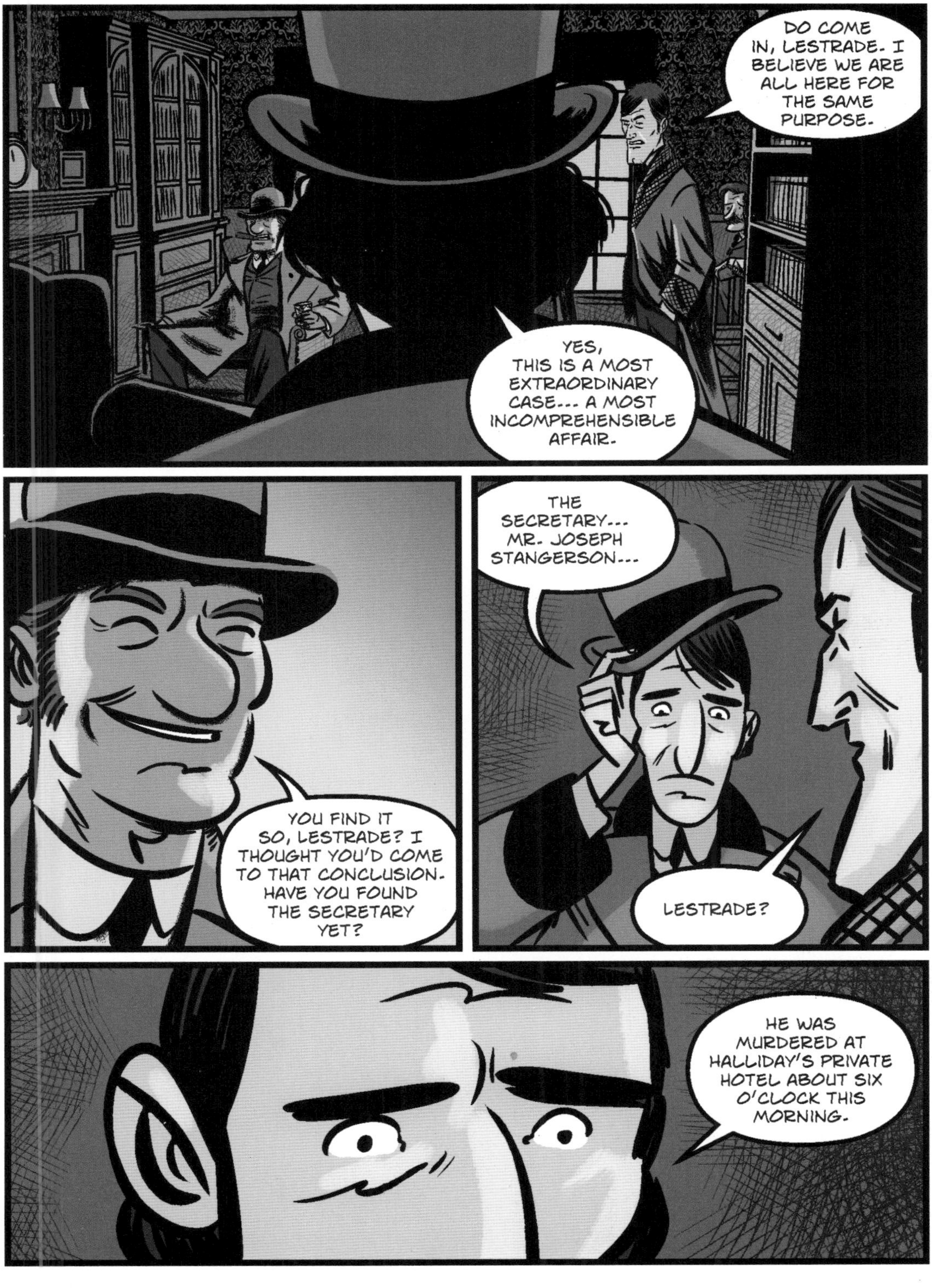
DO COME IN, LESTRADE. I BELIEVE WE ARE ALL HERE FOR THE SAME PURPOSE.
YES, THIS IS A MOST EXTRAORDINARY CASE... A MOST INCOMPREHENSIBLE AFFAIR.
YOU FIND IT SO, LESTRADE? I THOUGHT YOU'D COME TO THAT CONCLUSION. HAVE YOU FOUND THE SECRETARY YET?
THE SECRETARY... MR. JOSEPH STANGERSON...
LESTRADE?
HE WAS MURDERED AT HALLIDAY'S PRIVATE HOTEL ABOUT SIX O'CLOCK THIS MORNING.

LIGHT IN THE DARKNESS

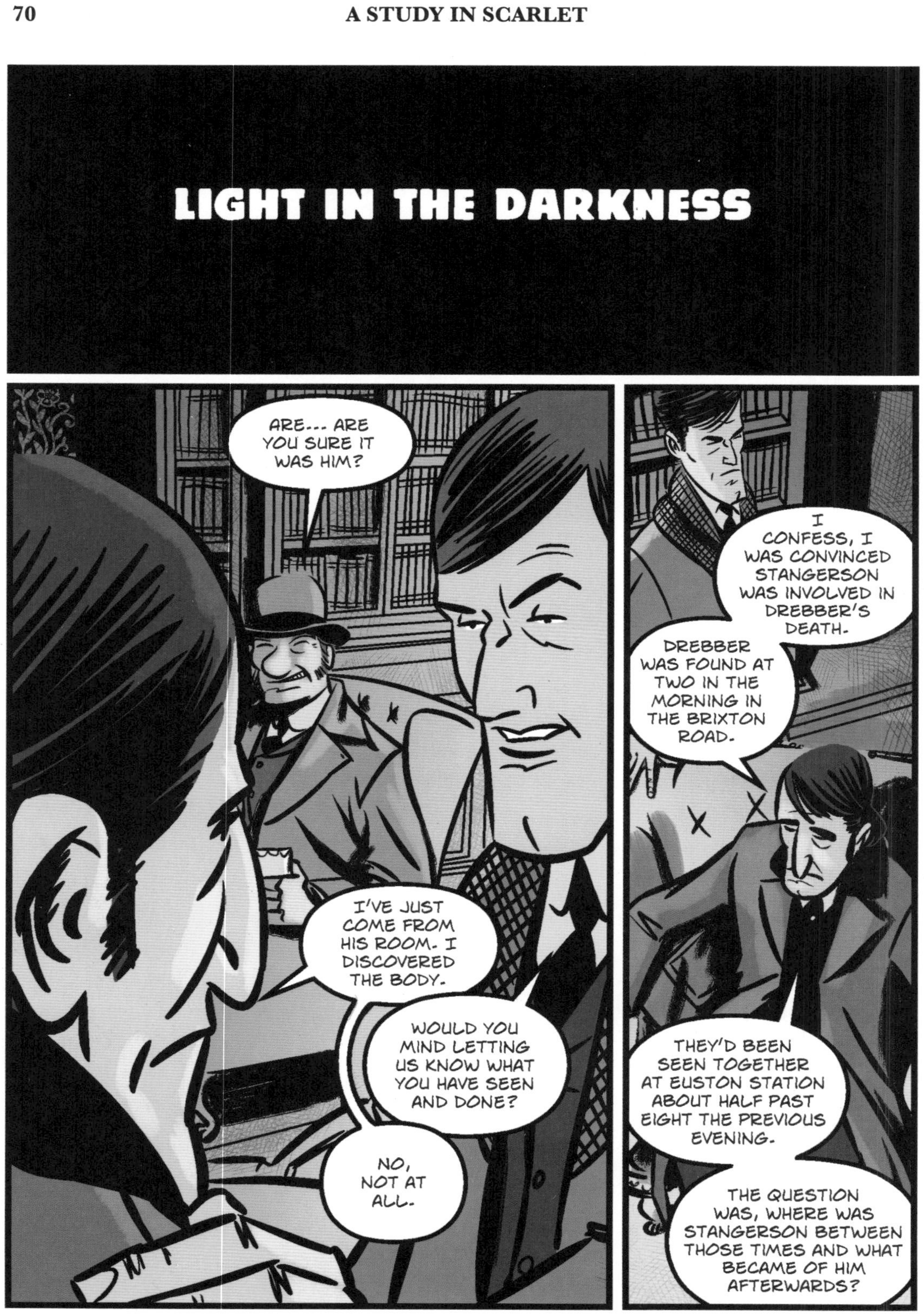
ARE... ARE YOU SURE IT WAS HIM?
I'VE JUST COME FROM HIS ROOM. I DISCOVERED THE BODY.
WOULD YOU MIND LETTING US KNOW WHAT YOU HAVE SEEN AND DONE?
NO, NOT AT ALL.
I CONFESS, I WAS CONVINCED STANGERSON WAS INVOLVED IN DREBBER'S DEATH.
DREBBER WAS FOUND AT TWO IN THE MORNING IN THE BRIXTON ROAD.
THEY'D BEEN SEEN TOGETHER AT EUSTON STATION ABOUT HALF PAST EIGHT THE PREVIOUS EVENING.
THE QUESTION WAS, WHERE WAS STANGERSON BETWEEN THOSE TIMES AND WHAT BECAME OF HIM AFTERWARDS?

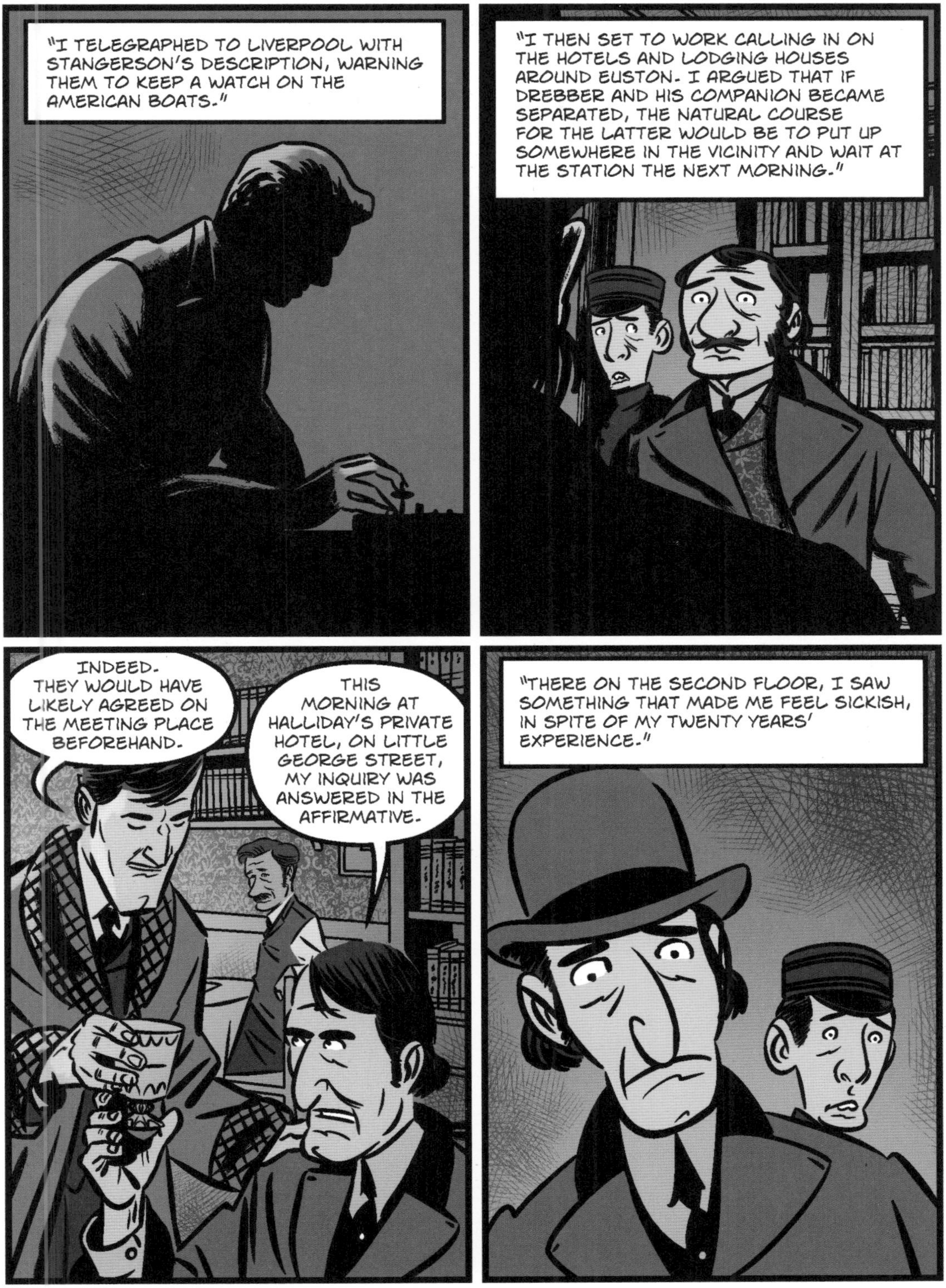
"I TELEGRAPHED TO LIVERPOOL WITH STANGERSON'S DESCRIPTION, WARNING THEM TO KEEP A WATCH ON THE AMERICAN BOATS."
"I THEN SET TO WORK CALLING IN ON THE HOTELS AND LODGING HOUSES AROUND EUSTON. I ARGUED THAT IF DREBBER AND HIS COMPANION BECAME SEPARATED, THE NATURAL COURSE FOR THE LATTER WOULD BE TO PUT UP SOMEWHERE IN THE VICINITY AND WAIT AT THE STATION THE NEXT MORNING."
INDEED. THEY WOULD HAVE LIKELY AGREED ON THE MEETING PLACE BEFOREHAND.
THIS MORNING AT HALLIDAY'S PRIVATE HOTEL, ON LITTLE GEORGE STREET, MY INQUIRY WAS ANSWERED IN THE AFFIRMATIVE.
"THERE ON THE SECOND FLOOR, I SAW SOMETHING THAT MADE ME FEEL SICKISH, IN SPITE OF MY TWENTY YEARS' EXPERIENCE."

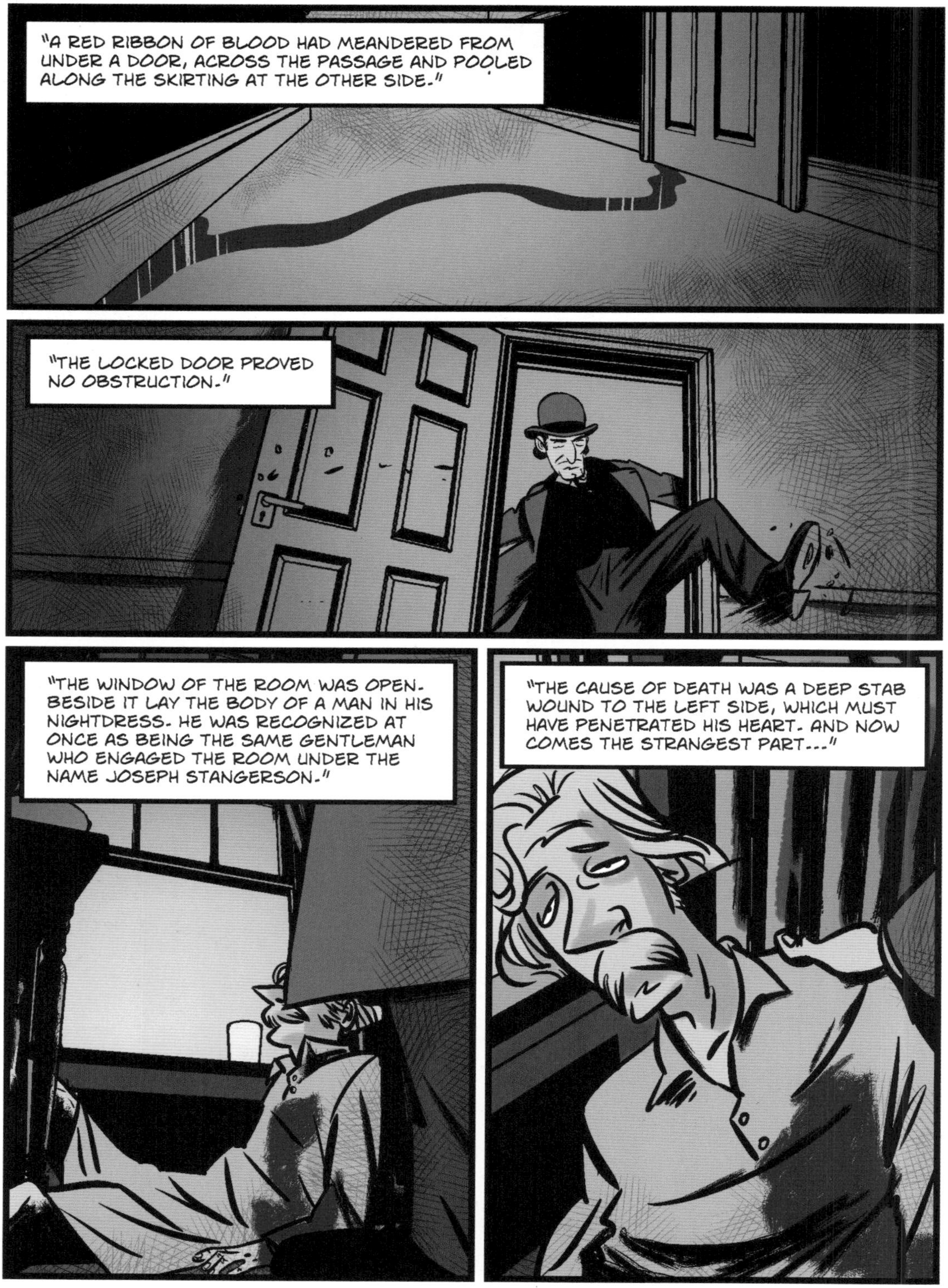
"A RED RIBBON OF BLOOD HAD MEANDERED FROM UNDER A DOOR, ACROSS THE PASSAGE AND POOLED ALONG THE SKIRTING AT THE OTHER SIDE."
"THE LOCKED DOOR PROVED NO OBSTRUCTION."
"THE WINDOW OF THE ROOM WAS OPEN. BESIDE IT LAY THE BODY OF A MAN IN HIS NIGHTDRESS. HE WAS RECOGNIZED AT ONCE AS BEING THE SAME GENTLEMAN WHO ENGAGED THE ROOM UNDER THE NAME JOSEPH STANGERSON."
"THE CAUSE OF DEATH WAS A DEEP STAB WOUND TO THE LEFT SIDE, WHICH MUST HAVE PENETRATED HIS HEART. AND NOW COMES THE STRANGEST PART..."

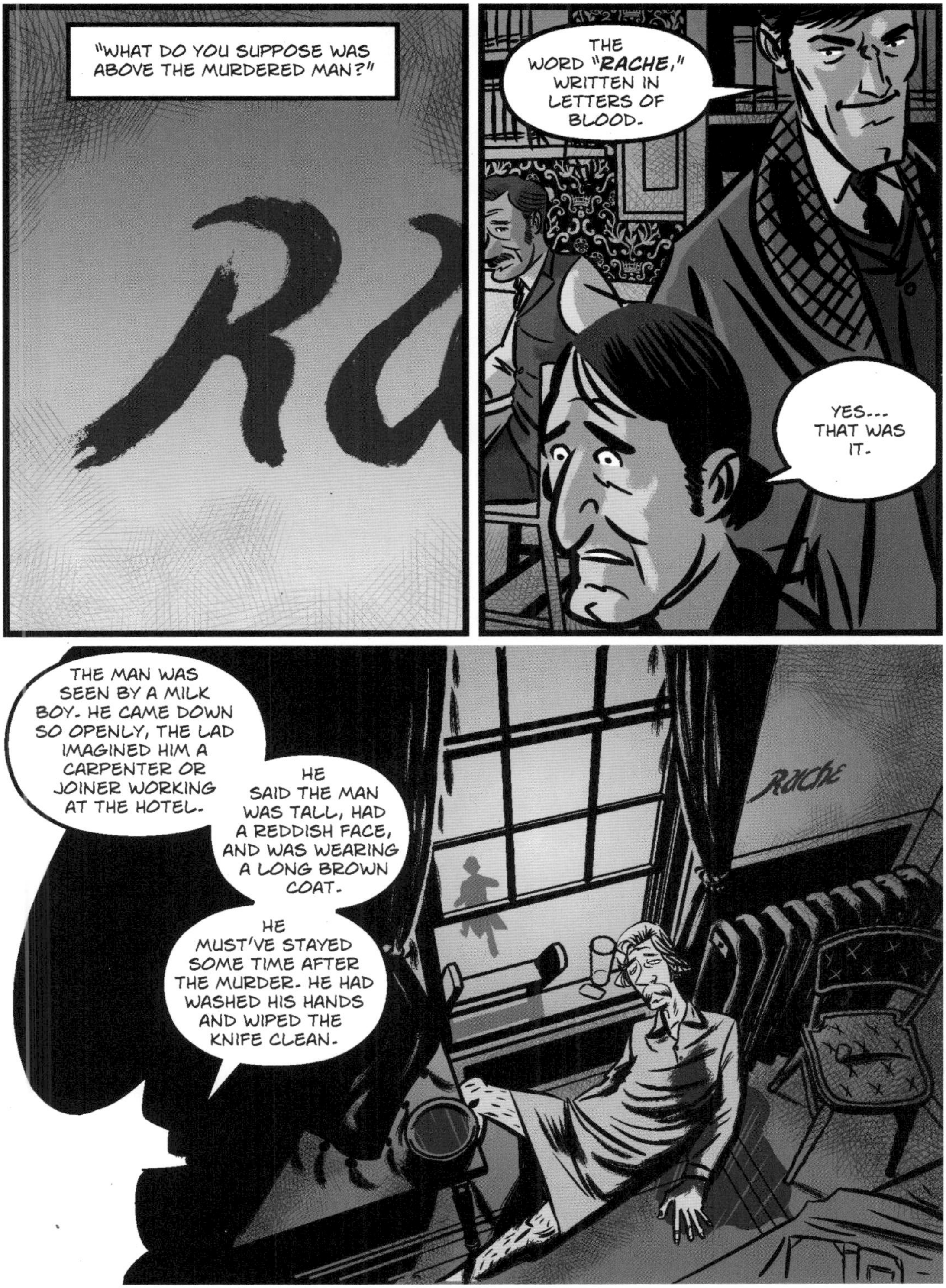
"WHAT DO YOU SUPPOSE WAS ABOVE THE MURDERED MAN?"
THE WORD "RACHE," WRITTEN IN LETTERS OF BLOOD.
YES... THAT WAS IT.
THE MAN WAS SEEN BY A MILK BOY. HE CAME DOWN SO OPENLY, THE LAD IMAGINED HIM A CARPENTER OR JOINER WORKING AT THE HOTEL.
HE SAID THE MAN WAS TALL, HAD A REDDISH FACE, AND WAS WEARING A LONG BROWN COAT.
HE MUST'VE STAYED SOME TIME AFTER THE MURDER. HE HAD WASHED HIS HANDS AND WIPED THE KNIFE CLEAN.
RACHE

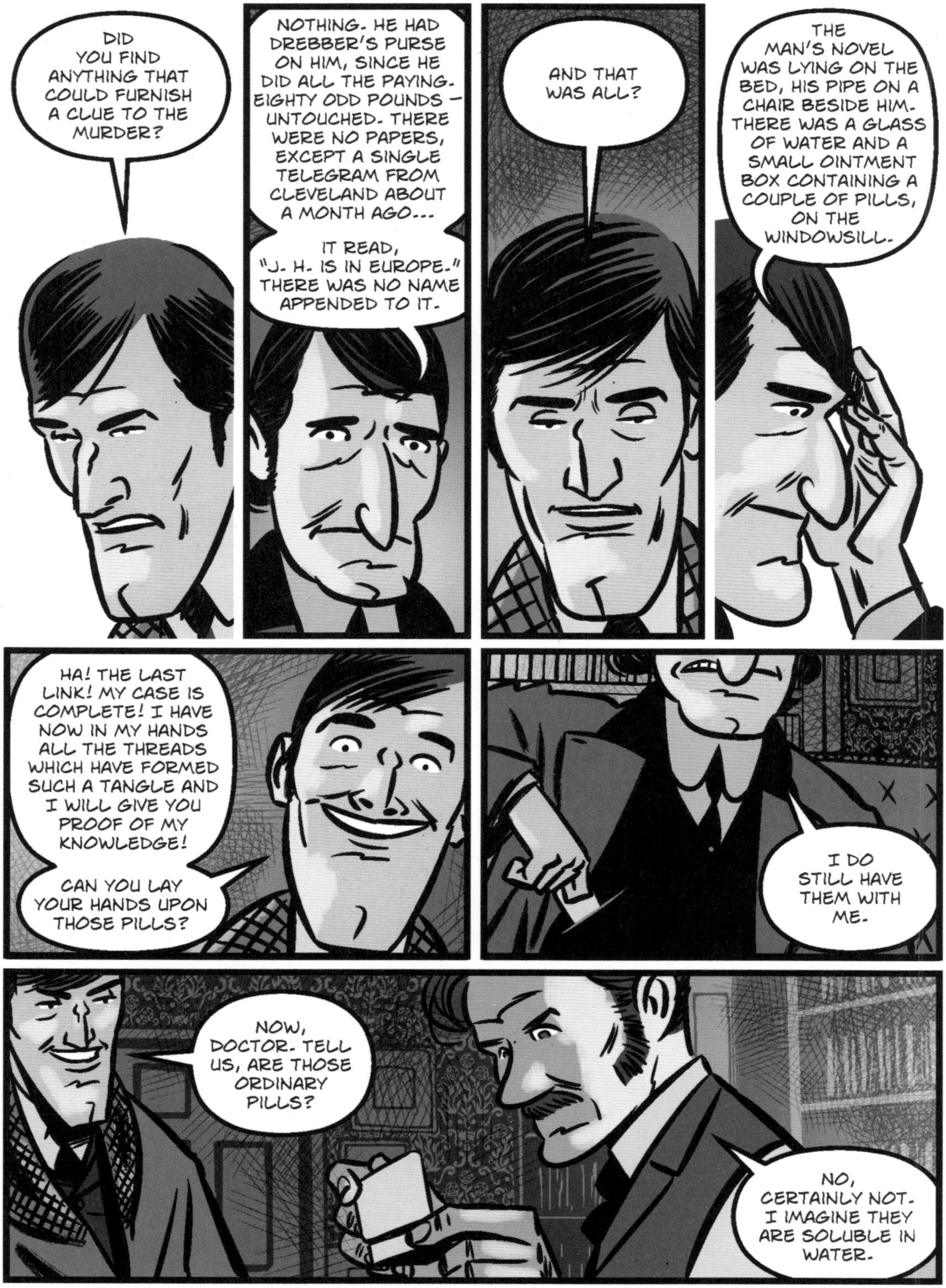
DID YOU FIND ANYTHING THAT COULD FURNISH A CLUE TO THE MURDER?
NOTHING. HE HAD DREBBER'S PURSE ON HIM, SINCE HE DID ALL THE PAYING. EIGHTY ODD POUNDS — UNTOUCHED. THERE WERE NO PAPERS, EXCEPT A SINGLE TELEGRAM FROM CLEVELAND ABOUT A MONTH AGO...
IT READ, "J. H. IS IN EUROPE." THERE WAS NO NAME APPENDED TO IT.
AND THAT WAS ALL?
THE MAN'S NOVEL WAS LYING ON THE BED, HIS PIPE ON A CHAIR BESIDE HIM. THERE WAS A GLASS OF WATER AND A SMALL OINTMENT BOX CONTAINING A COUPLE OF PILLS, ON THE WINDOWSILL.
HA! THE LAST LINK! MY CASE IS COMPLETE! I HAVE NOW IN MY HANDS ALL THE THREADS WHICH HAVE FORMED SUCH A TANGLE AND I WILL GIVE YOU PROOF OF MY KNOWLEDGE!
CAN YOU LAY YOUR HANDS UPON THOSE PILLS?
I DO STILL HAVE THEM WITH ME.
NOW, DOCTOR. TELL US, ARE THOSE ORDINARY PILLS?
NO, CERTAINLY NOT. I IMAGINE THEY ARE SOLUBLE IN WATER.

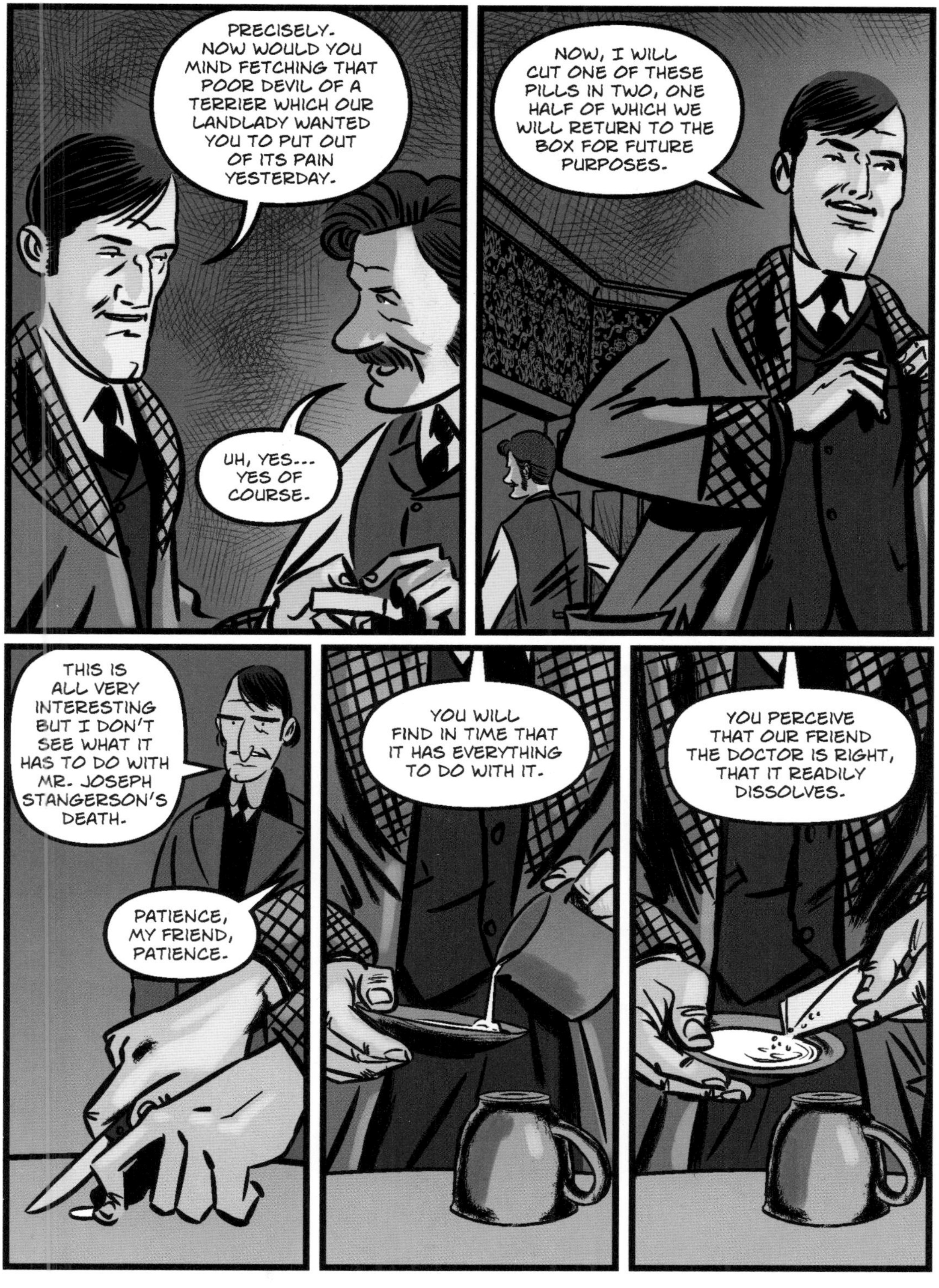
PRECISELY. NOW WOULD YOU MIND FETCHING THAT POOR DEVIL OF A TERRIER WHICH OUR LANDLADY WANTED YOU TO PUT OUT OF ITS PAIN YESTERDAY.
UH, YES... YES OF COURSE.
NOW, I WILL CUT ONE OF THESE PILLS IN TWO, ONE HALF OF WHICH WE WILL RETURN TO THE BOX FOR FUTURE PURPOSES.
THIS IS ALL VERY INTERESTING BUT I DON'T SEE WHAT IT HAS TO DO WITH MR. JOSEPH STANGERSON'S DEATH.
PATIENCE, MY FRIEND, PATIENCE.
YOU WILL FIND IN TIME THAT IT HAS EVERYTHING TO DO WITH IT.
YOU PERCEIVE THAT OUR FRIEND THE DOCTOR IS RIGHT, THAT IT READILY DISSOLVES.

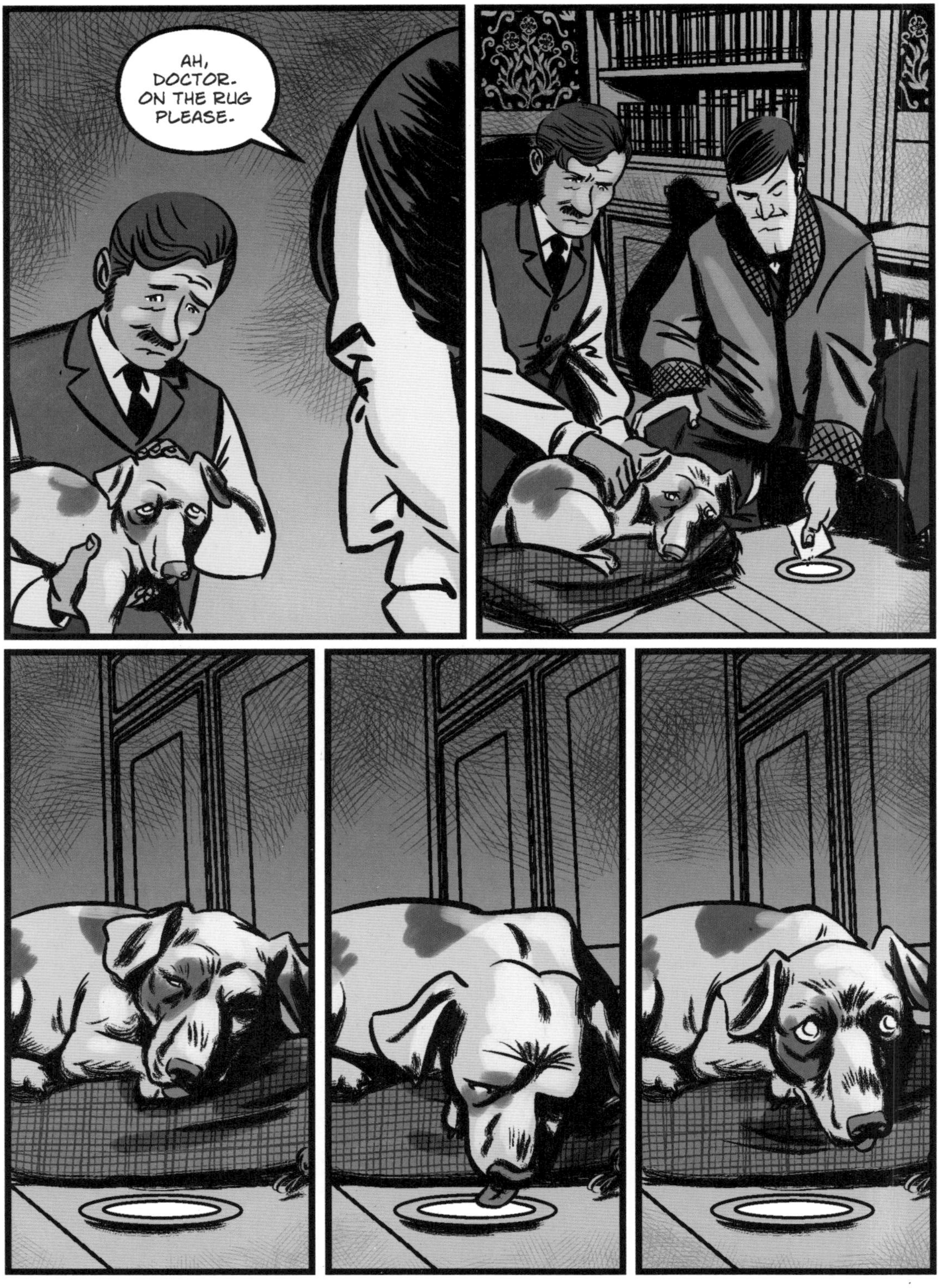
AH, DOCTOR. ON THE RUG PLEASE.

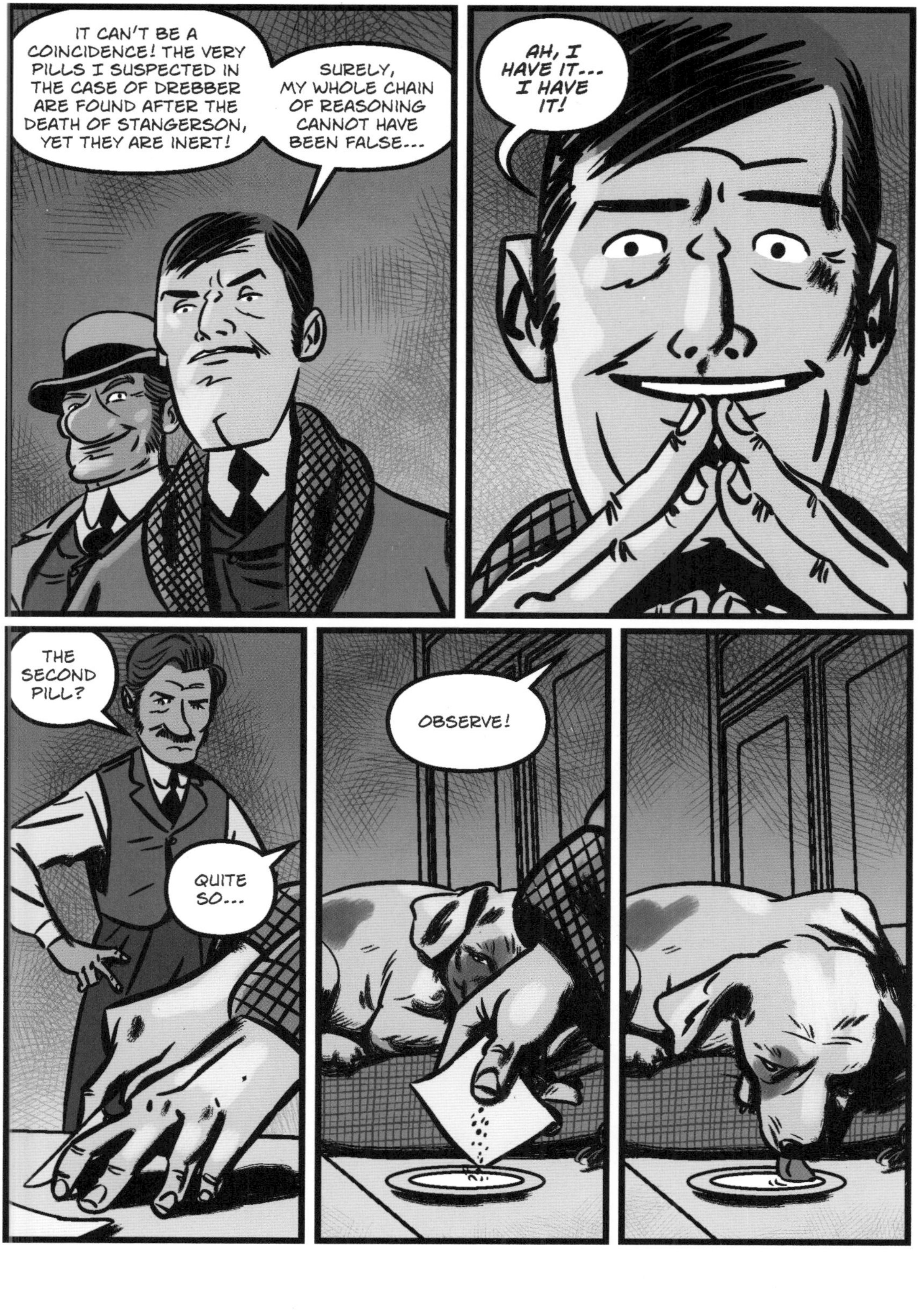
IT CAN'T BE A COINCIDENCE! THE VERY PILLS I SUSPECTED IN THE CASE OF DREBBER ARE FOUND AFTER THE DEATH OF STANGERSON, YET THEY ARE INERT!
SURELY, MY WHOLE CHAIN OF REASONING CANNOT HAVE BEEN FALSE...
AH, I HAVE IT... I HAVE IT!
THE SECOND PILL?
QUITE SO...
OBSERVE!

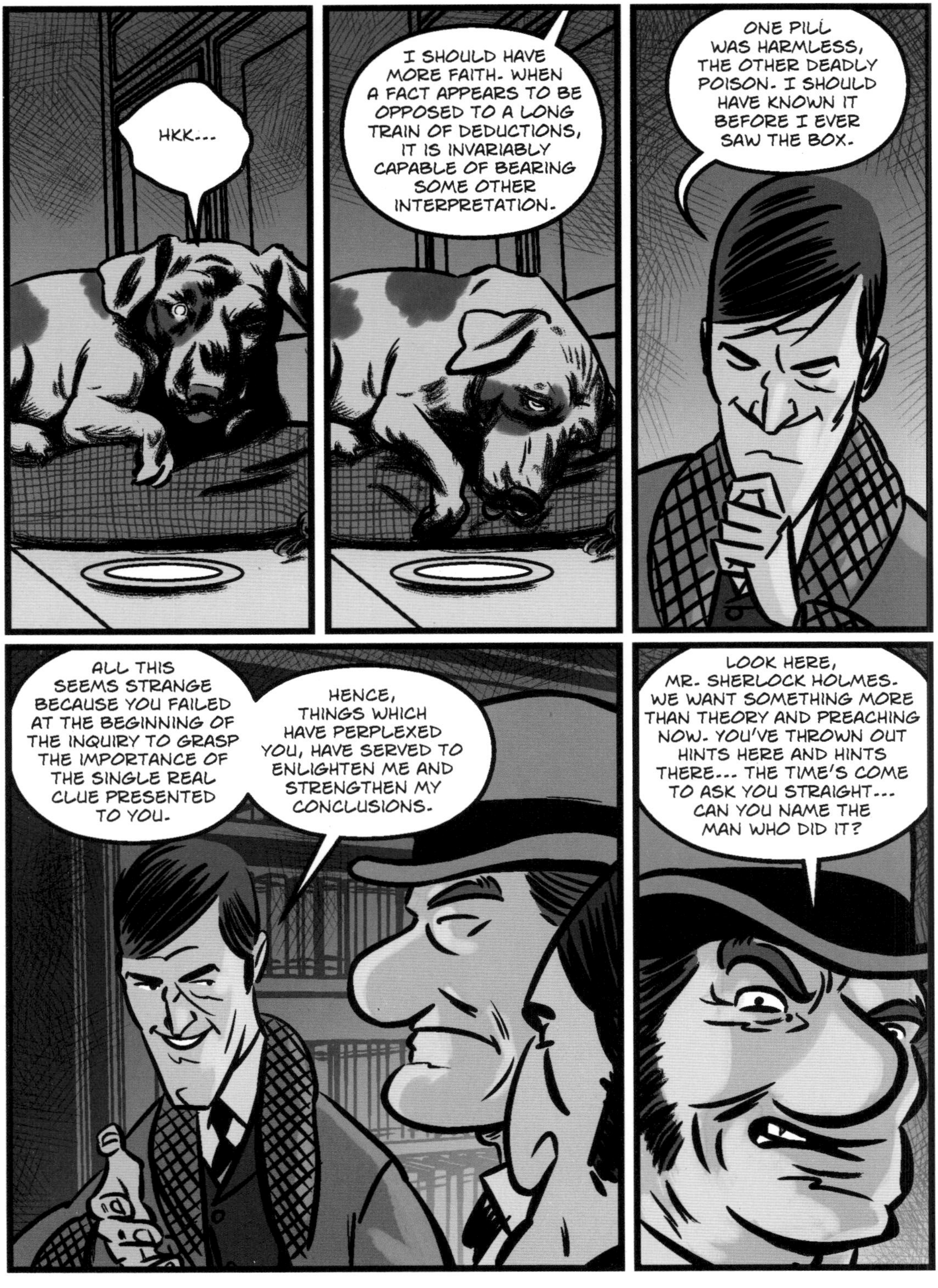
HKK...
I SHOULD HAVE MORE FAITH. WHEN A FACT APPEARS TO BE OPPOSED TO A LONG TRAIN OF DEDUCTIONS, IT IS INVARIABLY CAPABLE OF BEARING SOME OTHER INTERPRETATION.
ONE PILL WAS HARMLESS, THE OTHER DEADLY POISON. I SHOULD HAVE KNOWN IT BEFORE I EVER SAW THE BOX.
ALL THIS SEEMS STRANGE BECAUSE YOU FAILED AT THE BEGINNING OF THE INQUIRY TO GRASP THE IMPORTANCE OF THE SINGLE REAL CLUE PRESENTED TO YOU.
HENCE, THINGS WHICH HAVE PERPLEXED YOU, HAVE SERVED TO ENLIGHTEN ME AND STRENGTHEN MY CONCLUSIONS.
LOOK HERE, MR. SHERLOCK HOLMES. WE WANT SOMETHING MORE THAN THEORY AND PREACHING NOW. YOU'VE THROWN OUT HINTS HERE AND HINTS THERE... THE TIME'S COME TO ASK YOU STRAIGHT... CAN YOU NAME THE MAN WHO DID IT?

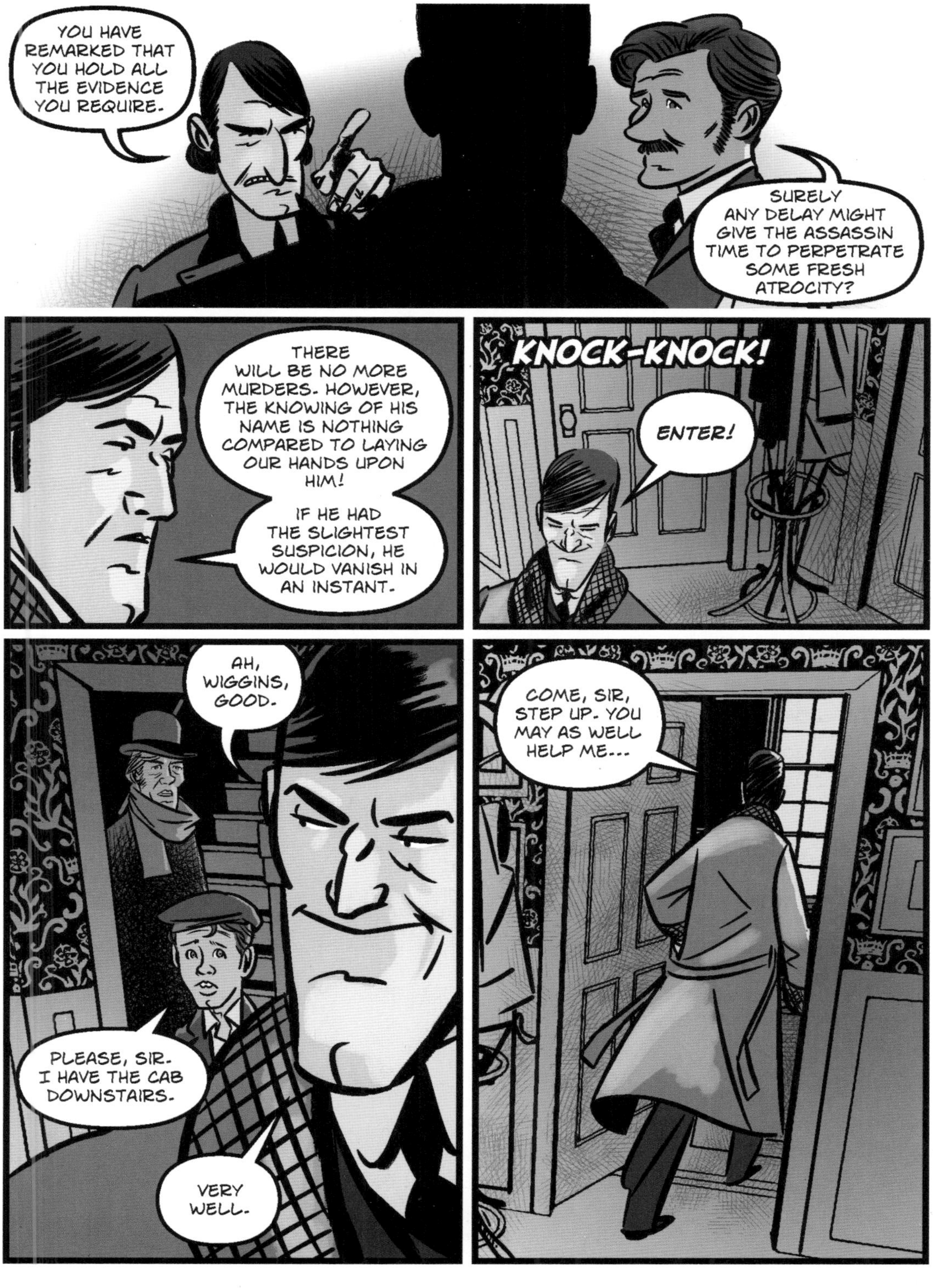
YOU HAVE REMARKED THAT YOU HOLD ALL THE EVIDENCE YOU REQUIRE.
SURELY ANY DELAY MIGHT GIVE THE ASSASSIN TIME TO PERPETRATE SOME FRESH ATROCITY?
THERE WILL BE NO MORE MURDERS. HOWEVER, THE KNOWING OF HIS NAME IS NOTHING COMPARED TO LAYING OUR HANDS UPON HIM!
IF HE HAD THE SLIGHTEST SUSPICION, HE WOULD VANISH IN AN INSTANT.
KNOCK-KNOCK!
ENTER!
AH, WIGGINS, GOOD.
PLEASE, SIR. I HAVE THE CAB DOWNSTAIRS.
VERY WELL.
COME, SIR, STEP UP. YOU MAY AS WELL HELP ME...

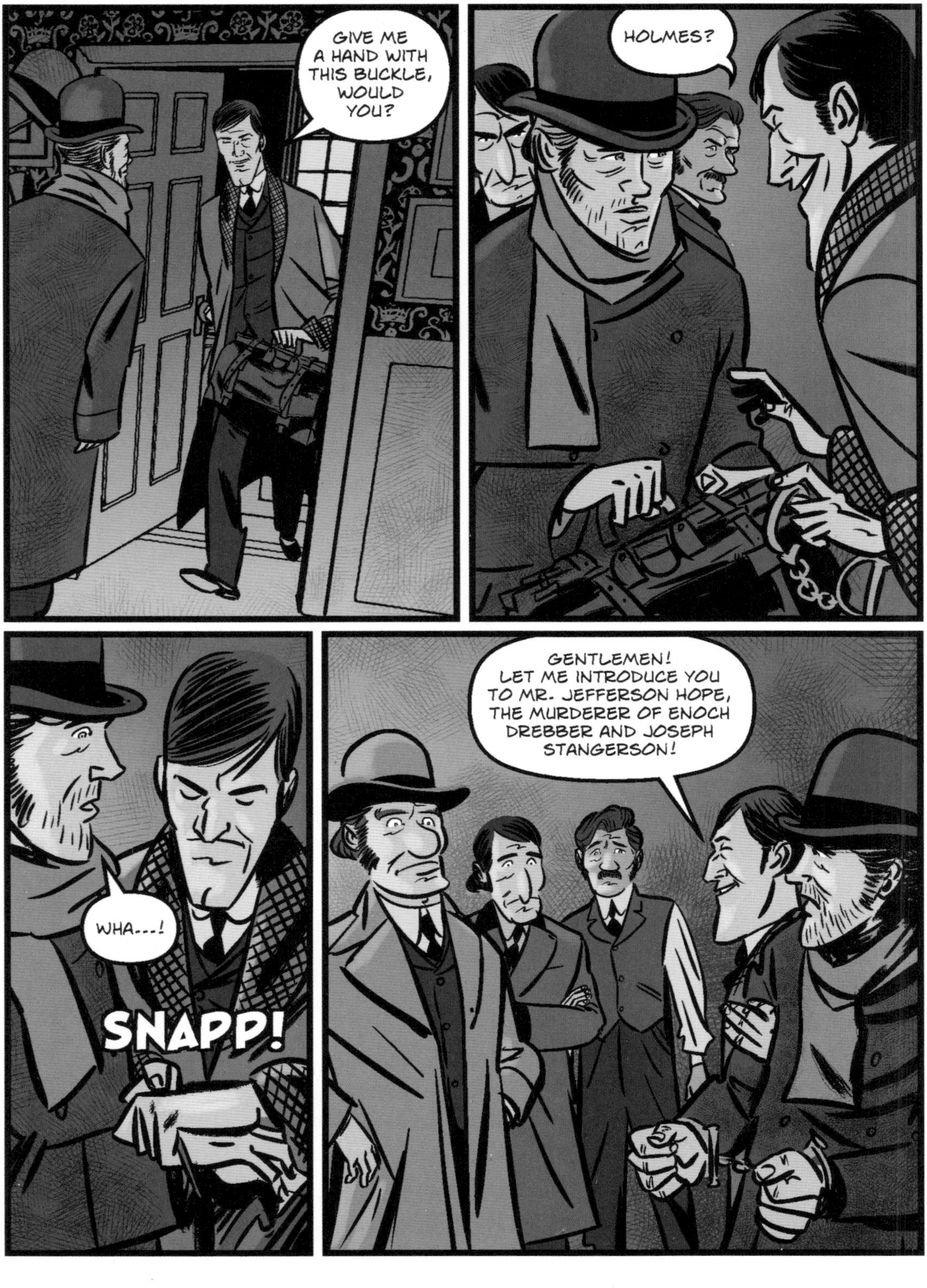
GIVE ME A HAND WITH THIS BUCKLE, WOULD YOU?
HOLMES?
WHA---!
SNAPP!
GENTLEMEN! LET ME INTRODUCE YOU TO MR. JEFFERSON HOPE, THE MURDERER OF ENOCH DREBBER AND JOSEPH STANGERSON!

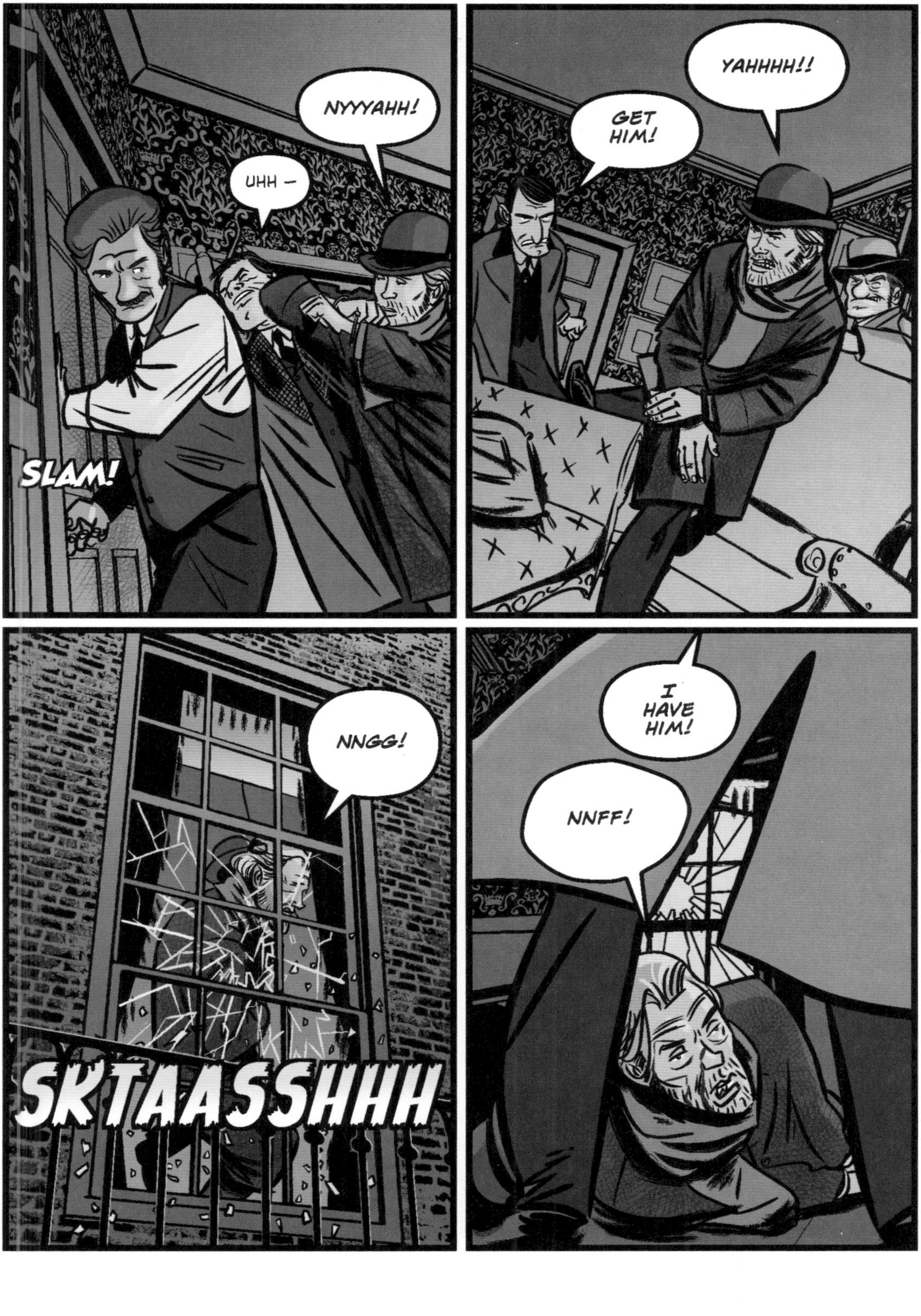
NYYYAHH!
UHH –
SLAM!
YAHHHH!!
GET HIM!
NNGG!
SKTAASSHHH
I HAVE HIM!
NNFF!

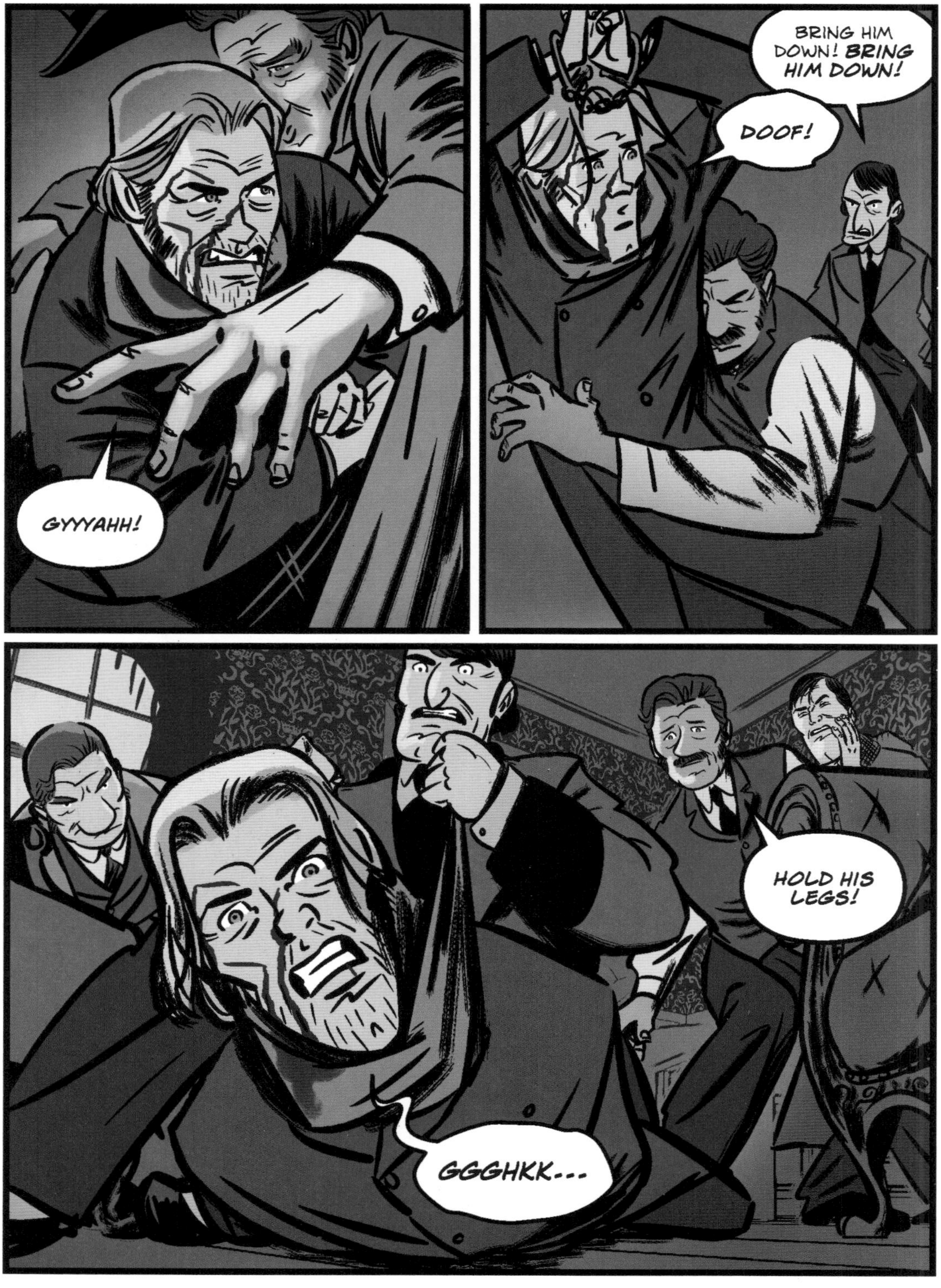
GYYYAHH!
BRING HIM DOWN! BRING HIM DOWN!
DOOF!
HOLD HIS LEGS!
GGGHKK...

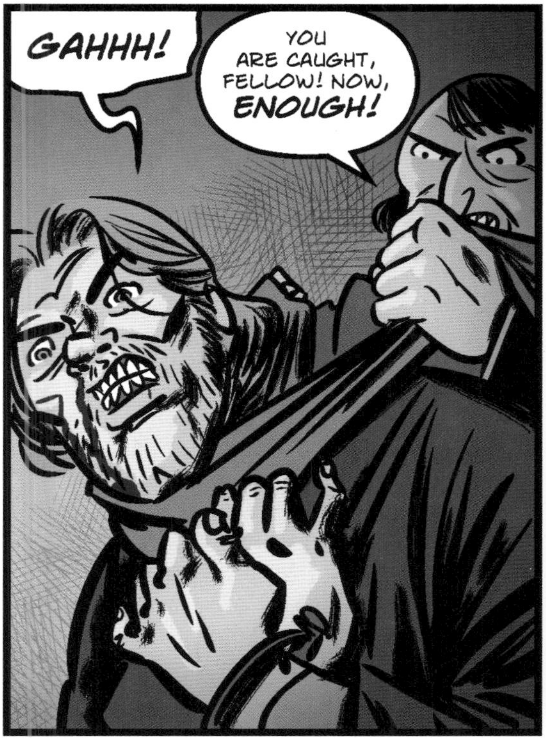
GAHHH!
YOU ARE CAUGHT, FELLOW! NOW, ENOUGH!

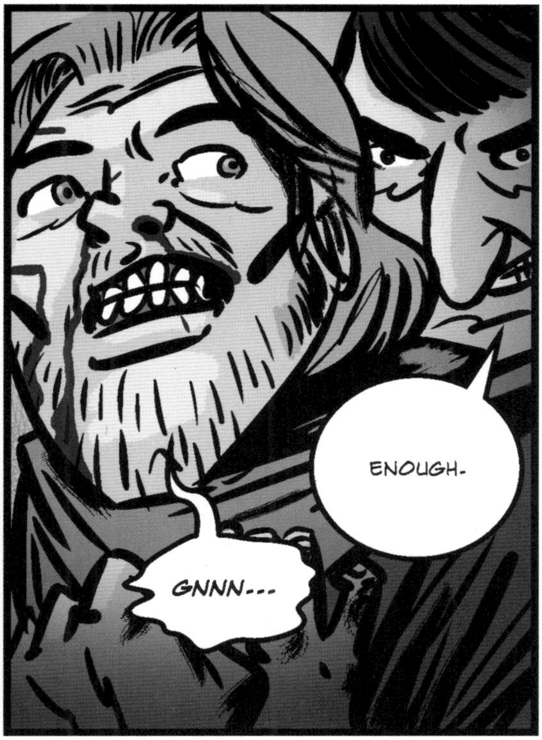
ENOUGH.
GNNN...

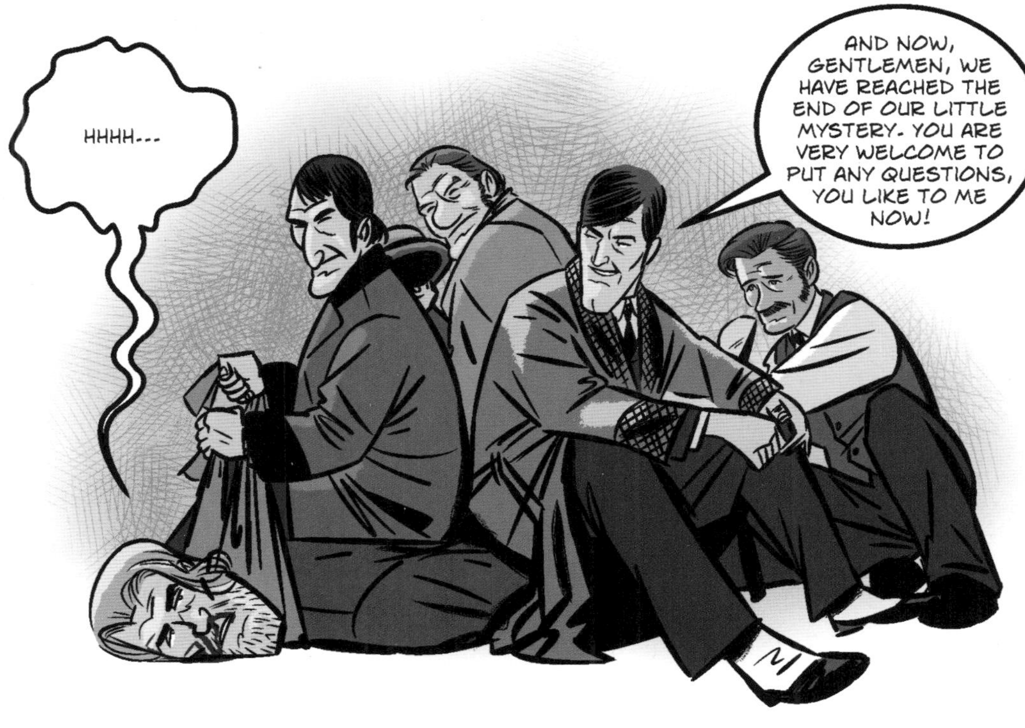
HHHH...
AND NOW, GENTLEMEN, WE HAVE REACHED THE END OF OUR LITTLE MYSTERY. YOU ARE VERY WELCOME TO PUT ANY QUESTIONS, YOU LIKE TO ME NOW!

PART 2.

The Country of the Saints

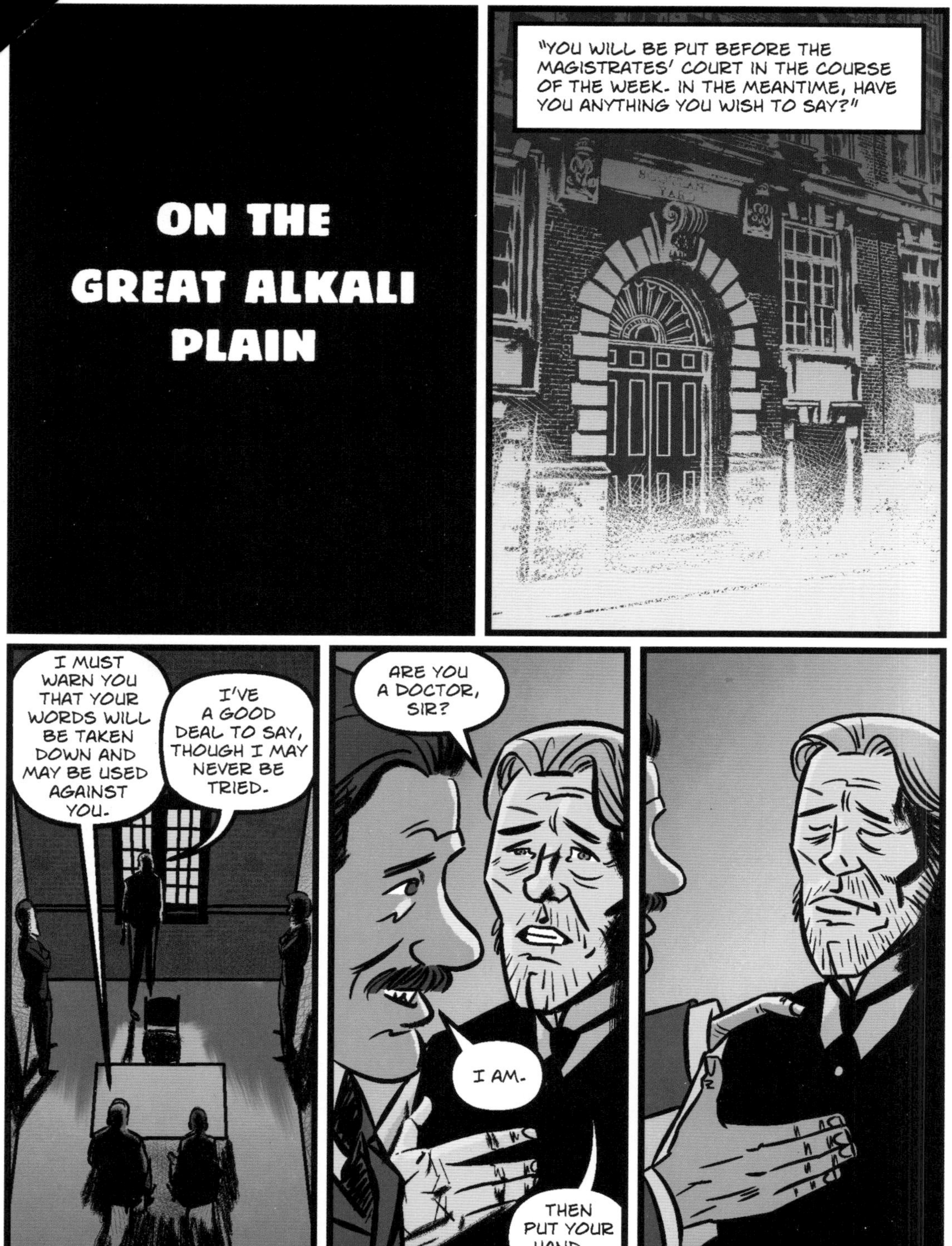
ON THE GREAT ALKALI PLAIN
"YOU WILL BE PUT BEFORE THE MAGISTRATES' COURT IN THE COURSE OF THE WEEK. IN THE MEANTIME, HAVE YOU ANYTHING YOU WISH TO SAY?"
I MUST WARN YOU THAT YOUR WORDS WILL BE TAKEN DOWN AND MAY BE USED AGAINST YOU.
I'VE A GOOD DEAL TO SAY, THOUGH I MAY NEVER BE TRIED.
ARE YOU A DOCTOR, SIR?
I AM.
THEN PUT YOUR HAND... HERE.

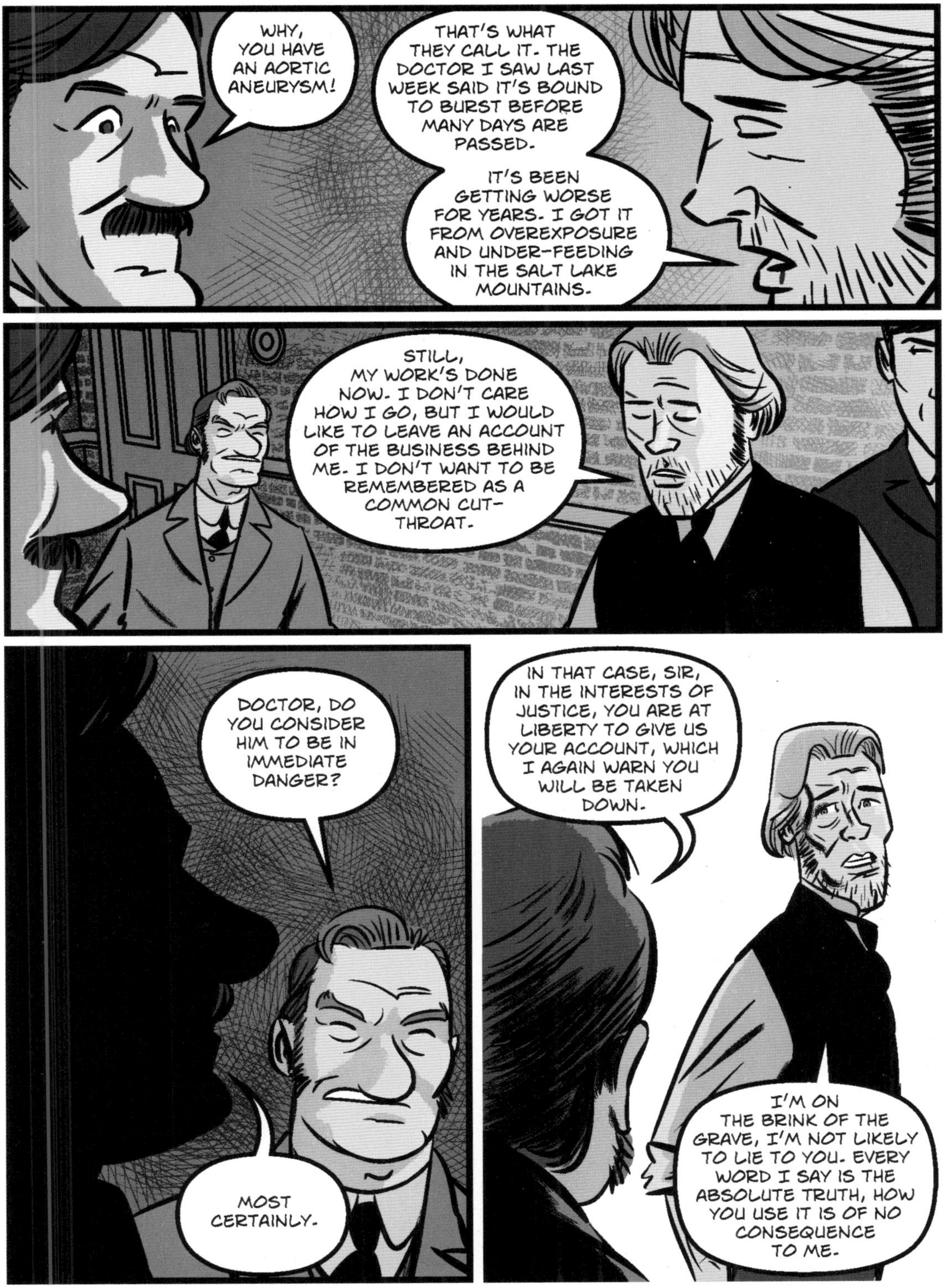
WHY, YOU HAVE AN AORTIC ANEURYSM!
THAT'S WHAT THEY CALL IT. THE DOCTOR I SAW LAST WEEK SAID IT'S BOUND TO BURST BEFORE MANY DAYS ARE PASSED.
IT'S BEEN GETTING WORSE FOR YEARS. I GOT IT FROM OVEREXPOSURE AND UNDER-FEEDING IN THE SALT LAKE MOUNTAINS.
STILL, MY WORK'S DONE NOW. I DON'T CARE HOW I GO, BUT I WOULD LIKE TO LEAVE AN ACCOUNT OF THE BUSINESS BEHIND ME. I DON'T WANT TO BE REMEMBERED AS A COMMON CUT-THROAT.
DOCTOR, DO YOU CONSIDER HIM TO BE IN IMMEDIATE DANGER?
MOST CERTAINLY.
IN THAT CASE, SIR, IN THE INTERESTS OF JUSTICE, YOU ARE AT LIBERTY TO GIVE US YOUR ACCOUNT, WHICH I AGAIN WARN YOU WILL BE TAKEN DOWN.
I'M ON THE BRINK OF THE GRAVE, I'M NOT LIKELY TO LIE TO YOU. EVERY WORD I SAY IS THE ABSOLUTE TRUTH, HOW YOU USE IT IS OF NO CONSEQUENCE TO ME.

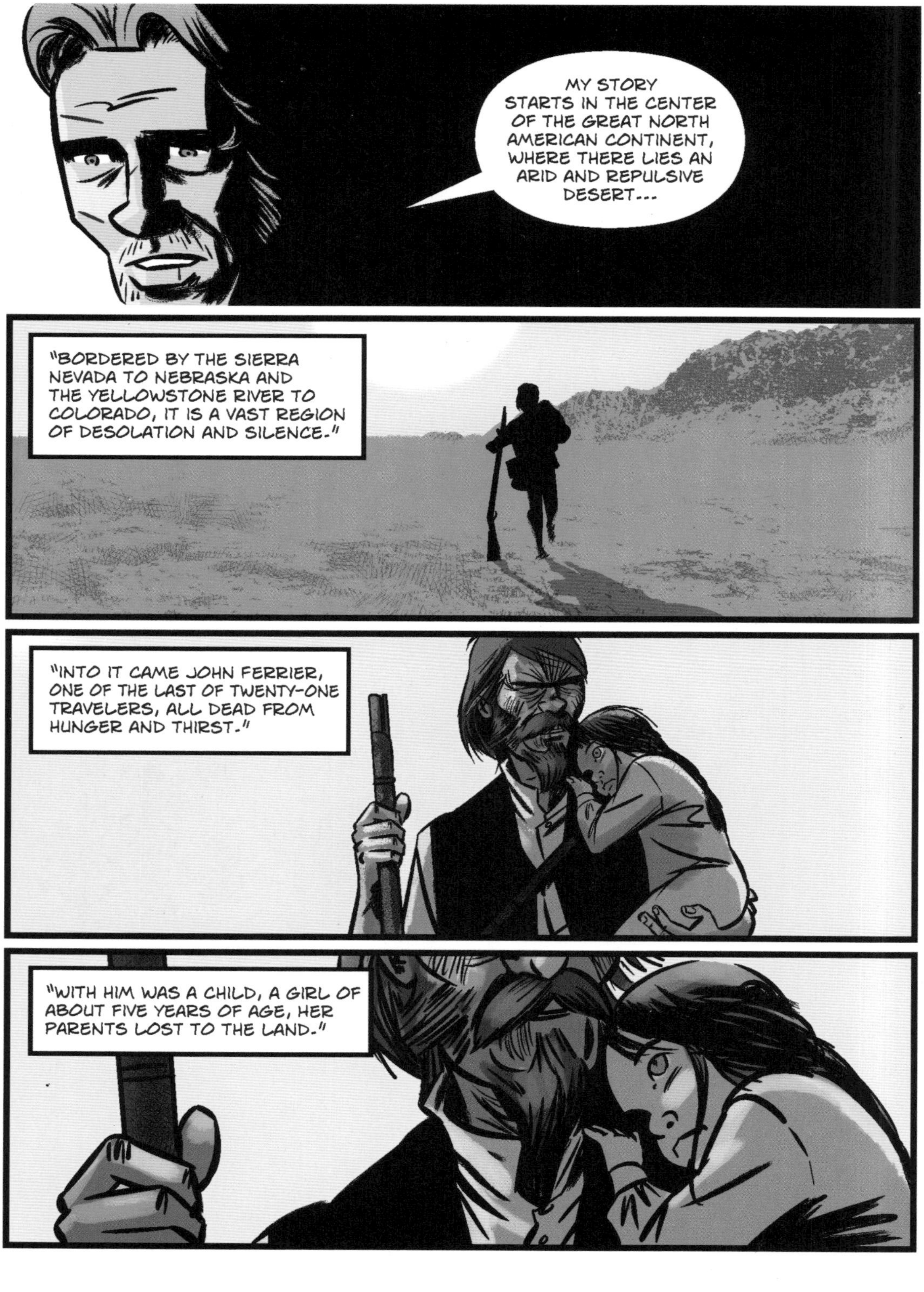
MY STORY STARTS IN THE CENTER OF THE GREAT NORTH AMERICAN CONTINENT, WHERE THERE LIES AN ARID AND REPULSIVE DESERT...
"BORDERED BY THE SIERRA NEVADA TO NEBRASKA AND THE YELLOWSTONE RIVER TO COLORADO, IT IS A VAST REGION OF DESOLATION AND SILENCE."
"INTO IT CAME JOHN FERRIER, ONE OF THE LAST OF TWENTY-ONE TRAVELERS, ALL DEAD FROM HUNGER AND THIRST."
"WITH HIM WAS A CHILD, A GIRL OF ABOUT FIVE YEARS OF AGE, HER PARENTS LOST TO THE LAND."

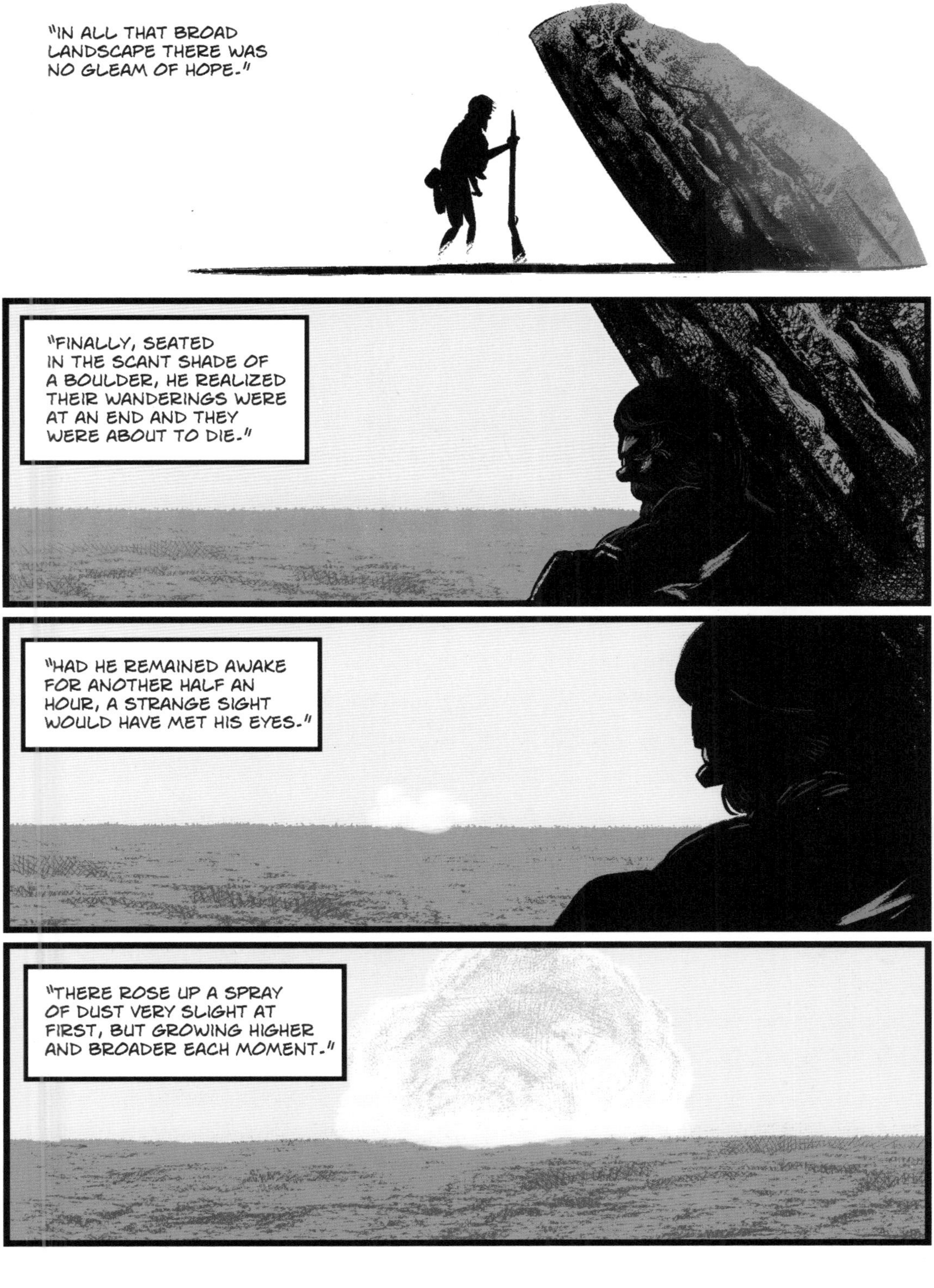
"IN ALL THAT BROAD LANDSCAPE THERE WAS NO GLEAM OF HOPE."
"FINALLY, SEATED IN THE SCANT SHADE OF A BOULDER, HE REALIZED THEIR WANDERINGS WERE AT AN END AND THEY WERE ABOUT TO DIE."
"HAD HE REMAINED AWAKE FOR ANOTHER HALF AN HOUR, A STRANGE SIGHT WOULD HAVE MET HIS EYES."
"THERE ROSE UP A SPRAY OF DUST VERY SLIGHT AT FIRST, BUT GROWING HIGHER AND BROADER EACH MOMENT."

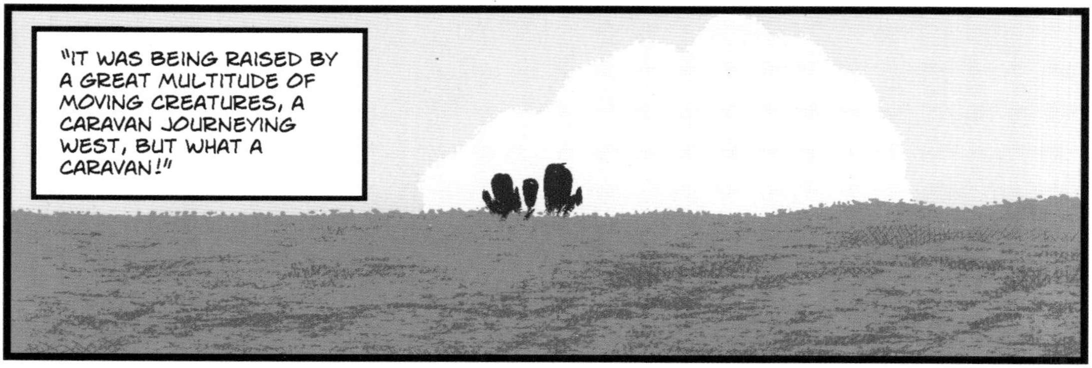
"IT WAS BEING RAISED BY A GREAT MULTITUDE OF MOVING CREATURES, A CARAVAN JOURNEYING WEST, BUT WHAT A CARAVAN!"

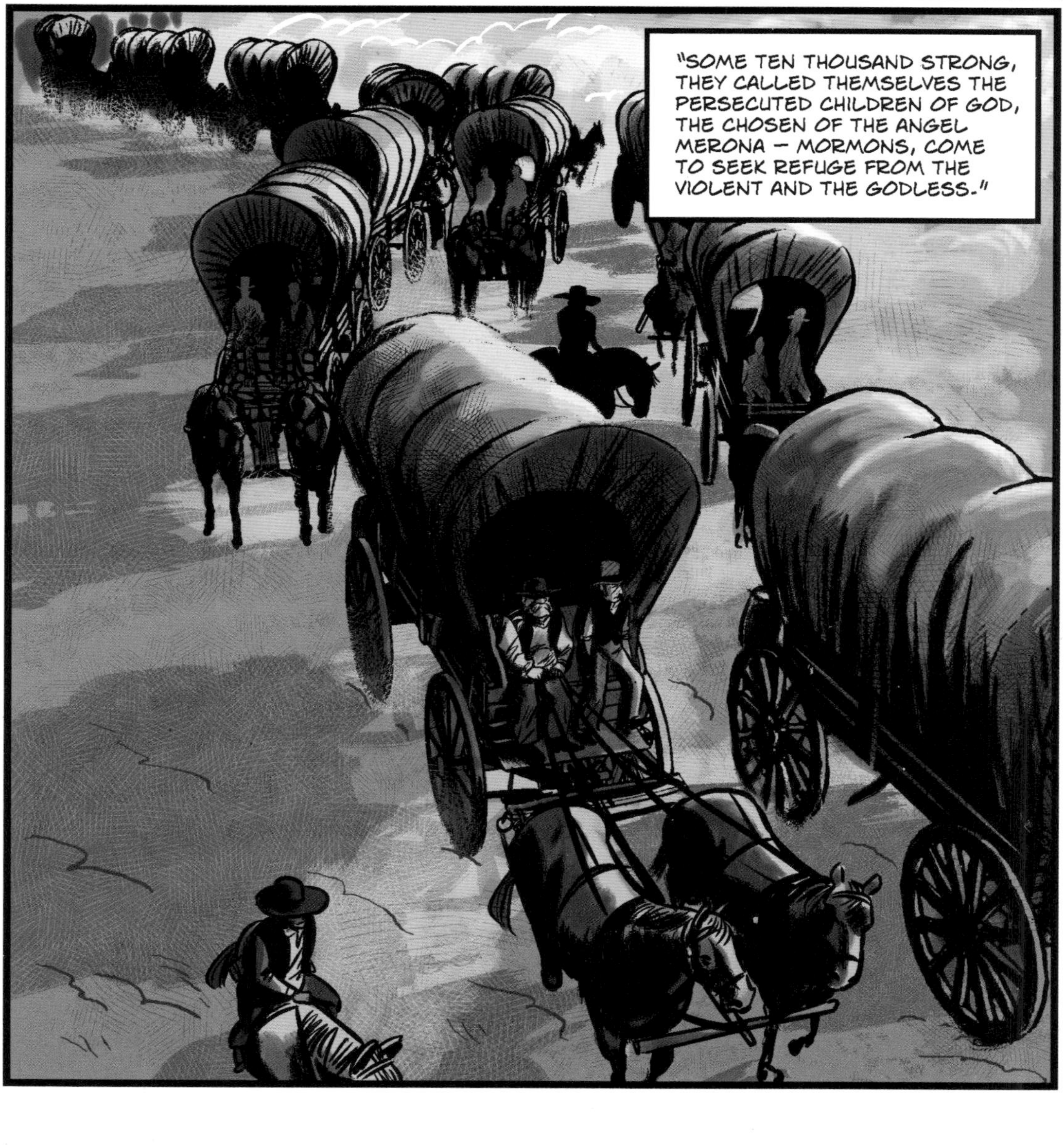
"SOME TEN THOUSAND STRONG, THEY CALLED THEMSELVES THE PERSECUTED CHILDREN OF GOD, THE CHOSEN OF THE ANGEL MERONA – MORMONS, COME TO SEEK REFUGE FROM THE VIOLENT AND THE GODLESS."

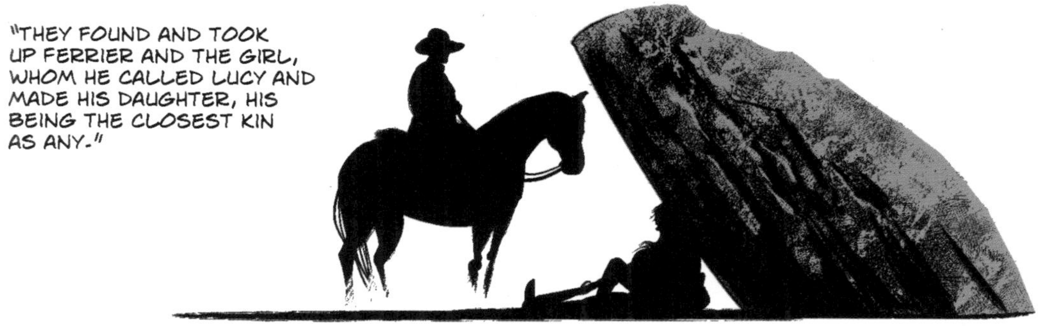
"THEY FOUND AND TOOK UP FERRIER AND THE GIRL, WHOM HE CALLED LUCY AND MADE HIS DAUGHTER, HIS BEING THE CLOSEST KIN AS ANY."

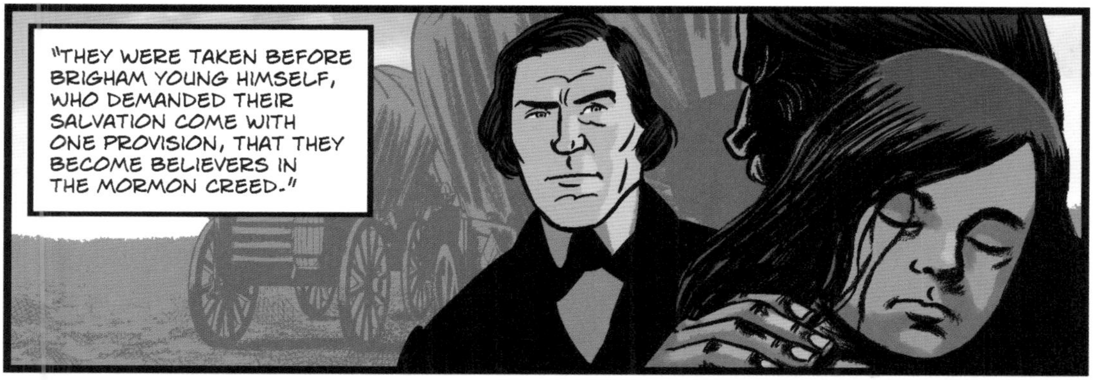
"THEY WERE TAKEN BEFORE BRIGHAM YOUNG HIMSELF, WHO DEMANDED THEIR SALVATION COME WITH ONE PROVISION, THAT THEY BECOME BELIEVERS IN THE MORMON CREED."

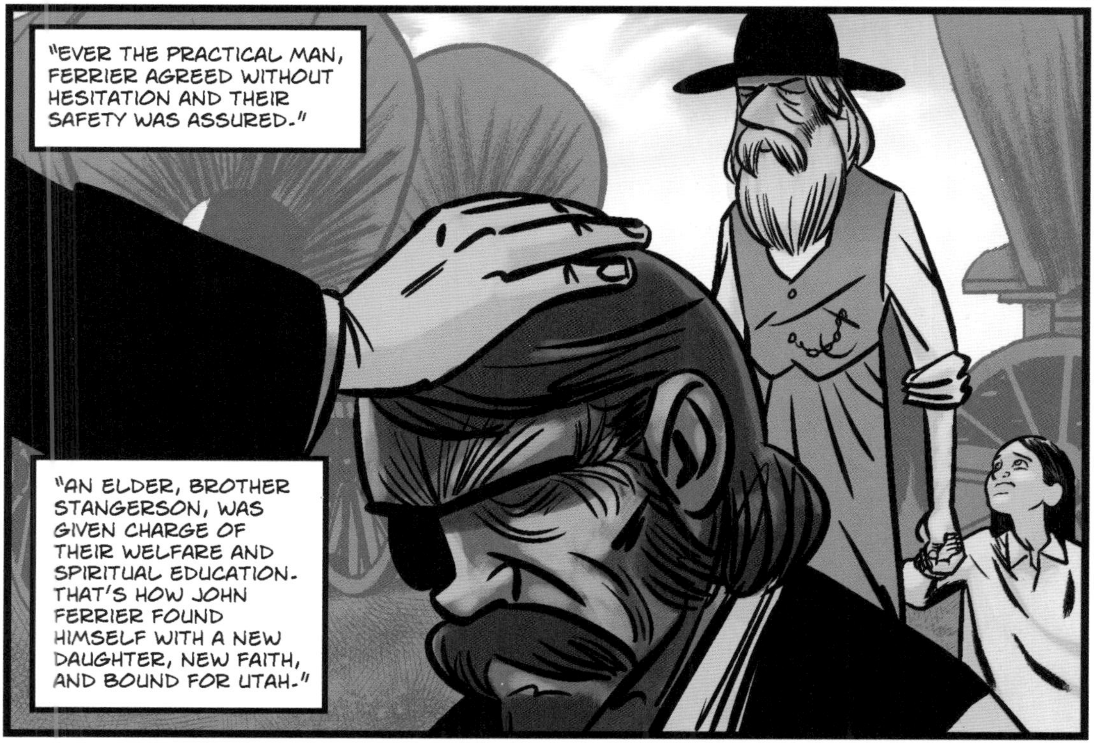
"EVER THE PRACTICAL MAN, FERRIER AGREED WITHOUT HESITATION AND THEIR SAFETY WAS ASSURED."
"AN ELDER, BROTHER STANGERSON, WAS GIVEN CHARGE OF THEIR WELFARE AND SPIRITUAL EDUCATION. THAT'S HOW JOHN FERRIER FOUND HIMSELF WITH A NEW DAUGHTER, NEW FAITH, AND BOUND FOR UTAH."

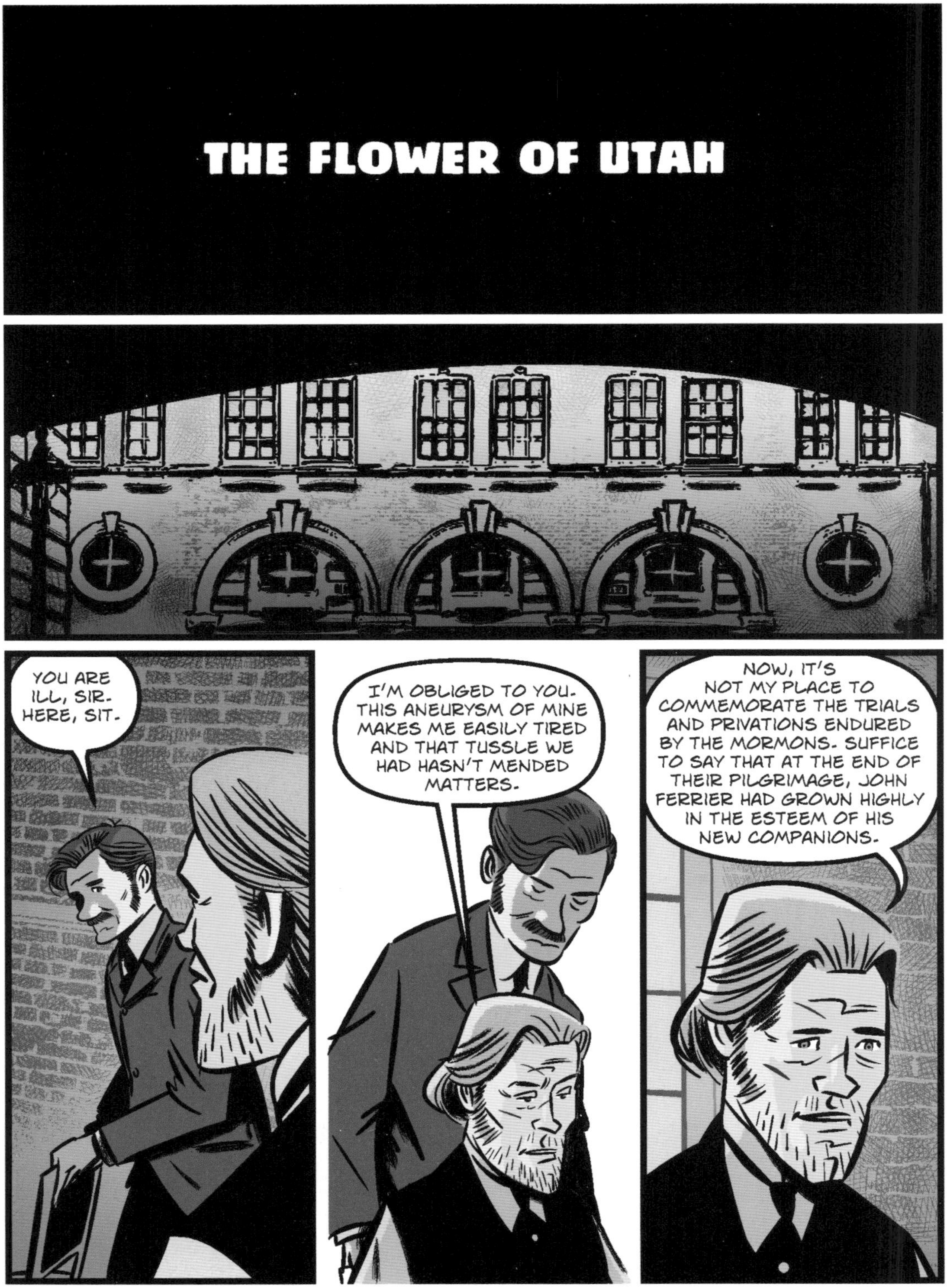
THE FLOWER OF UTAH
YOU ARE ILL, SIR. HERE, SIT.
I'M OBLIGED TO YOU. THIS ANEURYSM OF MINE MAKES ME EASILY TIRED AND THAT TUSSLE WE HAD HASN'T MENDED MATTERS.
NOW, IT'S NOT MY PLACE TO COMMEMORATE THE TRIALS AND PRIVATIONS ENDURED BY THE MORMONS. SUFFICE TO SAY THAT AT THE END OF THEIR PILGRIMAGE, JOHN FERRIER HAD GROWN HIGHLY IN THE ESTEEM OF HIS NEW COMPANIONS.

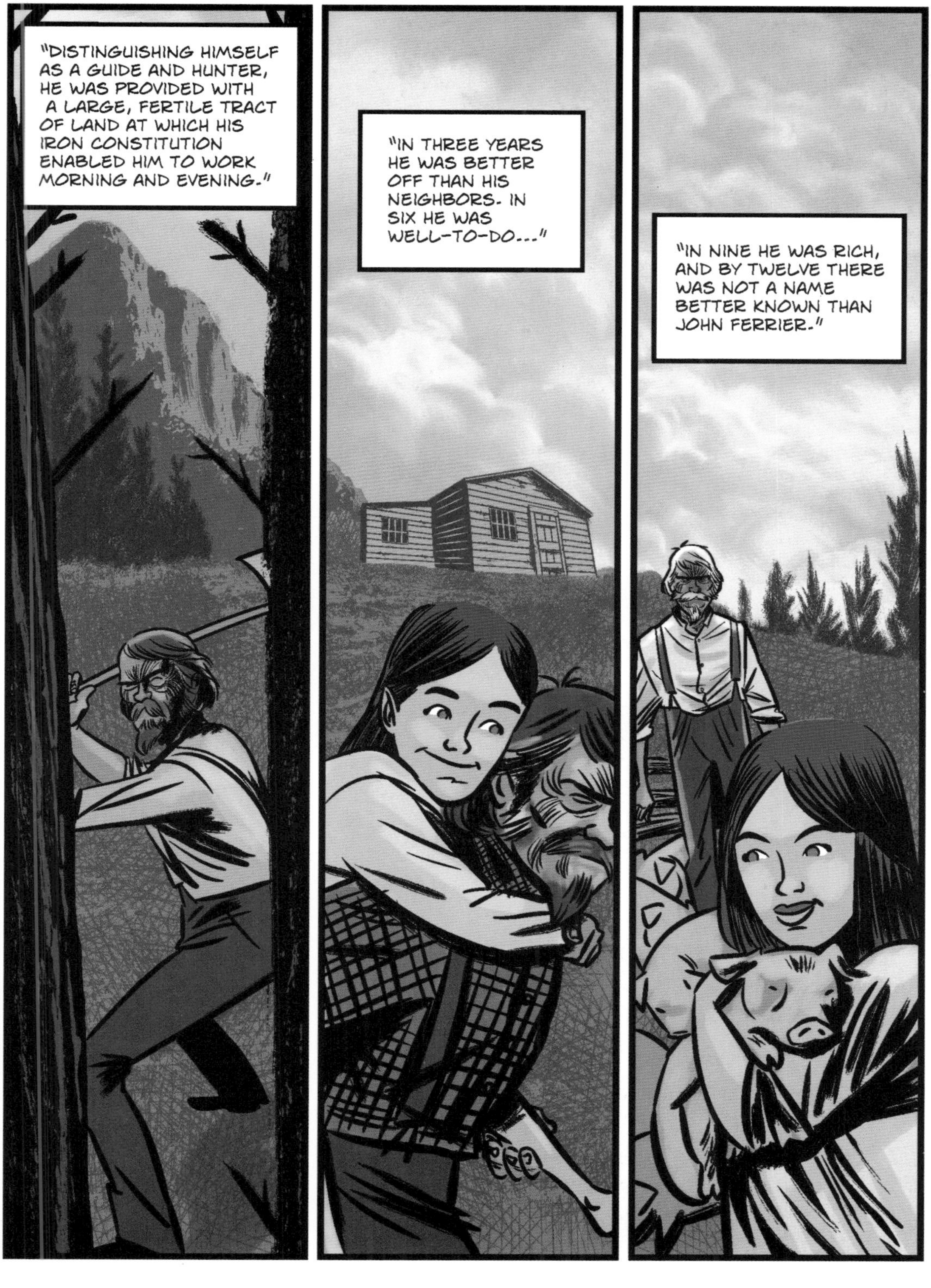
"DISTINGUISHING HIMSELF AS A GUIDE AND HUNTER, HE WAS PROVIDED WITH A LARGE, FERTILE TRACT OF LAND AT WHICH HIS IRON CONSTITUTION ENABLED HIM TO WORK MORNING AND EVENING."
"IN THREE YEARS HE WAS BETTER OFF THAN HIS NEIGHBORS. IN SIX HE WAS WELL-TO-DO..."
"IN NINE HE WAS RICH, AND BY TWELVE THERE WAS NOT A NAME BETTER KNOWN THAN JOHN FERRIER."

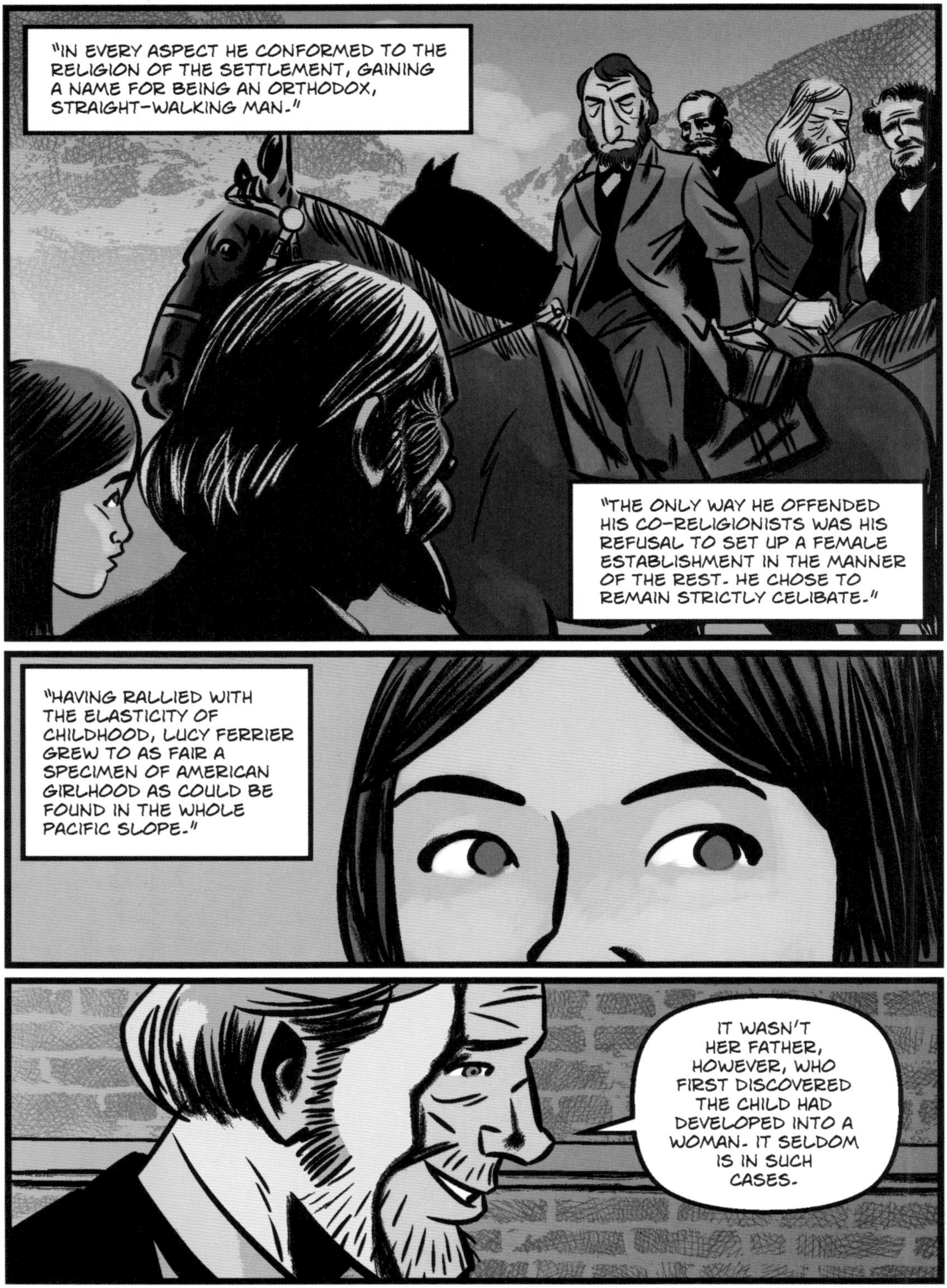
"IN EVERY ASPECT HE CONFORMED TO THE RELIGION OF THE SETTLEMENT, GAINING A NAME FOR BEING AN ORTHODOX, STRAIGHT-WALKING MAN."
"THE ONLY WAY HE OFFENDED HIS CO-RELIGIONISTS WAS HIS REFUSAL TO SET UP A FEMALE ESTABLISHMENT IN THE MANNER OF THE REST. HE CHOSE TO REMAIN STRICTLY CELIBATE."
"HAVING RALLIED WITH THE ELASTICITY OF CHILDHOOD, LUCY FERRIER GREW TO AS FAIR A SPECIMEN OF AMERICAN GIRLHOOD AS COULD BE FOUND IN THE WHOLE PACIFIC SLOPE."
IT WASN'T HER FATHER, HOWEVER, WHO FIRST DISCOVERED THE CHILD HAD DEVELOPED INTO A WOMAN. IT SELDOM IS IN SUCH CASES.

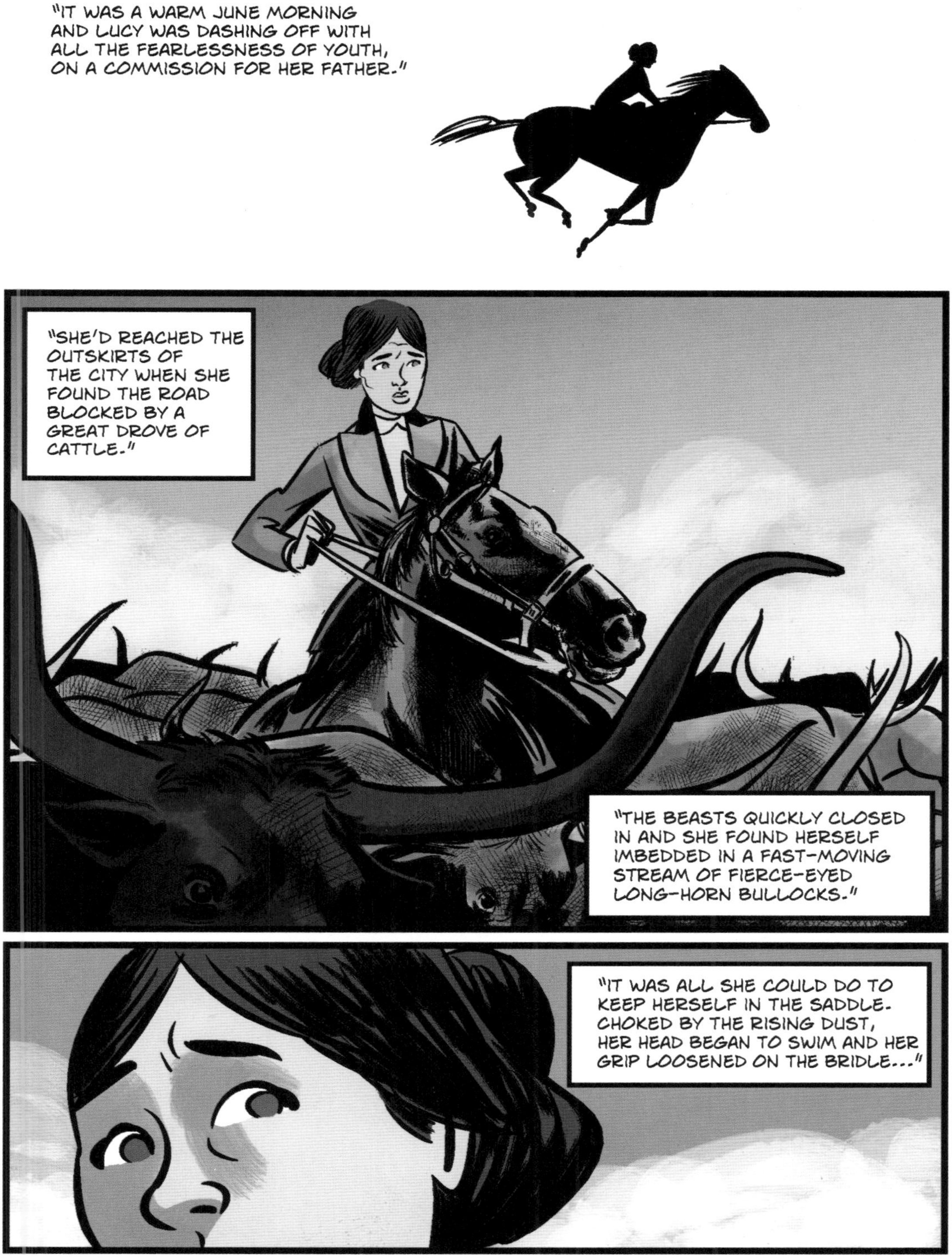
"IT WAS A WARM JUNE MORNING AND LUCY WAS DASHING OFF WITH ALL THE FEARLESSNESS OF YOUTH, ON A COMMISSION FOR HER FATHER."
"SHE'D REACHED THE OUTSKIRTS OF THE CITY WHEN SHE FOUND THE ROAD BLOCKED BY A GREAT DROVE OF CATTLE."
"THE BEASTS QUICKLY CLOSED IN AND SHE FOUND HERSELF IMBEDDED IN A FAST-MOVING STREAM OF FIERCE-EYED LONG-HORN BULLOCKS."
"IT WAS ALL SHE COULD DO TO KEEP HERSELF IN THE SADDLE. CHOKED BY THE RISING DUST, HER HEAD BEGAN TO SWIM AND HER GRIP LOOSENED ON THE BRIDLE..."

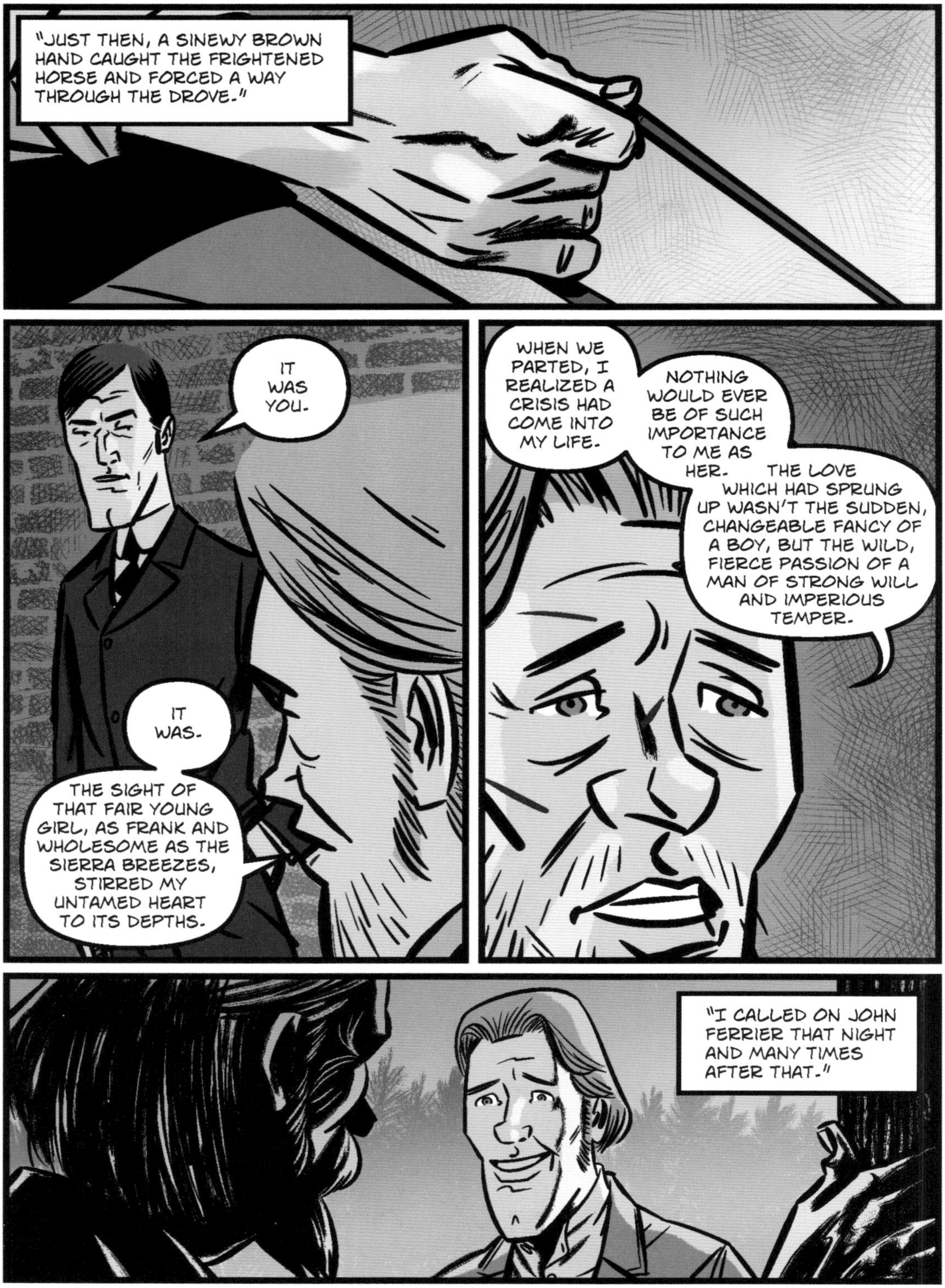
"JUST THEN, A SINEWY BROWN HAND CAUGHT THE FRIGHTENED HORSE AND FORCED A WAY THROUGH THE DROVE."
IT WAS YOU.
IT WAS.
THE SIGHT OF THAT FAIR YOUNG GIRL, AS FRANK AND WHOLESOME AS THE SIERRA BREEZES, STIRRED MY UNTAMED HEART TO ITS DEPTHS.
WHEN WE PARTED, I REALIZED A CRISIS HAD COME INTO MY LIFE.
NOTHING WOULD EVER BE OF SUCH IMPORTANCE TO ME AS HER. THE LOVE WHICH HAD SPRUNG UP WASN'T THE SUDDEN, CHANGEABLE FANCY OF A BOY, BUT THE WILD, FIERCE PASSION OF A MAN OF STRONG WILL AND IMPERIOUS TEMPER.
"I CALLED ON JOHN FERRIER THAT NIGHT AND MANY TIMES AFTER THAT."

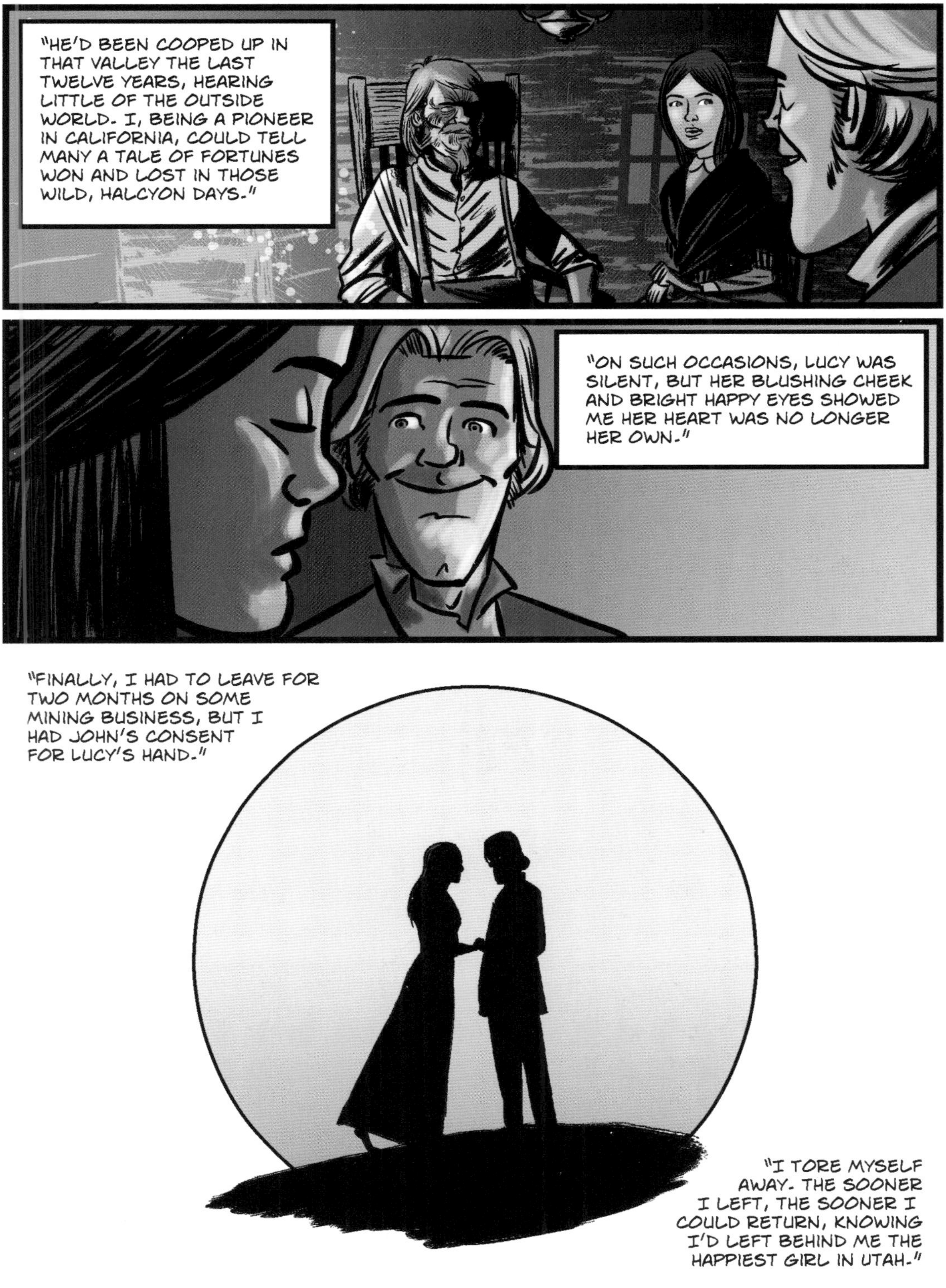
"HE'D BEEN COOPED UP IN THAT VALLEY THE LAST TWELVE YEARS, HEARING LITTLE OF THE OUTSIDE WORLD. I, BEING A PIONEER IN CALIFORNIA, COULD TELL MANY A TALE OF FORTUNES WON AND LOST IN THOSE WILD, HALCYON DAYS."
"ON SUCH OCCASIONS, LUCY WAS SILENT, BUT HER BLUSHING CHEEK AND BRIGHT HAPPY EYES SHOWED ME HER HEART WAS NO LONGER HER OWN."
"FINALLY, I HAD TO LEAVE FOR TWO MONTHS ON SOME MINING BUSINESS, BUT I HAD JOHN'S CONSENT FOR LUCY'S HAND."
"I TORE MYSELF AWAY. THE SOONER I LEFT, THE SOONER I COULD RETURN, KNOWING I'D LEFT BEHIND ME THE HAPPIEST GIRL IN UTAH."

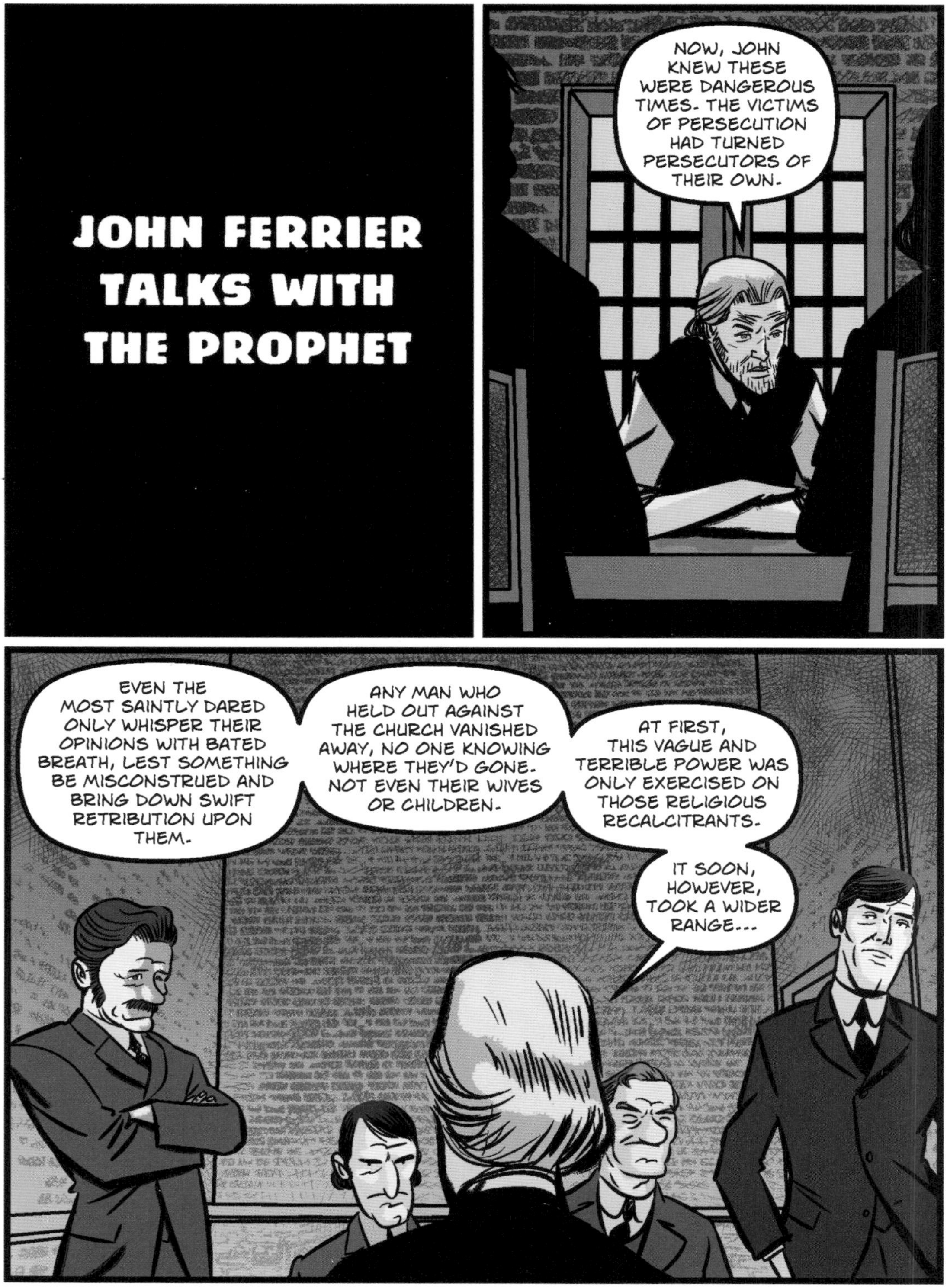
JOHN FERRIER TALKS WITH THE PROPHET
NOW, JOHN KNEW THESE WERE DANGEROUS TIMES. THE VICTIMS OF PERSECUTION HAD TURNED PERSECUTORS OF THEIR OWN.
EVEN THE MOST SAINTLY DARED ONLY WHISPER THEIR OPINIONS WITH BATED BREATH, LEST SOMETHING BE MISCONSTRUED AND BRING DOWN SWIFT RETRIBUTION UPON THEM.
ANY MAN WHO HELD OUT AGAINST THE CHURCH VANISHED AWAY, NO ONE KNOWING WHERE THEY'D GONE. NOT EVEN THEIR WIVES OR CHILDREN.
AT FIRST, THIS VAGUE AND TERRIBLE POWER WAS ONLY EXERCISED ON THOSE RELIGIOUS RECALCITRANTS.
IT SOON, HOWEVER, TOOK A WIDER RANGE...

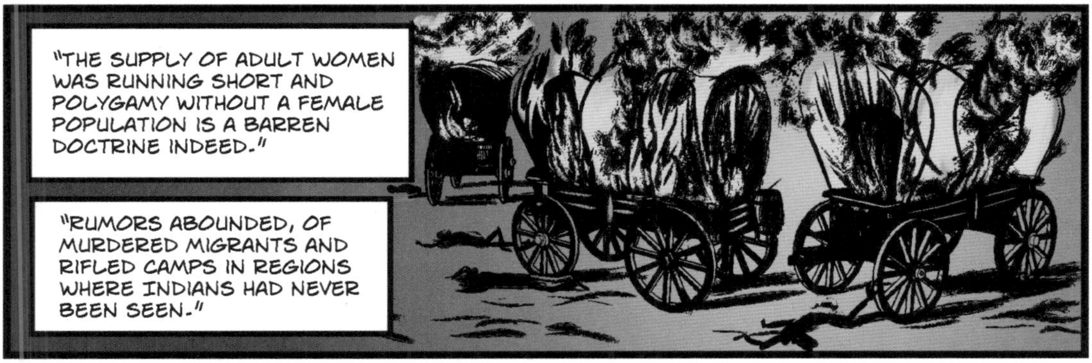
"THE SUPPLY OF ADULT WOMEN WAS RUNNING SHORT AND POLYGAMY WITHOUT A FEMALE POPULATION IS A BARREN DOCTRINE INDEED."
"RUMORS ABOUNDED, OF MURDERED MIGRANTS AND RIFLED CAMPS IN REGIONS WHERE INDIANS HAD NEVER BEEN SEEN."

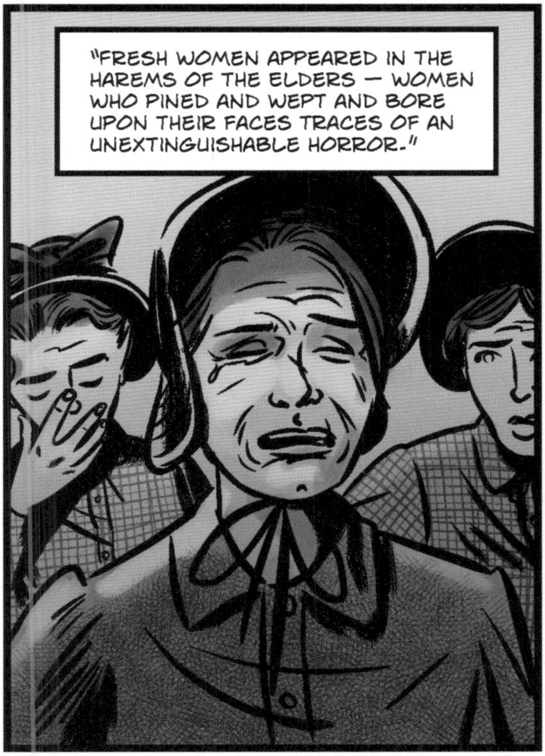
"FRESH WOMEN APPEARED IN THE HAREMS OF THE ELDERS — WOMEN WHO PINED AND WEPT AND BORE UPON THEIR FACES TRACES OF AN UNEXTINGUISHABLE HORROR."

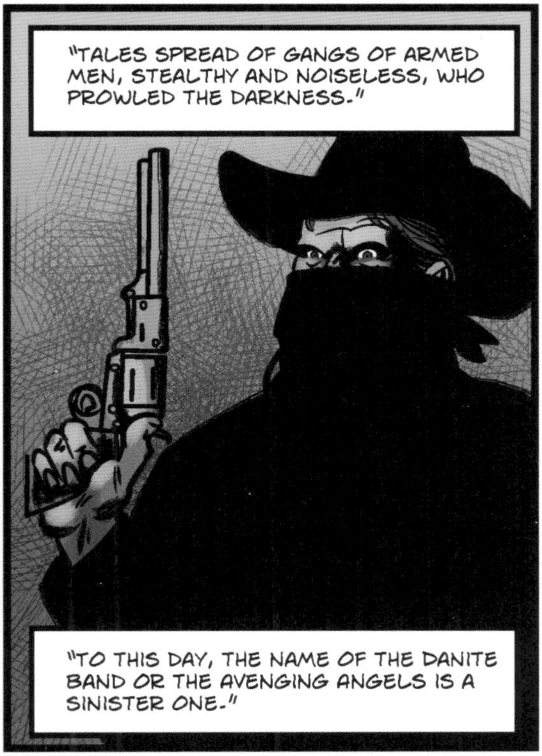
"TALES SPREAD OF GANGS OF ARMED MEN, STEALTHY AND NOISELESS, WHO PROWLED THE DARKNESS."
"TO THIS DAY, THE NAME OF THE DANITE BAND OR THE AVENGING ANGELS IS A SINISTER ONE."

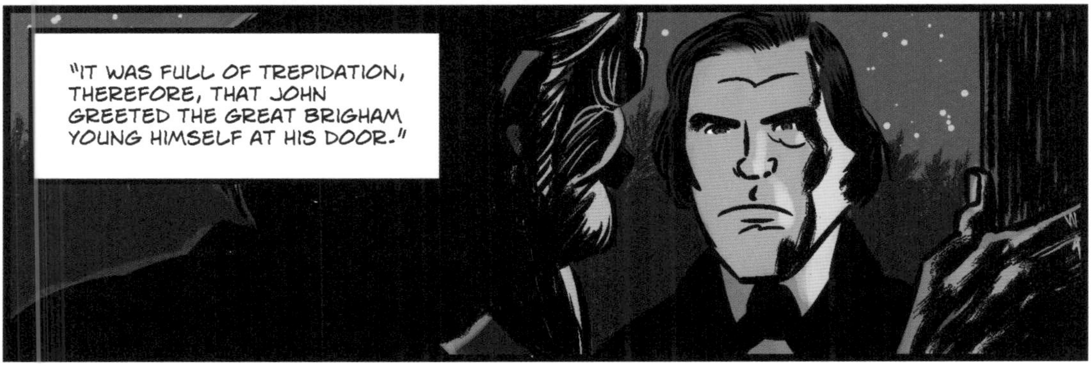
"IT WAS FULL OF TREPIDATION, THEREFORE, THAT JOHN GREETED THE GREAT BRIGHAM YOUNG HIMSELF AT HIS DOOR."

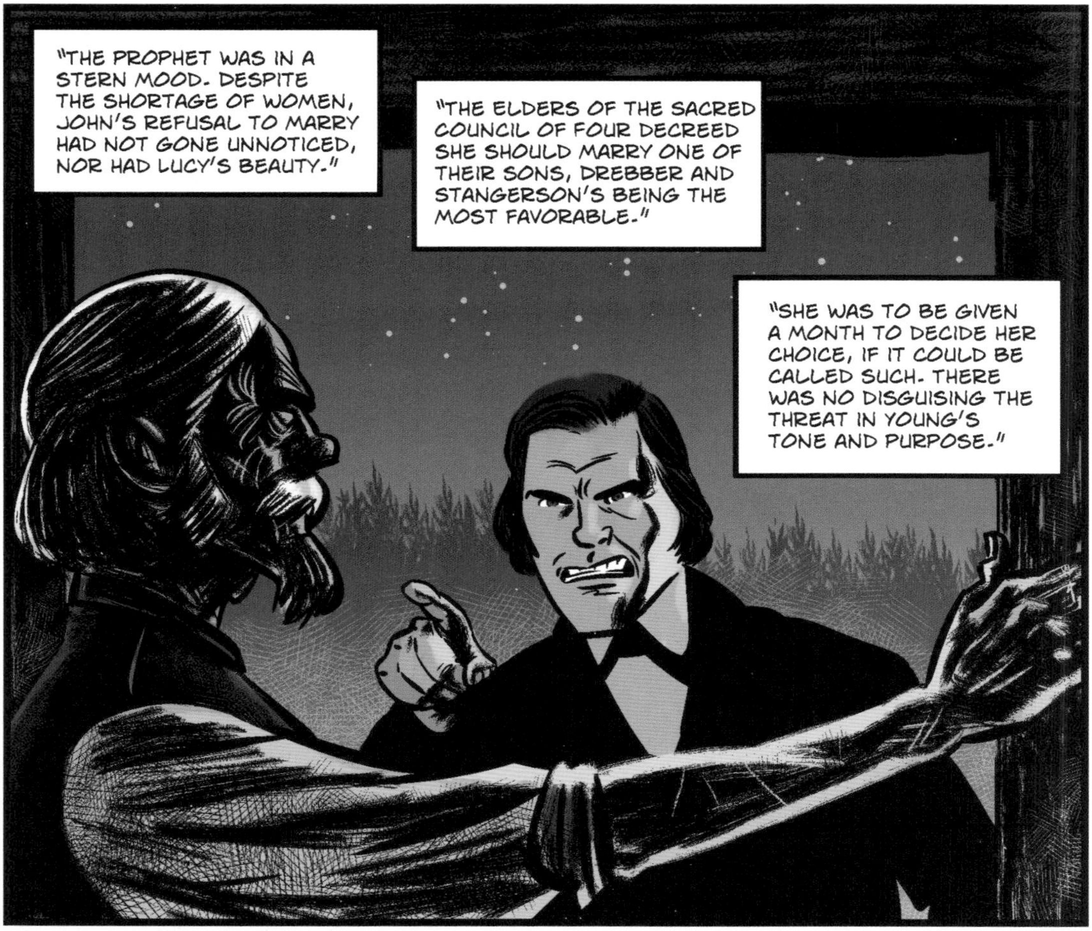
"THE PROPHET WAS IN A STERN MOOD. DESPITE THE SHORTAGE OF WOMEN, JOHN'S REFUSAL TO MARRY HAD NOT GONE UNNOTICED, NOR HAD LUCY'S BEAUTY."
"THE ELDERS OF THE SACRED COUNCIL OF FOUR DECREED SHE SHOULD MARRY ONE OF THEIR SONS, DREBBER AND STANGERSON'S BEING THE MOST FAVORABLE."
"SHE WAS TO BE GIVEN A MONTH TO DECIDE HER CHOICE, IF IT COULD BE CALLED SUCH. THERE WAS NO DISGUISING THE THREAT IN YOUNG'S TONE AND PURPOSE."

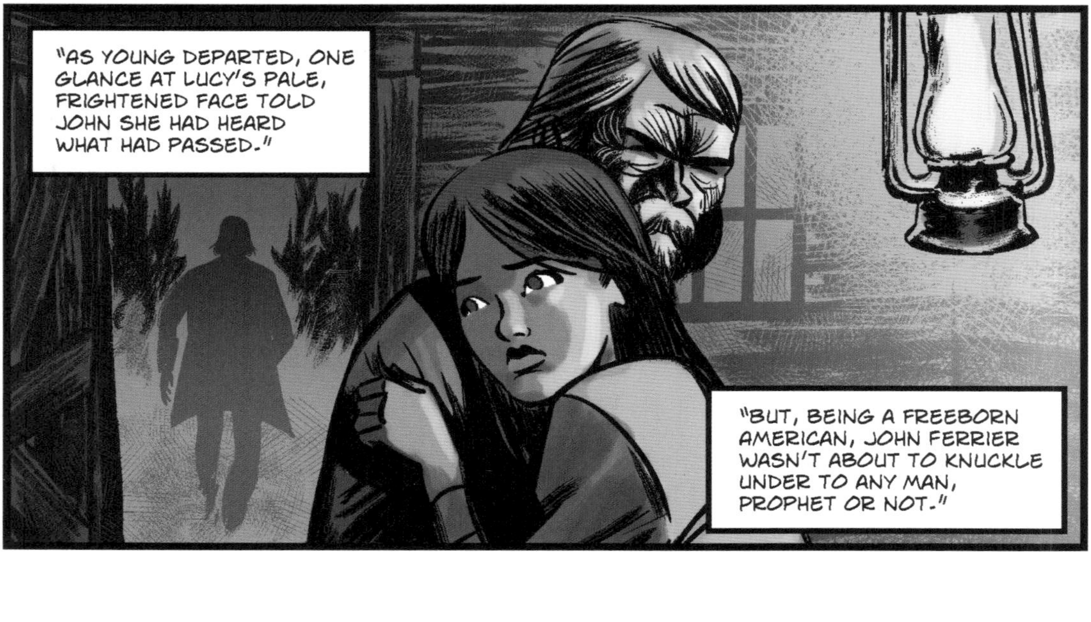
"AS YOUNG DEPARTED, ONE GLANCE AT LUCY'S PALE, FRIGHTENED FACE TOLD JOHN SHE HAD HEARD WHAT HAD PASSED."
"BUT, BEING A FREEBORN AMERICAN, JOHN FERRIER WASN'T ABOUT TO KNUCKLE UNDER TO ANY MAN, PROPHET OR NOT."

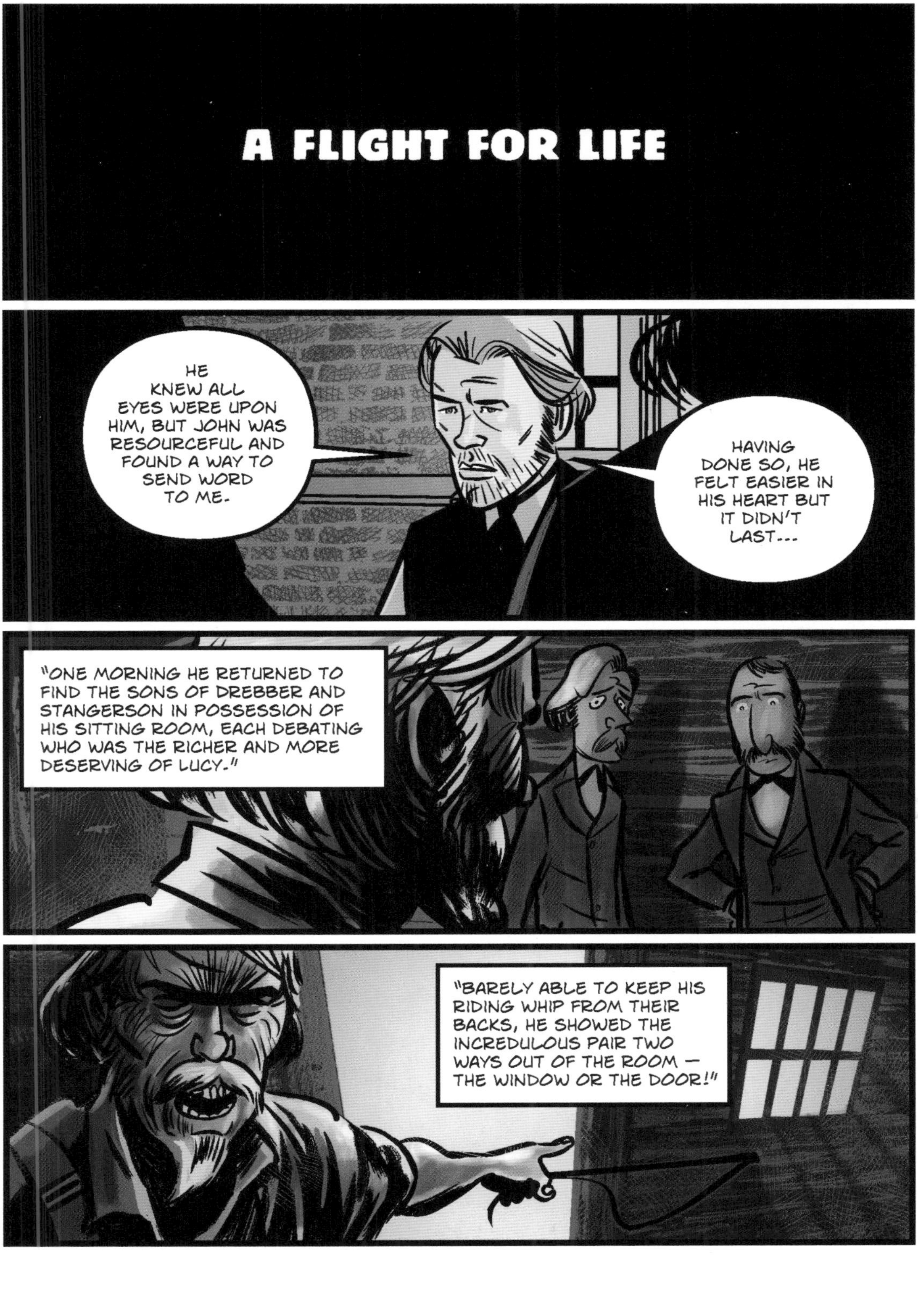
A FLIGHT FOR LIFE
HE KNEW ALL EYES WERE UPON HIM, BUT JOHN WAS RESOURCEFUL AND FOUND A WAY TO SEND WORD TO ME.
HAVING DONE SO, HE FELT EASIER IN HIS HEART BUT IT DIDN'T LAST...
"ONE MORNING HE RETURNED TO FIND THE SONS OF DREBBER AND STANGERSON IN POSSESSION OF HIS SITTING ROOM, EACH DEBATING WHO WAS THE RICHER AND MORE DESERVING OF LUCY."
"BARELY ABLE TO KEEP HIS RIDING WHIP FROM THEIR BACKS, HE SHOWED THE INCREDULOUS PAIR TWO WAYS OUT OF THE ROOM — THE WINDOW OR THE DOOR!"

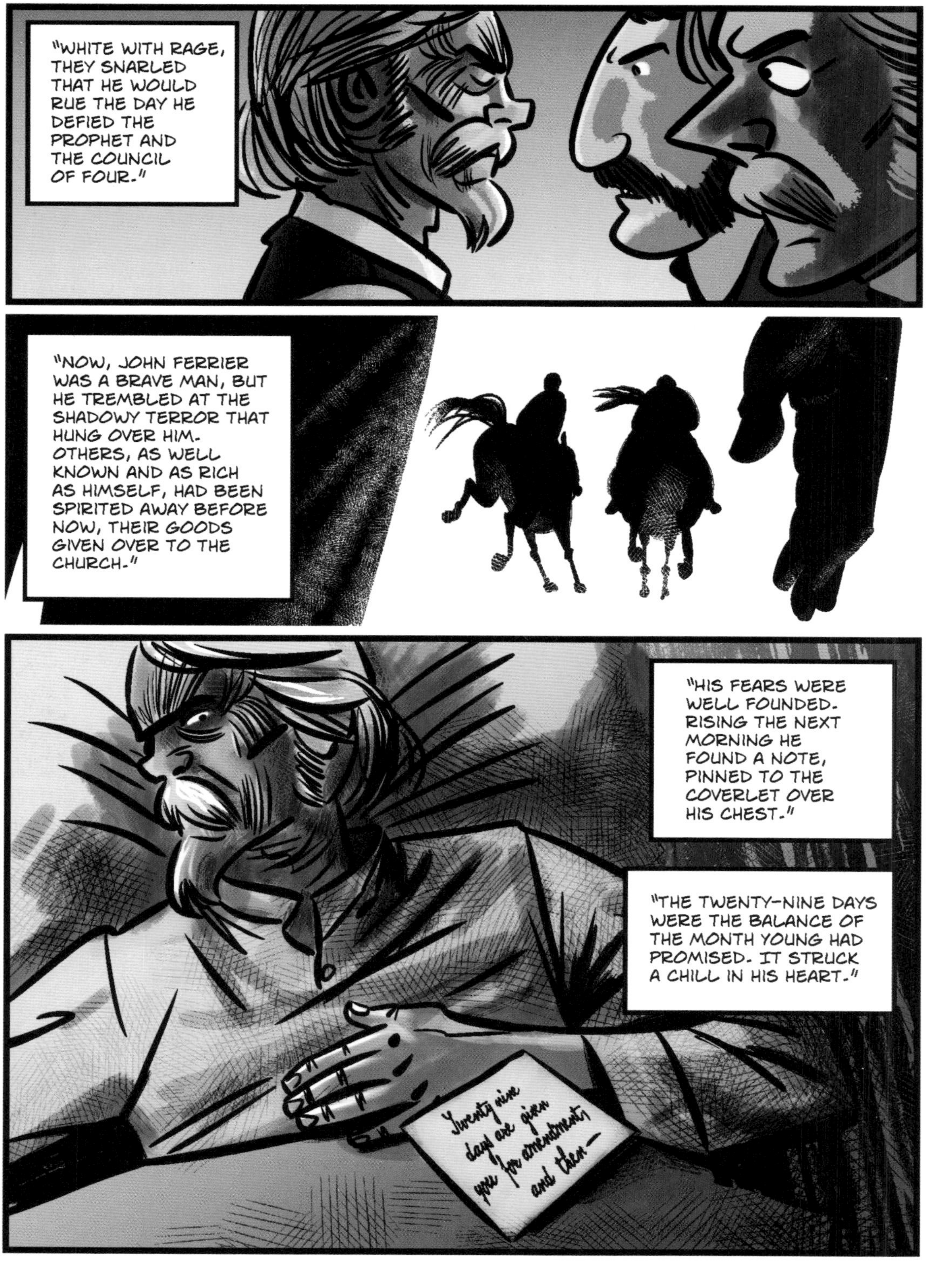
"WHITE WITH RAGE, THEY SNARLED THAT HE WOULD RUE THE DAY HE DEFIED THE PROPHET AND THE COUNCIL OF FOUR."
"NOW, JOHN FERRIER WAS A BRAVE MAN, BUT HE TREMBLED AT THE SHADOWY TERROR THAT HUNG OVER HIM. OTHERS, AS WELL KNOWN AND AS RICH AS HIMSELF, HAD BEEN SPIRITED AWAY BEFORE NOW, THEIR GOODS GIVEN OVER TO THE CHURCH."
"HIS FEARS WERE WELL FOUNDED. RISING THE NEXT MORNING HE FOUND A NOTE, PINNED TO THE COVERLET OVER HIS CHEST."
"THE TWENTY-NINE DAYS WERE THE BALANCE OF THE MONTH YOUNG HAD PROMISED. IT STRUCK A CHILL IN HIS HEART."
Twenty nine days are given you for amendment, and then—

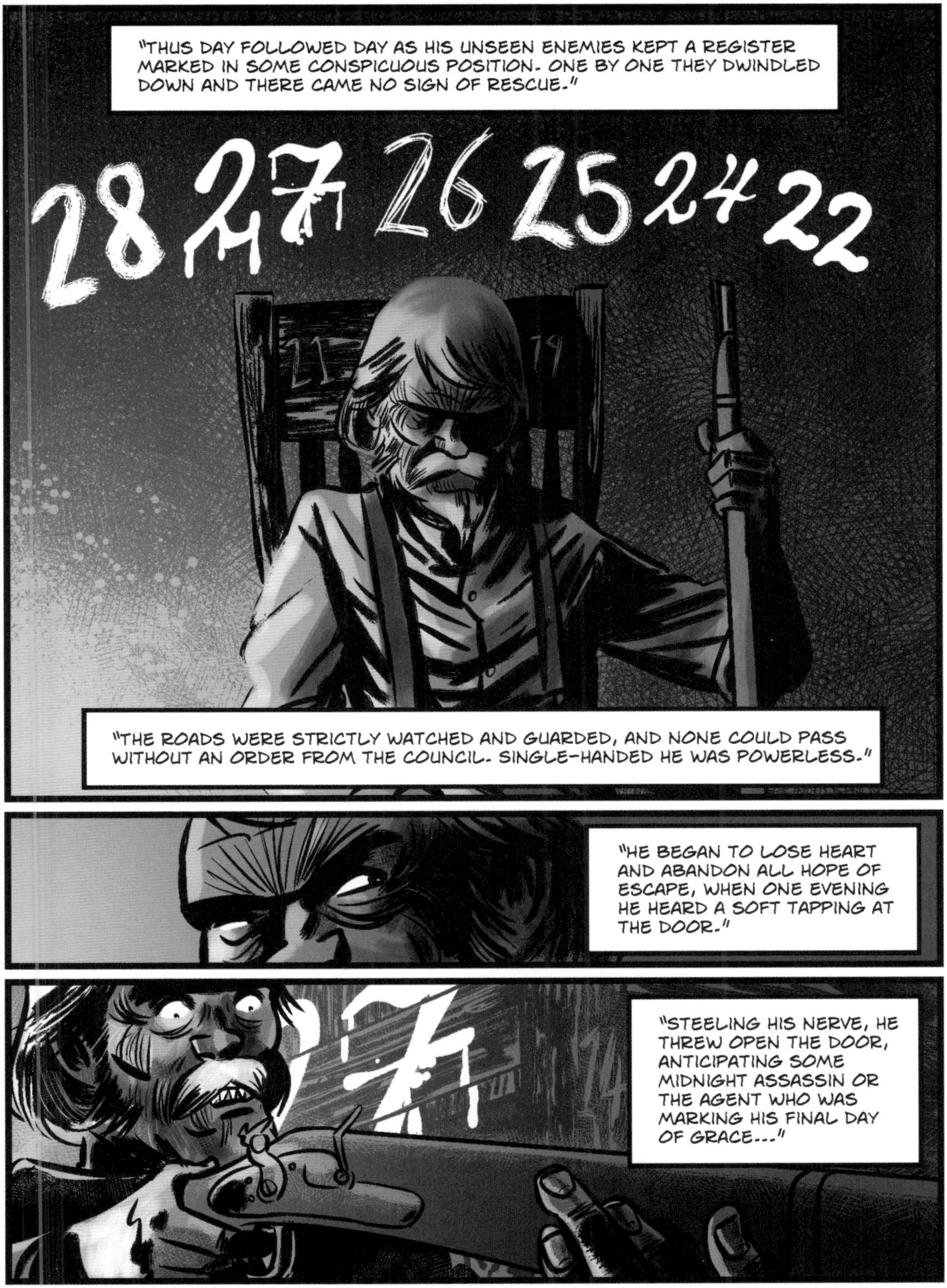
"THUS DAY FOLLOWED DAY AS HIS UNSEEN ENEMIES KEPT A REGISTER MARKED IN SOME CONSPICUOUS POSITION. ONE BY ONE THEY DWINDLED DOWN AND THERE CAME NO SIGN OF RESCUE."
28 27 26 25 24 22
"THE ROADS WERE STRICTLY WATCHED AND GUARDED, AND NONE COULD PASS WITHOUT AN ORDER FROM THE COUNCIL. SINGLE-HANDED HE WAS POWERLESS."
"HE BEGAN TO LOSE HEART AND ABANDON ALL HOPE OF ESCAPE, WHEN ONE EVENING HE HEARD A SOFT TAPPING AT THE DOOR."
"STEELING HIS NERVE, HE THREW OPEN THE DOOR, ANTICIPATING SOME MIDNIGHT ASSASSIN OR THE AGENT WHO WAS MARKING HIS FINAL DAY OF GRACE..."

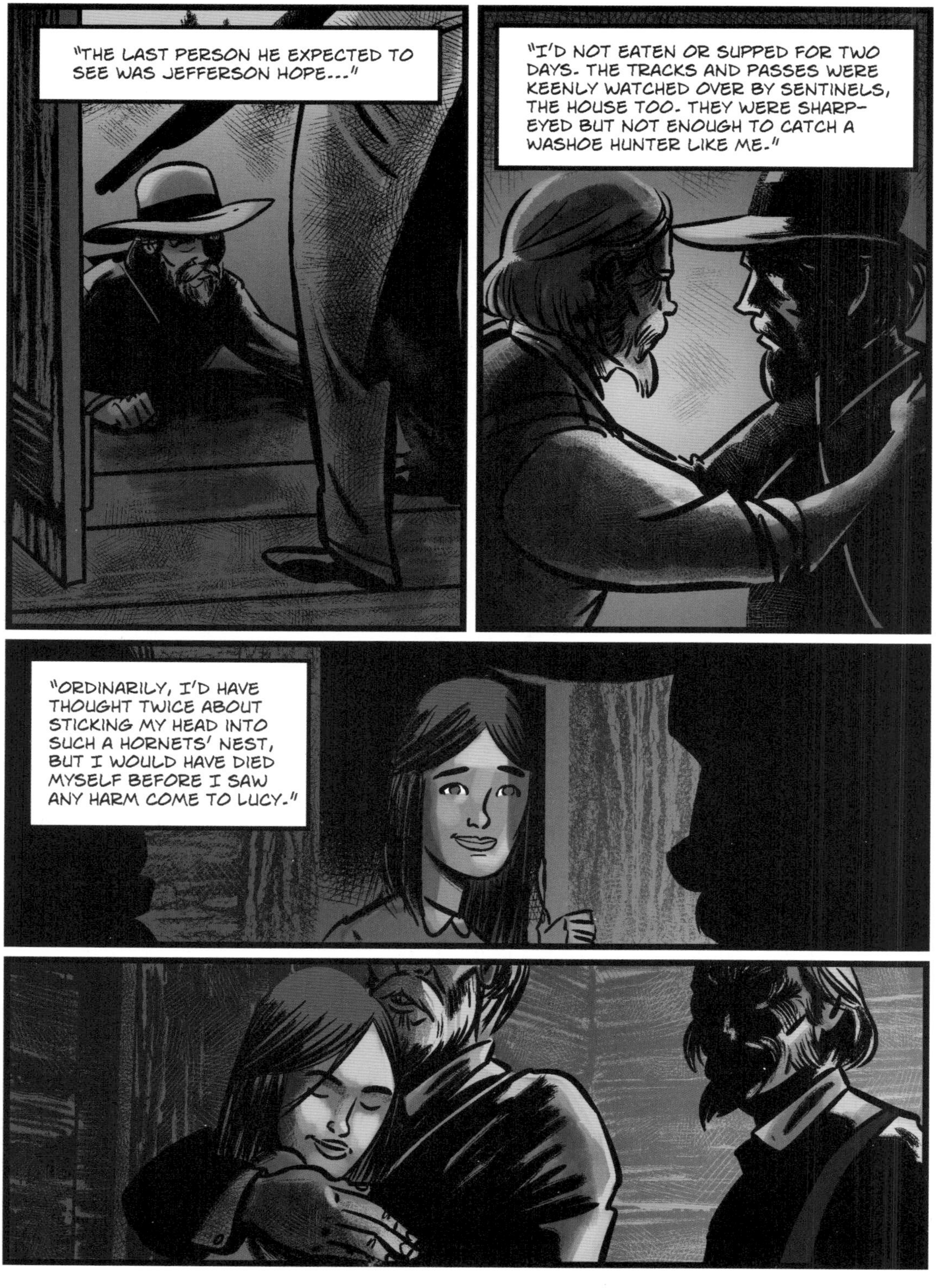
"THE LAST PERSON HE EXPECTED TO SEE WAS JEFFERSON HOPE..."
"I'D NOT EATEN OR SUPPED FOR TWO DAYS. THE TRACKS AND PASSES WERE KEENLY WATCHED OVER BY SENTINELS, THE HOUSE TOO. THEY WERE SHARP-EYED BUT NOT ENOUGH TO CATCH A WASHOE HUNTER LIKE ME."
"ORDINARILY, I'D HAVE THOUGHT TWICE ABOUT STICKING MY HEAD INTO SUCH A HORNETS' NEST, BUT I WOULD HAVE DIED MYSELF BEFORE I SAW ANY HARM COME TO LUCY."

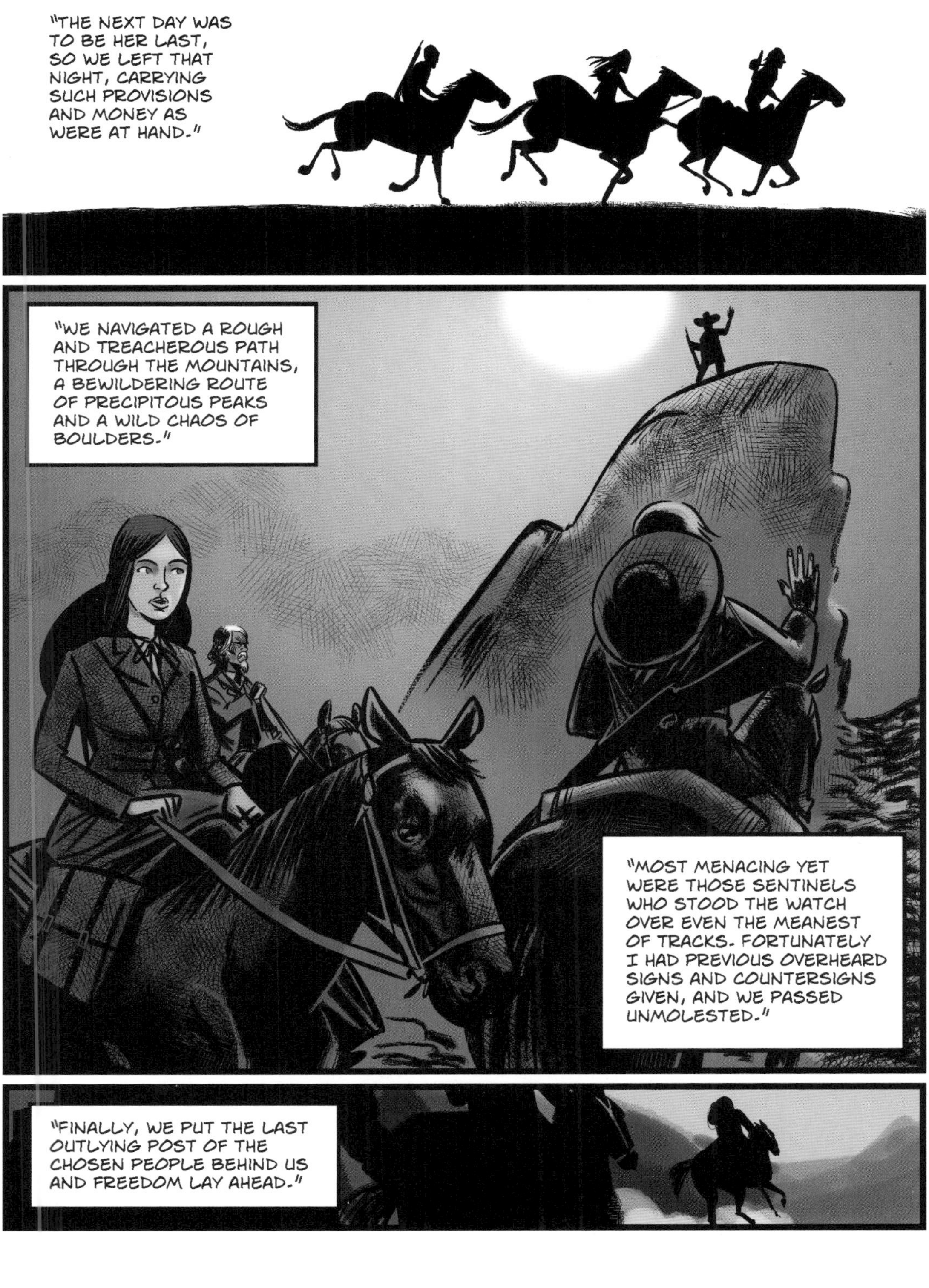
"THE NEXT DAY WAS TO BE HER LAST, SO WE LEFT THAT NIGHT, CARRYING SUCH PROVISIONS AND MONEY AS WERE AT HAND."
"WE NAVIGATED A ROUGH AND TREACHEROUS PATH THROUGH THE MOUNTAINS, A BEWILDERING ROUTE OF PRECIPITOUS PEAKS AND A WILD CHAOS OF BOULDERS."
"MOST MENACING YET WERE THOSE SENTINELS WHO STOOD THE WATCH OVER EVEN THE MEANEST OF TRACKS. FORTUNATELY I HAD PREVIOUS OVERHEARD SIGNS AND COUNTERSIGNS GIVEN, AND WE PASSED UNMOLESTED."
"FINALLY, WE PUT THE LAST OUTLYING POST OF THE CHOSEN PEOPLE BEHIND US AND FREEDOM LAY AHEAD."

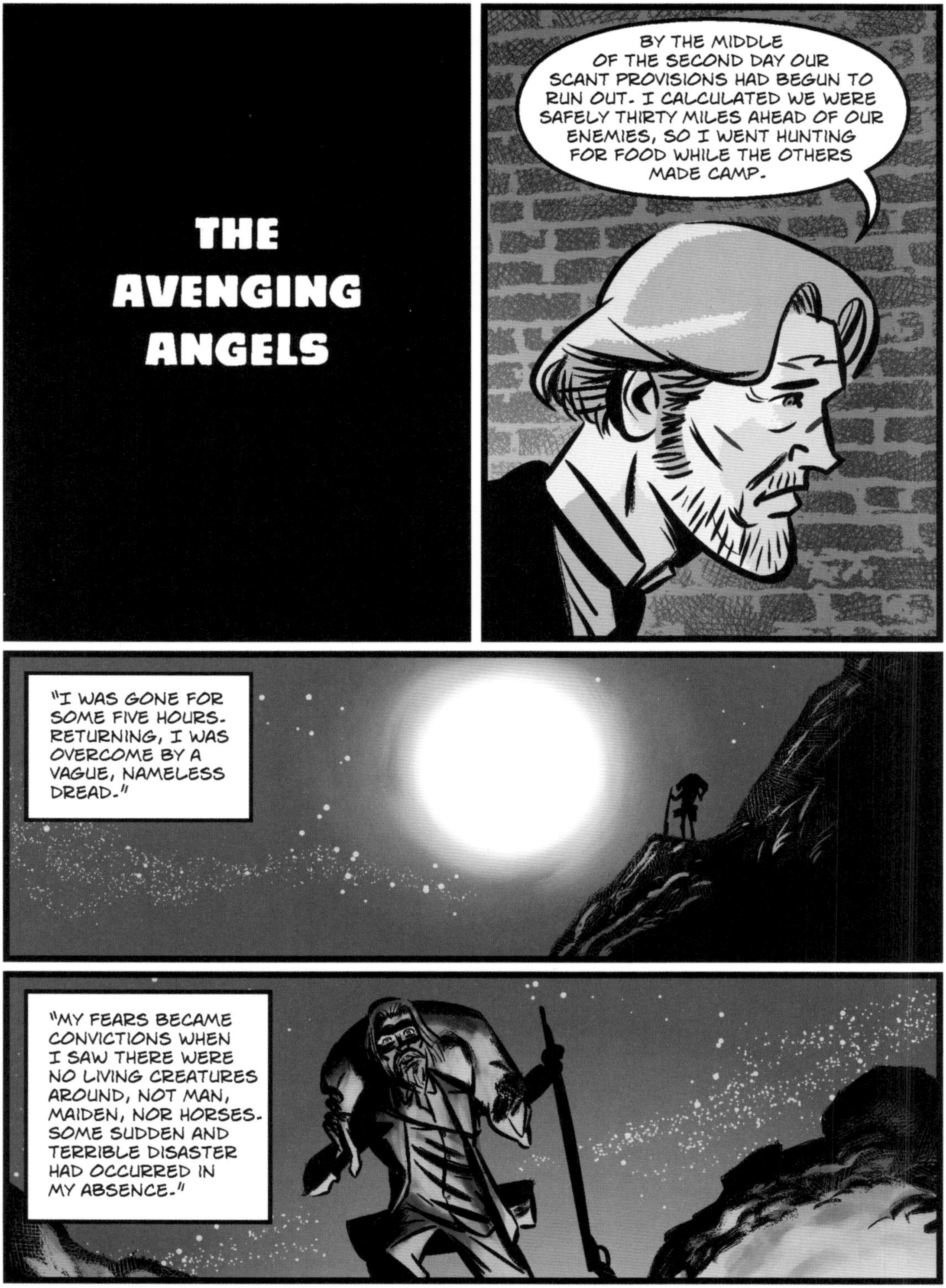
THE AVENGING ANGELS
BY THE MIDDLE OF THE SECOND DAY OUR SCANT PROVISIONS HAD BEGUN TO RUN OUT. I CALCULATED WE WERE SAFELY THIRTY MILES AHEAD OF OUR ENEMIES, SO I WENT HUNTING FOR FOOD WHILE THE OTHERS MADE CAMP.
"I WAS GONE FOR SOME FIVE HOURS. RETURNING, I WAS OVERCOME BY A VAGUE, NAMELESS DREAD."
"MY FEARS BECAME CONVICTIONS WHEN I SAW THERE WERE NO LIVING CREATURES AROUND, NOT MAN, MAIDEN, NOR HORSES. SOME SUDDEN AND TERRIBLE DISASTER HAD OCCURRED IN MY ABSENCE."

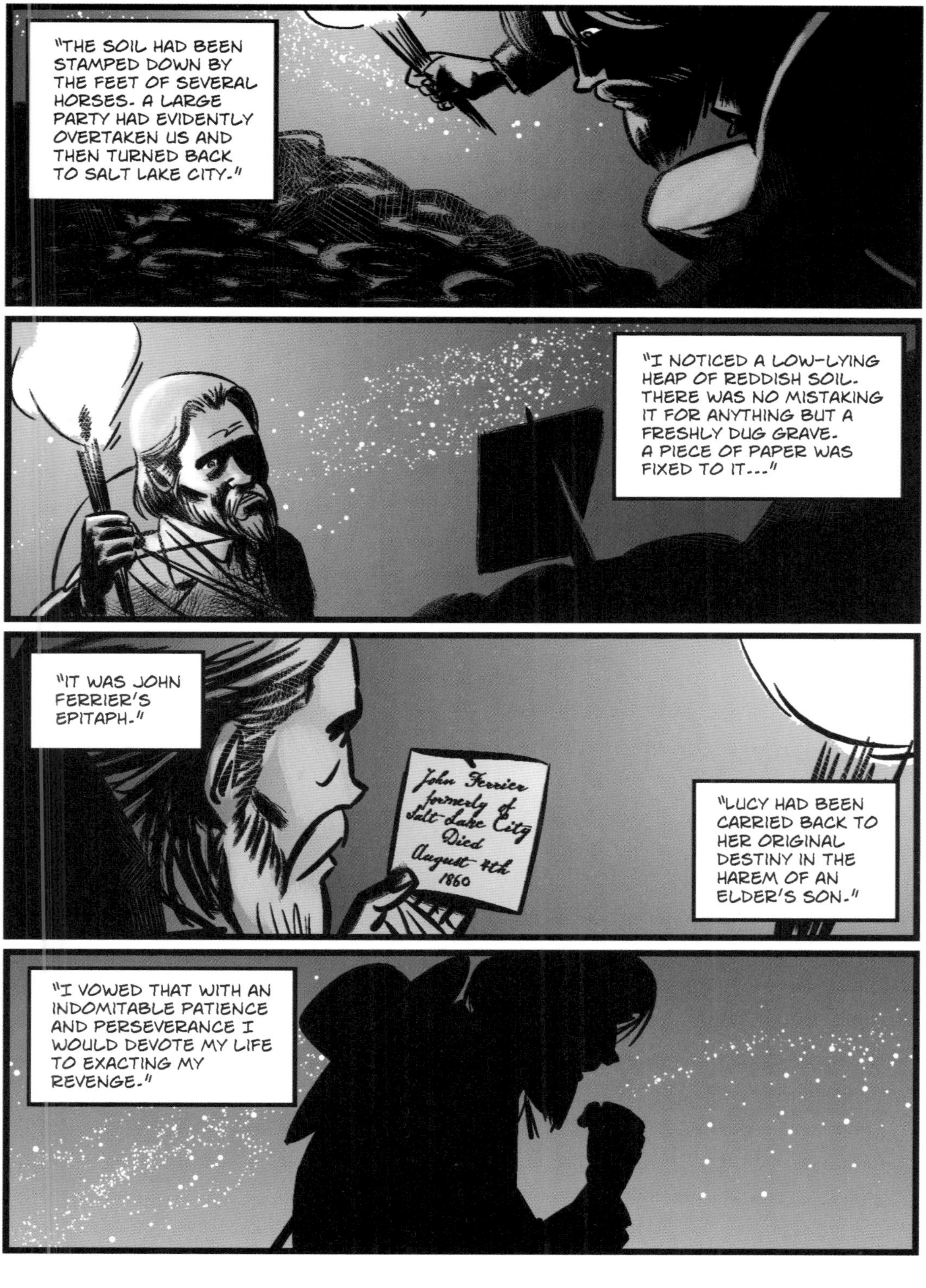
"THE SOIL HAD BEEN STAMPED DOWN BY THE FEET OF SEVERAL HORSES. A LARGE PARTY HAD EVIDENTLY OVERTAKEN US AND THEN TURNED BACK TO SALT LAKE CITY."
"I NOTICED A LOW-LYING HEAP OF REDDISH SOIL. THERE WAS NO MISTAKING IT FOR ANYTHING BUT A FRESHLY DUG GRAVE. A PIECE OF PAPER WAS FIXED TO IT..."
"IT WAS JOHN FERRIER'S EPITAPH."
John Ferrier formerly of Salt Lake City Died August 4th 1860
"LUCY HAD BEEN CARRIED BACK TO HER ORIGINAL DESTINY IN THE HAREM OF AN ELDER'S SON."
"I VOWED THAT WITH AN INDOMITABLE PATIENCE AND PERSEVERANCE I WOULD DEVOTE MY LIFE TO EXACTING MY REVENGE."

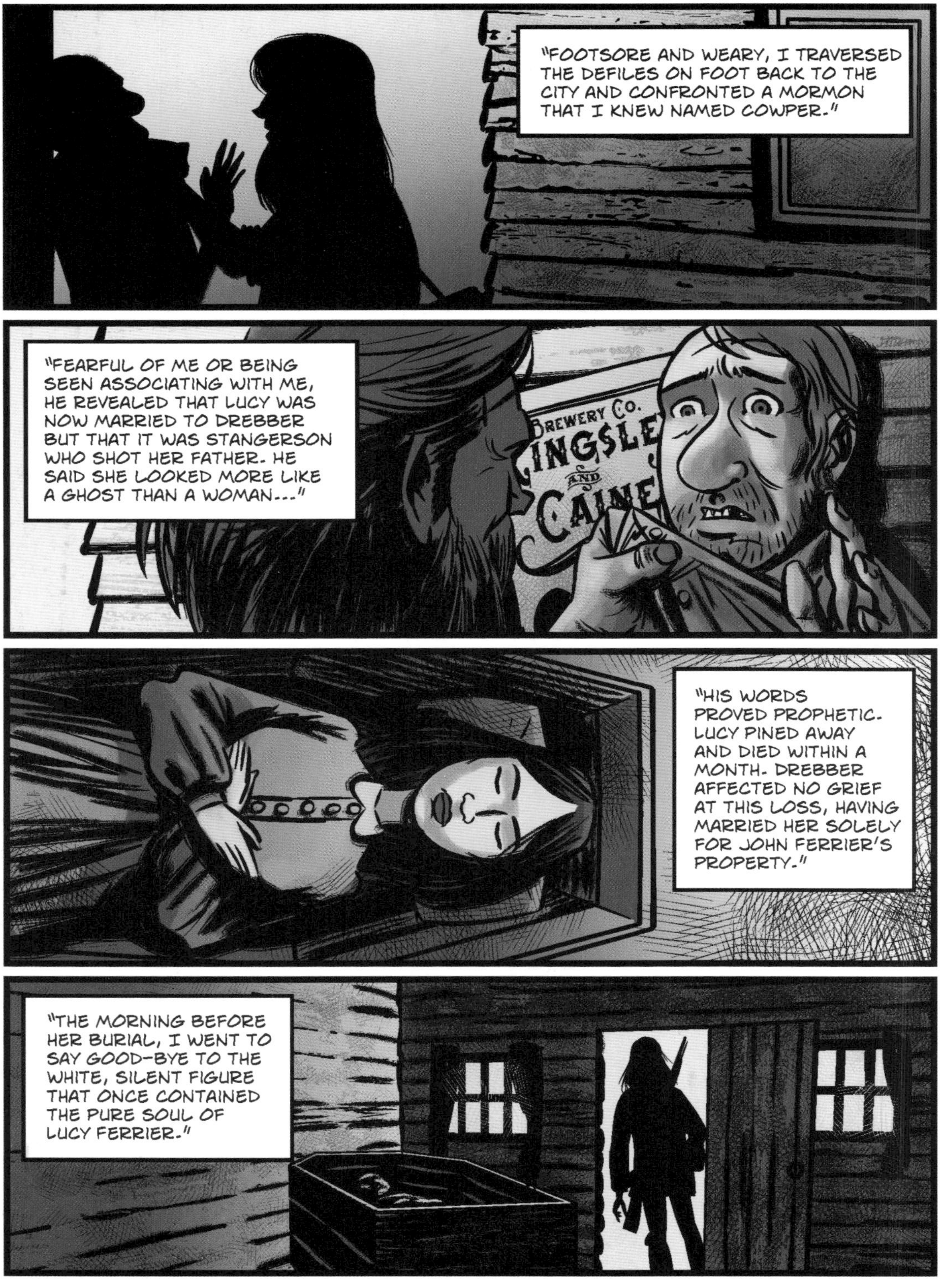
"FOOTSORE AND WEARY, I TRAVERSED THE DEFILES ON FOOT BACK TO THE CITY AND CONFRONTED A MORMON THAT I KNEW NAMED COWPER."
"FEARFUL OF ME OR BEING SEEN ASSOCIATING WITH ME, HE REVEALED THAT LUCY WAS NOW MARRIED TO DREBBER BUT THAT IT WAS STANGERSON WHO SHOT HER FATHER. HE SAID SHE LOOKED MORE LIKE A GHOST THAN A WOMAN..."
BREWERY CO.
INGSLE
AND
CAINE
"HIS WORDS PROVED PROPHETIC. LUCY PINED AWAY AND DIED WITHIN A MONTH. DREBBER AFFECTED NO GRIEF AT THIS LOSS, HAVING MARRIED HER SOLELY FOR JOHN FERRIER'S PROPERTY."
"THE MORNING BEFORE HER BURIAL, I WENT TO SAY GOOD-BYE TO THE WHITE, SILENT FIGURE THAT ONCE CONTAINED THE PURE SOUL OF LUCY FERRIER."

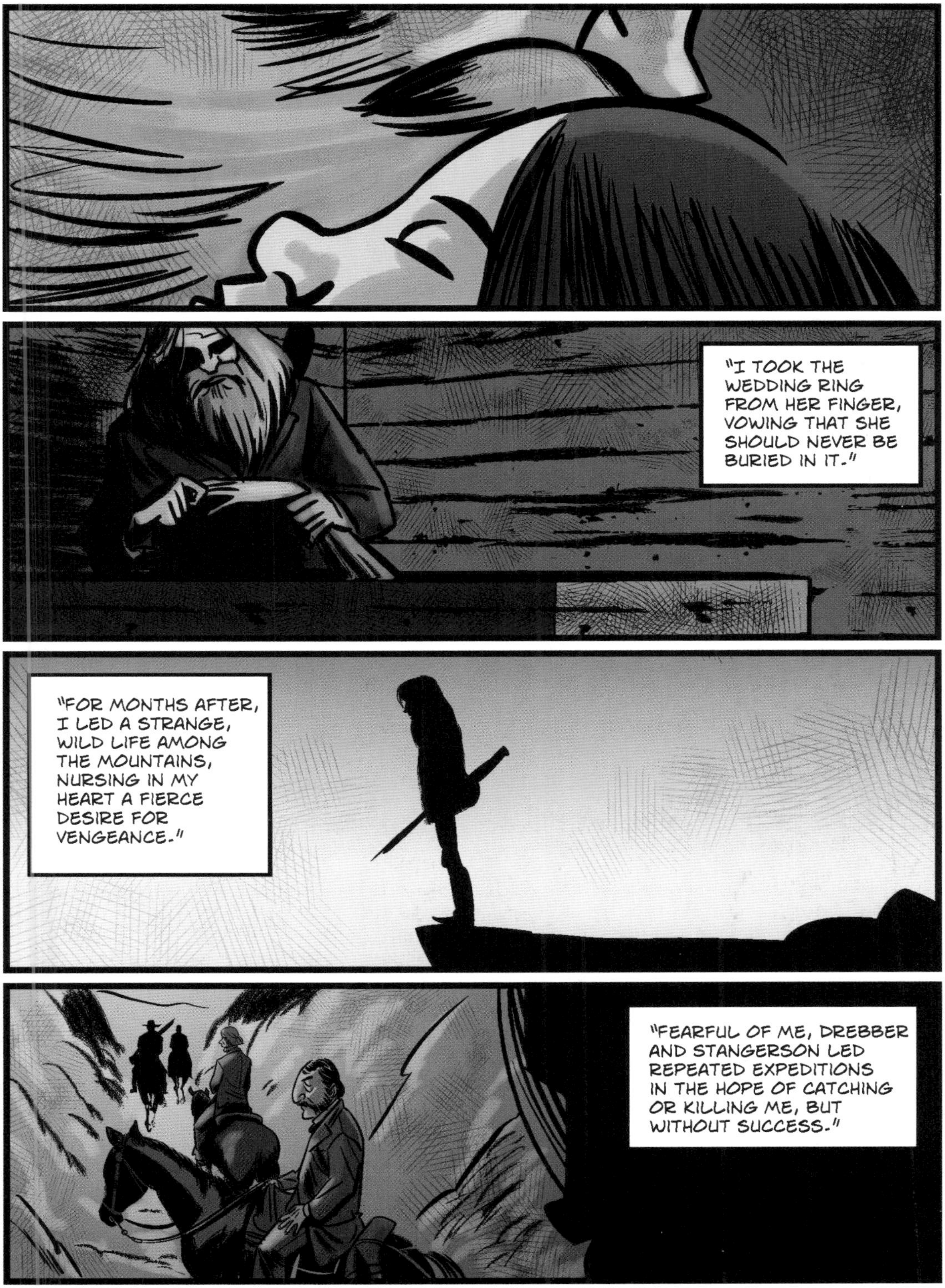
"I TOOK THE WEDDING RING FROM HER FINGER, VOWING THAT SHE SHOULD NEVER BE BURIED IN IT."
"FOR MONTHS AFTER, I LED A STRANGE, WILD LIFE AMONG THE MOUNTAINS, NURSING IN MY HEART A FIERCE DESIRE FOR VENGEANCE."
"FEARFUL OF ME, DREBBER AND STANGERSON LED REPEATED EXPEDITIONS IN THE HOPE OF CATCHING OR KILLING ME, BUT WITHOUT SUCCESS."

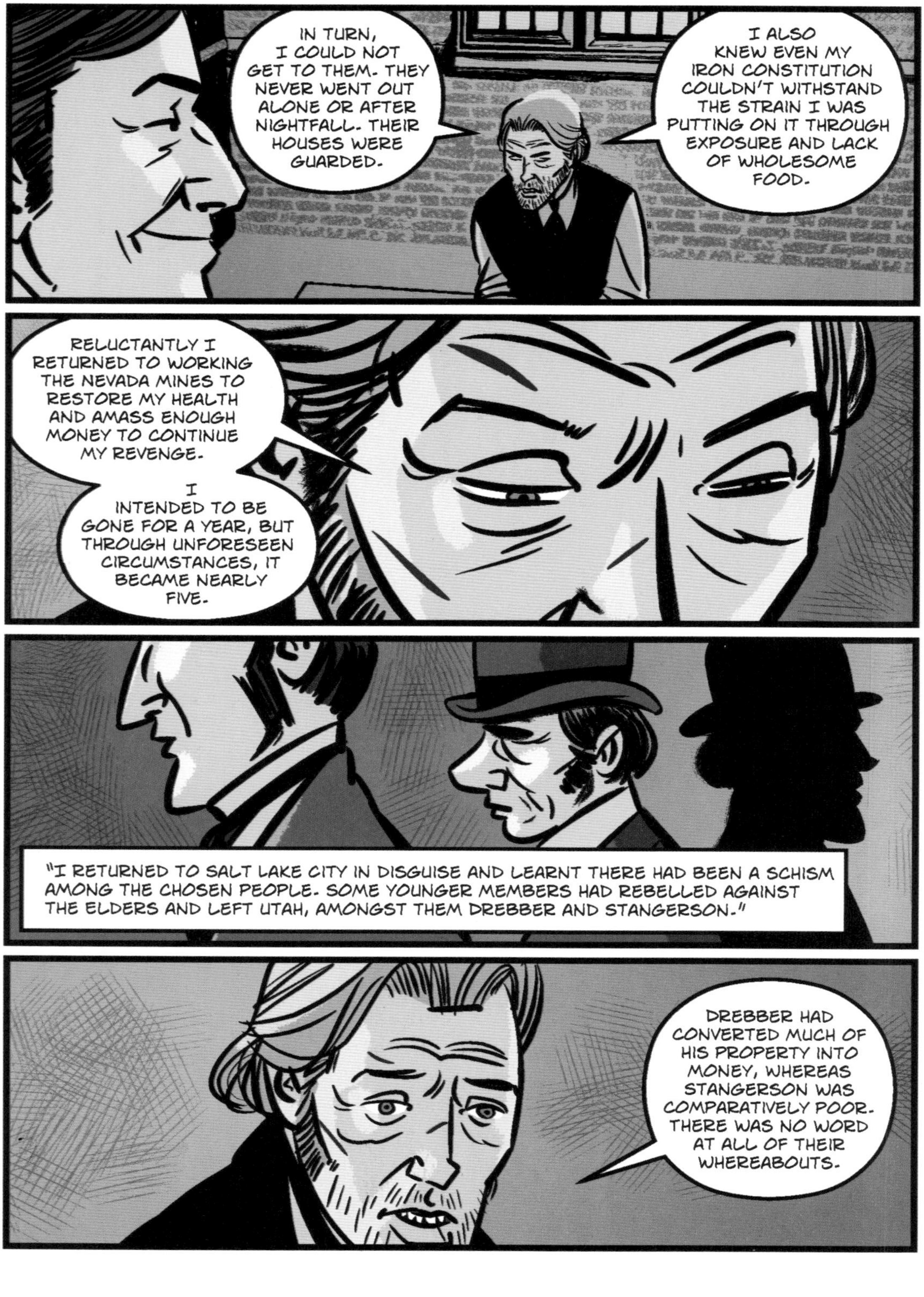
IN TURN, I COULD NOT GET TO THEM. THEY NEVER WENT OUT ALONE OR AFTER NIGHTFALL. THEIR HOUSES WERE GUARDED.
I ALSO KNEW EVEN MY IRON CONSTITUTION COULDN'T WITHSTAND THE STRAIN I WAS PUTTING ON IT THROUGH EXPOSURE AND LACK OF WHOLESOME FOOD.
RELUCTANTLY I RETURNED TO WORKING THE NEVADA MINES TO RESTORE MY HEALTH AND AMASS ENOUGH MONEY TO CONTINUE MY REVENGE.
I INTENDED TO BE GONE FOR A YEAR, BUT THROUGH UNFORESEEN CIRCUMSTANCES, IT BECAME NEARLY FIVE.
"I RETURNED TO SALT LAKE CITY IN DISGUISE AND LEARNT THERE HAD BEEN A SCHISM AMONG THE CHOSEN PEOPLE. SOME YOUNGER MEMBERS HAD REBELLED AGAINST THE ELDERS AND LEFT UTAH, AMONGST THEM DREBBER AND STANGERSON."
DREBBER HAD CONVERTED MUCH OF HIS PROPERTY INTO MONEY, WHEREAS STANGERSON WAS COMPARATIVELY POOR. THERE WAS NO WORD AT ALL OF THEIR WHEREABOUTS.

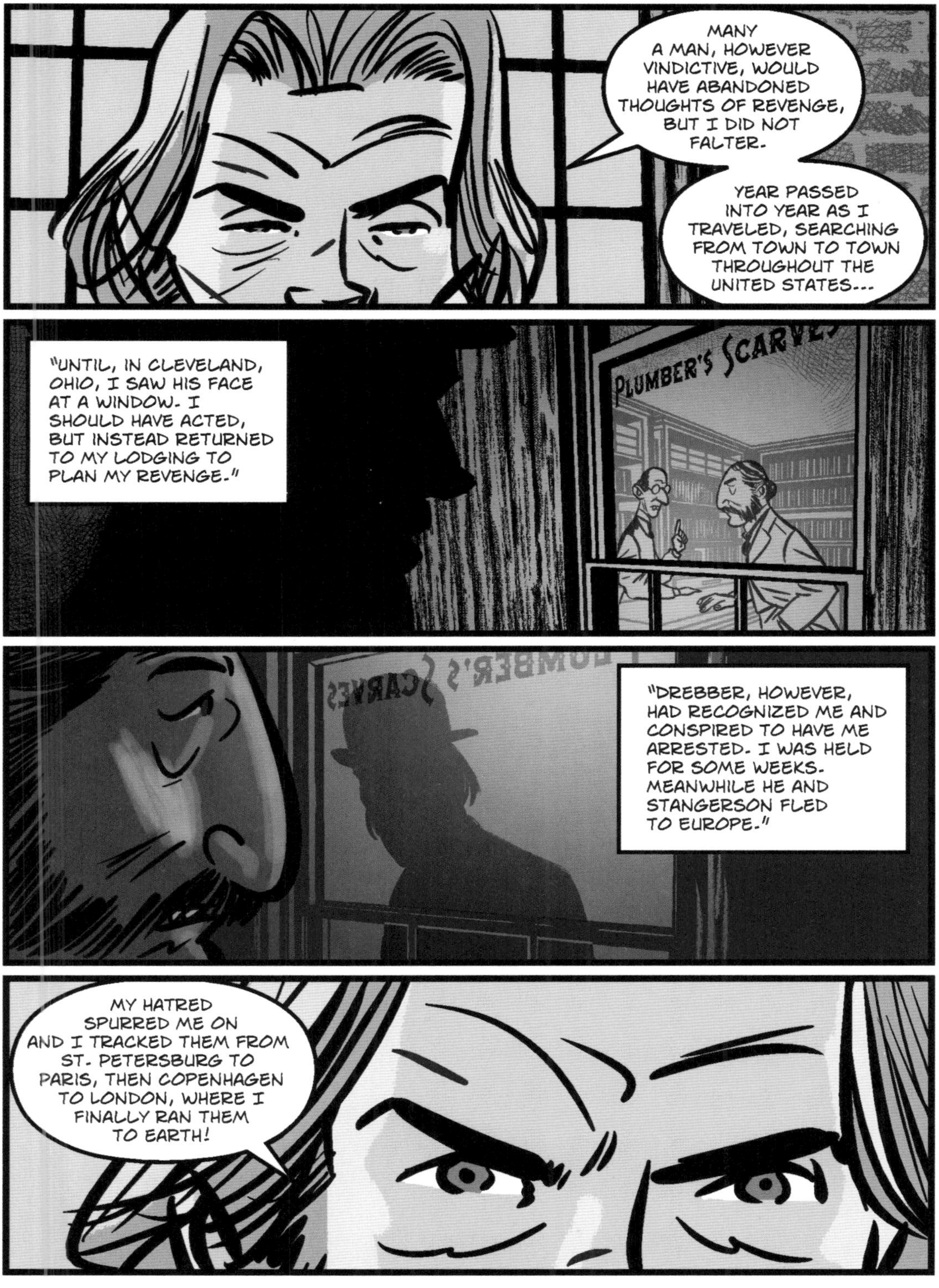
MANY A MAN, HOWEVER VINDICTIVE, WOULD HAVE ABANDONED THOUGHTS OF REVENGE, BUT I DID NOT FALTER.
YEAR PASSED INTO YEAR AS I TRAVELED, SEARCHING FROM TOWN TO TOWN THROUGHOUT THE UNITED STATES...
"UNTIL, IN CLEVELAND, OHIO, I SAW HIS FACE AT A WINDOW. I SHOULD HAVE ACTED, BUT INSTEAD RETURNED TO MY LODGING TO PLAN MY REVENGE."
PLUMBER'S SCARVES
"DREBBER, HOWEVER, HAD RECOGNIZED ME AND CONSPIRED TO HAVE ME ARRESTED. I WAS HELD FOR SOME WEEKS. MEANWHILE HE AND STANGERSON FLED TO EUROPE."
MY HATRED SPURRED ME ON AND I TRACKED THEM FROM ST. PETERSBURG TO PARIS, THEN COPENHAGEN TO LONDON, WHERE I FINALLY RAN THEM TO EARTH!

A CONTINUATION OF THE REMINISCENCES OF JOHN WATSON, M.D.

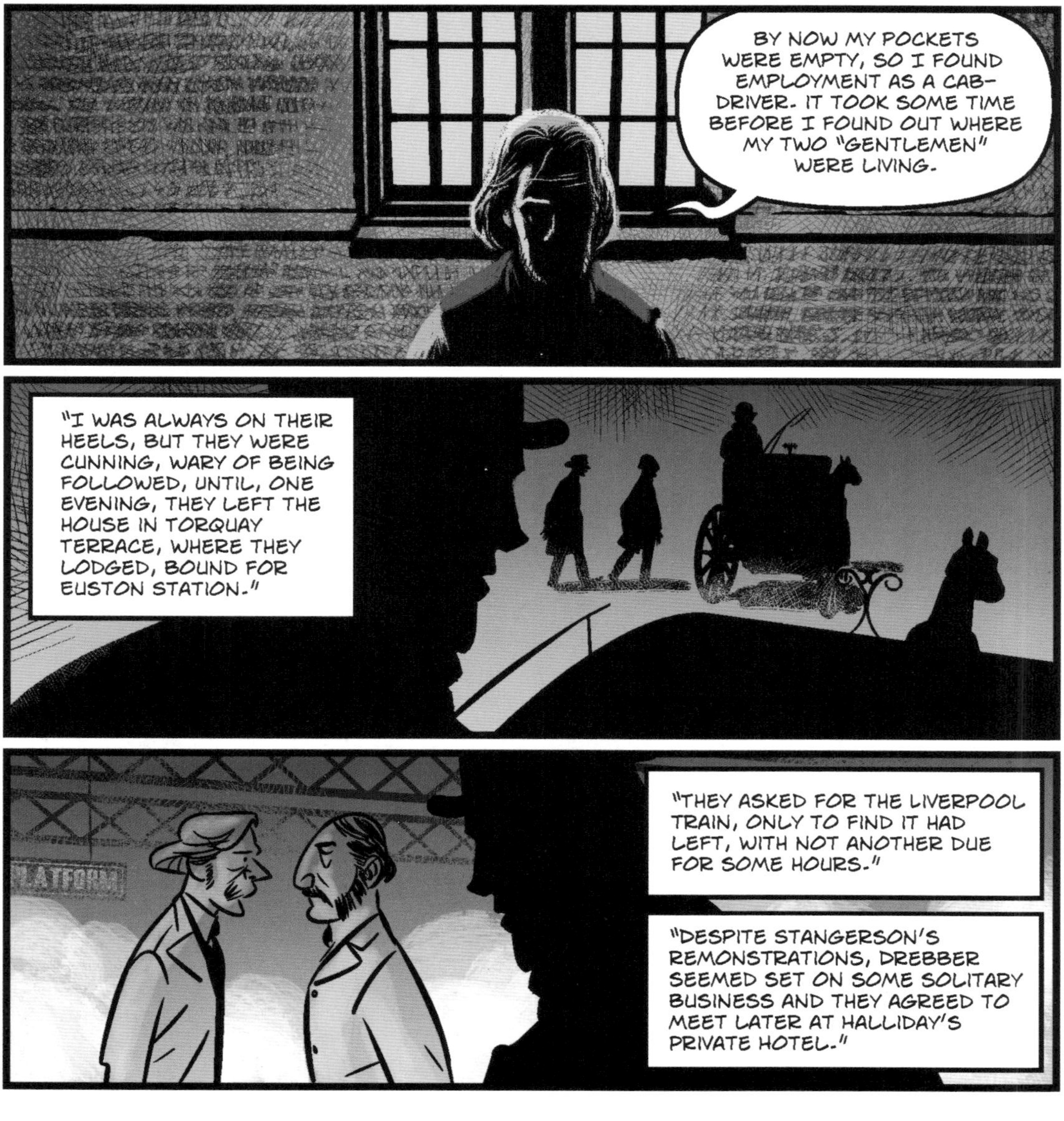
BY NOW MY POCKETS WERE EMPTY, SO I FOUND EMPLOYMENT AS A CAB-DRIVER. IT TOOK SOME TIME BEFORE I FOUND OUT WHERE MY TWO "GENTLEMEN" WERE LIVING.
"I WAS ALWAYS ON THEIR HEELS, BUT THEY WERE CUNNING, WARY OF BEING FOLLOWED, UNTIL, ONE EVENING, THEY LEFT THE HOUSE IN TORQUAY TERRACE, WHERE THEY LODGED, BOUND FOR EUSTON STATION."
"THEY ASKED FOR THE LIVERPOOL TRAIN, ONLY TO FIND IT HAD LEFT, WITH NOT ANOTHER DUE FOR SOME HOURS."
"DESPITE STANGERSON'S REMONSTRATIONS, DREBBER SEEMED SET ON SOME SOLITARY BUSINESS AND THEY AGREED TO MEET LATER AT HALLIDAY'S PRIVATE HOTEL."

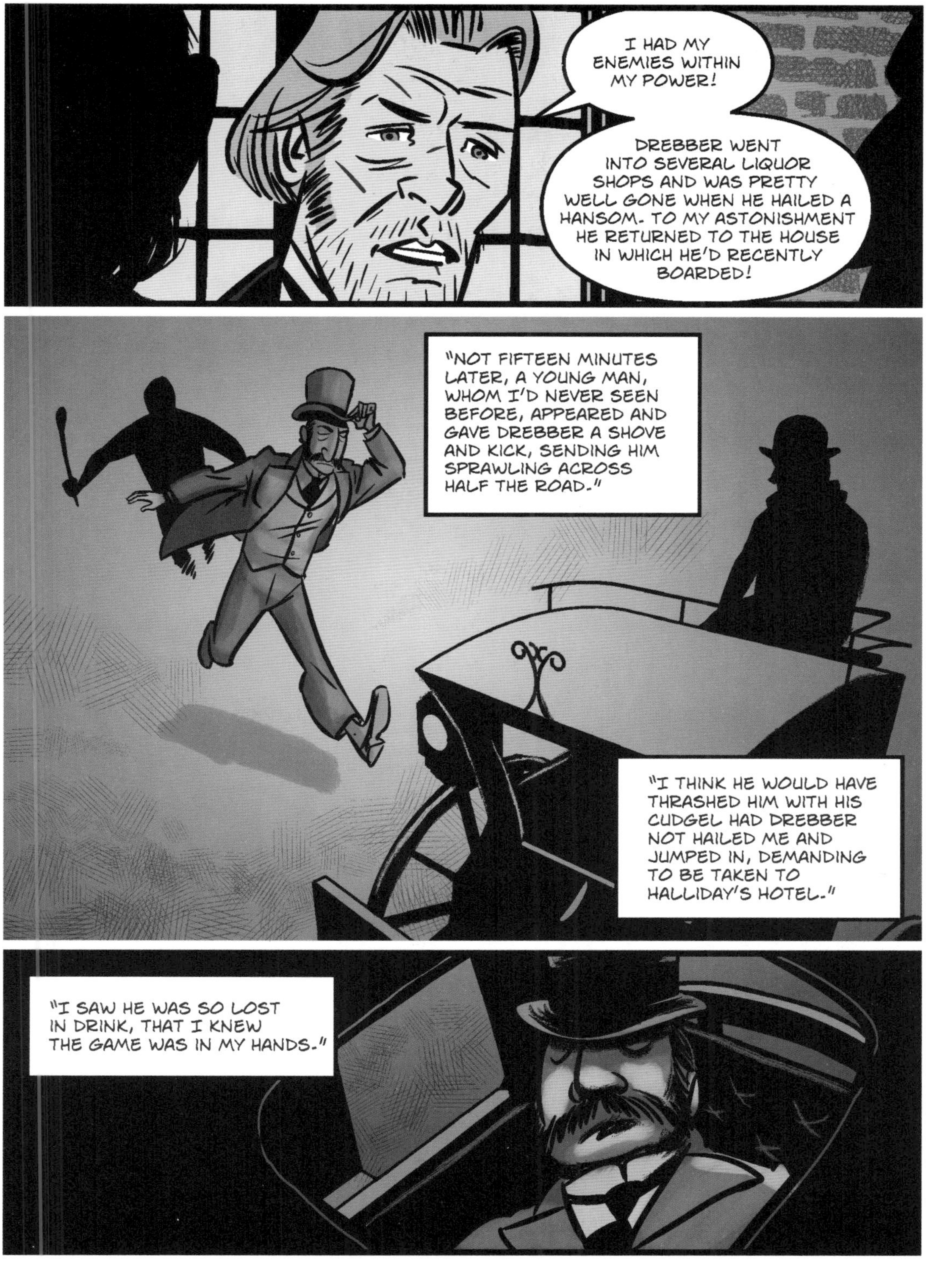
I HAD MY ENEMIES WITHIN MY POWER!
DREBBER WENT INTO SEVERAL LIQUOR SHOPS AND WAS PRETTY WELL GONE WHEN HE HAILED A HANSOM. TO MY ASTONISHMENT HE RETURNED TO THE HOUSE IN WHICH HE'D RECENTLY BOARDED!
"NOT FIFTEEN MINUTES LATER, A YOUNG MAN, WHOM I'D NEVER SEEN BEFORE, APPEARED AND GAVE DREBBER A SHOVE AND KICK, SENDING HIM SPRAWLING ACROSS HALF THE ROAD."
"I THINK HE WOULD HAVE THRASHED HIM WITH HIS CUDGEL HAD DREBBER NOT HAILED ME AND JUMPED IN, DEMANDING TO BE TAKEN TO HALLIDAY'S HOTEL."
"I SAW HE WAS SO LOST IN DRINK, THAT I KNEW THE GAME WAS IN MY HANDS."

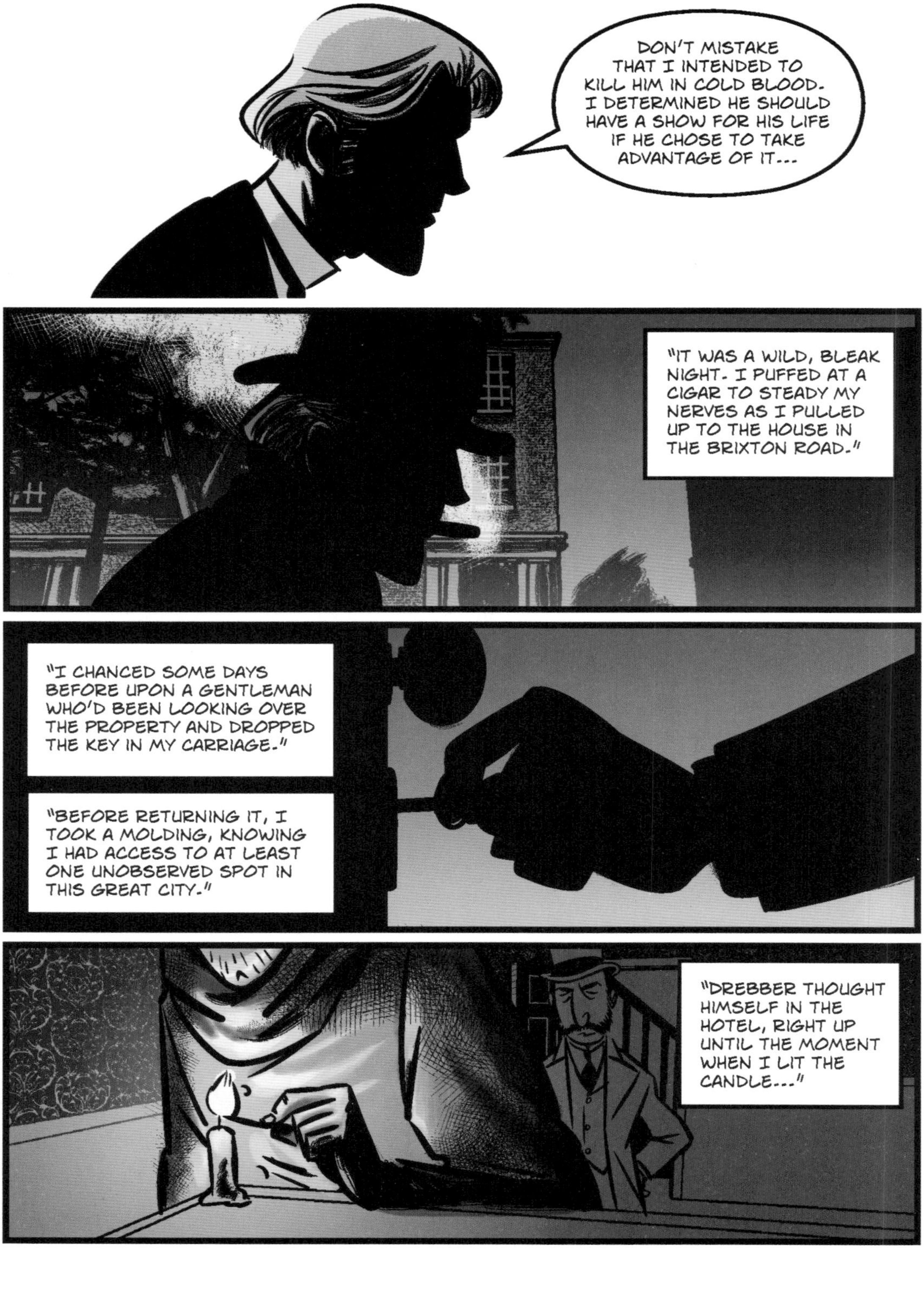
DON'T MISTAKE THAT I INTENDED TO KILL HIM IN COLD BLOOD. I DETERMINED HE SHOULD HAVE A SHOW FOR HIS LIFE IF HE CHOSE TO TAKE ADVANTAGE OF IT...
"IT WAS A WILD, BLEAK NIGHT. I PUFFED AT A CIGAR TO STEADY MY NERVES AS I PULLED UP TO THE HOUSE IN THE BRIXTON ROAD."
"I CHANCED SOME DAYS BEFORE UPON A GENTLEMAN WHO'D BEEN LOOKING OVER THE PROPERTY AND DROPPED THE KEY IN MY CARRIAGE."
"BEFORE RETURNING IT, I TOOK A MOLDING, KNOWING I HAD ACCESS TO AT LEAST ONE UNOBSERVED SPOT IN THIS GREAT CITY."
"DREBBER THOUGHT HIMSELF IN THE HOTEL, RIGHT UP UNTIL THE MOMENT WHEN I LIT THE CANDLE..."

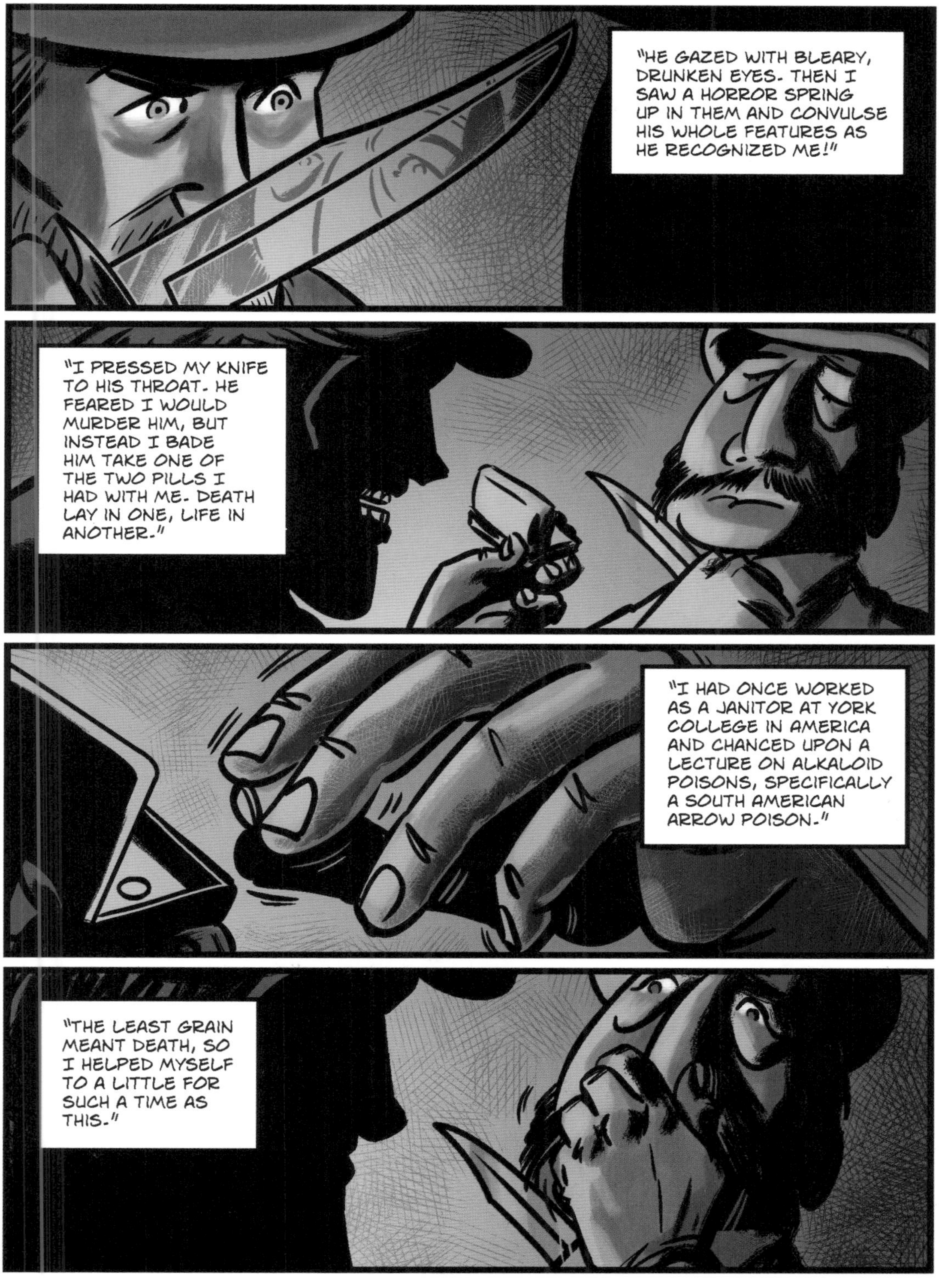
"HE GAZED WITH BLEARY, DRUNKEN EYES. THEN I SAW A HORROR SPRING UP IN THEM AND CONVULSE HIS WHOLE FEATURES AS HE RECOGNIZED ME!"
"I PRESSED MY KNIFE TO HIS THROAT. HE FEARED I WOULD MURDER HIM, BUT INSTEAD I BADE HIM TAKE ONE OF THE TWO PILLS I HAD WITH ME. DEATH LAY IN ONE, LIFE IN ANOTHER."
"I HAD ONCE WORKED AS A JANITOR AT YORK COLLEGE IN AMERICA AND CHANCED UPON A LECTURE ON ALKALOID POISONS, SPECIFICALLY A SOUTH AMERICAN ARROW POISON."
"THE LEAST GRAIN MEANT DEATH, SO I HELPED MYSELF TO A LITTLE FOR SUCH A TIME AS THIS."

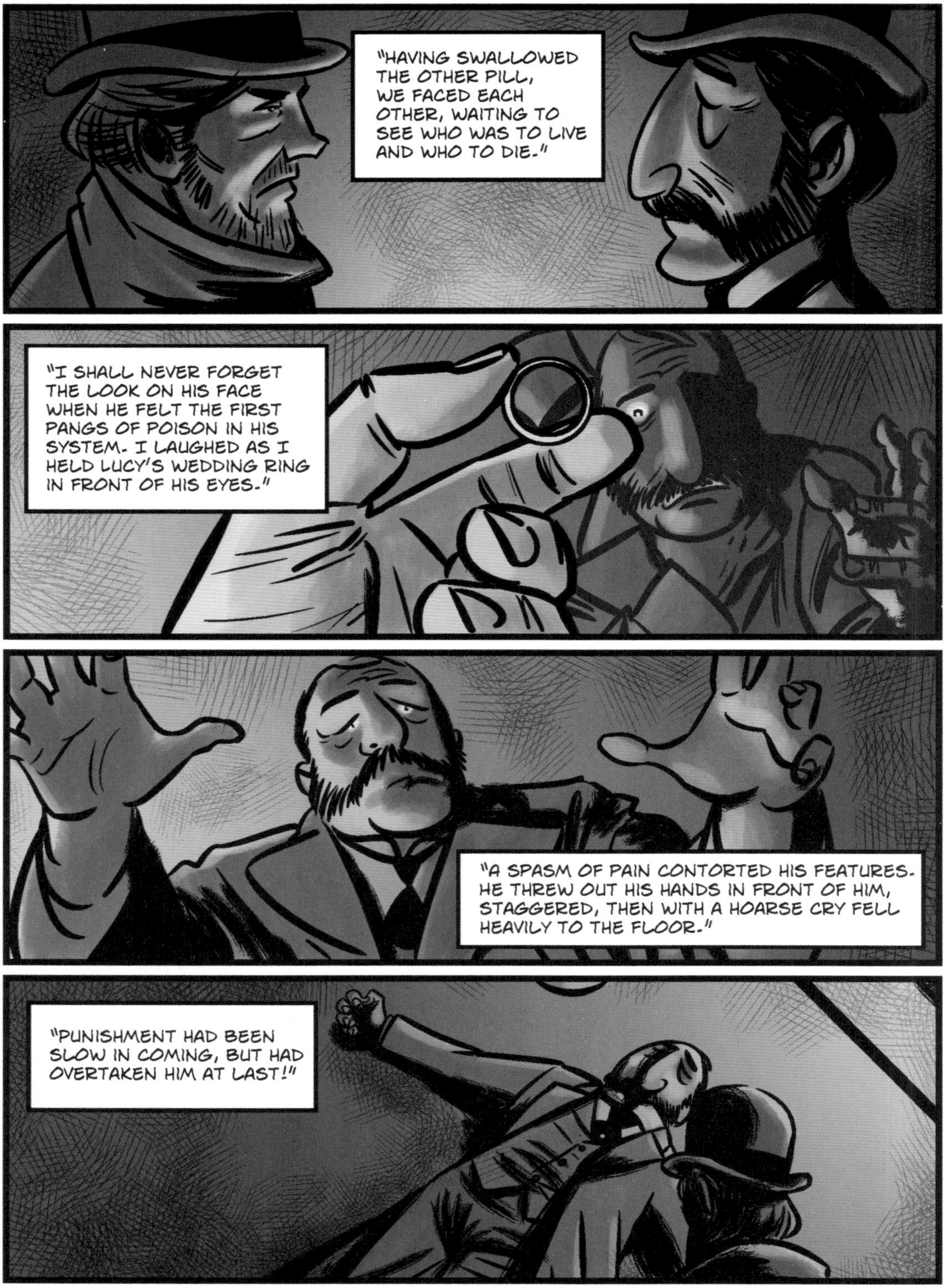
"HAVING SWALLOWED THE OTHER PILL, WE FACED EACH OTHER, WAITING TO SEE WHO WAS TO LIVE AND WHO TO DIE."
"I SHALL NEVER FORGET THE LOOK ON HIS FACE WHEN HE FELT THE FIRST PANGS OF POISON IN HIS SYSTEM. I LAUGHED AS I HELD LUCY'S WEDDING RING IN FRONT OF HIS EYES."
"A SPASM OF PAIN CONTORTED HIS FEATURES. HE THREW OUT HIS HANDS IN FRONT OF HIM, STAGGERED, THEN WITH A HOARSE CRY FELL HEAVILY TO THE FLOOR."
"PUNISHMENT HAD BEEN SLOW IN COMING, BUT HAD OVERTAKEN HIM AT LAST!"

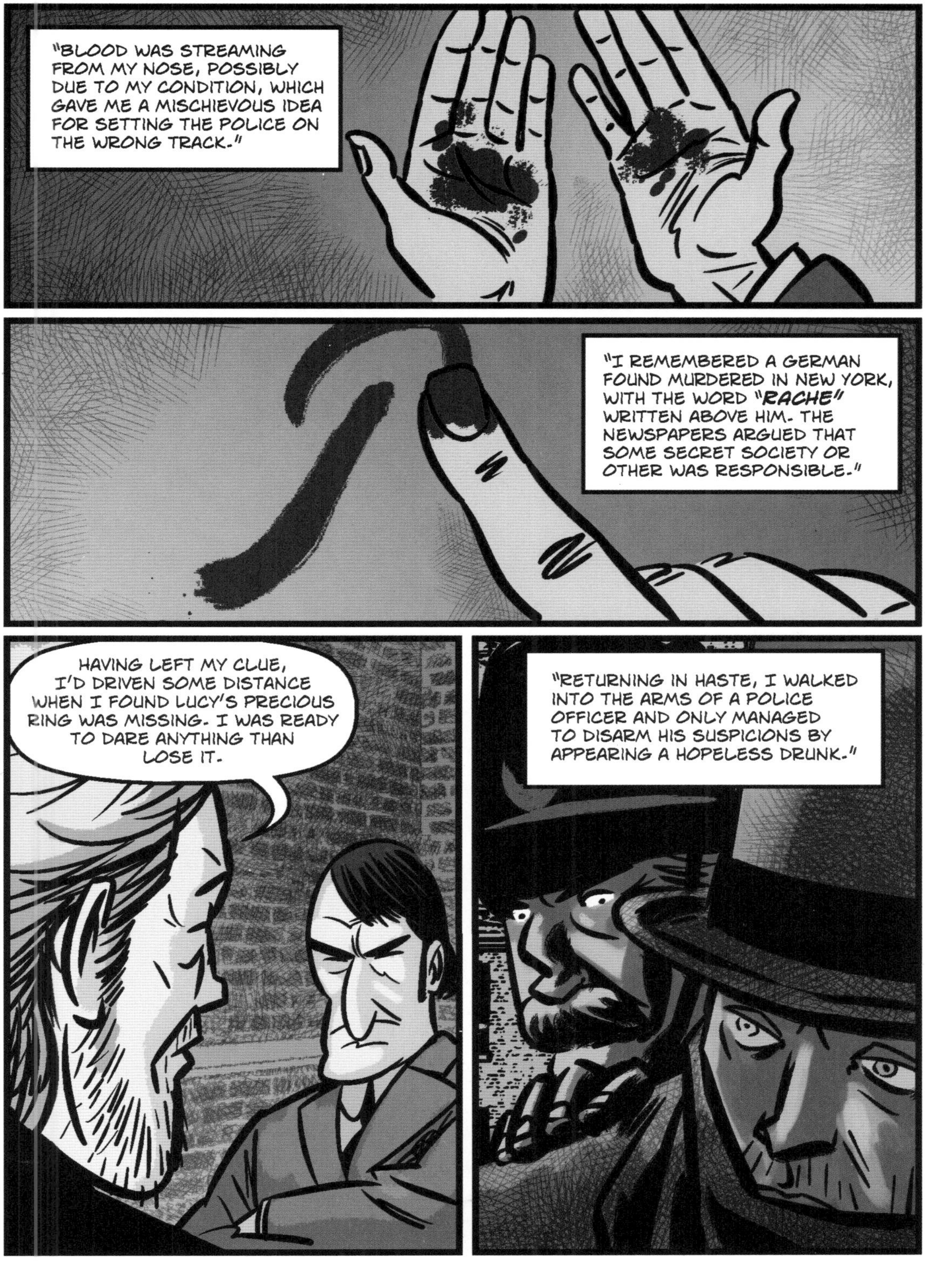
"BLOOD WAS STREAMING FROM MY NOSE, POSSIBLY DUE TO MY CONDITION, WHICH GAVE ME A MISCHIEVOUS IDEA FOR SETTING THE POLICE ON THE WRONG TRACK."
"I REMEMBERED A GERMAN FOUND MURDERED IN NEW YORK, WITH THE WORD "RACHE" WRITTEN ABOVE HIM. THE NEWSPAPERS ARGUED THAT SOME SECRET SOCIETY OR OTHER WAS RESPONSIBLE."
HAVING LEFT MY CLUE, I'D DRIVEN SOME DISTANCE WHEN I FOUND LUCY'S PRECIOUS RING WAS MISSING. I WAS READY TO DARE ANYTHING THAN LOSE IT.
"RETURNING IN HASTE, I WALKED INTO THE ARMS OF A POLICE OFFICER AND ONLY MANAGED TO DISARM HIS SUSPICIONS BY APPEARING A HOPELESS DRUNK."

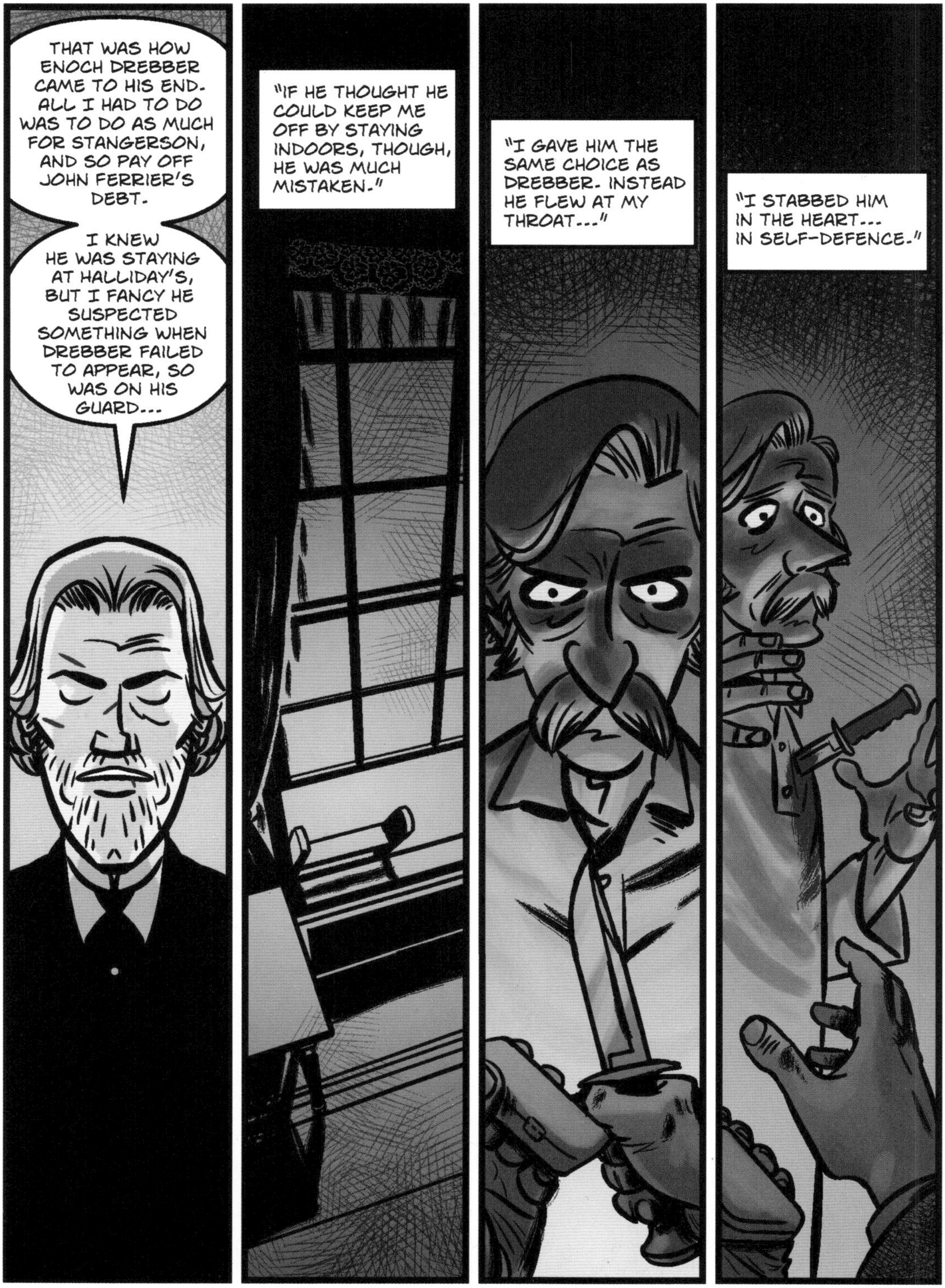
THAT WAS HOW ENOCH DREBBER CAME TO HIS END. ALL I HAD TO DO WAS TO DO AS MUCH FOR STANGERSON, AND SO PAY OFF JOHN FERRIER'S DEBT.
I KNEW HE WAS STAYING AT HALLIDAY'S, BUT I FANCY HE SUSPECTED SOMETHING WHEN DREBBER FAILED TO APPEAR, SO WAS ON HIS GUARD...
"IF HE THOUGHT HE COULD KEEP ME OFF BY STAYING INDOORS, THOUGH, HE WAS MUCH MISTAKEN."
"I GAVE HIM THE SAME CHOICE AS DREBBER. INSTEAD HE FLEW AT MY THROAT..."
"I STABBED HIM IN THE HEART... IN SELF-DEFENCE."

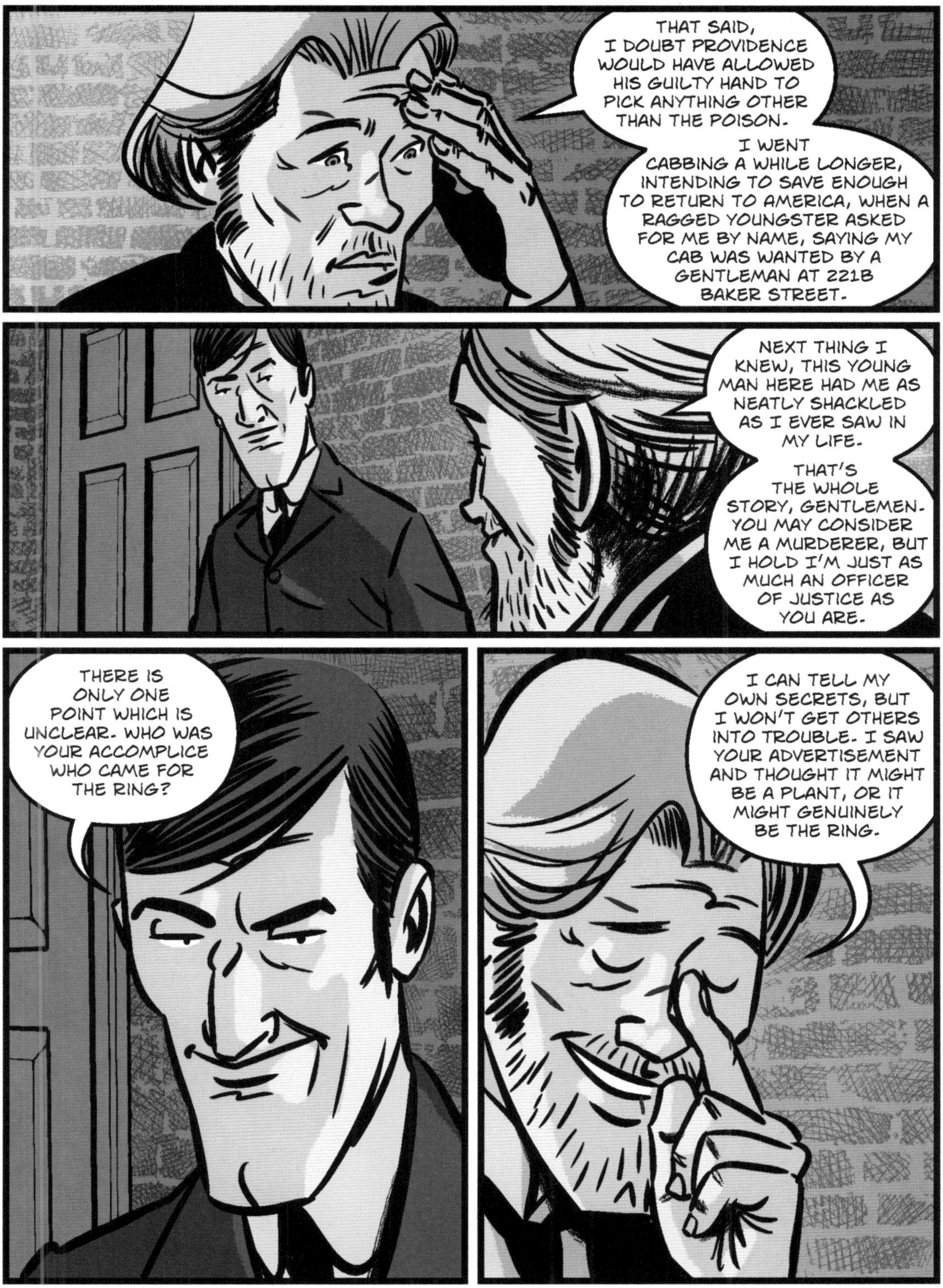
THAT SAID, I DOUBT PROVIDENCE WOULD HAVE ALLOWED HIS GUILTY HAND TO PICK ANYTHING OTHER THAN THE POISON.
I WENT CABBING A WHILE LONGER, INTENDING TO SAVE ENOUGH TO RETURN TO AMERICA, WHEN A RAGGED YOUNGSTER ASKED FOR ME BY NAME, SAYING MY CAB WAS WANTED BY A GENTLEMAN AT 221B BAKER STREET.
NEXT THING I KNEW, THIS YOUNG MAN HERE HAD ME AS NEATLY SHACKLED AS I EVER SAW IN MY LIFE.
THAT'S THE WHOLE STORY, GENTLEMEN. YOU MAY CONSIDER ME A MURDERER, BUT I HOLD I'M JUST AS MUCH AN OFFICER OF JUSTICE AS YOU ARE.
THERE IS ONLY ONE POINT WHICH IS UNCLEAR. WHO WAS YOUR ACCOMPLICE WHO CAME FOR THE RING?
I CAN TELL MY OWN SECRETS, BUT I WON'T GET OTHERS INTO TROUBLE. I SAW YOUR ADVERTISEMENT AND THOUGHT IT MIGHT BE A PLANT, OR IT MIGHT GENUINELY BE THE RING.

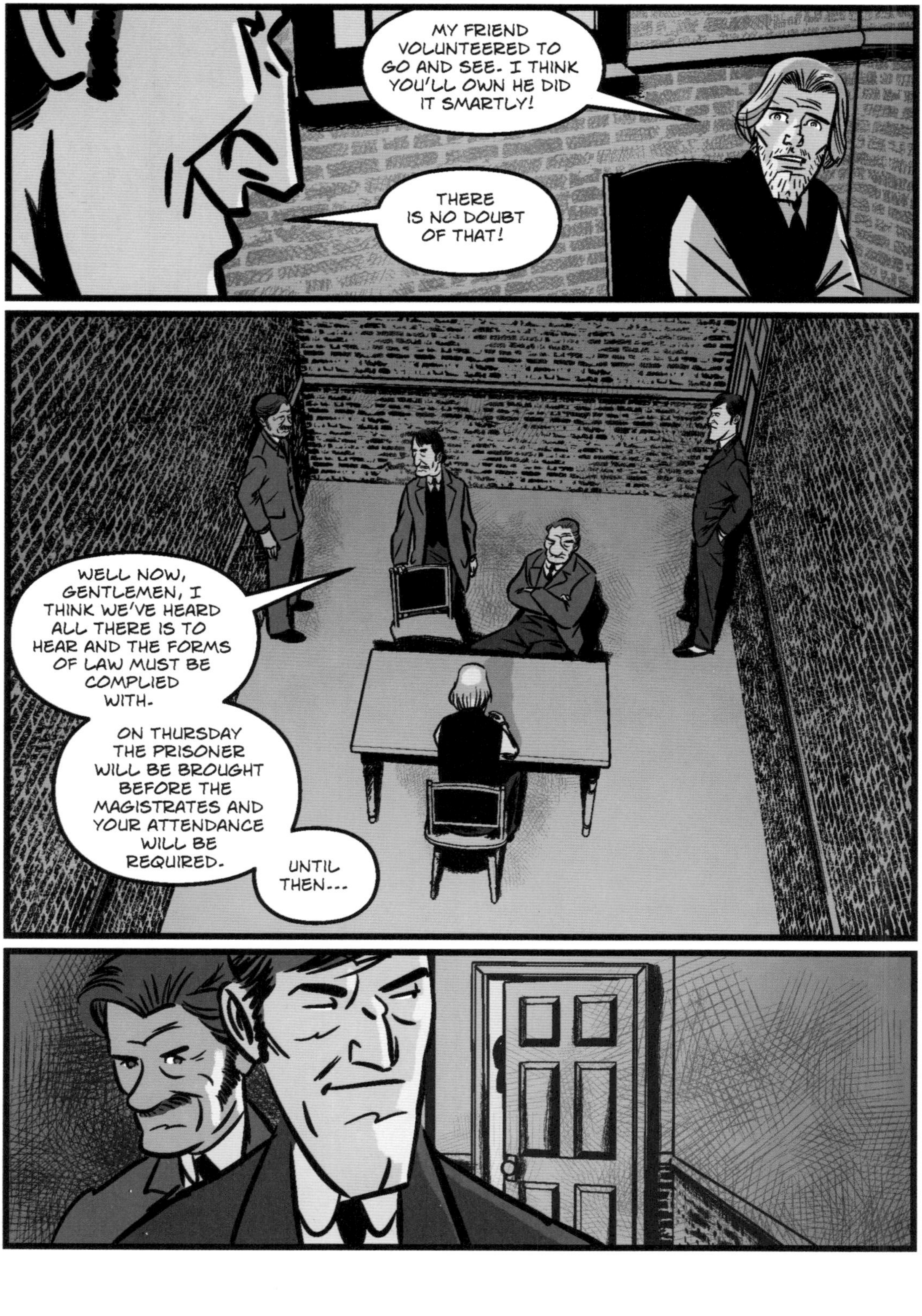
MY FRIEND VOLUNTEERED TO GO AND SEE. I THINK YOU'LL OWN HE DID IT SMARTLY!
THERE IS NO DOUBT OF THAT!
WELL NOW, GENTLEMEN, I THINK WE'VE HEARD ALL THERE IS TO HEAR AND THE FORMS OF LAW MUST BE COMPLIED WITH.
ON THURSDAY THE PRISONER WILL BE BROUGHT BEFORE THE MAGISTRATES AND YOUR ATTENDANCE WILL BE REQUIRED.
UNTIL THEN...

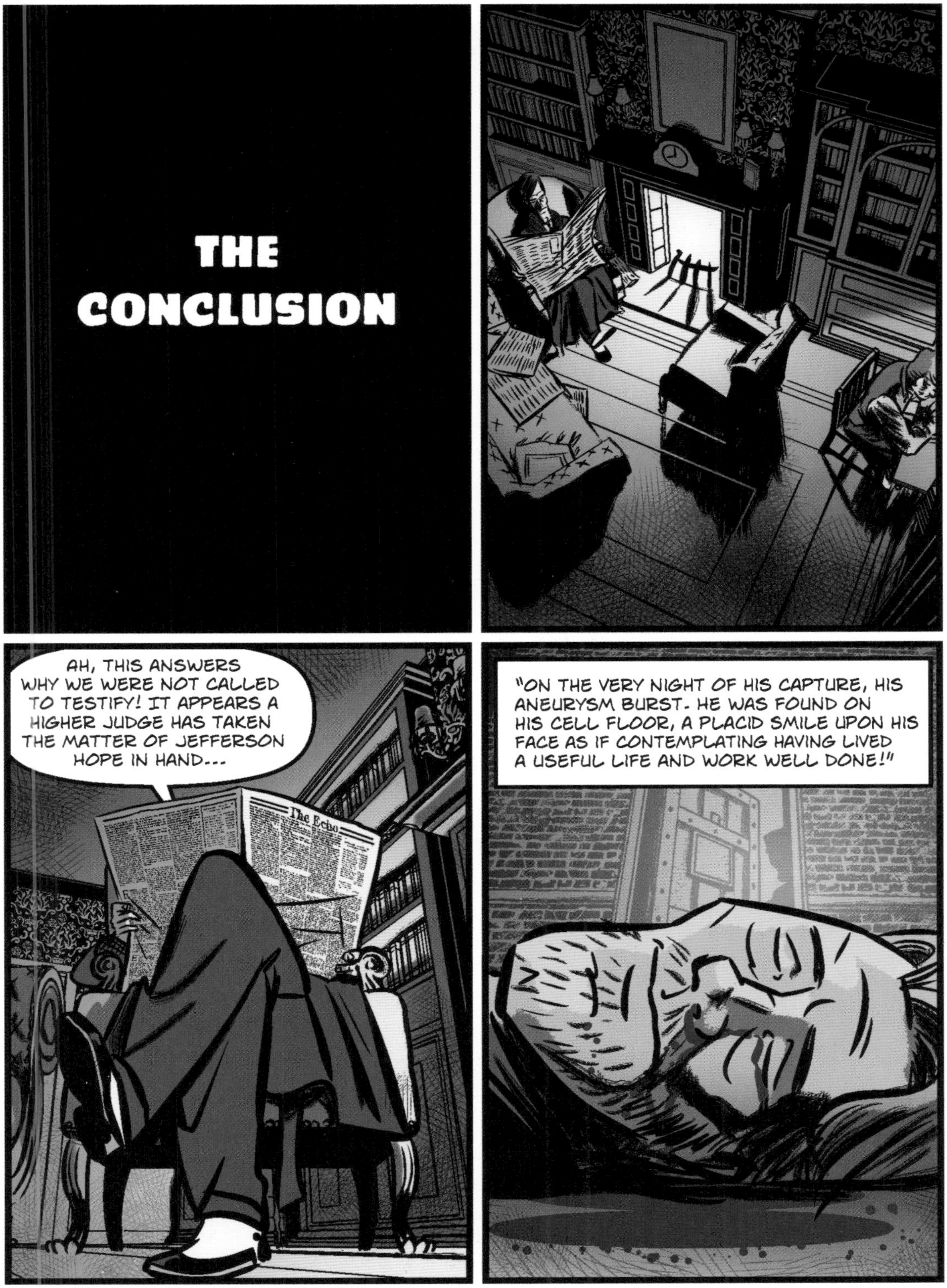
THE CONCLUSION
AH, THIS ANSWERS WHY WE WERE NOT CALLED TO TESTIFY! IT APPEARS A HIGHER JUDGE HAS TAKEN THE MATTER OF JEFFERSON HOPE IN HAND...
The Echo
"ON THE VERY NIGHT OF HIS CAPTURE, HIS ANEURYSM BURST. HE WAS FOUND ON HIS CELL FLOOR, A PLACID SMILE UPON HIS FACE AS IF CONTEMPLATING HAVING LIVED A USEFUL LIFE AND WORK WELL DONE!"

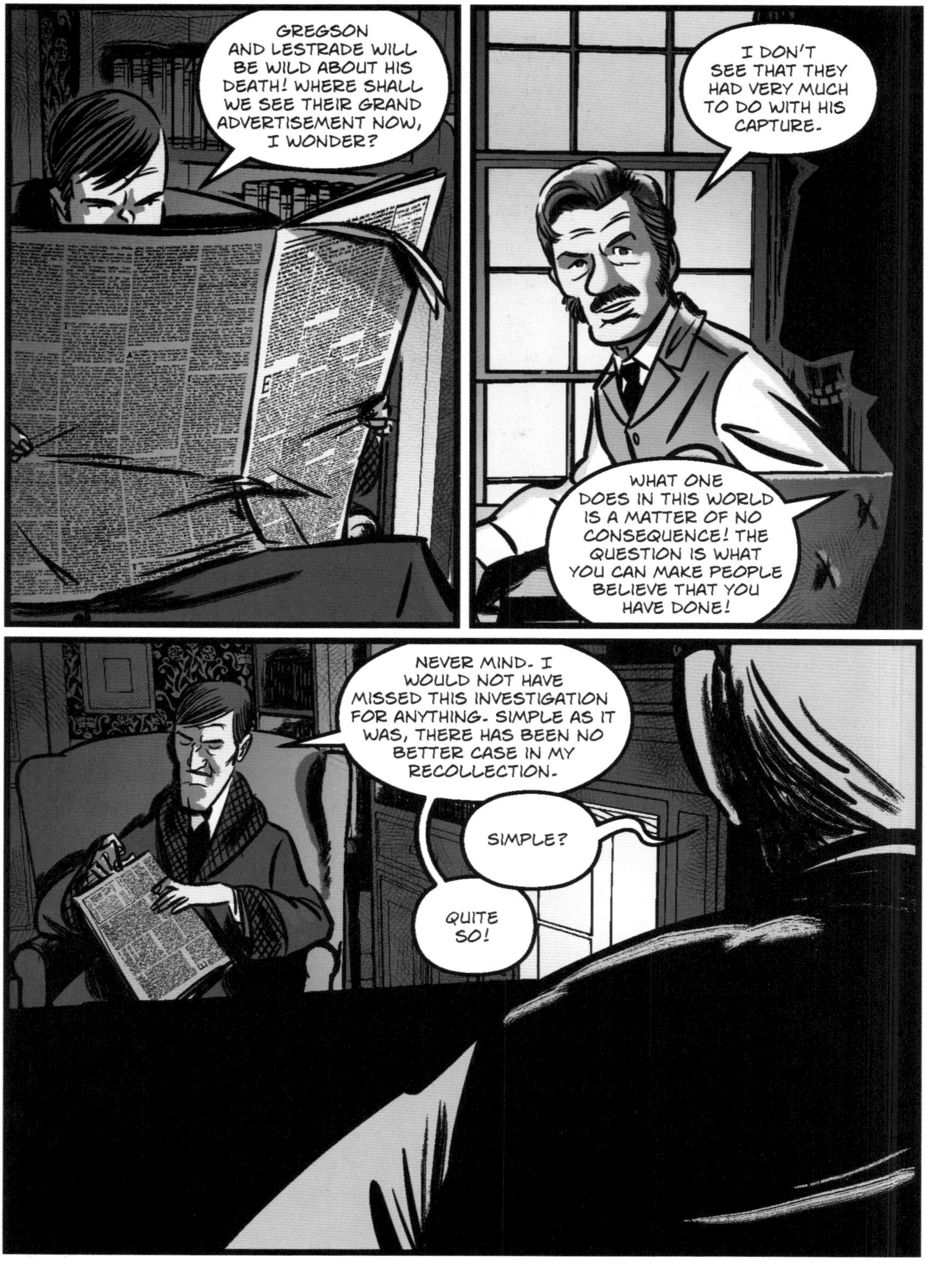
GREGSON AND LESTRADE WILL BE WILD ABOUT HIS DEATH! WHERE SHALL WE SEE THEIR GRAND ADVERTISEMENT NOW, I WONDER?
I DON'T SEE THAT THEY HAD VERY MUCH TO DO WITH HIS CAPTURE.
WHAT ONE DOES IN THIS WORLD IS A MATTER OF NO CONSEQUENCE! THE QUESTION IS WHAT YOU CAN MAKE PEOPLE BELIEVE THAT YOU HAVE DONE!
NEVER MIND. I WOULD NOT HAVE MISSED THIS INVESTIGATION FOR ANYTHING. SIMPLE AS IT WAS, THERE HAS BEEN NO BETTER CASE IN MY RECOLLECTION.
SIMPLE?
QUITE SO!

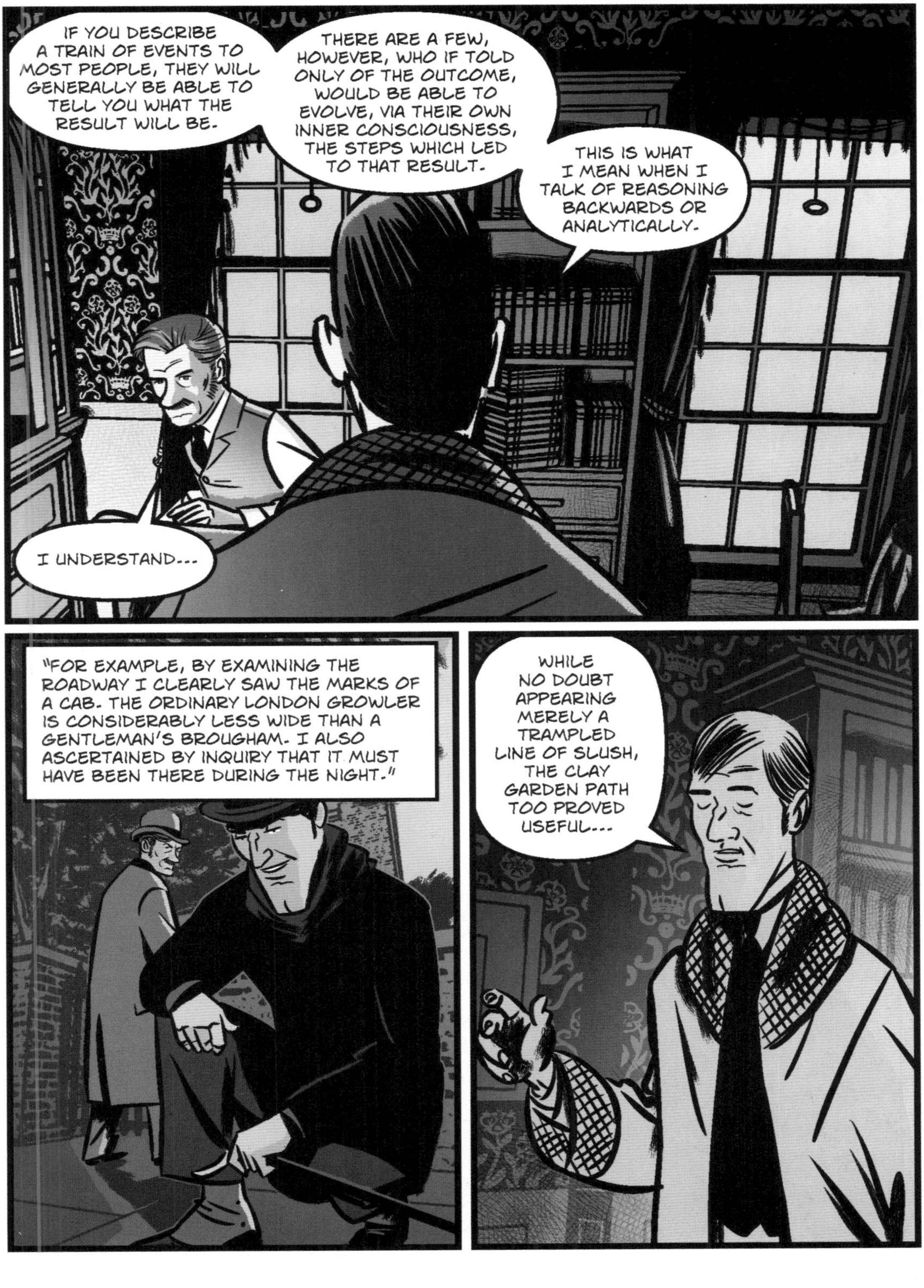
IF YOU DESCRIBE A TRAIN OF EVENTS TO MOST PEOPLE, THEY WILL GENERALLY BE ABLE TO TELL YOU WHAT THE RESULT WILL BE.
THERE ARE A FEW, HOWEVER, WHO IF TOLD ONLY OF THE OUTCOME, WOULD BE ABLE TO EVOLVE, VIA THEIR OWN INNER CONSCIOUSNESS, THE STEPS WHICH LED TO THAT RESULT.
THIS IS WHAT I MEAN WHEN I TALK OF REASONING BACKWARDS OR ANALYTICALLY.
I UNDERSTAND...
"FOR EXAMPLE, BY EXAMINING THE ROADWAY I CLEARLY SAW THE MARKS OF A CAB. THE ORDINARY LONDON GROWLER IS CONSIDERABLY LESS WIDE THAN A GENTLEMAN'S BROUGHAM. I ALSO ASCERTAINED BY INQUIRY THAT IT MUST HAVE BEEN THERE DURING THE NIGHT."
WHILE NO DOUBT APPEARING MERELY A TRAMPLED LINE OF SLUSH, THE CLAY GARDEN PATH TOO PROVED USEFUL...

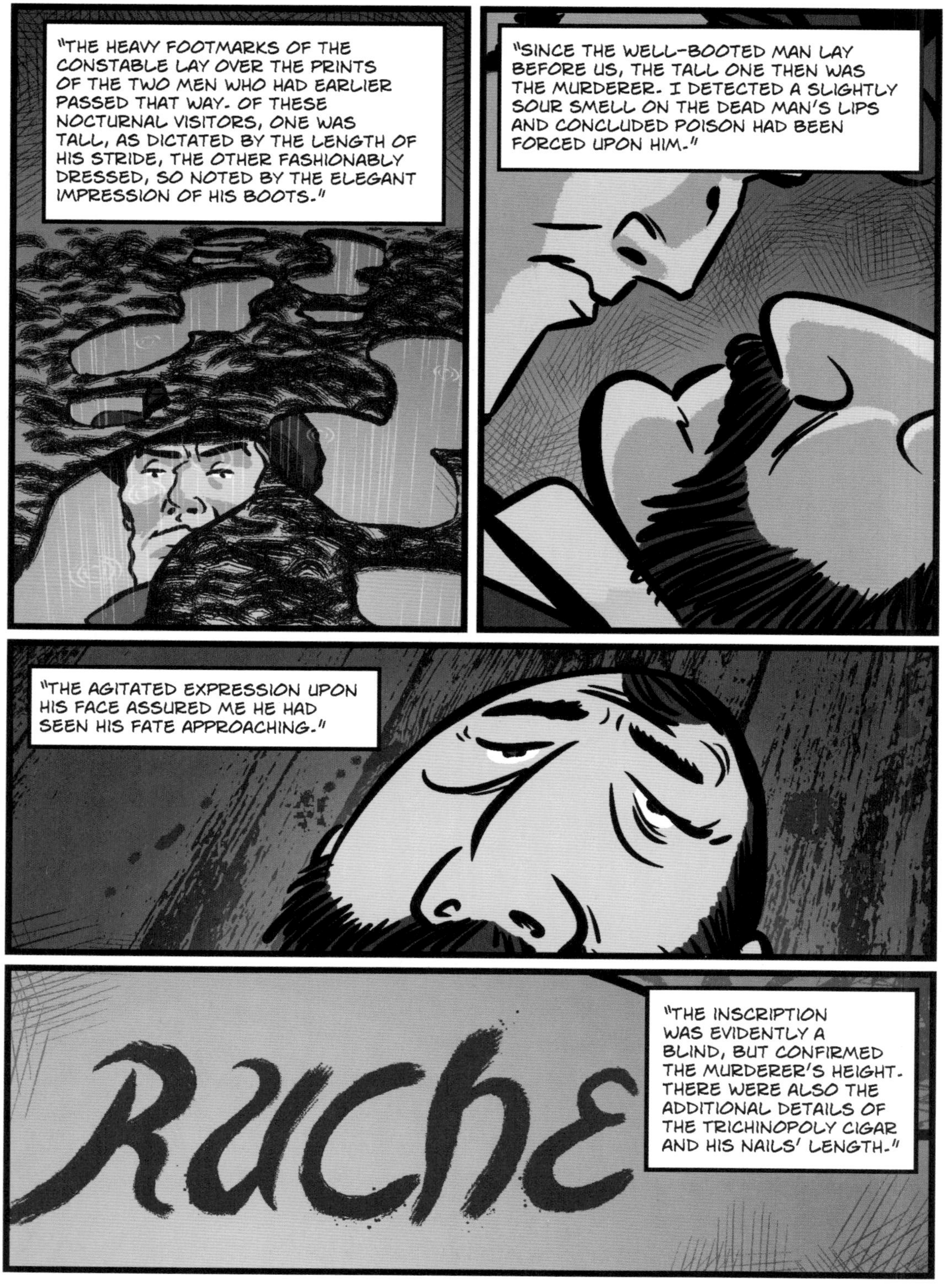
"THE HEAVY FOOTMARKS OF THE CONSTABLE LAY OVER THE PRINTS OF THE TWO MEN WHO HAD EARLIER PASSED THAT WAY. OF THESE NOCTURNAL VISITORS, ONE WAS TALL, AS DICTATED BY THE LENGTH OF HIS STRIDE, THE OTHER FASHIONABLY DRESSED, SO NOTED BY THE ELEGANT IMPRESSION OF HIS BOOTS."
"SINCE THE WELL-BOOTED MAN LAY BEFORE US, THE TALL ONE THEN WAS THE MURDERER. I DETECTED A SLIGHTLY SOUR SMELL ON THE DEAD MAN'S LIPS AND CONCLUDED POISON HAD BEEN FORCED UPON HIM."
"THE AGITATED EXPRESSION UPON HIS FACE ASSURED ME HE HAD SEEN HIS FATE APPROACHING."
RACHE
"THE INSCRIPTION WAS EVIDENTLY A BLIND, BUT CONFIRMED THE MURDERER'S HEIGHT. THERE WERE ALSO THE ADDITIONAL DETAILS OF THE TRICHINOPOLY CIGAR AND HIS NAILS' LENGTH."

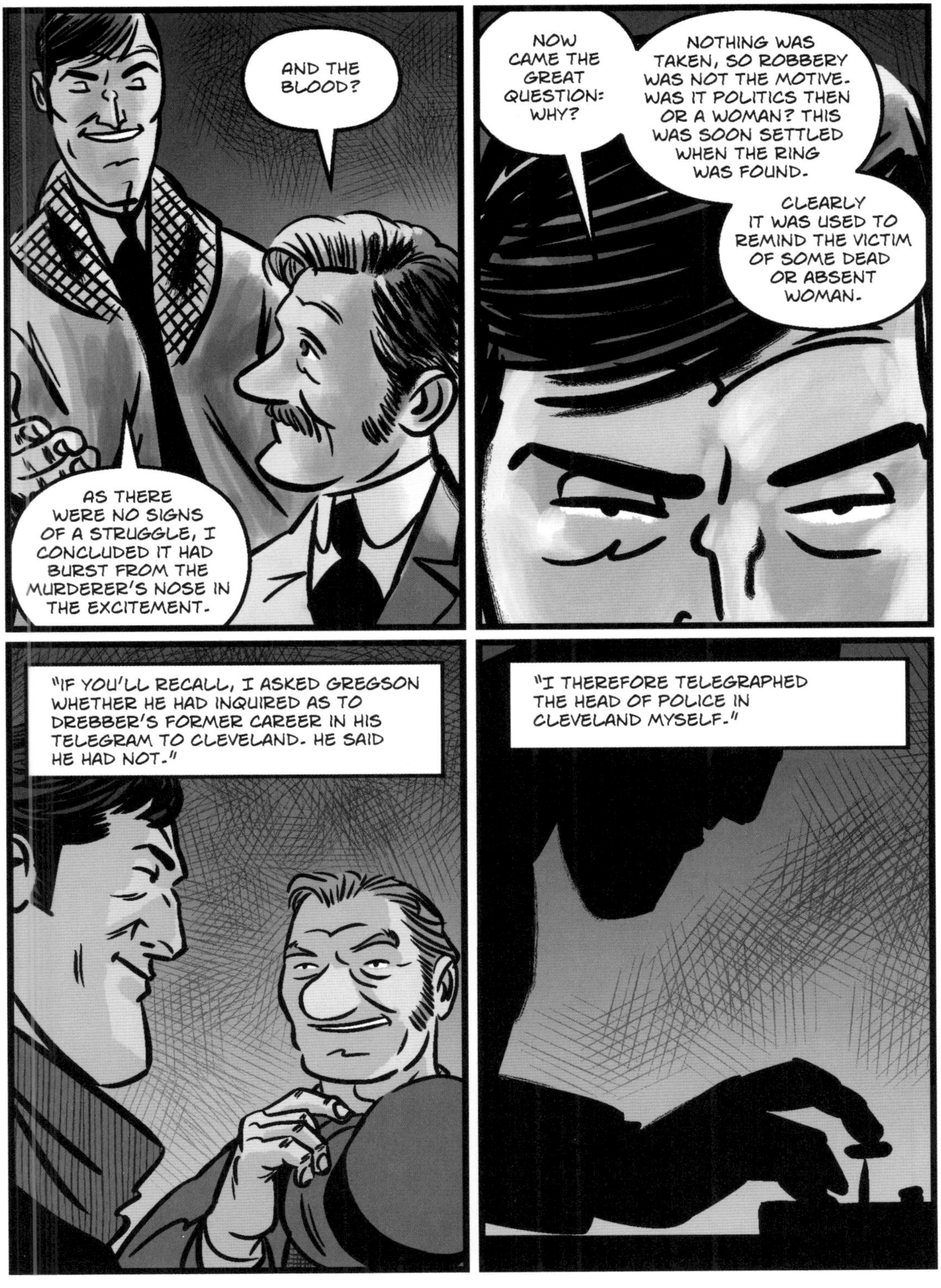
AND THE BLOOD?
AS THERE WERE NO SIGNS OF A STRUGGLE, I CONCLUDED IT HAD BURST FROM THE MURDERER'S NOSE IN THE EXCITEMENT.
NOW CAME THE GREAT QUESTION: WHY?
NOTHING WAS TAKEN, SO ROBBERY WAS NOT THE MOTIVE. WAS IT POLITICS THEN OR A WOMAN? THIS WAS SOON SETTLED WHEN THE RING WAS FOUND.
CLEARLY IT WAS USED TO REMIND THE VICTIM OF SOME DEAD OR ABSENT WOMAN.
"IF YOU'LL RECALL, I ASKED GREGSON WHETHER HE HAD INQUIRED AS TO DREBBER'S FORMER CAREER IN HIS TELEGRAM TO CLEVELAND. HE SAID HE HAD NOT."
"I THEREFORE TELEGRAPHED THE HEAD OF POLICE IN CLEVELAND MYSELF."

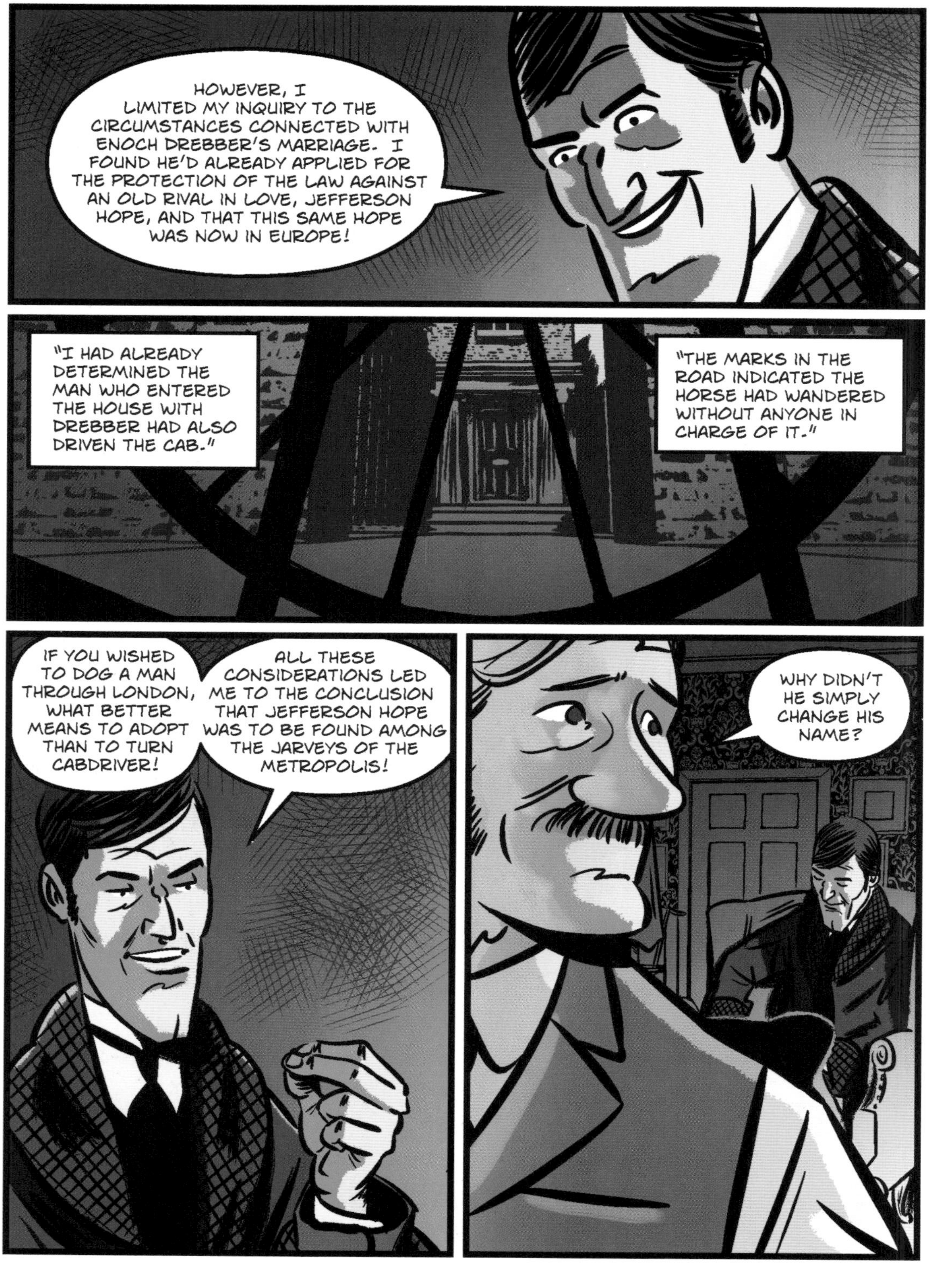
HOWEVER, I LIMITED MY INQUIRY TO THE CIRCUMSTANCES CONNECTED WITH ENOCH DREBBER'S MARRIAGE. I FOUND HE'D ALREADY APPLIED FOR THE PROTECTION OF THE LAW AGAINST AN OLD RIVAL IN LOVE, JEFFERSON HOPE, AND THAT THIS SAME HOPE WAS NOW IN EUROPE!
"I HAD ALREADY DETERMINED THE MAN WHO ENTERED THE HOUSE WITH DREBBER HAD ALSO DRIVEN THE CAB."
"THE MARKS IN THE ROAD INDICATED THE HORSE HAD WANDERED WITHOUT ANYONE IN CHARGE OF IT."
IF YOU WISHED TO DOG A MAN THROUGH LONDON, WHAT BETTER MEANS TO ADOPT THAN TO TURN CABDRIVER!
ALL THESE CONSIDERATIONS LED ME TO THE CONCLUSION THAT JEFFERSON HOPE WAS TO BE FOUND AMONG THE JARVEYS OF THE METROPOLIS!
WHY DIDN'T HE SIMPLY CHANGE HIS NAME?

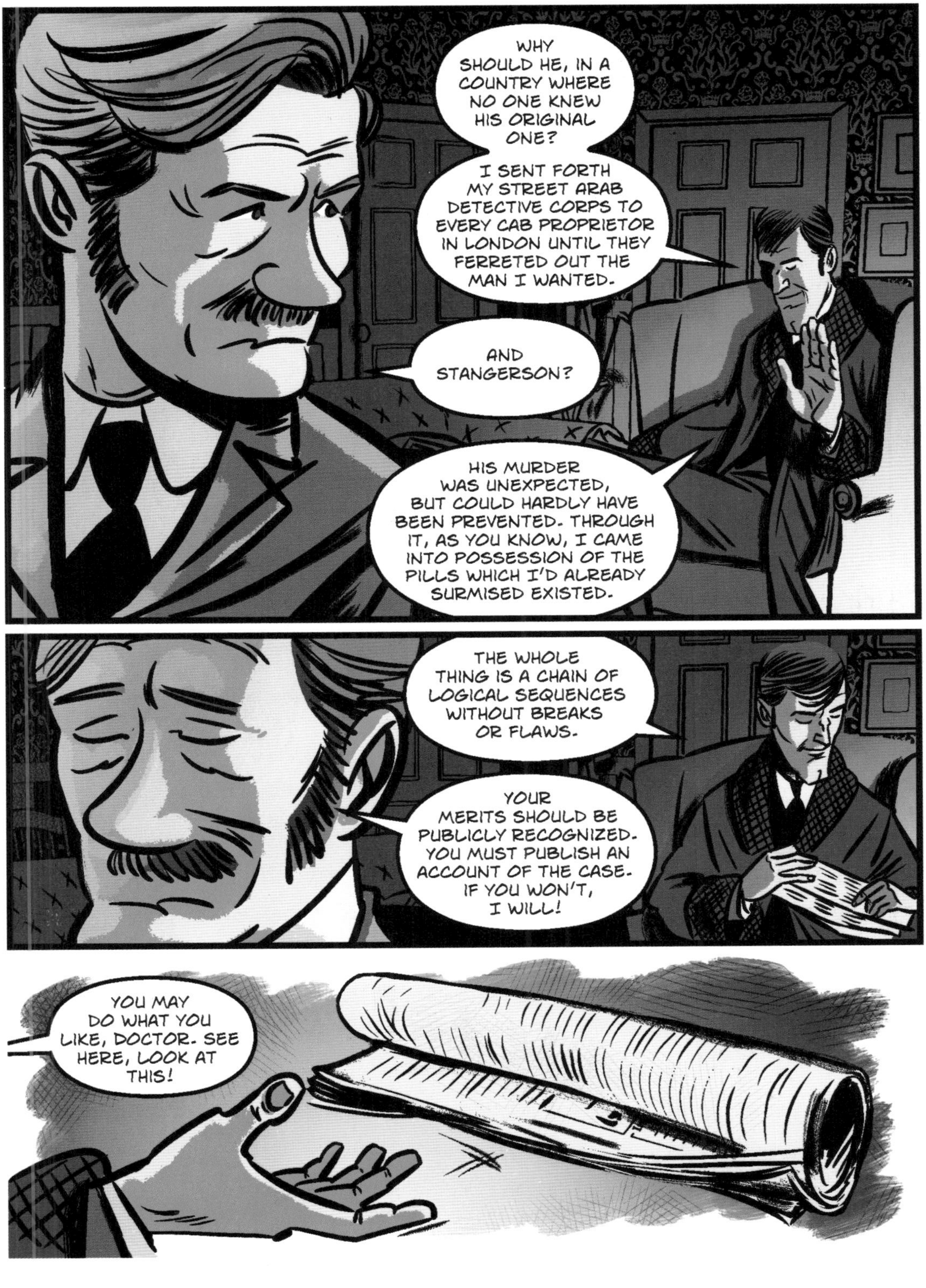
WHY SHOULD HE, IN A COUNTRY WHERE NO ONE KNEW HIS ORIGINAL ONE?
I SENT FORTH MY STREET ARAB DETECTIVE CORPS TO EVERY CAB PROPRIETOR IN LONDON UNTIL THEY FERRETED OUT THE MAN I WANTED.
AND STANGERSON?
HIS MURDER WAS UNEXPECTED, BUT COULD HARDLY HAVE BEEN PREVENTED. THROUGH IT, AS YOU KNOW, I CAME INTO POSSESSION OF THE PILLS WHICH I'D ALREADY SURMISED EXISTED.
THE WHOLE THING IS A CHAIN OF LOGICAL SEQUENCES WITHOUT BREAKS OR FLAWS.
YOUR MERITS SHOULD BE PUBLICLY RECOGNIZED. YOU MUST PUBLISH AN ACCOUNT OF THE CASE. IF YOU WON'T, I WILL!
YOU MAY DO WHAT YOU LIKE, DOCTOR. SEE HERE, LOOK AT THIS!

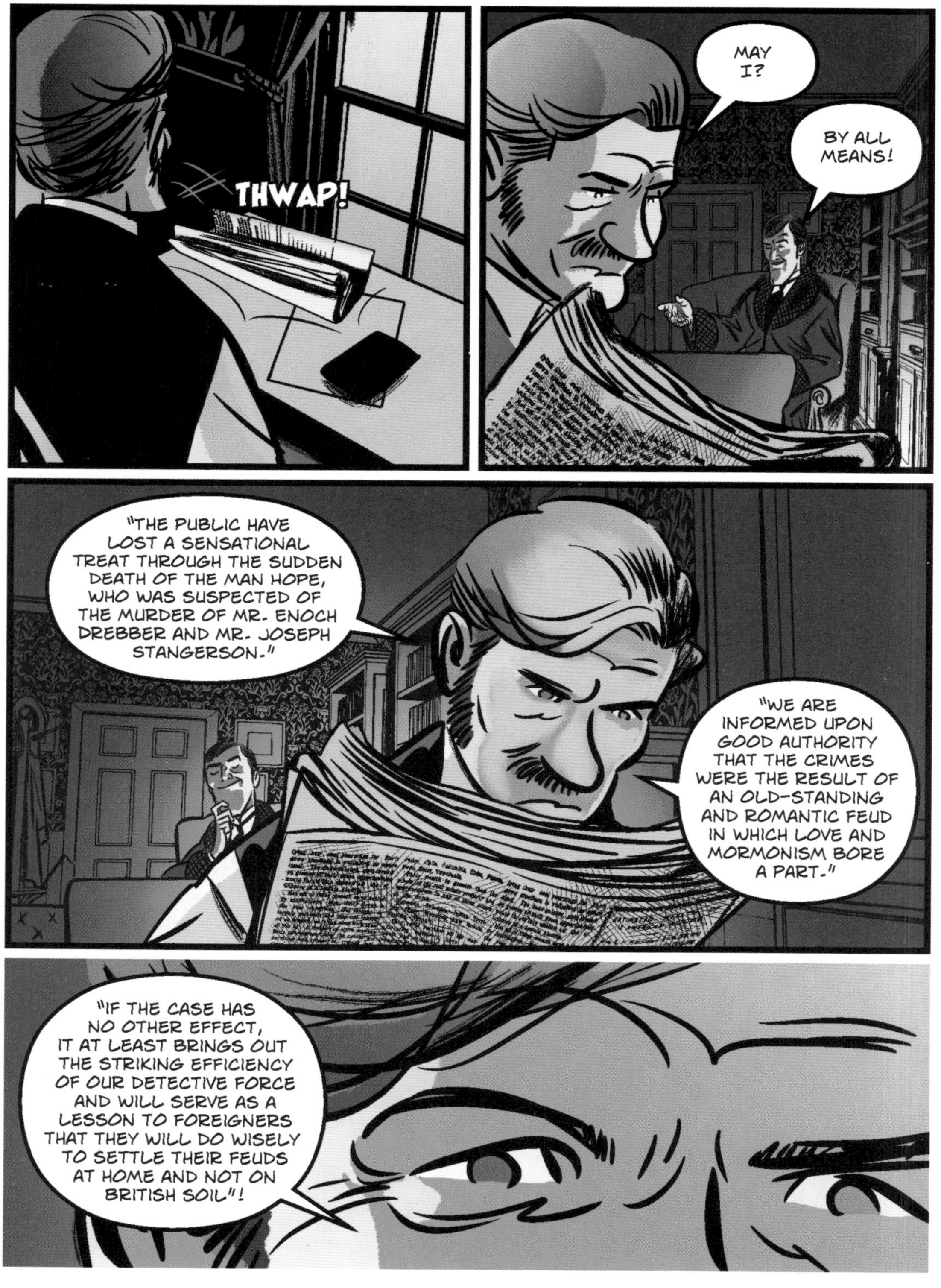
THWAP!
MAY I?
BY ALL MEANS!
"THE PUBLIC HAVE LOST A SENSATIONAL TREAT THROUGH THE SUDDEN DEATH OF THE MAN HOPE, WHO WAS SUSPECTED OF THE MURDER OF MR. ENOCH DREBBER AND MR. JOSEPH STANGERSON."
"WE ARE INFORMED UPON GOOD AUTHORITY THAT THE CRIMES WERE THE RESULT OF AN OLD-STANDING AND ROMANTIC FEUD IN WHICH LOVE AND MORMONISM BORE A PART."
"IF THE CASE HAS NO OTHER EFFECT, IT AT LEAST BRINGS OUT THE STRIKING EFFICIENCY OF OUR DETECTIVE FORCE AND WILL SERVE AS A LESSON TO FOREIGNERS THAT THEY WILL DO WISELY TO SETTLE THEIR FEUDS AT HOME AND NOT ON BRITISH SOIL"!

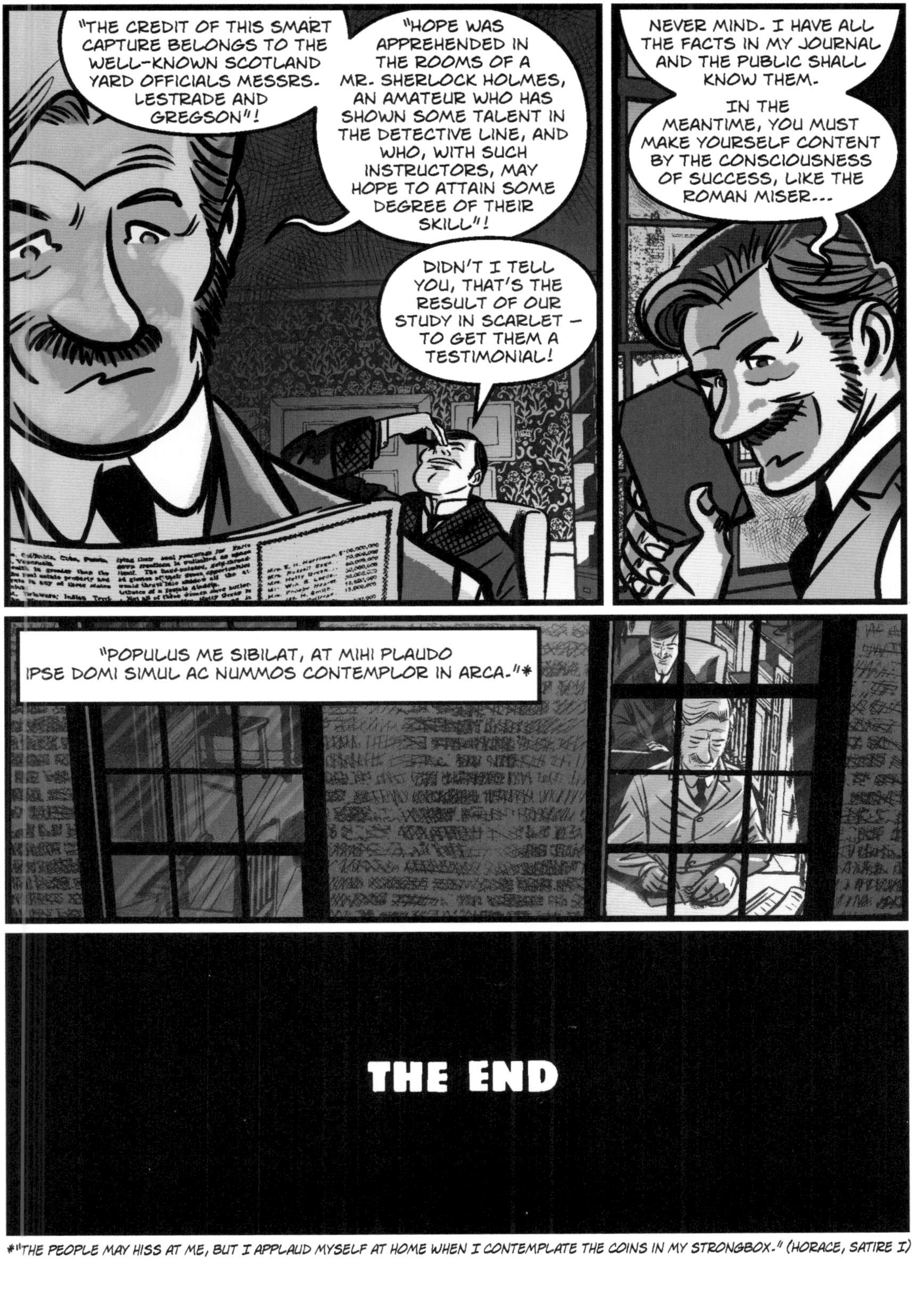
"THE CREDIT OF THIS SMART CAPTURE BELONGS TO THE WELL-KNOWN SCOTLAND YARD OFFICIALS MESSRS. LESTRADE AND GREGSON"!
"HOPE WAS APPREHENDED IN THE ROOMS OF A MR. SHERLOCK HOLMES, AN AMATEUR WHO HAS SHOWN SOME TALENT IN THE DETECTIVE LINE, AND WHO, WITH SUCH INSTRUCTORS, MAY HOPE TO ATTAIN SOME DEGREE OF THEIR SKILL"!
DIDN'T I TELL YOU, THAT'S THE RESULT OF OUR STUDY IN SCARLET — TO GET THEM A TESTIMONIAL!
NEVER MIND. I HAVE ALL THE FACTS IN MY JOURNAL AND THE PUBLIC SHALL KNOW THEM.
IN THE MEANTIME, YOU MUST MAKE YOURSELF CONTENT BY THE CONSCIOUSNESS OF SUCCESS, LIKE THE ROMAN MISER...
"POPULUS ME SIBILAT, AT MIHI PLAUDO IPSE DOMI SIMUL AC NUMMOS CONTEMPLOR IN ARCA."*
THE END

*"THE PEOPLE MAY HISS AT ME, BUT I APPLAUD MYSELF AT HOME WHEN I CONTEMPLATE THE COINS IN MY STRONGBOX." (HORACE, SATIRE I)